the Wolf
at Twilight

Also by Kent Nerburn

Calm Surrender
Chief Joseph and the Flight of the Nez Perce
A Haunting Reverence
The Hidden Beauty of Everyday Life
Letters to My Son
Make Me an Instrument of Your Peace
Neither Wolf nor Dog
Road Angels
Simple Truths
Small Graces

Edited by Kent Nerburn

The Wisdom of the Native Americans
The Soul of an Indian
Native American Wisdom

the Wolf
at Twilight

An Indian Elder's Journey
through a Land of Ghosts and Shadows

Kent Nerburn

New World Library
Novato, California

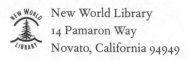 New World Library
14 Pamaron Way
Novato, California 94949

Text design by Tona Pearce Myers

Library of Congress Cataloging-in-Publication Data
Nerburn, Kent.
 The wolf at twilight : an Indian elder's journey through a land of ghosts and shadows / Kent Nerburn.
    p.   cm.
ISBN 978-1-57731-578-0 (pbk. : alk. paper)
 1. Dan, 1913–2002. 2. Dakota Indians—Biography. 3. Dakota philosophy.
4. Dakota Indians—Social life and customs. I. Title.
E99.D1D345 2009
978.004'9752—dc22   2009032689

First printing, November 2009
ISBN 978-1-57731-578-0
Printed in Canada on 100% postconsumer-waste recycled paper

g New World Library is a proud member of the Green Press Initiative.

10   9   8

Dedicated to Dan, 1913–2002,
and all those who dared not speak

If you lose something important to you, go back and search for it and you will find it.

— SITTING BULL

CONTENTS

◇◈◇◈◇◈◇◈◇◈◇◈◇◈◇◈◇◈◇◈◇◈◇◈◇◈◇◈◇◈◇

FOREST SILENCE

THE GATHERING DAWN

◇◇◇◇◇◇◇◇◇◇◇◇◇◇◇◇◇◇◇◇◇◇◇◇◇◇◇◇◇◇◇

A TRUTH THAT LODGES
DEEP IN THE HEART

"I am no longer myself. I am someone else."

The Wolf at Twilight might never have come into being had it not been for a chance encounter in a dusty roadside café on the high plains of the Dakotas on a sweltering July afternoon. I had stopped for a glass of water and noticed an elderly Indian man sitting by himself at a table in the corner. He was the only other person in the café.

Feeling a need for conversation, I asked if I could sit with him. Much to my delight, he agreed.

Our conversation was casual, as might be expected of two men sitting together on a hot summer afternoon. I made passing mention of the Indian boarding schools — a strangely cruel but little-known era in American history when Indian children were taken from their families and placed in residential institutions far from their homes so that they could be stripped of their Native identities and reeducated into Euro-American values and ways. As I had expected, he had been part of that system.

"Oh, I learned," he said. "I can speak good English. I became a Christian. But it changed me. I am no longer myself. I am someone else."

His tone was matter-of-fact — almost fatalistic. But his words were chilling. It was at once one of the saddest and most damning comments I had ever heard about the situation of the Native people on this American land, and it brought me face-to-face with a promise I had made almost twenty years earlier.

THE YEAR WAS 1988. I had taken a job helping young people on the Red Lake Ojibwe Reservation in northern Minnesota to collect the memories of the tribal elders. It was a wonderful job, and tremendously rewarding. As well as working with young people, I had the good fortune to meet and share time with the elders. I sat at their tables, heard their stories, shared their laughter, and felt their sadness. It was a profoundly human time, and I valued it more than I can express.

But through it all, what struck me most deeply was the almost sacred value the elders placed on the importance of stories, and their hunger to pass these stories along. Stories were not mere entertainment to them, nor were they simple reminiscences; they were the traditional way of handing down the values and the memories of their culture — the way they had been taught by *their* elders — and they approached the task with something close to reverence.

There were times when I was near tears as I watched them struggle to communicate the knowledge their grandparents had passed to them and to hold back the pain that had been part of their lives. It was as if they held a precious fragment of the past in their hands and they were desperate to pass it on.

"No one has ever asked us before," they said. "And we were made to feel so much shame about our traditional ways."

This experience had a profound effect on me. It showed me how fragile the vessel of cultural knowledge really was, and how close it had come to being completely shattered. And it showed me how hungry the young people were for knowledge of their past, and how difficult it was for the elders to give voice to that knowledge in a language not completely their own.

When I finished my work at Red Lake, I made a private promise that I would use such skills as I possessed to help the Native people tell their stories. It was the least I could do in gratitude for the gifts and trust that had been given to me.

NEITHER WOLF NOR DOG, the predecessor to *The Wolf at Twilight*, was one of these acts of gratitude. It was the story of a journey across the Dakota plains with a Lakota elder I identified only as Dan. During that journey he offered his thoughts about his people and their ways of understanding the world. It was a story intended to engage the reader and offer a glimpse into the contemporary Native life and heart.

My hope was that *Neither Wolf nor Dog* would give non-Natives a glimpse into a way of understanding they had never imagined. But, more important, I hoped that through Dan's story I would give voice to beliefs and points of view that had been too long ignored. It was a chance to use the traditional art of storytelling to teach and to heal. To a great extent, I believe it was successful.

But things quickly took an unexpected turn.

Non-Native readers, hungry for Dan's voice, began asking how to contact him. Native readers, appreciative of his insights, began asking where to find him. His thoughts were quoted in journals, on websites, in government reports. I was sought out to serve as cultural translator for non-Natives who were more comfortable with one of their own people than they were with the people they were seeking to understand.

Soon colleges, universities, high schools, tribal gatherings; Germans, Dutch, Chinese, Japanese; all began using Dan's words.

Everyone from missionaries in South America to the Maori in New Zealand found touchstones of meaning in *Neither Wolf nor Dog* that caused them to reach out to me, and, by extension, to Dan.

This was a great compliment as well as a great surprise. The book's intentions had been humble, even personal; suddenly, its effects were international. It had taken on a life of its own — the dream of all authors — and it had helped me fulfill my promise to share the stories and to help rebuild the narratives by which the Native people were understood.

But in doing so, it had placed both Dan and me in a difficult position. Dan was a real person. But I had fictionalized his story and distorted his identity to protect his privacy. I had also used him as he had suggested — as a vehicle around which to craft a story that gave voice to truths that had remained unspoken for too long.

He did not wish to be perceived as a spokesperson for all things Native, and I had no wish to be seen as an historian or documentarian. Our goal had been to counter the tragic and reprehensible misrepresentation of Native people in this country and to articulate Native values through a powerful story. As he had once told me, people learn by story, because stories lodge deep in the heart. Our creation, *Neither Wolf nor Dog*, had been a teaching story in the Native tradition, and, by all indications, it had lodged deep in people's hearts.

Then, sadly, Dan died.

It was a loss to me and to everyone who knew him. It seemed like an appropriate time for me to withdraw and let the book make its own way.

But it was not so simple. Dan had captured peoples' hearts and imaginations. His story had touched readers who had never before given a thought to Native America. He had articulated the feelings of many Native people who had been seeking a voice by which to explain themselves to their non-Native friends. Most important, his story had contributed in some small fashion to the reshaping of the

American cultural narrative that for too long has depicted Native peoples as savages on horseback, drunks in gutters, and wisdom-bearing elders possessed of some mystical earth knowledge.

People wanted to hear more from Dan and more about him. They wanted me to tell more of his story.

I resisted. I was proud of what we had accomplished. But Dan was gone, and I was uncomfortable serving as a spokesman for a Native point of view and weary of trying to explain the literary method of the project we had undertaken. The book spoke for itself. There was no need to say more.

But then came that chance meeting in the café. In that old man's simple, off-handed comment, I heard the echoes of all the yearning and struggle in the voices of the elders at Red Lake. They, too, had lost their identities. They, too, were no longer themselves, and it was this fate that they so wanted to help the young people avoid by sharing their stories. More than anything else I had written, *Neither Wolf nor Dog* had let people be themselves and see themselves.

Was I breaking my own promise and abdicating my moral responsibility by refusing to tell more of Dan's story, simply because I did not want to deal with the questions and challenges that it posed?

I carried this quandary with me until the following summer, when I was invited to participate in a sweat lodge on the Pine Ridge Reservation in South Dakota.

A sweat, truly done, is a hard thing. What on the outside looks to be only a crude mound of blankets and tarps piled over a low, convex frame is, on the inside, a place of sweltering, breathless blackness that pushes you to the very limits of your physical endurance and strips away all spiritual artifice and pretense. As I huddled on the dirt floor in the steaming darkness of the sweat lodge, I prayed, as best I could, for guidance in how to proceed with this story I had been given.

I asked the Great Spirit, *Tunkashila*, God, Grandfather — whatever you choose to call him or her or it — to give me courage to do what was right, whether that was walking away from Dan's story or traveling farther down the trail of its telling.

Almost in a swoon, somewhere between trance and unconsciousness, I heard the echo of Dan's words from years before come floating back to me: "You're here for a reason. The Creator has given you a task. It is not for you to decide. If you are afraid or if you are too small, it is too late."

It was as if I was being reminded that my involvement with Dan's story was not a choice; it was a gift and an obligation. Dan's words — "I am reaching out for the grandchildren. You must help the grandchildren, too" — echoed deep in my conscience.

I thought of the young people at Red Lake, sitting rapt at the tables of the elders, trying to take in the truth of what they were hearing. I thought of the elders themselves, so hungry to help shape the lives of the young people with their stories. I thought of the quiet words of the man in that dusty café: "I am no longer myself. I am somebody else." And I thought of Sitting Bull's earnest entreaty, "Come, let us put our minds together to see what kind of lives we can create for our children."

I emerged from that sweat knowing what I had to do.

I had to tell more of Dan's story.

I had to tell it so that Native children do not lose who they are, so they do not become somebody else. I had to tell it so that an America that has closed its ears and hearts to the presence of its first inhabitants would be reminded that there is more to the Native experience than hatchets and tomahawks and casinos and powwows. I had to tell it so that the dry bones of historical fact could be animated with the heartbeat of a human story.

I had to tell it because it was the only honorable way to fulfill the promise that I had made on the Red Lake Reservation almost twenty years earlier.

This, then — *The Wolf at Twilight* — is the fruit of that promise. It is the part of Dan's life I had left untold. It takes us to places that for too long have been hidden in shadow and reveals truths about what has been taken from Native people and what the rest of us have lost in that taking. But it also reveals what we may all yet become if we heed Sitting Bull's poignant entreaty and put our minds together to see what kind of lives we can create for the children.

I hope you find it worthy of your time. If it opens your eyes to another way of understanding, I am grateful. If it simply entertains you, I am pleased. But what matters most is that it touches you.

For it is, above all, a story of Native America, and its goal is to lodge deep in your heart.

Distant Voices

◇◇◇◇◇◇◇◇◇◇◇◇◇◇◇◇◇◇◇◇◇◇◇◇◇◇◇◇◇◇◇◇◇

CHAPTER ONE

"FATBACK'S DEAD"

The words on the slip of paper struck me like a blow.
"Fatback's dead."

It was not just the news itself, though the words cut deep. It was the very fact of the note, stuck on my windshield on the Red Lake Indian Reservation in northern Minnesota, hundreds of miles from where Fatback had lived and, apparently, died. That, and the small deerskin pouch of tobacco that was tied to it.

Fatback was a black Lab — a good dog — who had belonged to Dan, an elderly Lakota man who lived far out on the Dakota plains. Years before, as a result of a book of elders' memories I had done with students at Red Lake, Dan had contacted me to come out to his home to speak with him. His request was vague, and I had been both skeptical and apprehensive. But, reluctantly, I had gone, and it had changed my life. We had worked together, traveled together, and created a book together in which the old man told his stories and memories and thoughts about Indian people and our American land.

However, for reasons that I cannot easily explain, after the book was published he and I had not stayed in touch. Perhaps it was because we were from such different worlds. Perhaps it was because the intimacy we had achieved was uncomfortable to both of us — he was, in some measure, allowing me to make up for my guilt about what I had left unsaid and undone with my father at the time of his passing, and I, in some measure, had served as a surrogate for Dan's son who had died an untimely death in a car accident and to whom he had initially entrusted the task of writing his story and collecting his thoughts.

But whatever it was, when we had stood together on the dusty Dakota roadside fifteen years ago, hands clasped in a bond of promise and friendship, we had both known, in some deep part of ourselves, that our time together was finished. We had shared a moment in time; we had done something worthy; and that, for each of us, was enough.

But now it was all coming back to me. He had reached out to me again — if, indeed, it was him — and had reopened a door that I thought had been closed forever.

"WHAT MAKES YOU THINK IT'S REAL?" Louise asked. "You *were* on the rez, and there are lots of practical jokers up there."

"Tobacco's no joke," I said, pulling out the small deerskin pouch.

To the Indian people, tobacco is the Creator's gift. It comes from the earth and rises up to heaven. When the Creator sees it, he pays attention. So when tobacco is presented to someone, it's a sacred statement. It means that the Creator is being called upon to witness the interaction. I knew of no Indian people who would use it as part of a hoax or a trick.

"I can't just let it rest," I continued. "I've got to find out."

"You could go back up to Red Lake and ask around."

"Where? It was a powwow. There were hundreds of cars parked in that field — folks from North Dakota, South Dakota, Montana, Canada."

"Maybe you should try to contact Dan or his family."

I looked down. I knew she was right. But, in truth, I was scared. I had never really talked to any of the participants since *Neither Wolf nor Dog* — the book Dan and I had created together — had been published. I had heard that it had been well received. But there were depictions within it that might have given offense, and I was afraid of the disapproval and recriminations that might surface if I allowed myself to get involved again.

And then there was the deeper, more tawdry issue: Dan had received nothing for the book. Though this is the way he had wanted it, I had always harbored the gnawing guilt that I should have done more for him and his family.

I looked down at the small pouch in my hand. It was not just a gift, it was a command. If it really was from Dan or someone close to him, it was a reaching out I could not ignore.

I placed it carefully back in my shirt pocket and turned toward the phone. Perhaps this was just a necessary contact too long deferred. Perhaps this was a chance to return the gift that his friendship had given to me.

When I had last been in contact with Dan, he had been unwilling to speak on the telephone — an elder's quirk. I assumed nothing had changed — if, indeed, he was even still alive. But in the intervening years phone service had increased, cell phones had come into existence, and I was certain that some of the other people I had known would now be able to be contacted without difficulty.

However, it did not prove to be so simple. As I scoured the Internet and dialed up directory assistance, I realized, much to my chagrin, that I hadn't learned anyone's last name. The only person who had ever been called by a last name was me — I was always just

"Nerburn." They had all been simply Dan, Grover, Wenonah, or whatever strange nickname they were known by on the rez. When you were introduced at all, it was without any air of formality. Just, "This is Nerburn. This is Wenonah." So I had no reasonable way to proceed.

Finally, it came to me that the only chance I had was to look for the number of a business establishment. There was only one business establishment on the rez whose name I could recall.

"YEAH?" CAME THE VOICE. It was as I remembered — deep, dark, and slow, as if coming from the bottom of a well.

"Jumbo?" I said.

"Yeah."

I could almost see him standing there in his huge sagging jeans and filthy laceless tennis shoes, with a dirty white T-shirt hanging like a tent over his astonishing belly, his massive ham of a hand wrapped around the grease-covered phone receiver.

"This is Nerburn. The guy..."

"The Nissan," he interrupted. "We got a lot of 'em out here now."

The comment made me smile. Who but Jumbo would answer a business phone with "Yeah?" But, then again, his had not been an ordinary business. His primary occupation had been car repair, but he worked on toasters, pumps, and anything else that had springs or levers or any moving parts. His sign had been a dripping, hand-painted affair that said something about "broke stuff fixed" with a variety of quotation marks and underlinings that corresponded to no grammatical rules that I or anyone else had ever learned. His tool collection had run toward pipe wrenches and hammers, all covered with layers of grease and scattered randomly on a filthy black work-bench. Close tolerances and delicate repairs were not his forte.

"Truck got troubles?" he asked.

"No, no. I sold it years ago," I said.

"I'd have took it," he answered. "Good truck."

"Good as a Chevy?" It was an inside joke.

"What you got now?" he asked.

"A Toyota wagon."

He emitted a low grunt. The meaning was indecipherable.

It was good to hear Jumbo's voice, but I knew I was pressing my luck by engaging him in too much conversation. The last time I had been with him he had seldom said more than two words at a time, and those had usually concerned meals or machines. So I cut to the chase. "Jumbo, I got a note on my car in Red Lake. It said Fatback was dead."

"Yeah, just keeled over last winter. Really old."

"But Dan's still alive?"

"Was yesterday."

I could hear the rustling of a wrapper being opened, followed by a chewing sound.

"So, when you coming out?" he said.

The question caught me by surprise.

"Coming out? I hadn't really thought about it."

"Probably should. The old man's counting on you."

"Counting on me? For what?"

"Don't know. Just counting on you."

"How do you know this?"

"Just do."

I probed for more information, but he had nothing more to say.

I hung up the phone completely mystified. None of it made any sense. Fatback had been dead for months, so why the note now? And how did Jumbo know that Dan had contacted me? And what was he counting on me to do?

Again, reservation protocol had put me in a box. Jumbo was not about to speak for Dan or attempt to assay his motives. He simply passed on information.

For Jumbo, it was enough that Dan wanted me out there. "Why" was none of his business, and how he had known was none of mine.

"I DON'T KNOW WHAT TO DO," I said to Louise. "Why couldn't he just have written a note saying he wanted to see me? Or why didn't he have Wenonah call me, like the last time, if he doesn't want to talk on the phone? And how'd they know my car?"

Louise just shrugged. She, too, had worked on reservations. She knew that my questions were futile.

"What do you want to do?" she asked. "That's the only real question."

I shook my head and sighed. "I think I'd better go out there. He seems to be expecting me."

"Then you'd better go," she said. "You won't feel very good about yourself if you don't."

"But only a week. No more."

She gave me a look of healthy skepticism.

But I was serious. I had writing obligations, speaking obliga- tions. And our short northern Minnesota summer was already on the wane. Louise was a wonderfully patient wife, but she cherished our summer visits from family and friends and didn't want me to miss them. I couldn't allow myself to get trapped like I had during my previous visit to Dan when he and his friend Grover had, in effect, kidnapped me. This time I needed to get back. No "Indian time." My obligations were white obligations, and they were bound by clocks and deadlines.

A week. No more.

CHAPTER TWO

RETURN

The green WWII canvas aviator bag that had been my traveling companion for years had long been demoted to tasks like carrying wood to the house or shoes to the gym. But somehow it seemed more appropriate and less conspicuous for a trip to the reservation than a black nylon suitcase made for racing through airports.

I threw in a few pairs of jeans and several T-shirts, added a few gifts, a sleeping bag, and the old beat-up tape recorder that I carried when I went out on one of my "little trips," and called it a night.

The following morning I gave Louise a peck on the cheek as she slept, checked the oil in the old Toyota wagon, and headed west on U.S. Highway 2. Despite my concerns about what I might find, the lure of the open road soon overtook me, and the day spread out like a promise before me.

By midday I had left the dark forests of northern Minnesota behind and had crossed into the broad, flat expanse of the Dakota prairies. Fields of wheat and sunflowers, redolent with the scent of summer, stretched resplendently toward the horizon. Solitary farmsteads with their prim white two-story houses sat far back from the road in copses of trees. Under the warm summer sun they conjured up images of family picnics with white tablecloths and men in rolled-up shirtsleeves playing horseshoes by the barn. The smell of the earth was so rich that I drove with the windows down just to breathe the air.

By evening I had fallen completely under the Dakota spell. All was earth and sky. Only the occasional vertical of a distant small-town grain elevator broke the flat line of the horizon. A French station out of Canada scratched in on the radio from some far distance, and I listened with appreciation to the round tones of the unfamiliar language as I made my way into the growing prairie twilight.

Soon the pooling lights of Bismarck appeared before me. I skirted their beckoning warmth and turned south into the rolling hill country that flanked the broad waters of the Missouri. The slow, languid river moved silently in the darkness, conjuring up images of Lewis and Clark, the fur traders, and the distant outposts of Omaha and St. Louis hundreds of miles downstream. The echoes of our nation's frontier past were washing over me.

But other echoes, too, were rising. The voices of the Hidatsa and the Mandan and the Nakota and the Arikara — people whose pasts had been obliterated, or, at least, pushed far below the surface of our national consciousness — whispered through the shapeless prairie night. They gave a dark edge to my reverie, reminding me that another history, far less sanguine and hopeful, lay deeper than the memories of sodbusters and settlers and pioneers.

Deeper and deeper I drove into the Dakota darkness. The wind blew warm and intimate, like a voice trying to reveal a secret. Now and then a small town with a broken-down roadside bar would announce its presence with a few lonely neon signs and ghostly sodium yard lights, then quickly disappear into the prairie darkness. But soon they, too, thinned, then ceased altogether, and I was left alone with my thoughts and reveries in the great star-drenched night.

I was tired almost beyond redemption, but I forced myself to keep driving. I wanted to arrive at Dan's house in the early morning before he went out for the day. I needed to find out what had motivated him to reach out to me in such an enigmatic way.

By dawn I had reached the breaking point. I grabbed a few hours of sleep at a roadside pull-off, slapped some river water on my face, and gave my teeth a quick brushing in a gas station restroom. A cup of weak convenience-store coffee, and I was back on the road. By eight I was approaching the reservation line; by nine I was headed out the old familiar highway toward the turnoff to Dan's home.

Everything was just as I remembered it. The path up to his house was unchanged, except for a few more holes and ruts. The same rusted automobile carcasses hulked in the weeds on either side of the roadway. The same desiccated gray trees with broken branches stood in wounded isolation on the same distant rises. Only the brush around the house seemed different. It was now so thick and brambly that it almost totally hid his home from view.

The old Toyota creaked and groaned as I crawled up the path toward the house. Gully washes a foot wide and a foot deep cut raw diagonals across the white clay of the roadway, and even at the slowest, most careful speed, the wagon dropped into them with a sickening clunk, then pushed and surged as it struggled to make its way out the other side.

It was hard to imagine that anyone could navigate this path in a normal automobile during the winter or the rainy season. Yet this was the kind of road that people on the reservation took for granted. It was small wonder that the fields and yards were littered with junk cars.

As I approached Dan's house, a wave of nostalgia overtook me. The old half-dismantled car that had been Fatback's doghouse still sat on blocks to the right of the steps. The three planks that formed the steps to his door were more warped and weathered but otherwise unchanged. The door still hung loosely on its hinges, and the screens were still torn. Even the patchy, peeling paint on the clapboard siding seemed the same. Nothing had been moved, nothing had been repaired. The place had simply deteriorated from an old man's house into an old man's shack.

Though it was barely 9:00 a.m., I could hear a television blaring through the open front door. I had expected someone to come out at the sound of the engine, but no one appeared. It seemed strange, since an unexpected car coming up the driveway of an isolated rural home usually draws attention, if not outright concern. Perhaps the sound from the television had masked my arrival.

I stepped out cautiously, apprehensive about the reception I was about to receive.

I walked quietly up the steps, not wanting to wake Dan if he was still asleep, and was about to knock, when the old man's voice came rattling from inside.

"About time, Nerburn."

The greeting shocked me; I had no idea how he knew it was me. His voice had the same twinkle in it, the same wry playfulness that I remembered so well from my last visit. The dark edge of disapproval that I had so feared was nowhere to be heard.

"Come on in. Come on in."

I opened the old screen door and stepped across the threshold. Memories flooded over me. The same yellow Formica kitchen table sat in the middle of the one large living area. The floor was still a dingy patchwork of cheap linoleum with chunks torn up in various places, revealing the black mastic underneath. The fluorescent light still buzzed from the ceiling, but the plastic cover had been broken off, making the light from the two long cylindrical tubes even more harsh and unsettling.

Dan was sitting in the middle of the room in a four-wheeled rolling "medical equipment" kind of chair with chrome framework and brown vinyl arm pads. He was facing away from me, staring at a large, flat-panel television set. His long white hair hung down to the middle of his back and, despite the growing warmth of the morning, he had a shawl draped over his shoulders. To a casual observer, he might have been mistaken for an infirm old woman.

"Hello, Dan," I said, not knowing quite how to proceed. "How'd you know it was me?"

He didn't turn, but kept facing the television. The bright colors from the screen looked out of place in the grimy surroundings.

"Remembered your footsteps. Hearing gets good when your eyes go bad."

Dan lifted his hand over his shoulder, as if waiting for me to take it. He kept his eyes glued to the screen.

"How you been, Nerburn?" he asked. I grasped his gnarled root of a hand and squeezed it in an awkward approximation of a handshake.

He seemed somehow smaller and more fragile than I had remembered. The wheels of the chair squeaked as they shifted on the hard linoleum.

"I'm fine," I said. "You got a new chair."

It was a stupid comment, but I was casting about for an entry into our old friendship. I wanted to pour forth questions about how he had known how to find me and why he had sent the note, but I knew that silence and patience would get me further than a series of rapid fire questions.

"Yep. New TV, too," he answered. "Got a remote." He held up the small black rectangle and clicked through several stations, as if to show off the technology he now had under his control. "Grover made me get a satellite. Now I don't know whether I'm watching them or they're watching me."

Since he was making no attempt to face me, I walked across and stood next to the TV so I would be directly in his line of vision. He cocked his head a bit, then turned his lined and leathery face upward toward me. For a second it seemed as if he didn't recognize me. Then he broke into a grin. "Christ, Nerburn, you're getting old," he said.

I burst out laughing. The comment brought back everything — the intimacy, the hint of a challenge, a devilish sense of humor, and a sense that in his life there was no passage of time.

"Still kicking," I said.

He jerked his right leg straight out. "Me, too." His pale, mottled shin protruded like a stick from his pajama leg. On his feet were the same filthy sheepskin-lined slippers I remembered him wearing when I had last visited him.

"Sit down," he said, flapping his hand toward the sagging, motel-style couch against the wall. I eased myself into it and sunk almost to the floor.

"Well, this sure isn't new," I said.

"Good enough for the visitors I get," he answered. I imagined Grover and the others who always camped out in Dan's living room watching TV. The wooden arms of the brown couch were covered with cigarette burns.

"It's good to see you, Dan," I said, trying to give some sense of significance to the moment. "It's been a while."

"Yep. Long time," he answered. "How's the family?"

"Wife still puts up with me. The boy's almost grown." They were shorthand answers to shorthand questions, but I had learned long ago that my usual circumlocutions were both unnecessary and unwelcome. Just answer the question and shut up — that was the way to do it on the rez. Besides, I was anxious to get past the small talk.

"Wait a minute till I finish my show," he said. "It's almost over."

We sat silently for a few minutes while Dan stared at the conclusion of his talk show. The fluorescent lights buzzed, and some unfamiliar birds twittered outside the window.

I looked more carefully at his face. He had always been one

whose character was etched in every line — smile wrinkles at the sides of the eyes, tight puckery wrinkles framing his mouth in a way that spoke of conscious silence and withholding of information. All that was still present, but there was a greater air of weariness about him now. His one good eye seemed droopy and withdrawn, and his white, wounded eye seemed ever more disengaged, as if looking deeper into an unfathomable distance.

Finally, he cocked his head and flashed me the old, familiar, impish grin. "You've gotten better, Nerburn."

"What do you mean?"

"Not filling up every silence with words."

He knocked me in the shin with the old willow cane he had propped against his chair. "Going Indian on me."

"Nope, just getting older and wiser."

He whacked me again with the cane. "Getting old don't make you wise."

It was a comforting bit of repartee. This was the Dan I remembered.

He threw another great silence at me to see how I'd respond. I just sat quietly, waiting for him to tell me what was on his mind. He stared at the TV for a while, then turned his face toward me.

"Want to know what I called you for?" he asked.

"Never crossed my mind."

He broke into a hearty, phlegmy laugh and thumped his cane several times on the floor. "That's good. That's good."

He leaned forward in his squeaking chair. "Come here," he said. I leaned closer to him. "Got a job for you," he said in hushed, conspiratorial tones, as if letting me in on a secret.

"I don't need a job, Dan," I said.

It was an idle comment, made more in jest than to make a point. But he didn't take it that way. His eyes flashed and his back stiffened. Immediately I wished I could take the words back.

"I didn't ask if you needed a job. I said I got a job for you."

"Sorry," I said. "Just joking."

"This isn't a joke. I want you to help me bury Fatback."

I looked at him, half confused and half disbelieving. "Bury Fatback? Jumbo said she died last winter."

"That's right," he said. "January."

"So how am I supposed to help bury her?"

"With a shovel. How else?"

"You know what I mean."

"No, I don't."

"It's July. She died in January. She must be buried already."

"I guess you're not up on things," he said.

He nodded slightly toward the far corner near the kitchen door.

A white, oblong, top-loading freezer stood against the wall, piled high with old shoes, jackets, and a few pizza boxes.

"Amana," he said. "The guy at the store said it's the best you can buy."

CHAPTER THREE

BURIAL

I had imagined many things during my drive. But burying Fatback had not been among them. That Dan would put her body in a freezer certainly had never occurred to me.

"She's fine," he said. "Go take a look."

"That's okay. I'll trust you."

"Go on," he insisted.

I walked over and lifted the lid, dreading what I was likely to see. But Dan had made some proper preparations. He had placed the old dog in a green plastic garbage bag and secured it with a twist tie. She was nestled in the center of the freezer among what appeared to be frost-covered pieces of elk and various boxes and cartons of frozen food.

"Have some ice cream," he said. "It's in there somewhere. I got some stuff to do."

He wheeled himself off into the bedroom and began splashing around in the bathroom sink.

I had no desire to spend any more time staring at a green plastic bag containing the carcass of a dog, and I certainly had no desire for any of the ice cream that was wedged in around her, so I shut the lid and moved quietly toward the kitchen area.

One cupboard door was partly open. The shelves were completely full of cans of Campbell's cream of mushroom soup and packs of saltine crackers. There were several jars of grape jam and a half-empty, institutional-size jar of generic peanut butter with its lid askew. About a hundred packs of convenience-store ketchup were stuffed in a corner. A loaf of white bread lay open on the counter. It was a diet that would have killed a lesser man.

I was about to check Dan's refrigerator when I heard him rolling back toward the living room. I hurried back over to the freezer and acted as if I had been waiting casually for his return. He emerged with his hair tied back in a ponytail and a string tie with a turquoise pull hanging around his neck. His face smelled of cheap cologne.

"Did you get some ice cream?" he said.

"A little early for me."

"Suit yourself," he said. "Then let's get it done."

"What?" I asked.

"Bury her."

"Bury her? Now?"

"Hell, yes. If you wait too much longer, you might have to put me in the Amana."

He pushed himself upward slowly from his chair. "Just grab my arm a little bit. Once I'm up I'm okay."

I took his elbow, trying to make my grip seem like casual assistance rather than a prop of support. But he was weak and unsteady; I could feel his fragile bones through the sleeves of his old flannel shirt.

"I'm okay," he said. "Just get me out to the car, then come back and get Fatback."

I assisted him down the steps and led him toward the Toyota's passenger door.

"Nah, not here," he said. "Put me in the backseat. This is a funeral, Nerburn, for Christ's sake."

I did as he requested, then returned to the freezer and hoisted out the green garbage bag. I could feel the old dog's stiff corpse through the plastic.

"Put her next to me," Dan shouted through the window as I struggled down the steps with the weight.

He swept a few wrappers and CD cases onto the floor, and I placed the frost-covered bag on the seat next to him. I wished I had spent more time cleaning out the car before I had driven out to his house that morning, but things were what they were.

"Now, go back into the house, get them two walking sticks next to the door and that buckskin bag on the counter. Be careful, it's got my pipe in it. And bring the shovel on the side of the house."

Despite the informality, I knew I was involved in something important. Dan had loved that dog like a child — indeed, he had always believed that his son's spirit had lived in Fatback. By letting me be involved in burying his old dog, he was allowing me to participate in some kind of ritual burial of his own son. I wanted to do everything right. It was all very complicated and deep, but it was not mine to judge, or even to understand.

"You remember the hill where we used to go to talk?" he said.

"The one with the prairie dog holes?"

"That's the one. Take her up there."

We drove to the base of the hill where he had often taken me on my earlier visit to the reservation. Two tire tracks wound through the grasses toward the top.

"Park here," he ordered. He knew my little car was no match for the rutted trail before us.

"You can't climb that, Dan," I said.

"I can if you carry Fatback," he said.

I shrugged and opened the door for him, then hoisted Fatback's body and the shovel onto my shoulder as he took his two willow walking sticks and started making his way up the hill.

The sun had burned off the morning haze and was beating down with raw intensity. I would have liked to have given Dan some assistance, but I had all I could handle with the heavy plastic bag and the shovel. I was concerned that the heat would thaw things out, and I'd be left carrying something that I didn't even want to imagine.

I labored toward the top of the steep hill, stopping frequently to put down the bag and catch my breath. Dan was too engrossed in his own climb to notice my struggles. I was tempted to make some comment about most funerals having more than one pallbearer, but this seemed to be no time for levity.

When I reached the top, I set the bag down and stood there, doubled over with my hands on my knees, wheezing and gasping in an effort to catch my breath. Dan was still making his way upward, chanting softly.

Despite my exhaustion, I was filled with an almost palpable sense of nostalgia. This was the place I always associated most with Dan and Fatback. It was here where Dan had first spoken to me about the beliefs of his people, here where he had wordlessly called Fatback to him to show me how little I understood of the forces of the world into which I had entered.

I looked out over the hills toward the horizon. It stretched, unbroken, as far as the eye could see in either direction. I could almost hear the old dog snuffling and rushing about, examining the scents and sounds of the hill's unseen life. On the far rise was the spot where she had liked to dig for gophers. Under the lone tree was the place where Dan had bent down and gently pulled burrs and foxtails from between her toes while she had looked up at him with an almost human gaze of love and appreciation.

◇◇◇◇

BY THE TIME DAN MADE IT TO THE TOP, I had begun to remember the true, almost animal power of this land. The wind keened, the grasses hissed as they bent and flowed, the hills rolled endlessly toward the horizon like an amber sea. Far above, in the cobalt sky, a hawk circled and floated. In this world of whisperings and unseen forces, it was easy to imagine that it was watching us and had come to bear witness to the burial of a fellow being.

"Bring her out," Dan said. He was breathing hard, but his voice was clear and filled with purpose.

Cautiously, reluctantly, I took the twist tie off, fearing the worst. But Fatback looked surprisingly ordinary and peaceful, changed only by the cold stiffness of death and the few remaining icy crystals of white on the edges of her fur. She was still the same old hog-backed black Lab with swollen joints and a gray-tinged muzzle.

Dan walked over and stroked her head. "That's a damn good dog," he said, running his gnarled fingers across her icy fur. "Damn good."

"Where do you want to bury her, Dan?" I asked quietly.

"Right there," he said, pointing to the base of the single tree that stood on the top of the hill. "That's the spot."

I lifted her into my arms and carried her like a baby up to the place that Dan had indicated. The ice crystals on her fur were beginning to melt and run down my skin.

I set her down at the base of the tree on the highest point on the hill. Dan handed me the shovel, and I began framing a grave in the hard prairie earth.

"Don't make it square," he said. "Just make a hole."

I did my best to follow his instructions, digging hard against the tough prairie-grass roots. Finally, I was able to hollow out a depression about two or three feet deep. Dan had begun a low chant — the same one I remembered from the first time he had brought me up on the hill.

I glanced around for some clues as to what I should do next, but he had closed his eyes and was lost in his chant. Slowly and carefully I began to pull Fatback down into the hole by her hind legs.

"Wait," Dan said, pulling a small buckskin bag of sage from inside his shirt. "Sprinkle this in the hole and light it," he said.

The wind took the green leaves and scattered them across the hillside, but I was able to gather together enough to create a small pile in the bottom of the depression and get it lit. The leaves darkened and smoldered, filling the air with sweetness and sending the smoke upward in a sinuous dance.

When the pile had burned down to ash, Dan instructed me to pull Fatback's body into the hole.

"I'm going to talk now," he said. His eyes remained lowered, looking only at the body of his beloved dog. He began a long speech or prayer in Lakota. I recognized only *shunka*, the word for dog, and *Tunkashila*, the word for grandfather or the Great Spirit.

He finished with a few *hunh*'s, then abruptly switched to English, probably for my benefit.

"*Shunka*'s the best animal," he said. "Teaches us how to be faithful. How to be kind. Has the purest heart. You always know how *shunka* feels."

He sprinkled some more sage or sweetgrass onto the body, then fell silent. I reached for the shovel and began to pick up some dirt, but he stopped me.

"Aren't you going to say anything?"

"Should I?" I asked.

"Lots of guys can shovel dirt."

I stuck the point of the shovel in the ground, placed both hands on its handle, and bowed my head.

"Fatback was a good dog," I began. "One of the best."

"What the hell you doing?" Dan blurted. "You were her favorite. That's why I invited you here. Don't give a damn lecture; talk to her. Or talk to the Great Spirit."

He shook his head several times. "Get him around white people, and he forgets how to pray and starts giving speeches. Christ."

"Okay, okay," I said, and drew in a deep breath. "Fatback, my buddy, my friend. You were a special dog. You had the kindest eyes. I remember you eating my cheeseburgers, sleeping with your head on my lap in the back of Grover's car. You always seemed to be looking out for me, just like you were looking out for Dan."

Tears welled up in my eyes as I stared down at the lifeless body of the old Lab curled up in the hole.

"*Tunkashila*. Grandfather. Grant this dog's spirit a good journey. She gave us the best of what she had."

I paused and swallowed hard. "I really loved her."

"*Hau, hau*," Dan responded.

I reached for the shovel.

"Wait," Dan said. He dug in his pocket and pulled out a piece of fry bread and threw it in the grave. "For the journey," he said. "Now, give me the shovel."

I handed it across to him.

His arms were feeble. He could only lift a small scoop of dirt. He threw it on the body, then handed the shovel back to me. It was left to me to fill in the grave.

I shoveled until my arms were sore, building a kind of mound on the top of the grave so it would not cave in as the earth settled.

"Make it look like everywhere else," he said. "I want it to disappear. I'll know where to find it."

When I had finished, Dan reached in his pocket and pulled out several red ribbons. "Tie them on the tree," he said. "Keep them long so they can blow in the breeze."

I had seen prayer ribbons before, on the fence at Wounded Knee, on Chief Joseph's teepee site at the Big Hole battlefield in Montana, on old Joseph's grave in the Wallowa Valley in Oregon. But I had never been asked to tie them before. I wondered if there was some special way I was supposed to do it, or if I even dared ask.

But Dan was paying no attention. His eyes were closed and he was holding his hands out as if in supplication. He was speaking again in Lakota, leaving me alone with a task I barely understood. After a short time, he opened his eyes and looked at the ribbons I had tied. He nodded in approval.

He nodded again and moved his hands slightly, as if to give me a hint.

The gesture confused me; I didn't know what he wanted.

He did it again, raising his hands higher toward the sky with his palms up and his fingers out.

He looked at the tree, then at me. Catching on, I raised my hands in imitation of his gesture, mimicking the branches of a tree. "*Utahu can*'s a reminder for us," he said. "Always in prayer. Arms always up, facing the sky. Reminds us we need to pray. When the ribbon moves in the wind, we know the spirit's listening."

Then he closed his eyes and began speaking in Lakota again. After a few minutes of private prayer he put his hands down and gestured me toward the path.

"I want to be alone now," he said. "You go on."

"I'll wait in the car," I said.

He turned and glared at me. "I didn't say, 'Wait in the car.' I said, 'Go on.' I'm just old, I'm not dead."

I stood, unmoving, unsure of what to do. I didn't want to leave him there in the growing heat. We were at least half a mile from his house, and he had barely been able to get up the hill.

"Go on," he said, as if I were a bad dog who refused to leave the premises.

I made my way down the rutted path, glancing over my shoulder at intervals to make sure that he was all right. When he saw me pause, he would shake his finger at me in reprimand. By the time I reached the car he was just a small figure silhouetted against the blue prairie sky.

The last glimpse I had of him was in my rearview mirror. He was holding the stem of his pipe toward the sun. A thin stream of smoke was rising skyward — toward the heavens, toward the Creator, toward the land of *Wakan Tanka* where the spirit of Fatback was traveling her final journey.

CHAPTER FOUR

◇◇◇◇◇◇◇◇◇◇◇◇◇◇◇◇◇◇◇◇◇◇◇◇◇◇◇◇◇◇◇◇

SCARS ON THE MOON

I wanted to stay close by in case Dan needed help getting home, but the lack of sleep had gotten to me. Between the long drive, carrying Fatback up the hill, and the emotions I felt about the old dog's burial, I was overwhelmed with exhaustion. I decided to leave the old man, check into a motel, take a quick nap, then drive back out to see how he was doing. I had to trust that his decision to stay alone on the hill was born of knowledge, not grief, and that no harm would come to him in an environment he knew so well.

Luckily, the motel I had stayed in the last time I had visited was still in operation. It was out on the main highway — an old two-lane that had been almost abandoned by long-distance travelers in favor of the distant, more efficient interstates. I had worried that it would be shut down; it was the only one I knew of for about a hundred miles.

The motel had been dilapidated before, but now it was almost uninhabitable. Most of the units had plywood over the windows. The few still in operation had their shades pulled and the cracks in the windows patched with pieces of duct tape. The paint on the sign was worn and faded to the point where it was only the ghostly image of the word *motel* on a faded gray background. The only indication of life was a garish blue-and-white Pepsi vending machine whirring away in front of the door to the office unit.

The woman at the desk checked me in with an indifferent shrug. "Room nine," she said, and threw me a key attached to a wooden block with the number 9 written on it in ballpoint pen. "It's the one on the end." There were no other cars anywhere.

The interior of the unit was worse than the exterior. The seal around the window air conditioner had been stuffed with pieces of cloth. The carpet was stained and sticky. When I went to track down the source of a drip in the bathroom I discovered that the trap under the sink had been wrapped with a sock in an effort to stop a slow leak. The drip was the sound of the water landing in a rusty coffee can that had been placed underneath to catch any overflow.

I threw my aviator bag on one side of the bed and myself onto the other. I could hardly keep my eyes open. I figured I'd grab a few minutes' rest, then go back out and make sure Dan was okay. After I was sure he was safe I'd return to the motel and really catch up on my sleep.

WHEN I AWOKE, the light through the cracked window had the soft glow of early twilight.

In something close to panic I jumped in my car and set out toward the hill, terrified that I had just contributed to the injury, or possibly even the death, of a frail old man.

When I got there I could see the lone tree silhouetted against the sky, but Dan was nowhere in sight. There were a few small objects on top of Fatback's grave, but beyond those there was only the hissing of the wind and the snapping of the ribbons in the breeze.

I hurried back to the car and sped off in the direction of the old man's house.

The sun was cutting below the hilltops as I bounced my way up the rutted drive. As I stepped out and slammed the car door a figure appeared in the doorway. It was Dan.

Half relieved, half amazed, I climbed the steps and opened the door. "How'd you get back?" I asked.

He ignored the question. There was a disconcerting air of distance and isolation around him. I stood quietly beneath the cold glare of the fluorescent lights, unsure if I should come in or leave. Dan padded from sink to table, moving things distractedly. It struck me that the television was off. I had never heard such a large silence in his house before.

"Is everything okay?" I asked.

"Yeah," he said. It was a terse and closed answer.

I took a few steps forward. He seemed oblivious to my presence. After a few seconds I turned to leave.

"Just a minute," he said, and shuffled over to the kitchen cabinets. He reached into a jumble of papers and grabbed what appeared to be a small photograph and put it in his shirt pocket.

"Come on," he said. "Let's go out back. I want to talk."

I could not understand what had caused this sharp change in mood, and I dared not ask.

I helped Dan down the wooden steps, around the junk car that had served as Fatback's doghouse, and into the back field that opened onto the wide Dakota prairie. The sky was darkening, and purple shadows were filling in the draws and gullies.

"Get me something to sit on," Dan said.

I grabbed an old wooden bench that had been leaned up against the house and helped ease him onto it. He was more morose than I had ever seen him. Far to the southwest a red antenna light blinked its lonely, rhythmic message.

I sat quietly as the dark grew around us, allowing him to choose the moment to speak. For almost twenty minutes we sat in absolute silence.

Finally, he spoke up.

"Look at that moon, Nerburn," he said, gazing at the spectral orb that was rising in the east. "Looks all bright and hopeful. But if you look at it close, you can see that it's all full of scars."

He kept fingering the photograph in his shirt pocket. From somewhere in the distance came an animal's piercing cry.

"That old dog," he said, "her spirit's gone now. We let her loose today."

"I was happy to help," I said.

He poked at the ground with his walking stick.

"There's too many deaths," he said softly. "Too many deaths. From the first day we see them. Babies dying. A week, two weeks old, just been around long enough for the mom and dad to get to know their little spirits. Kids drunk, killing themselves in cars. Diabetes. Cancer. Our old medicines don't work. Dying everywhere. There's a wake and a funeral every damn week on this reservation. Hell, every damn day. Sometimes seems they're the only thing happening around here."

He spit once into the darkness, like a shaman trying to rid himself of a poison.

"Makes scars, Nerburn. Scars on the heart. Even our little kids got scars on the heart. Your folks got big hospitals, your babies all grow up. When someone dies you put them in a box and drive them out to some cemetery where right down the block there's people laughing and eating in restaurants who don't even know what's going on. Here, you feel every death. Everyone knows. Everyone gets a new scar."

Ground animals rustled in the grasses. The shadowy form of some kind of night bird passed swiftly overhead.

Quietly he pulled the photograph from his pocket.

"Make a fire, Nerburn," he said. "I got something to tell you."

IT WAS WELL PAST MIDNIGHT BEFORE I LEFT. The fire had grown, flared, and settled into embers. I had hardly spoken a word in all the time we had sat there. In those hours Dan had let me into his life in a way that he never had before.

His parents had been born right before the Wounded Knee massacre in 1890, he said. His grandmother was among those killed. She had been hiding in the gully of the creek with her little boy when the government soldiers opened fire from the hill with their Hotchkiss guns. No one knew exactly when she had been hit, or if she had died instantly. All they knew is that she was said to have been dragged by her arms up the hill to the mass grave and thrown in by the white volunteers who were paid five dollars a body to dispose of the government carnage.

"They threw quicklime on her so she'd decompose," he said, his voice shaking with rage and grief. "They threw quicklime on her face so it would rot faster. That was my grandmother, Nerburn. That was my grandmother."

I had heard such stories about the burial of Sitting Bull at Fort Yates, though never about the grave at Wounded Knee. But I kept silent, not wishing to interrupt his story.

His grandfather had been out on the battlefield fighting when his grandma was killed. He'd taken the boy and gone north.

Dan wasn't sure how they'd escaped — there were a lot of different stories. But his grandpa set up a little homestead back in the hills, then married a woman from Wind River. They'd had some kids together, but she wanted to go home to Wyoming, so she took her kids, and Dan's grandpa raised Dan's dad mostly by himself.

It was a hard time with no mom and almost no food in the house. His grandfather had planted a little garden, and they hunted deer and quail to supplement their diet. When things got bad they ate prairie dogs, but mostly they got by on government commodities and the game they could shoot out in the hills.

When Dan's dad was old enough he went to Canada, where he met a woman from Sitting Bull's band who had remained up at Fort Walsh. They'd gotten married and had two children. Dan came first; his little sister, Yellow Bird, was born three or four years later.

It had been a happy childhood. Yellow Bird was a quiet girl. She mostly stayed at home with their mother. She was always singing and playing with dolls. Dan spent his time with other boys from the reservation, riding horses along the hills and ridges and pretending it was the old days when there were buffalo to hunt and enemies to fight.

Everything had been fine until Yellow Bird got sick. She got the disease with spots — measles, he thought, or smallpox. It was everywhere on the reservation. For days she lay in her bed as if she were dead. When she finally woke up, she had a look of terror in her eyes. Her mother said something to her, and she started crying. She began shouting and twisting in bed, and it took two people to hold her down. It turned out she couldn't hear anything. The disease had stopped up her ears.

That's when everything changed. After that Yellow Bird never went out of the house. She could still talk some, but she couldn't hear anyone. If Dan spoke very slowly, or very close to her face, she could make out something, but mostly she couldn't understand what anyone was saying. She told Dan it was like being under water.

The grandmas from the village would come up and sit with her. They made special dolls for her with beaded dresses and little buckskin moccasins. Yellow Bird would talk to the dolls, and the grandmas would move the dolls around to talk back. Other than that, no one could get her to say anything. Dan was the only person she'd talk to.

One day when Dan was about ten the family was sitting in the house eating breakfast when they heard a car drive up. In those days only white people had cars, and white people visiting their house usually meant no good. Dan's dad told the kids to run out the back door and hide in the grass and not to look up or make any noise until they heard the car drive away.

Dan grabbed Yellow Bird and pulled her up to a hollow on the ridge. She kicked and screamed, but he just lifted her up and carried her. When he put her down she lay quiet for a second. But when he wasn't looking, she jumped up and ran back toward the house.

"I want Pehanska. I want Pehanska," she screamed. That was the name of her favorite doll. Dan had never heard her scream so loud since she had gotten sick.

The white man must have heard her screaming, too, because he came out in back. When Dan saw him coming, he ducked his head down like his father had told him. There was some loud shouting, then Dan heard the car door slam and the sound of the car going down the dirt path from the house.

He waited for a while to make sure the car wasn't coming back, and then he ran down the hill as fast as he could. His mother was standing in the backyard, just staring. She grabbed him and hugged him. He could still remember the fresh-washed smell of her dress after all these years.

When he went inside his father was sitting in the old brown chair, facing the wall. He was just sitting there, not saying a word.

"Where's Yellow Bird?" Dan asked.

His father didn't look up or say anything.

"Where's my sister?" Dan said again. "I want Yellow Bird."

"Let your father be," his mother said softly.

"No. I want to know what happened to my sister."

His mother pulled him closer and stroked his hair. "Yellow Bird's gone," she said. "The school men took her."

Dan ran to the corner and began gathering up his clothes. "Then I'm going to the school, too," he said.

His mother wrapped her arms around him. He fought with her to get away until his father slowly turned around in his chair. His eyes were dark and empty.

"You will stay here," he said. It was a tone Dan had never heard before.

For the next several weeks the house was silent, like a house of the dead. His mother cried and spent a lot of time out in the yard. His father just sat in his chair like a ghost, as if the spirit had gone out of him.

Dan kept pleading to go be with Yellow Bird, but his father wouldn't listen to him. "You're not going to that school," he said. "I've already lost one child to the white man. I'm not going to lose another."

His mother tried to reason with him. But Dan wouldn't listen. He just wanted to find his sister. He felt responsible for letting her break free so the white man could catch her.

Finally he had worked up his courage to challenge his father. It was not something a Lakota boy would normally do.

"I'm going to go," he said. "You have to let me."

His father said nothing, just listened.

Dan pleaded with him. "It's not like the old days, not even like when you were young. There's no buffalo to hunt. I can't fight the enemies to prove my courage. All I can do is ride around on my pony and shoot at prairie dogs. Please, father," he said. "This is my chance to become a man. I can go take care of little Yellow Bird. You've got to let me."

His father sat with his hands folded in front of his mouth. Dan remembered the sadness in his eyes. When he finally spoke, his voice was very soft and quiet.

"The white man's world is very strong," he said, "but it has no heart. You are my son. I don't want to lose you to that world. I don't want you to be like one of those boys who goes to the white man's school and comes back calling the elders 'savages.'"

"You won't lose me," Dan promised. "I won't become a white man."

His father put his hand on Dan's shoulder. "All young men think they are strong. But something happens to them when they go off to the white man's world. They go thinking about their people, but they come back thinking only of themselves."

"Please," Dan asked, "let me go." He had never begged his father for anything.

His father thought for a long time. He walked to the window and stared out at the hills. Then he turned and looked at Dan.

"Maybe you're right. Maybe this is your path to manhood. My fears should not be your fears. Maybe the time has come for you to do with your life what I can no longer do with mine."

He'd brought out his pipe and attached the two parts together. It was a pipe he had gotten from his grandfather.

"Here. Let us smoke together. You can go. You can go to the white man's world. But you must promise me that you will never give up your Indian heart and that you will always take care of little Yellow Bird."

At that point, Dan went silent. We sat together without speaking, staring into the fading fire. Strange, muffled sounds came from his chest. He fingered the piece of paper that he had put in his shirt pocket. When he spoke again his voice was so soft you could barely hear it above the nighttime rustle of the grasses.

"I smoked with my father," he said. "I made the promise. And I have never given up my Indian heart."

He paused and inhaled deeply. The embers shifted and settled. His silence carried the weight of an entire lifetime.

He took the piece of paper from his pocket and handed it to me. It was a small faded photo of a little girl.

"But I lost little Yellow Bird," he said. "I lost little Yellow Bird. Now I want you to help me find her."

CHAPTER FIVE

◇◈◇◈◇◈◇◈◇◈◇◈◇◈◇◈◇◈◇◈◇◈◇◈◇◈◇◈◇◈◇

RESERVATION FORTUNE COOKIE

I helped Dan into the house, then left quietly. My mood was pensive and somber. We both understood that the hard question had been asked.

I was confused and frightened. I didn't understand what had just happened. Why had Dan waited until now to look for his sister? And why had he chosen me? None of it made any sense.

I lay on the lumpy motel bed listening to the whir of the air conditioner and the drip from the pipe under the sink.

Dan had insisted that I keep the photo of Yellow Bird. When I had tried to hand it back to him he had refused it and had folded my hand around it. "You keep it," he said. "Maybe it will help."

I turned on the bedside light and stared at the grainy image. It was small — no more than two inches square — and had been roughly cut from a larger photo, probably of a group of girls standing in front of a church or boarding school.

Yellow Bird wore a checked dress and a sweater buttoned at the neck. Her hair was cut short into a ragged pageboy. Though the image was faded almost beyond recognition, it was impossible to miss the fierceness in her gaze. She stared directly into the camera as if challenging it. Her mouth was tight, and her jaw was clenched. But her eyes betrayed a sadness and loneliness that almost broke my heart. She could not have been more than eight years old.

The night dragged on, with the seconds measured by the incessant drip from the leaking pipe. It was like a heartbeat, a drumbeat, the tick of a clock. Finally, as the darkness turned slowly toward the dawn, I fell into a fitful sleep.

When I awoke the room was awash in daylight. The red numbers on the cheap bedside clock said 10:45.

I washed up in the weak dribble from the shower, then checked out of the motel and headed toward Dan's house.

The night of sleep had cleared my head, but I was still filled with questions and doubts. Why me? Why now? Why had no one sought little Yellow Bird before, or, if they had, why hadn't they found her? And why couldn't Wenonah or Grover or one of Dan's other friends give him the same assistance he was asking of me?

But I put those questions aside. This wasn't about reasons, it was about heart. I owed the old man, not only out of respect for him as an elder but for all he had done for me. If he wanted my help, I would give it.

I drove up the path to his house with a lilt in my spirit. I would get any information that he had, go back to my home, and begin the research. I knew systems; I could talk the proper administrative talk. I could get past the walls of governmental obfuscation and find out what had happened to a little Indian girl who had disappeared from her family almost eighty years ago.

The task would be difficult but not impossible. In fact, it would be almost a pleasure. This was my chance to help a man I respected deeply answer a lifelong question, my chance to help him find peace at the end of his life.

I drove toward his house with a new resolve. I would leave the gifts, say my good-byes, and be on the road by noon.

But my good spirits were dashed when I turned into the clearing and found my way blocked by a welter of cars. Something must have happened during the night. Perhaps Dan had exhausted himself on the climb and fallen ill, or worse.

I could hear commotion inside as I ran to the door. Without knocking, I pushed open the screen and rushed in. The room was full of people. The television was blaring on the far side of the room.

"Hey, Nerburn," came a gruff and raspy voice. It was Dan's buddy, Grover, sitting at the kitchen table, eating a bowl of cold cereal. Dan was sitting next to him, washed and dressed and laughing.

I was amazed and relieved. Not only was the old man okay, but something akin to a party was going on. It made no sense in light of what I had seen only a few hours before, but I had learned long ago that reservation ways were not my ways. Perhaps this was some post-burial feast. Perhaps this was the way things were done after a funeral for an animal. But whatever it was, the old man was safe. And he seemed to be in high spirits. The mood was positively festive.

Wenonah, Dan's granddaughter, was standing at the counter rolling dough into balls. Several young children, who were either hers or her grandchildren, were crawling under the table and pushing toy cars across the dirty linoleum floor. A gaunt, pasty man I had never seen before was sitting in a chair in the corner watching the television. The entire couch was taken up by the massive body of Jumbo. If he had weighed four hundred pounds before, he must have been pushing a quarter of a ton by now. He sank down so far into the couch that he looked like some huge robin sitting on a nest.

"You made it," he said. "That Ti-yota need any work?"

It was as close to humor as Jumbo was likely to get, and as close to intimacy, as well. I was still in shock at the unexpected situation, but I tried to enter into the spirit of the gathering.

"Why, you got a new pipe wrench you want to try out?"

He let out a rumble that shook the entire couch. The others joined in the laughter.

Wenonah walked over and put her hand on my arm. "Thank you for helping Grandpa," she said. She had never made physical contact with me before, and there was a softness in her manner that I did not remember. "This is the happiest I've seen him in years."

I was confused but delighted. These people had been part of my life when I was here before. I never felt that they had really liked me, with the possible exception of Jumbo, who had liked me because he liked my truck. But their enthusiasm to see me now seemed genuine.

It was a shock to see how much we had all aged. Jumbo's bowl haircut had turned gray around the temples, and he had made a failed attempt to grow a mustache and a beard. A full-blood, or close to it, he did not grow facial hair easily, and the strands that hung from his chin and neck were sparse and patchy. His few remaining teeth either had been removed or had fallen out, so his grin was a great gaping gash that made him look like a chestnut-colored jack-o'-lantern.

Grover still looked harsh and ashen with his gray crew cut and leathery skin, but his sinewy forearms had started to cave in on themselves. He seemed less wiry than stringy, more sunken than solid. He had given up his trademark gleaming white T-shirts for the less naval, more Western look of a striped long-sleeved shirt with pearl buttons. He still wore the pointed-toe, high-heeled cowboy boots, but everything about him seemed less robust and more tentative. The endless cigarettes he smoked had clearly taken their toll.

Wenonah alone seemed to be in the bloom of life. She had put on weight, but it was the rich fullness of motherhood, and she wore it well. With her hair pulled back and her long, blousy dress tied loosely at the waist, she seemed every bit the Indian mother, guiding her kids with a steady hand and caring for the needs of the men

with a quiet efficiency. The children playing on the floor just under-
scored the reality of how the wheel of life had turned and how
another generation was coming up strong behind us.

"Want something to eat, Nerburn?" she asked. I smiled at the
question. It was the same thing she'd said to me when we'd first met
in this same kitchen almost fifteen years before.

"What do you have?" I asked.

"Fry bread."

I could see the golden balls leaning against each other like puck-
ered doughnuts on a piece of newspaper next to the stove.

"Absolutely," I said. The doughy lard pastry had to be one of the
world's least healthy foods, but it was a staple of most Indian diets,
and it tasted wonderful.

She handed me a piece of fresh fry bread wrapped in a napkin,
then two more to pass to Jumbo. The grease leached through and
covered my fingers.

"Better look inside, Nerburn," Grover said from his seat across
the room. "Reservation fortune cookie. Might have a food stamp
inside of it."

The others roared with laughter. It was inside humor and far
from politically correct. But it was a sign that I was no longer an outsider. They were willing to make fun of themselves in my presence,
and their barbs were directed at each other, not at me.

I pulled open the fry bread and gave a shrug.

"Just not a lucky guy," Grover said.

It wasn't much, but it heartened me. Grover had always been
Dan's guardian and protector, and he watched over the old man with
a fierce vigilance. I had learned during my last visit that he kept his
emotions close, and that any sort of relaxed attitude or casual gesture
was a signal of approval. This gentle bit of banter was a clear message of acceptance. It was the first time that I hadn't felt measured or
judged in his presence.

Dan flapped his hand toward the stringy man on the chair in the corner. "This is Shitty," he said. A crude, skinny man with heavy welfare glasses, bad teeth, and a cat-whisker mustache looked up at me and nodded, then turned his attention back to the blaring television.

Dan had never introduced me to anyone before. I had always been forced to find my way into a group by hanging around and just drifting into the conversation. Usually I never even knew a name unless I happened to overhear it being used. Suddenly I was being introduced. This was the single most welcoming gathering I had ever attended on the reservation.

Grover stood up, walked to the counter, pushed down the handle on Dan's old silver toaster, and lit a cigarette from the glowing filaments.

"So, you helped bury Fatback?" he said.

"I did my best," I answered.

"Good thing," Grover said. "I was afraid the old man was going to eat her if he ran out of soup."

Jumbo let out a great, booming guffaw. His heaving belly vibrated across the room.

"Why have you been such a stranger?" Wenonah said. "People ask about you. Sit down. Have another piece of fry bread."

I moved across and took a place at the table next to Dan. I noticed that his hair was washed, and he smelled of cheap cologne.

"You're pretty dressed up," I said.

"Big day," he replied.

"Coffee?" Wenonah asked.

"No, thanks. I can't stay long. It's a long drive home."

Suddenly the room fell silent. I looked around for some sign as to what I'd done wrong. Jumbo and Shitty were staring at their feet; Grover was looking past me at a place on the wall. Even the children had stopped their playing and were staring at me.

Wenonah fixed me with a dark, angry glare.

"I thought you said you were going to help Grandpa," she said.

"I am. I just came by to get a little more information before I take off."

Her glare got harder and darker.

I looked around, frantic. Dan was idly spooning sugar into his bowl of cereal. He would not look at me.

Grover gestured with his lips toward the far corner of the room. An old brown suitcase was sitting behind the door.

"Take it out to your car," he said.

"What's going on?" I asked.

He pulled another cigarette out of his pocket and tapped it on the back of his hand.

"Sometimes you've got to do what you're supposed to do, not what you want to do," he said.

Dan reached over and put his bony hand on my forearm.

"I knew I could count on you, Nerburn," he said. "I always could."

CHAPTER SIX

◇◈◇◈◇◈◇◈◇◈◇◈◇◈◇◈◇◈◇◈◇◈◇◈◇◈◇◈

THE JARBURETOR

I wasn't sure what was going on. I had a faint hope that I was simply being asked to drop Dan off at some friend's house on the rez. But, in my heart, I knew better.

Wenonah handed me a brown paper bag filled with fry bread. "Take good care of him," she said.

"This is a good thing, Nerburn," Jumbo added.

Grover took the old man's arm and helped him down the stoop. I followed behind with the old suitcase and the greasy bag of fry bread.

"Lucky you got this station wagon," Dan said as Grover helped him into the front seat. "It would have been kind of tight in that truck of yours."

Grover positioned himself in the backseat and lit up a cigarette.

The kids from under the table were standing on the front stoop waving. "Bye, Grandpa. Bye, Grandpa," they called.

Dan waved at them like a dignitary passing in a parade.

"So, where am I taking you, Dan?" I asked.

"Just follow Shitty," Grover said. "Soon as he gets his truck started."

Shitty and Jumbo had left the house before we had and were busying themselves with some kind of operations around what was easily one of the worst vehicles I had ever seen.

It was an early 1980s blue Chevy half-ton pickup — or, at least, it probably once had been blue. Where there was any color left, the relentless Dakota sun had faded it to a nondescript off-gray. Almost all the body panels were covered with dings, dents, and bashes. The left front fender, which was of a completely different color, was so rusted that the wheel well looked like it was framed in sharks' teeth.

On the front passenger side, the door had been replaced by a piece of weathered plywood with a rough approximation of a window jigsawed out of it. The window opening was covered with opaque plastic held in place by a border of duct tape. A rock or bird or some other heavy object had hit the windshield at some point, leaving a deep depression that spiderwebbed in all directions, making any sort of visibility nearly impossible.

But all this paled in comparison to the engine. The vehicle had no hood, and a mason jar or something like it was held in place over the center of the engine compartment by a few rods of construction rebar that were welded to either fender. The jar sat in a roughly crafted metal cradle directly above the carburetor. A tangle of copper tubing protruded from the jar and disappeared somewhere down into the engine.

"What in the world is that?" I said.

"Shitty's truck," Dan said.

"I figured that. But the jar? What's that about?"

"It's the jarburetor," Grover answered. "Temporary fix. He's waiting for a part."

"Will it run that way?"

"Has for two years."

I was about to question him further when Jumbo lumbered around from the back of the pickup, took the top off the jar, and poured what I assumed was gasoline into it from a rusted can he had taken from the truck bed. He flipped the jar over into some kind of cradle constructed from the tubing and shouted something to Shitty, who had taken his place in the driver's seat. I heard a grinding and chuffing, then a sound like a rifle shot, followed by a tremendous flame from the vicinity of the jarburetor and a billowing of blue smoke that emerged from the tailpipe and all parts of the undercarriage, making the truck look like it was floating on a blue cloud of exhaust.

I expected the gasoline in the mason jar to explode from the flame, but it didn't. Meanwhile, Jumbo hurried around to the passenger door, pulled off the piece of plywood, threw it in the pickup bed, and wedged himself in. The truck sagged noticeably, then began issuing ear-splitting reports from the tailpipe. The flame subsided, there was a horrible grinding sound, and the vehicle moved forward on its cloud of blue smoke. It made its way past me on through the grasses and coughed its way down the path.

"What's that all about?" I asked.

"Bad fuel pump," Grover said. "You have to add gas by hand."

"He's been waiting two years for a fuel pump for an old Chevy?"

"He's saving up."

"I've seen some bad vehicles in my life, but that's . . ."

"It's ahead of you," Grover interrupted.

There was nothing more to say. I fell in behind Shitty's smoke cloud and followed him down toward the highway.

Once on the main road, Shitty's truck was even more astonishing. It must have been drinking gasoline at the rate of about a gallon every five miles. When the carburetor became overloaded, the car hiccuped, another flame shot out, and there was a backfire that echoed against the reservation hills. The blue-black smoke that poured from the tailpipe and undercarriage made it almost impossible to breathe, even at a distance of a hundred feet. To avoid the noxious fumes I fell back even farther.

"Don't lose him," Dan said.

"Doing my best," I said. "Who is this Shitty, anyway?"

Grover leaned over from the backseat. "Jumbo's business associate."

"The result of a national search, I presume?"

"Hired him on as his foreign car mechanic after your Nissan. He works on Ti-yotas, too."

Shitty and Jumbo popped and thundered down the road ahead of us. We were moving farther from town and deeper into the backcountry of the reservation. Here and there an old tire with a name painted on it would be hooked on a pole beside a rutted path that wound back into the hills. There were no houses visible anywhere.

Every mile or so Shitty would pull over, Jumbo would climb out and add more gasoline to the jar, and the whole starting process would be repeated. The flames would shoot, the exhaust would fire and report, and the truck would surge forward, leaving a cloud of inky smoke lingering behind us in the azure summer sky.

After half an hour I was beginning to wonder if we were going to leave the reservation entirely, when Shitty's bony arm emerged from the smoke, signaling that he was turning left. His car slowed, and he turned off into a pair of ruts that looked as if they had not been traveled since the days of buckboards.

"Now comes the fun part," Grover said, clapping me on the shoulder.

Within a minute of entering the buckboard trail, it became evident to me that my little wagon couldn't make it down this washed-out, cratered path for more than a hundred yards.

"How far do we have to go on this?" I asked.

"Couple, five miles," Grover said.

"Can't do it."

"Shitty's doing just fine," he answered.

Up ahead, over the next hill, I could see the smoke from the truck rising into the clear summer sky.

"Yeah, but I don't want my car to end up like Shitty's."

"So, you expect me to walk?" Dan said.

"If I try to drive on this, we'll all be walking in a few minutes. Where are we going, anyway?"

"Damn it, Nerburn," Grover snapped, starting to open the door. "I'll drive."

I was more than a little irritated. "If you wanted to drive, we should have taken your car."

"I wouldn't take my car on a road like this," he said. "It's a classic."

From somewhere over the rise I could hear Shitty honking.

"God," I said. "His horn actually works."

"Got to," Grover said. "It's the law."

It was obvious that Dan was getting impatient. "You going to let an old man die out here in the sun?"

Shitty's horn was blaring insistently in the distance.

"Okay, okay," I conceded. "I'll give it a try." I comforted myself by remembering all the news footage I had seen of various revolutionaries and guerilla groups pounding across deserts in pickup trucks. They were always driving Toyotas. Perhaps, with luck, my wagon could survive what was ahead of us. "But if this car breaks down...," I said.

"Then Shitty can fix it," Grover interjected.

I tried to navigate the trail in my lowest gear. But the situation was hopeless. The road, such as it was, was crisscrossed with gullies a foot deep. Here and there a rock the size of a small boulder protruded from the middle of the path, and I had to ease one tire up onto it because the undercarriage of the car would be torn apart if I tried to straddle it.

As we got deeper into the hills, the path gradually became a groove in the earth, with chalky, two-foot-high banks on either side. I had no idea how it had been created or for what kind of vehicle it was intended. All I knew was that the cross-wash gullies were becoming deeper and more frequent, and there was no place either to pull over or to turn around. Had another vehicle been coming from the opposite direction — unlikely as that was — there was no conceivable way we could have gotten past each other.

About every half mile we came to a barbed-wire gate strung across the road. They were nothing more than three strands of barbed wire attached to a desiccated post that was hitched to a stationary post on the other side of the road by a loop of wire. If you lifted the loop off, you could pull the gate back and continue on your way.

I wondered why Jumbo and Shitty hadn't left these gates open, knowing that we were close behind. But each gate we approached was properly rehooked, requiring one of us to get out, push on the freestanding post, lift off the loop, and drag the gate out of the way until the vehicle was past. Then, once the car was through, the gate had to be closed again.

When we got to the first gate, I slowed to an idle, expecting Grover to get out and do the hooking and unhooking. But he remained in the backseat. "I'm an elder now, Nerburn," he said. Dan said nothing.

I bit my lip, then shoved the car into park, climbed out, pushed as hard as I could on the post of the gate, and tried to jimmy the loop over its top. It must have been Jumbo who had closed it last, because every loop was shoved so far down on the post that it required the strength of Hercules to move it.

I managed to do the first gate — both the opening and closing

— with only minimal cutting and tearing of my hands. But by the time we were at the fourth gate, maybe two miles back into the hills, my hands were raw and bloody.

"Shitty's getting pretty far ahead of us, Nerburn," Grover said, leaning back and lighting up another cigarette.

Despite my irritation and concern for my car, I couldn't help but marvel at the beauty of the landscape. This was the way this country had looked before the arrival of the white man — mile after mile of rolling, amber grasslands beneath a cloudless sky, with the chirping of plover and curlew and swarms of buzzing insects filling the clear afternoon air. I kept telling myself, "It's just a car. This is for the old man. You're doing it for the old man," though what it was I was doing for him was still unclear.

We traveled through the hills for almost an hour. The actual distance we covered was probably no more than five miles, but it was the most difficult five miles I have ever driven. After a while I simply closed my ears to the groaning and clunking of the suspension as my car dropped into foot-deep gullies and climbed over half-buried boulders.

I comforted myself with the knowledge that other vehicles had made it. Indeed, Shitty's old pickup was making it. If I drove carefully and with an eye to the tracks where vehicles had driven before, it was possible to keep the car from hanging up on some dirt ledge or rock outcropping and to move forward with a certain degree of confidence. Still, I had a feeling that these five miles were taking more out of my little Toyota wagon than the hundred and some thousand miles that it had traveled up to that time.

After maybe seven or eight gates, we topped a rise that overlooked a small line of trees huddled against a dry creek bed in the bottom of a gully. Shitty had already made it to the bottom and parked; his truck was smoldering in a nearby clearing next to three or four other vehicles. A few Indian men were walking around in swimsuits and T-shirts and laceless tennis shoes, with towels thrown over their shoulders or around their necks. A young man in a black hooded sweatshirt was racing up and down the gully in a four-wheeler. Two children, neither more than six or eight years old, were balanced precariously on the back of the vehicle. At least half a dozen dogs were running around, tussling with each other and chasing after the four-wheeler.

"Here it is," Grover said.

"Here what is?" I said.

"Orv's."

I had no idea who or what "Orv's" was, but I drove down the hill with a great feeling of relief. Wherever we were, at least we were at the end of the journey, and, by all appearances, my Toyota had survived.

As we got to the bottom Grover pointed to a man in his late fifties who was sitting on a fallen tree trunk at the edge of the clearing.

"That's Orv," he said. "Shitty's dad."

Orv was fitting the parts of a pipe together. The stem of the pipe was about two feet long and carved from a piece of light-colored wood. The bowl, a long cylinder about six inches tall, was fashioned from red pipestone. Orv was attending to the task with the focus and precision of a surgeon.

"Come on, Nerburn," Grover said. "You should meet him."

We walked across the clearing. "This is Nerburn," Grover said, as if what mattered was that I be introduced to Orv, not that Orv be introduced to me.

Orv looked up at me with warm, kind eyes. "Welcome," he said. "I hear you're going to help Dan."

"I hope to," I said, though I was still unsure what "helping Dan" meant.

"We'll do a good sweat for you," he said. "Get you ready. Try to make things right with the spirits."

He finished with the pipe and handed it to Grover. Grover took it in his hands with an unashamed reverence.

"Come on," Orv said to me, pushing himself upward. "Time to get the wood. I can use your help. We'll get Shitty and Jumbo."

I could see Shitty and Jumbo on the far side of the clearing talking to some young girls who must have arrived in one of the other vehicles. I could not imagine how they had gotten here or what they were doing here. It was impossible to imagine that this was a common gathering place or that people drove in here as a matter of course.

Orv waved his hand toward Jumbo and Shitty. Immediately, as if this was some kind of signal, the two men leaped into action — or at least as close to "leaped" as Jumbo was able to do. He poured some more gasoline into the mason jar, and Shitty fired up the engine. Then Jumbo pulled the plywood door out of the pickup bed, threw it on the ground next to the truck, and settled himself on the tailgate. They thundered across the clearing to where we were standing. Orv got in the passenger seat next to Shitty and gestured me toward the back.

I climbed into the pickup bed next to Jumbo. There were probably fifty Mountain Dew cans scattered around, along with various tire jacks and bolts and greasy, unidentifiable pieces of metal. I took a seat on a spare tire that was lying flat next to an oily orange chain saw and several dented cans of what I assumed to be gasoline. I did not like the idea of riding in a pickup bed filled with gasoline containers in a vehicle that spewed flames from its carburetor. But any expression of concern on my part would have sounded too suburban and prissy. So I put my fate in the hands of the gods and prepared to offer such assistance as I could.

I soon learned that the gas cans were the least of my concerns. At least their toxins were encased. But the exhaust from Shitty's truck was another matter altogether. When Shitty pushed on the accelerator, the thick, acrid smoke poured right up from beneath us and engulfed us in a black stinking cloud that almost made me gag. My eyes started burning, and I pulled my shirt up over my face. Jumbo, who was sitting on the tailgate with his legs dangling, looked at me with amusement and calmly lit up a cigarette.

"Who needs cigarettes when you can breathe this stuff?" I shouted.

Jumbo tapped his ear to indicate that he couldn't hear, then went back to placidly inhaling cigarette smoke and exhaust while eating chunks of Wenonah's fry bread from the napkin he had stuffed into the pocket of his bib overalls.

I truly thought that I might asphyxiate, and probably would have, had we not been out in the open. But the blue skies absorbed most of the smoke, and I was able to get a breath of fresh air every time Shitty shut off the engine to gather wood or refill the jar, which was about every thirty or forty feet. As soon as the truck stopped, Orv would climb out, grab the chain saw, and cut limbs from fallen trees that lay everywhere along the dry creek bed.

The young man on the four-wheeler had fallen in behind us. At each stop he ran over and assisted Orv by pulling out deadfall or shifting the position of the branches so that Orv could get a clear cut at them. The two young girls who were riding with him assisted by picking up small pieces of kindling that they then threw into the back of the truck.

I tried to help as best I could, taking the logs and bigger branches from the young man as soon as they were cut, and either handing them to Shitty or throwing them in the back of the truck myself. I noticed that Orv always paused right before cutting and said a few words under his breath. I assumed it was a prayer of some sort, or an invocation. The young man stood still during this pause, only moving again when Orv revved up the saw for the next cut.

It was obvious that Orv was a good man. Though only in his

fifties, he was clearly the patriarch of this group. He had an ample belly and a cauliflower nose and pock-scarred face that would have made him seem ugly had it not been for the kindly manner he exuded in everything he did. From calling Shitty and Jumbo into action, to starting the chain saw and cutting the tree limbs, there was calmness in his demeanor. When he touched things, he did so gently. When he moved, he was patient and deliberate. There was something almost prayerful in his approach to every task. He seemed at peace with his work, with himself, and with the world around him.

At one point I heard him tell Shitty to stop, and he climbed out and walked past a number of downed trees to a limb that was freshly fallen and still covered with leaves. He paused for a moment, said a few words under his breath, then deftly sheared off the leaf-bearing branches and cut the remaining limb into precise two-foot pieces.

"This one will give us good smoke," he said as I gathered up the freshly cut logs. "It still remembers being up in the sky."

He lifted one of the shorn branches and said a short prayer. "Oak," he said, as if teaching me. "Oak's a good tree. Lots of courage. It'll stand on a hill all by itself, even when there's no other tree around. Holds out its arms to protect the animals during a storm. It's good wood for a sweat."

We proceeded this way up along the gully. Orv cut, the young man handed the logs to me, and I handed them to Shitty, who then handed them to Jumbo, who piled them in the pickup bed. It was like a water brigade, and it made me feel good to be part of a collective effort.

After about a half hour, the pickup bed was almost full. We were all sweating and exhausted from the heat. Orv sat down on a fallen log and gestured me to do the same. He nodded to the sweatshirt boy, who immediately ran back to the pickup and grabbed a plastic milk jug filled with water. He sat down next to us and handed the jug to Orv.

"This will be a good sweat," Orv smiled. "We're getting good wood."

The sweatshirt boy nodded. I had the distinct impression that he was serving an apprenticeship or was in some kind of training.

I was fascinated by Orv's concern for the wood. I had sculpted in wood for almost twenty years before turning to writing, and it was the spirit and presence of trees that had first piqued my interest in the Native world. It was the Native peoples alone who seemed to understand the almost mystical life force of trees in the way I had come to experience it when I worked for six or eight months on a single tree. Now I was with a man who seemed to accept this spiritual presence as a matter of course, and who sprinkled his conversation with casual references to a way of seeing the world that few, if any, white men I had met could even begin to understand.

"So, the tree you choose is important?" I asked.

"Oh, yeah. You want trees with a good spirit."

"How do you decide which trees to choose?"

"Oh, I just kind of drive along until I get a feeling. Maybe I'll see a tree and I'll feel like it's calling out to me. Cottonwood's the best. That's the sacred tree. The best cottonwood is from a tree that's been used for a Sun Dance. Some guys, they'll use anything — old two-by-fours, scrap, whatever they have. I don't think that's a good way to do it."

He took a leaf from a branch that was lying nearby and put it in his mouth and started chewing it.

I decided to take a chance.

"I used to carve wood," I said. "I did big sculptures from trees. Six months, a year with one tree, and you learn something about it."

I was nervous that I'd sound like some New Age seeker. But I wanted to continue the conversation. This was one of the few men I'd ever met who was willing to talk about spirit in trees.

Orv nodded understandingly.

Emboldened, I continued. "There was an oak tree once. It had been down for years. I didn't like to kill trees to carve in. It seemed wrong."

Orv nodded again.

"I worked on that tree for months. It was the saddest tree I'd ever known. Something about the way it responded to the chisel. Sometimes after six or eight hours alone with it, I'd just start crying. It seemed so lonely."

"It must have had a hard life," Orv said. "Oaks are pretty strong. They can take a lot."

"That's what I thought. That's why this one surprised me so much. Oak always seemed pretty masculine, almost military. I expected a struggle, or at least something that challenged me. But this one was crying."

I had never said words out loud like this to anyone before.

"It's good to listen to them," Orv said. "What kind of tree did you like best?"

"Walnut was my favorite. Walnut and butternut. They seemed so giving, so feminine."

"We don't have them out here. They have fruits or nuts, right?" I nodded.

"Trees that have nuts, fruits — they're used to giving things away."

In a strange way it was one of the headiest conversations I had ever had. I felt like a boy in a confessional. These were thoughts I had never shared with anyone, and here I was carrying on a perfectly matter-of-fact conversation with a man I had just met, telling him things that I didn't even share with my wife and children.

The boy in the hooded sweatshirt was sitting across from us, saying nothing.

Shitty shouted something from over at the pickup. Orv took a final swig of water and hoisted himself upward. "Time to get back," he said.

He looked over at me with his kind, smiling eyes. "Why don't you pick a couple of logs? We can use a few more."

IT WAS NOT AN EASY RIDE BACK TO THE CLEARING. We had filled the truck bed to overflowing with logs and branches until there was hardly enough room in the bed for us to sit. Jumbo had managed to clear off a place on the tailgate and had situated himself there. I had found a little space for my feet in the front of the pickup box and had propped myself on the one undented side panel.

While we had been cutting and loading, the two young girls from the four-wheeler had climbed on the roof of the cab and were lying flat with their fingers grasping a thin ridge of metal at the top of the shattered windshield. No one, from Orv to Jumbo to Shitty or the boy on the four-wheeler, seemed to think it was strange or dangerous.

"Hold on tight," Orv shouted up to the girls.

They gripped the windshield lip hard, laughing and squealing as Shitty jounced the pickup through the gully, tossing us violently from side to side.

I sat in the choking haze of exhaust trying to protect the girls by holding onto their ankles without losing my own precarious balance. A half-dozen dogs ran alongside the truck, barking and jumping. Occasionally Jumbo threw tiny pieces of fry bread in their direction, and they would all peel off and gather in a noisy scrum until the prize had been claimed. Then, with a few final snarls and bites at each other for good measure, they would fall in behind the truck again, barking and yipping and jumping toward Jumbo, hoping for one more bite of Wenonah's fry bread prize.

We surged forward in this fashion — a quarter-ton Indian, a gray-bearded white man, a cat-whiskered mechanic named Shitty, and a sweat lodge keeper who talked about the personalities of trees

— all jammed together in a truck that got its fuel from a mason jar, while two girls, barely old enough to ride bikes, lay splayed on its roof, laughing and squealing, and a young man wearing a hooded sweatshirt in 100-degree heat led a pack of random hounds who moiled and barked and fought each other for fry bread.

I closed my eyes and thought of my wife and son and our quiet house in the northern Minnesota woods. I was a long way from home.

◇◇◇◇◇◇◇◇◇◇◇◇◇◇◇◇◇◇◇◇◇◇◇◇◇◇◇◇◇

CHAPTER SEVEN

LOOKING FOR MR. PEANUT

O rv's sweat lodge was little more than a large hump of blankets and hides and pieces of plastic maybe twelve feet in diameter and four feet high. It was nestled comfortably among the aspen and birch on the bank of the dry creek bed. To an outsider, it might have looked like some kind of homeless person's shelter. The phrase that kept coming to mind was "a beaver lodge made by a hobo."

Orv started the fire with the help of the young man in the sweat-shirt, then took a seat on one of the logs that were scattered randomly near the lodge.

"The Creator's gonna give us a good sweat," he said.

Dan and Grover said a few *hau*'s in agreement, and then we all lapsed into a comfortable Indian silence while the fire grew and the leaves in the surrounding birch trees whispered and danced in the afternoon sun.

The mood had become almost totally calm and pacific when the peace was shattered by Jumbo crashing toward us through the underbrush. He emerged from the foliage holding a bulging green garbage bag. He tossed it in front of me and said, "Here, Nerburn."

"What's this?" I asked.

"Look inside," Grover said.

I gingerly opened the bag, remembering all too well what had been in the last green trash bag I'd been asked to open. Jumbo was watching in anticipation.

"It ain't too clean," he rumbled as I looked inside at a jumble of wadded-up underwear and T-shirts. "It's at the bottom."

I had no interest in digging around in a bag of Jumbo's unwashed laundry.

"Here, I'll get it," he said, and thrust his hand deep into the bag.

"There," he said, pulling out a huge, ragged red and white swimsuit the size of a small tent.

He held it aloft, like a prize catch, then tossed it in my direction. "For the sweat."

I looked at it with amazement. Its size was astonishing, and the prospect of putting on anything that Jumbo had worn, much less anything that had come out of his bag of dirty laundry, did not appeal to me in the least.

I picked it up gingerly. It was covered with grease and other substances that did not bear close examination.

"Think it'll fit, Nerburn?" Grover asked.

"I'll probably have to cinch it up a bit."

"Yeah, you're kind of a *teʐi tanka*, but not like Jumbo. Jumbo's a really big guy."

"Big everywhere," Jumbo grinned, pointing toward his crotch.

"Home of Mr. Peanut," Grover said.

The men roared with laughter. It must have been an old joke, and I had no interest in entertaining the visuals it conjured up.

The young boy from the four-wheeler had taken over building the fire. I could not believe that he continued to wear the sweatshirt in the overwhelming heat. But he not only kept it on, he kept the hood up. I had no idea if it was part of some ritual, or if he was hiding from something. But none of the other men seemed to notice or care, so I soon gave up thinking about it and let myself settle into the beauty and sanctuary afforded by this small grove of trees in the sweltering Dakota landscape.

It took about an hour for the fire to get hot enough to heat the rocks for the sweat. The young man tended the fire with the seriousness of an acolyte, turning rocks with a set of deer antlers and adding new ones with a pitchfork. When he added the two pieces of wood that I had chosen to the fire, he turned to me and nodded.

Dan and Orv and Grover carried on a sporadic conversation, consisting mainly of short, one-line comments that evoked laughter from the others. Half were spoken in Lakota. Others were said so low, or so offhandedly, that I couldn't understand them. But there was no malice or exclusion in what was said. These were just old friends, sitting together, enjoying each other's company as part of an old, comfortable ritual. I felt honored to be among them.

Occasionally, one of them would pick up the old plastic milk jug filled with water and pass it around to keep us cool in the growing afternoon heat. Orv kept sprinkling what I assumed was sage onto the flames, and his helper kept turning the rocks with the forked antler. Every time Orv added another log, he made that same incantation I had heard back while we were cutting the deadfall. Again, there was a quiet sense of ceremony in everything he did.

"Orv pours a gentle sweat," Dan said.

"I could not imagine him doing it any other way," I smiled, appreciative of the comment but not sure exactly what it meant.

"I've been doing sweats with him . . ." He turned to Orv. "When did you get out, Orv?"

"Ninety-eight, ninety-nine," he said.

"Army?" I asked.

"Prison," Orv said. "Eight years."

The comment stunned me. I had known men who had done hard time before, and the experience had always left a mark on them. Orv had none of the hard-edged rectitude or inviolable self-containment that was so much a part of most ex-cons' demeanor. I couldn't imagine what sort of crime this soft-spoken, gentle man had committed to get him incarcerated for almost a decade.

Dan seemed to want to explain the circumstances to me. He glanced once at Orv. Orv gave him an almost imperceptible nod.

"Orv did Shitty's time," Dan said, gesturing toward the sallow figure sitting over by the truck with Jumbo.

"Shitty used to drink pretty heavy," Grover added. "One day he got a gun and tried to hold up a liquor store over toward Rapid."

The idea of Shitty trying to rob a liquor store was as stunning as the idea of Orv in prison.

"Shitty doesn't strike me as a stickup man," I said.

"He isn't," Grover said. "That's why he got caught."

Orv shook his head. "He just got lost in the brown bottle. I tried to tell him he was going down a bad road. But he wouldn't listen."

"So you did his time?" I asked.

"I know what prison does to a boy."

I was confused and amazed. "They let you do time for a crime you didn't commit?"

"They just wanted an Indian. I said what they wanted to hear." He paused and poked the fire several times, as if trying to gather his thoughts. "Shitty's my son. I figured I could straighten him out once I got out a lot better than prison could."

He smiled a kind, distant smile. "You got a boy, Nerburn?"

"Yes," I answered. "He's a teenager now."

"Would you let him go to prison?"

"If he did the crime, I guess I probably would."

Orv shook his head. "Then you haven't been to prison. You'd never get your son back. It cuts the heart out of them."

I looked over toward the truck at the skinny, dirty man with the bad teeth and the heavy welfare glasses and the cat-whisker moustache. Orv was looking at him, too. There was a sad love in his eyes.

"Shitty hasn't had it easy. No kid around here does. There's nothing to do. Lots of drugs, booze. Unless you fight it, something bad is going to catch you. Shitty just got caught by the brown bottle."

"It's a sad story," I said.

"That's why I started doing the sweats," Orv said. "Too many sad stories. I want to give the boys their traditions. I want to set them on the red road."

He looked over again at Shitty, who was smoking a cigarette and drinking a can of Mountain Dew.

"I just got to Shitty a little late."

The fire had settled to embers, and the rocks had been heated almost to glowing.

"Well, about time to get in," Orv said. "I'll go tell the fellas we're ready."

He walked across the clearing and said a few words to the two men. I went off into the woods to change into Jumbo's swimming trunks.

When I returned, Grover looked me up and down. "A few more Indian tacos, and it will fit just fine," he said.

I could see Shitty and Jumbo over by the trucks pulling on their own suits. Thankfully, they both had their backsides to us. Grover saw me looking. "Better cover your eyes, Nerburn. Might see something that'll be hard to forget."

"Like Mr. Peanut?"

"No one's ever seen Mr. Peanut. Not even Jumbo."

Dan gave a low cackle and shook his head.

With Orv across the clearing I decided to ask a question that had been gnawing at me.

"I can't believe Orv calls his son 'Shitty,'" I said. "That can't be his real name."

"It isn't," Grover said. "His real name's Marvin. But everyone just calls him Shitty. I guess his old man just gave in and started calling him that, too."

"So how'd he get a nickname like that?" I asked. Every reservation was full of nicknames, and there was usually a story behind them.

Grover dug the point of his buck knife into the stump. "Indian way. He earned it. You know, a man goes hunting and kills a couple of buffalo, they might name him, 'Kills Two' or 'Kills Buffalo.'"

"This isn't about buffalo," I said. "This is a guy named Shitty. How do you earn a name like that?"

Grover sat silently for a second, as if trying to decide whether or not to answer seriously. Then he looked at me in a way that let me know the time for joking was over. "If your dad has to go to jail for you, that makes you kind of shitty, doesn't it?" he said.

Across the way, Shitty was running toward us in torn, worn-out tennis shoes. He looked like a lonely kid hurrying to get in the clubhouse before the older boys closed the door. The young man in the sweatshirt, who had been standing silently by the fire listening to our conversation, looked up for a moment, then quietly went back to tending the embers.

WHEN EVERYONE HAD GATHERED BY THE LODGE, Orv stood up and announced, "Let's get her started." The young man opened the canvas flap, and we all crawled in, with Orv leading the way. Dan turned a full circle once before he entered — then we all filled in around the inside wall of the lodge. It was a small space, no more than a dozen or so feet across and barely tall enough at the center for a man to stand up. The air was stifling.

Orv said a few quiet prayers and lit a pipe, which he passed, in turn, to each of us. We all took a few puffs, pulled the smoke around us with our cupped hands, then passed it on to the next person with the Lakota phrase *Mitakuye oyas'in* — "all my relations."

Orv gave us each a bit of sage to chew or place behind our ears. "It will help if you get thirsty," he said. Then he instructed the sweat-shirt boy to bring in the hot rocks and place them in the fire pit. While the boy carried the glowing rocks in on the antlers, Orv continued chanting a low prayer. Then he took a ladle of water and touched it to the rocks. The boy closed the flap, and the world as I knew it disappeared into darkness.

In all honesty, I don't remember much of what went on in the sweat. The intense heat, the suffocating closeness, the strange and hypnotic Lakota prayers all combined to annihilate my sense of time and move me to a place that was as much dream as memory.

I remember Jumbo's heavy grunts, my burning lungs, and the wafting smell of the sweet grass. I recall Dan's low chants in Lakota, and Grover's prayers. But beyond that all is lost in a shapeless fog.

I do know that at one point we each had to pray out loud, directing our prayers to *Tunkashila*, the Grandfather spirit. I remember that when it was my turn I prayed for the courage and grace to help Dan in his journey and to do it with a pure heart. I finished my prayer with the ritual "*Mitakuye oyas'in.*" The others signaled their approval with low *hau, hau*'s.

At intervals that could have been minutes or an hour, the flap of the door was opened, and a life-giving waft of cool air rushed in. We each took a sip of water from the ladle. Then, just as quickly as it was opened, the flap was closed, fresh water was poured onto the rocks, and the burning, choking steam rose again and plunged us back into the shapeless, suffocating darkness.

After several rounds of this, the blanket was lifted from the door for the last time. Orv said a final prayer, and those of us who wished to leave were allowed to do so.

I crawled out and fell on the cool earth like a newborn child on the bosom of its mother. I lay there in the unbearable freshness of the summer breeze, completely renewed, alive with a humble appreciation of the beauty of everything around me.

Jumbo had crawled out after me and lay, wheezing, like a beached whale, on a filthy blanket. Shitty was huddled up in his towel taking deep breaths. Grover and Dan remained inside with Orv. It was beyond my comprehension that a human being, much less a frail one almost ninety years old, could willingly endure more than we had just experienced.

Despite my physical depletion, I was filled with an overwhelming sense of peace. I felt like I had gone to the other side of death and returned renewed, refreshed, rebaptized. It was like all the sacraments rolled into one, rising up whole and inseparable from the very center of the earth.

BY THE TIME ORV AND DAN AND GROVER EMERGED, I had almost regained full consciousness. I was weak and unsteady but awash in this indescribable sense of well-being. Shitty and Jumbo and I had drunk our fill of water from the plastic jugs, passing the remainder on to the next person.

Finally, I felt life flowing back into me sufficiently that I could sit up. Grover was standing next to me, taking in deep breaths of the dry Dakota air.

"Cleaned out, Nerburn?" he said.

I nodded weakly. "That was a gentle sweat?"

"White boy special," he grinned.

In the distance, over by Jumbo's truck, a group of women had set up tables and covered them with containers of food. They were laughing and joking and playing with the children. It was hard to associate such levity with the spiritual ordeal that had taken place in the crude shelter of blankets only a few yards away.

Soon Orv and Dan walked over. They each took a great drink of water from the ladle in the bucket and sat down on the logs, laughing and joking in Lakota. I looked at Dan's ninety-year-old body. It was like a fading memory — you could see the echoes of muscles, but they had no power, no strength. The skin hung limply from his bones, thin as parchment. Only the hands still seemed strong. Otherwise, it was all bones pushing to the surface, as if his skeleton was trying to escape.

Shitty, too, was all bones, but in a very different way. His was a sickly thinness, exuding ill health and poor living. His skin was sallow, and there was a long scar across his abdomen. On his left bicep was a crudely rendered tattoo of a warrior's head made by poking holes in his flesh with a straight pin and filling them with ink. There was some equally crude writing underneath it, but at this distance I couldn't read what it said.

The young boy in the sweatshirt closed up the lodge and began sweeping around the area with a tree branch. Orv went around to each of us, saying a few private words of encouragement and thanks. I continued to sit there, legs out, arms back, head lifted skyward into the life-giving breeze.

The sweat had cleansed me of much of my concern about the journey. In a strange way, it had been like an artificially induced fever: when it breaks, your concerns with the minutiae of life seem absurd and meaningless. You are thankful simply to be alive, and filled with joy at the presence of the smallest things around you. I sat on the cool earth, staring up at the clouds moving across the sky and listening to the gentle whisper of the wind. I was awash in gratitude and love for everything.

Grover walked over to me. "The old man was praying for you in there, Nerburn," he said. "It was a good thing you said what you said. It made him feel good."

I nodded weakly.

"Want some more water?" he asked. He was carrying a bucket and a ladle. I took a long draft and smiled up at him gratefully. He winked once and gave me a broad grin.

"There's a feast ready over there, when you want it."

The "feast," as Grover called it, had as its main course a large pot of watery soup that was mostly vegetables and a flavorless broth. A few lumps of unidentifiable gray meat floated ominously on the surface. A large basket of fry bread and a couple of institutional-size packages of cheap store-bought cookies graced the far end of the table, along with a huge half-eaten sheet cake. Two coolers of various kinds of soft drinks sat on the ground nearby.

I ladled myself a Styrofoam bowl full of soup and took a seat on a flatbed hay wagon at the far edge of the clearing. My exhaustion was total. I was happy to sit alone and catch my breath while life flowed back into my limbs and lungs.

Soon I felt a presence behind me. I expected it to be Dan or Grover, but when I turned I saw it was the boy in the hooded sweatshirt. He was standing quietly on the far side of the flatbed. It was obvious that he wanted to sit with me.

I gestured him over, and he took a seat next to me.

"Thanks for the sweat," I said. It was a stupid comment, but I didn't know what else to say.

He nodded and sat silently.

Self-consciously, I continued to sip away at my soup. I knew that he wanted something, but I also knew enough not to force the issue. If he wanted to talk, he would. But his presence and proximity were unnerving. He had never spoken a word in all the time I had been there, and I had no idea who he was or what he was about, beyond

the fact that he seemed to be Orv's acolyte or assistant. But even
that was unclear. I was about to break the silence and ask him his
name when he said, in a voice so soft I could barely hear him, "I
carve, too."

He pulled a small, crude stone eagle's head out of the pouch of
his sweatshirt and handed it to me, keeping his eyes averted the
whole time. It was rudely shaped but full of the kind of close obser-
vation and heart that showed a deep earnestness and hunger to learn.

I cradled it in my hand. The eagle's fierce eyes stared directly
into mine; it was clear that the boy had carved it by holding it just as
I was holding it now. Like all young artists anxious to communicate,
he had concentrated on the expression at the expense of the form.

"It's really powerful," I said.

"I'm making it for my dad," he answered.

"It'll be a beautiful gift."

We sat together in an awkward silence. I wanted to say something more to encourage him, but I was not sure what he was after.

Finally, after a few moments, he asked the hard question: "Any
good?"

I had to choose my words carefully. I wanted to encourage him
but give him some advice as well.

"It has a powerful sense of presence," I said. "I can feel the eagle
trying to come out."

"That's what I wanted."

"But you need to get the shape right first. You should start a
sculpture as if it's a figure emerging from the fog. Go for the detail
later." It was a comment I had made to many young artists before. I
hoped he would see it as helpful and not take offense.

I handed the eagle back to him, trying to seem respectful and
appropriately reverential. I knew how great a gift it was for a young
artist to show another person his work.

"You've got a lot of talent," I offered.

"I want to go to school in New Mexico," he said.

"The IAIA?"

He brightened visibly. "Yeah. You know it?"

The IAIA — Institute of American Indian Arts — is an art school in Santa Fe that has produced many successful Indian artists.

"Allan Houser used to teach there, didn't he?" I asked. Houser was a well-known Apache sculptor whose figures of Indian men and women were characterized by strong, simple forms and powerful, dignified presence. He was the only Indian sculptor I knew.

"I got a book of his," the boy said.

Then, as if he had revealed too much, he stood up abruptly and pulled his hood over his head. "I got to go now," he said, then took off across the clearing toward the trees. I could see him holding the eagle's head and staring at it as he walked.

THE FEAST WENT ON LONG INTO THE TWILIGHT. Nothing much happened, just folks sitting around talking while the children played and the dogs barked and ran through the trees along the draw. It was a relaxed, convivial gathering of friends, made all the more delicious by the exhilarating sense of exhaustion from the sweat and the shifting oranges and magentas of the enveloping evening sky. I felt grounded and at peace.

But the lack of clarity about our journey was beginning to gnaw at me. I had meant it in the sweat when I had said I wanted to help Dan, and I had felt honored that they would give a sweat to help me in my efforts. But I did not know exactly what Dan wanted of me, and I wanted to go home.

The sky was almost dark as the campsite began to be packed up. I helped carry the cooler to a big conversion van that sat at the edge of the clearing. How it had gotten in on the road we had navigated, I hadn't a clue.

Dan and Grover had already moved across to the Toyota and were leaning against its hood.

"Come on, Nerburn," Grover shouted. "Time to saddle up."

We loaded ourselves in and took our place in a line of cars that started off on a road that headed west.

"Where to now?" I said casually, hoping to get some kind of meaningful answer. But Dan and Grover had settled back in their seats and closed their eyes. Neither of them offered a response.

The route out was different from the route in and was both shorter and less pockmarked. In the growing dark the line of head-lights was like a string of pearls moving across the lonely Dakota landscape.

Both Dan and Grover were depleted from the sweat. They dozed in their seats as I followed the other cars out through the darkness. A passing storm spat lightning on the far horizon. The short flashes illuminated the tops of the distant hills, followed by a low grumble of distant thunder. The heat was thick, and the sky was alive with night sounds.

It was clear we could not begin any major leg of our trip tonight; the hour had gotten far too late. I did not even know where Dan expected us to go. All I could do was follow the line of cars. So I settled in and drove in silence, listening to the slow breathing of the two men beside me and the creaking and groaning of the Toyota's suspension. I had no idea what I had gotten myself into.

CHAPTER EIGHT

◇◇◇◇◇◇◇◇◇◇◇◇◇◇◇◇◇◇◇◇◇◇◇◇◇◇◇◇◇◇

BIBLES AND BROOMSTICKS

We soon found ourselves in a grassless front yard at the end of a long, rutted trail somewhere even deeper in the hills. The procession of cars had taken a turn off the main path at one point and wound its way up to a small compound consisting of three government-issue houses, a house trailer, and a collection of cars and vans in various stages of disrepair.

A sodium yard light fixed on a utility pole cast a sickly halo of illumination as we all drove in and parked our cars in whatever spot we could find. I navigated through a collection of scruffy dogs and tried to situate the Toyota so we could escape if necessary, but I was quickly boxed in by cars pulling in behind me. Wherever we were, this was very likely where we were going to spend the night.

Dan and Grover roused themselves and took in the scene. Without saying anything, they each got out of the car and went up to the first house on the left. I followed behind, hoping I would finally be given some kind of explanation.

The house was like almost every other on the reservation: a

small rectangular structure with fading fiberboard siding and a rickety set of warped, wooden steps leading up to the front door. From the outside, it was but one more deteriorating, cheaply built government tract home. But once inside I was surprised to find a cheery, freshly painted robin's-egg blue living room with family photos on the wall and a wood stove sitting on a brick platform in the corner. As usual, there were no books anywhere, but a collection of ceramic eagles was proudly displayed in a glass knickknack cabinet. Five young children were sitting on a couch in front of a big-screen television watching a video full of car crashes and police chases. The whole place was neat, orderly, and cheerful, albeit cramped and crowded.

As soon as we entered, one of the children jumped up and turned down the volume on the television. It was the kind of house where too many people lived together but had managed to find a way to coexist with civility and grace.

Orv was seated at a cheap wooden dining room table reading a local penny shopper. He must have left the sweat almost immediately after we had finished. He smiled as we entered, greeting Dan and Grover in Lakota. They responded in kind, and the three men laughed heartily. Orv gestured warmly toward me and said, "Sit down, Mr. Nerburn. I'm glad you came."

"Thank you for having me," I said. "But *Mr. Nerburn*'s my dad's name. Just call me Kent."

Orv nodded but said nothing more. It was clear he was used to dealing with white men as authority figures.

Here in his living room, with the television blaring and family members coming and going, he had none of the aura of spiritual authority I had felt at the sweat lodge. He seemed like one more middle-aged Indian trying to get by on the rez.

"You like the sweat?" he asked.

"Very much," I answered. "Thank you."

It was an awkward answer to what had felt like an awkward question. It was like being asked, "Did you like the Mass?" or, "Did you like the baptism?"

Orv made a comment to the children in Lakota, and they hopped down from the couch, turned off the TV, and scurried to their bedroom. A woman I assumed was Orv's wife appeared briefly in a doorway, smiled, and withdrew.

I had no idea where all the people in all the cars were, or why we alone seemed to have come directly to this house.

"We'll get some shut-eye here, then start in the morning," Dan said.

I wanted to grab the opportunity to ask about the purpose of our trip, but I resisted. We were in Orv's house as his guests, and it seemed like an insult to his quiet hospitality to begin pushing my personal concerns.

Orv reached over and took a deck of cards from a nearby shelf. "Game?" he asked.

Dan and Grover pulled up chairs without answering. It was obviously a well-practiced ritual.

"You, Nerburn?" Grover said.

"Nah," I answered.

"That's right. I forgot. You don't play cards."

"I'd play if I knew how," I said.

Dan had dredged a few pennies and nickels out of his pocket and laid them on the table. "Now ain't the time to learn," he said. "Stakes are too high for a beginner." Orv and Grover chuckled, then turned their attention to the cards.

The game went on for an hour, becoming ever more jocular. Unlike other similar situations I'd encountered on the rez, everyone kept me included in the conversation. At one point Shitty came in and took a seat at the table. Numerous women came and went. Orv kept pulling soft drinks out of the plastic cooler that had been at the sweat and shoving them across the table to us. I noticed that there was no alcohol anywhere.

Orv kept winning and soon had a substantial pile of pennies and other small change in front of him.

"At least prison was good for something," he said. "I got a lot of practice with the cards."

The mention of prison gave me an opening. I screwed up my courage and turned toward Orv.

"You don't seem like a guy who's been in prison," I said.

"How would you know?" Grover asked.

"I used to work for the governor in Minnesota," I said. "I had to deal with cons. Most of them got hard and cold. Orv doesn't seem like them."

"He's cold at poker," Dan said, pointing to the pile of pennies.

Orv smiled. "Oh, I suppose it's in there. But I just spent my time trying to help the younger guys. Prison's tough on Indians. They've got no respect for us and our ways."

"Were there lots of Indians doing time?" I asked.

"Around here? Yeah," Grover interjected. "We don't have enough black guys. They've got to fill the joints with 'Skins."

Orv smiled. "There's way more than there should be. We've got no lawyers. We're not much for talking. They throw the book at us. Then when we get inside they treat us bad."

"Worse than other people?"

"In some ways. They don't respect our beliefs. I wanted to start a sweat lodge for the men, but they wouldn't let me. I knew the men needed it. Every Indian there was in because of something to do with alcohol or drugs. Every one.

"At first they said they couldn't let us have a lodge because they didn't want us to go inside a place where they couldn't see us. They thought we might be planning something. Then they didn't want us to have a dirt floor, because they said we'd use it to bury knives and weapons. Then they wouldn't let us have a pipe. They said we might smoke marijuana in it.

"They'd let the Catholics have wine, and they'd let their priests come in and say Mass. But they wouldn't let us have eagle feathers or prayer beads or anything. And they wouldn't let our medicine men come in because they didn't have some piece of paper saying they were spiritual leaders.

"They let anyone go to Mass or go talk to ministers. They thought that was great — it was helping the men get religion. But if those men wanted to be part of our spiritual ways, they were told they couldn't because they weren't Indian."

He set his can of soda down and sat back in his chair. The card game had ground almost to a halt.

"Tell him about the hair," Dan interjected.

Orv smiled. "Oh, yeah, the hair. Some of us who followed the old ways didn't want to cut our hair. We tried to explain that it was part of our beliefs, but the prison said that long hair wasn't sanitary and that we could hide weapons in it. They said it was a trick we were using so we could change our appearance by cutting it if we escaped. They wanted us all to look like Grover there." Grover grinned and ran his hand over his ashen gray flattop.

"Let me show you something," he said.

He got up and went into the back room. I could hear papers rustling, then he emerged with a yellowed sheet of newsprint.

"Here," he said, handing it to me. It was a faded Xerox of an article from the *San Francisco Examiner* in 1902.

"What's that?" Dan asked.

"It's a copy of an old newspaper article," I said, unsure of why Orv had given it to me. "It's about some lieutenant who thought he could civilize the Apaches by forcing them to cut their hair."

Orv gestured me to keep talking.

I squinted hard at the image of the faded newsprint. "It says that the guy was cutting their hair so they would be 'transformed from naked, drunken, idle savages into well-dressed, sober and industrious builders of the commonwealth.' "

"Read it to me," Dan said.

"Go ahead. It's a good article," Orv urged.

Grover sat back picking his teeth with his buck knife.

" 'They stole for pastime and murdered for pleasure . . . the squaws of the tribe had to submit to being traded back and forth among the braves for horses and cattle, a hungry father frequently preferred to trade away his comely daughter to working for food.' "

"A good daughter should be worth at least a six-pack and a pickup," Grover said.

Dan shot him a hard glance.

"Read the part about the hair," Orv said. "The part at the end."

I went to the final paragraph. " 'They were run down one by one, thrown to the ground and fleeced, their hair coming off in patches and slashes as though it were cut with a scythe. Today there isn't a long-haired buck in the tribe, nor is there an uncivilized one.' "

Orv nodded his approval. "See, that's almost a hundred years ago. Things haven't changed that much. At least not in prison. They still thought our long hair made us savages. Being scalped by a soldier isn't all that different from being scalped by a prison guard."

Dan had closed his eyes and leaned his head back. I could see that he was retreating to one of those dark places in his memory.

"Makes me think of boarding school," he said. "The first thing they did when we got there was to take us into a back room, hold us down, and cut off all our hair."

I sharpened my attention. This was the first time Dan had spoken about his boarding school experience. Perhaps this conversation would lead him into the subject of his little sister, and I'd be able to gain some information that would help me find out what had happened to her.

"Christ, I fought. Oh, how I fought. But those matron ladies were strong. They held me down and chopped my hair off with scissors. Then that priest in his black dress, he came in and started talking really mean to me in English. I couldn't understand anything. The women, they poured some kerosene on my head, put some tar stuff there that burned like the devil. They said it was for bugs. Burned my head so bad I could hardly stand it. Got in my eyes, I thought I was blind. Oh, Christ, I was scared."

The men put down their cards. Their respect for Dan kept them from returning to the levity of the game, and it was clear that the mention of the cutting of hair had opened a wound.

"I had an aunt, went to the boarding school over by Rapid," Orv said. "They used to take the girls down into the basement and make them sit naked on a cold iron stove if they did something wrong. Made them take down their pants and sit there until they got blisters. They were just little girls."

Dan was staring down at the table. "Yeah, those were hard times," he said. "Those priests, some of them were really bad. One boy hanged himself because of what a priest made him do. There was one priest, we used to jump out of windows when we saw him coming." He didn't pursue the story but left it to our imaginations.

"They must have learned all that stuff from a special part of their Bible," Grover said. "Some part that never got translated into Indian."

The men chuckled grimly and took swigs of their sodas.

Dan lifted his eyes and turned his attention toward me.

"You know about the boarding schools, Nerburn?" he asked.

"A little."

"Well, let me tell you," he said. "My dad was right. They tried to beat the Indian right out of us." He lifted his gnarled, arthritic hand and started shaking it at me, like a man trying to make a point. "See, that's all they were — places to beat the Indian out of you.

They kidnapped kids, just like they did with Yellow Bird. Made them go there, then beat the hell out of you. They took us away from our families. They stole our lives from us."

"They got my dad by tricking him," Orv said.

"How'd they trick him?" I asked.

"Well, if they couldn't convince a kid to go, or they couldn't scare the parents into sending them, sometimes they'd come by and bribe you with candy. They'd tell you they were taking you to town for something. I think there was like a bounty on us, like for gophers or beavers. Some guy got paid to come out and get us. The more Indian kids he got, the more money he was paid."

"And kids would get in their car?"

"Sure. Those were different days, especially when my dad was young. When a white man told you to do something, you did it. Besides," he grinned, "Indians like candy."

"That's how they got my uncle," Grover said. "Damn piece of licorice."

Dan turned back to me. "Remember what I told you about how I begged my dad to let me go so I could protect little Yellow Bird? It wasn't that I didn't know what I was getting into. They'd been taking kids for years. But I wanted to protect her."

"Lots of us actually wanted to go," Grover said. "We didn't want the damn white man's education. We wanted to test ourselves. We figured we'd stand up against the white man, become new kinds of warriors. That's what a lot of us thought."

"It's what I thought," said Dan.

He opened up another can of Coke and started drinking it down in large gulps.

"Boy, was I wrong."

Grover let out a short "hnn" of approval or support.

Though I was fascinated and honored to be present at these kinds of revelations, I felt uncomfortable with the direction the conversation was taking. I had been raised in the Christian tradition and loved much of what it had to offer. But the Indian boarding schools, like the Inquisition and the Salem witch trials, had exposed a dark underbelly of the Christian faith. I couldn't defend them, nor did I want to. They were, to my mind, the worst of all crimes — crimes committed in the name of religion.

"I'm going to show you something now," Dan said. "Go over there and get that broom."

I looked at him quizzically. "That one," he said, pointing to a broom propped up next to the woodstove.

Without speaking, I walked over and picked it up. I did not want to anger him.

"Now, lay it down on the floor in front of me."

I was not sure what was going on, but I dared not question. I simply did what he requested.

"Now, get down and kneel on it."

I hesitated.

"Just do it."

Slowly I got down on the floor in front of him and slid the broomstick under my knees. It dug into the soft spot right below my kneecaps.

The other men were still looking down. None of them would raise their eyes to look at me.

"Now just stay there."

I knelt there, balanced unsteadily on the broomstick. It created an uncomfortable pressure in my shins and thighs.

"Having fun yet?" Dan asked.

The pressure was rapidly turning to pain. I reached for the arm of a chair to give myself support.

Dan whacked my fingers with his walking stick. "No support."

The pain was increasing, moving up my legs.

"Stay there," Dan commanded. "Jesus is mad at you."

"Come on, Dan," I said, putting my hands on the floor. "I get the point."

He whacked at my forearms viciously.

"No, you don't," he said. "You aren't going to get the point for a half hour."

I didn't know what to do. I couldn't stay there for a half hour. But I didn't want to defy him.

"Just stay there," he said angrily.

I teetered on the broomstick, my knees throbbing with pain. Finally, in spite of my embarrassment, I just rolled off the broomstick and lay on the floor.

Dan spit — a gesture of undisguised contempt.

"Too hard for a grown white man," he said. "But not for a little Indian boy."

"That's how it was for us," he said. "Every day. Didn't know your lesson? Kneel on the broomstick. Speak Lakota? Kneel on the broomstick. 'Jesus is mad at you. Jesus will send you to hell.'

"Christ, Nerburn. We were just little kids. Cut off our hair, drag us away from our parents. Don't let us talk in our own language. Tell us our parents are savages and are going to burn up in a fire that lasts forever. No wonder I pissed my bed."

He looked down at me seated on the floor and holding my knees. His eyes were filled with a cold and empty rage. He was looking at every white man who had ever abused him.

He tapped the floor next to my knees with his walking stick. "You think that broomstick was bad? You should try marbles. One day they caught me talking my own language. They brought out two Bibles. Big black books, heavy as hell. They put some marbles on the floor, made me kneel on them. I cried and cried, but they hit me and made me do it. Made me kneel there with my arms out, holding one of those Bibles on each hand, balanced. Told me to pray.

"I prayed all right. I prayed. You know what I prayed for?"

I shook my head.

"I prayed for the goddamn broomstick."

Grover let out a soft chuckle. Orv stayed silent. I could see he was uncomfortable for me, uncomfortable for Dan. But it was clear he knew what Dan was talking about.

He reached out his hand to help me up.

"You're too old for floors," he said.

I accepted his assistance gratefully.

"So that's the answer to your question, Nerburn," Dan said.

"What question?" I asked. My knees were still throbbing.

"About Orv and prison. Why it didn't change him."

I looked at Orv. His eyes were still cast downward.

"Prison couldn't change him. It was too late. Prison wasn't nothing. He'd been in a boarding school."

A small, sad smile crossed Orv's lips.

"Want to finish the game?" he said.

CHAPTER NINE

◇◇◇◇◇◇◇◇◇◇◇◇◇◇◇◇◇◇◇◇◇◇◇◇◇◇◇◇◇

TIOSPAYE

The card game never really got going again. The anger swirling around the talk of the boarding schools had dampened everyone's enthusiasm.

Slowly, the men filtered out. I moved over to the couch and began to doze. The sweat had exhausted me, and my knees and legs were still throbbing from the broomstick. I remember seeing some of the women come in and hearing the screen door slam several times. But I was too tired to care. I fell off into a night of restless sleep and shapeless dreams.

When I awoke there were birds singing outside and bright light coming in through the window. The table was littered with cigarette ashes and half-finished cans of soda. There was no one else in sight.

I shifted on the couch. My knees were still sore, and the cigarette smoke had given me the edge of a headache.

I slipped my shoes on quietly and stepped outside into the morning.

The front yard was empty. Only the junk cars and my Toyota

remained in the clearing. A shiny Dodge crew-cab pickup sat by the side of the white house trailer. It was as if the whole party had disappeared overnight, like a village packing up and silently moving on at the first light of dawn. I was amazed that the departure of Shitty's truck had not jolted me awake. I must have been more exhausted than I realized.

The sky was a deep, empty blue, and the air had a crisp, intoxicating freshness. You could feel the heat growing, but it was still hours away. For now, the wind blew gently and the songs of plover and meadowlark filled the air.

I inhaled deeply and stared out toward the horizon. For the first time I could get a good sense of where we were. The little grouping of houses — Orv's *tiospaye* — sat on the flank of a low short-grass rise. Soft rounded hills receded in all directions as far as the eye could see. A rutted trail of white clay led down to the main path several hundred yards away. There were no other houses in sight, no sign of human habitation other than this small cluster of cars and buildings. In this early summer morning, it felt like a peaceful oasis. But I could only imagine what it was like in winter, with winds howling across the high plains and snow burying everything under an indifferent blanket of white.

I tried to coax one of the dogs to come over and sit with me, but they were close to feral and did not want to approach. One came near enough to see that I had no food, then bared its teeth and withdrew. I leaned back on the steps and breathed deeply. The conversation during the card game had given me a sense of Dan's deep rage and pain about the boarding school, but it hadn't told me much about Yellow Bird, and it hadn't given me any clear guidelines about what we were doing or where we were going.

I was about to walk up the rise behind the house in a futile attempt to see if I could get any cell phone reception when the door of the house trailer adjacent to the houses opened. It was the young

man who had tended the fire at the sweat. He was still wearing the
hooded sweatshirt, but at least he had the hood pulled back. Slowly
he walked across the patch of grass and dirt and took a place on the
steps beside me. He lit up a cigarette and leaned back on his elbows.

"Morning," I said.

He drew on the cigarette and stared into the sky, saying nothing.

With his hood off, he afforded me a better look at him. He was
a good-looking kid with high, hard cheekbones. His face was broad,
and he wore his hair pulled back into a tight ponytail. There was
seriousness in his manner, like someone who had been asked to be the
man of the house at a very early age. I had the distinct impression
that he might have been in some trouble earlier in his life. There was
a thin scar of the kind made by a swift stroke of a knife on his left
cheek, and he had homemade tattoos of crosses and daggers on the
backs of his hands.

We sat there in silence staring out into the lavender dawn. The
sky was taking on a morning brightness; the heat was on its way.

The boy kept his eyes on the horizon. When the morning insects
buzzed around him he just brushed them away and kept his focus on
the far hills or the hawks wheeling in the sky. His whole manner was
one of finely tuned vigilance. I could imagine that in a former time
he might have been an advance scout for the tribe.

"You like coffee?" he said suddenly.

I was surprised and delighted.

"Absolutely," I said.

Without saying another word, he got up and walked toward the
trailer. He beckoned me with a slight nod of his head, so I got up
and followed.

As always, I was unsure about the protocol. I trailed behind him
as he entered the door. He gestured me in, so I followed, letting the
screen door slam behind me.

I heard a small cry from the back room and realized that there was a baby somewhere.

"I'm Donnie," he said, as if entry into his house required that I know his name.

"Kent," I responded.

He made no effort to shake my hand.

The child cried again.

Donnie smiled at me — the first real personal contact he had made — to indicate that it was okay; we hadn't awakened the child. I waited patiently as he poured two cups of coffee from a discount store drip pot. It was so weak you could see the daylight through it, but it was coffee, and the gesture of friendship was most welcome.

He shoved a half-full cylinder of powdered creamer and a small jar of sugar packets toward me and sat down on the chair next to me.

"I fixed it," he said.

"Good," I said. I didn't know what he was talking about, but I didn't want to sound stupid.

"Want to see?"

"Sure."

He reached into the pouch of his sweatshirt and pulled out the stone eagle head. He had reshaped everything so that the profile, even from a distance, was now fully resolved and accurate. With a few deft touches he had transformed the rough piece into a fully formed, well-wrought sculpture. It was obvious that he had talent.

"I did what you said."

"You sure did," I smiled. "You're a quick study."

He cast his eyes downward as if the compliment embarrassed him.

"Want to see something?" he said. It was less a question than an offer.

"Absolutely."

He led me down the short hall into a small room with cheap

paneling and vinyl baseboards. Through the wall I could hear a woman talking to the baby.

In one corner he had set up a homemade workbench that was covered with a motley assortment of small carving tools — dental picks, files, a few stone chisels, some sandpaper. Everything was arranged in perfect rows. The walls were covered with pencil drawings of eagles, Indians on horseback, and closely observed sketches of specific individuals. I walked over and stared at a highly detailed sketch of an old woman's face. He had overemphasized the wrinkles and obviously had encountered some difficulty in rendering the eyes, but it was, nonetheless, a carefully and lovingly crafted portrait.

"My grandma," he said.

"She looks like a kind woman," I answered.

He smiled shyly and pulled out a dusty book with a torn cover. "Here," he said, handing it to me.

It was a collection of the work of Allan Houser, the man I had mentioned while we were sitting together after the sweat. It was filled with images of strong, simplified forms of Indian people in robes and blankets. The faces were simple but well defined, while the robes and blankets were stylized to the point of being little more than slabs and flat surfaces. It gave the characters at once a sense of personality as well as a sense of timelessness.

The book was well worn; the edges of the pages were smudged with fingerprints, and the creases between the pages were filled with stone dust.

"I guess you really like Houser's work, don't you?" I said.

In the next room the baby cooed and gurgled.

"His sculptures look really proud," he said.

"That's what they're about," I answered. The sculptor and teacher in me was coming to the surface. "Strength, pride, presence."

"Like Indian people," he added.

He bent over behind the bench and lifted out a piece of white limestone. The face of the old woman in the drawing was carved crudely into its surface. Again, he had pursued detail before he had established the form, but his fidelity to the drawing was impressive. It was obvious he had looked closely at Houser's work. He sipped quietly on his coffee while waiting for my response.

"It's good," I said. "Here, let me see that book for a minute."

He handed the Houser book across to me. I opened it to a sculpture of an Indian woman standing with an eagle feather fan.

"Look at how he does faces," I said, trying to use his mentor's work as a teaching tool. "They don't have much detail. They're more about a general emotion or spiritual feeling than about individual character." I knew I was sounding too academic, but Donnie seemed hungry for my thoughts.

"Now look at your carving. You've really focused on the individual. That's okay. But it makes it more of a portrait."

He nodded solemnly. It was hard to know what he was thinking.

He pointed to a flat surface just below the face. "How do you do letters?" he asked. "I want to put her name there."

"Well," I said, "you can either have them stand out by chiseling out the background, or you can incise them into the stone."

"Incise?"

"Yeah. You cut the letters into the stone."

"Here. Show me," he said. He handed me a black metal tool like a railroad spike with teeth on the end of it. I recognized it as a basic *gradina*, the first tool of stone sculpture that I had ever used when I was in Italy.

"I'm not very good with stone," I told him. "I like wood."

"Like my dad."

"Orv is your dad?"

"Yeah."

I smiled. "Yeah, like your dad. Stone's a little too heroic for me."

He blushed a bit, as if my words revealed too much about his aspirations.

I turned the stone over so I wouldn't ruin his work, then showed him how to mark the center of a letter, carve a groove into that center line, then carve down to that groove by beveling the sides.

"If you don't get the bevel right, you can use your files to flatten the surfaces. Then mix up some of the stone dust with oil and polish the surface with it. It will give it a beautiful shine." I made a simple serifed capital *I* to show him.

It was a short, clumsy lesson full of gaps. But it was the best I could do under the circumstances. I was worried that the hammering would upset the baby in the next room, and I wanted to get back outside in case Dan and Grover had gotten up and were ready to go.

"Where'd you learn this stuff?" he asked.

"Italy."

"Italy?"

"Yeah, I spent a few months there working with stone carvers."

He ran his finger over the rough letter I had carved as if by touching it he was touching some kind of sacred knowledge.

"Thanks," he said.

"You're welcome. My gift to you for the gift of the sweat."

He smiled and put the stone carefully back behind the bench.

As we walked back toward the kitchen a young heavyset girl wearing an oversized gray athletic T-shirt and jeans emerged from the next room holding a baby.

"This is Angie," Donnie said. She didn't look a day over seventeen. We exchanged a soft handshake.

"What's the baby's name?" I asked, looking at the wide-eyed infant wrapped in a star quilt.

"Shantell," she said.

Shantell had a full head of dark brown hair, and tiny, pudgy fingers. She was screwing up her face and fussing and squirming.

"She's very beautiful," I said.

"She's been crying a lot."

"Is she sick?" The prospect of a sick infant this far out in the hills concerned me.

"The doctor at the clinic says she has an ear infection. But my grandma thinks it's the spirits talking to her from the other side. She thinks there's some things her little spirit didn't finish up before she was born."

I placed my hand on little Shantell's forehead. Her skin was hot. The baby's temperature concerned me. Too many infants never made it to their first birthday on the reservation.

"You take good care of her," I said.

"I've got some medicine," she answered.

"That's good. You get her well. She's a little beauty."

Angie beamed and adjusted the star quilt behind the infant's head.

Donnie was standing at the door.

"Well, I better be going," I said. "I've got to be ready for Dan and Grover."

"Bye," Angie said. She lifted Shantell's pudgy hand and waved it toward me.

"Bye, Angie. Bye, Shantell."

Donnie held the screen door for me as I stepped out into the light. The sun had moved higher, and the hills were starting to bake.

"Thanks for showing me that stuff," he said. "I want to make my dad proud."

He paused as if trying to decide if he wanted to go further.

Then, almost under his breath he added, "Kind of make up for my brother."

THE SUN HAD REACHED ITS ZENITH by the time Dan and Grover emerged from wherever they had spent the night. Orv was laughing and joking with them as they walked across the dusty yard toward the car.

"Nerburn," Grover said. "You're dressed and loaded. You must be on white man's time."

"Comes with the territory."

Orv gave us a plastic jug of Kool-Aid and a bag of cookies. He said something to Dan in Lakota. Both men laughed.

He took my hand in a gentle handshake. "You come again. You're always welcome." He handed me a small piece of paper folded to the size of a postage stamp. "Here's my phone number. You call any time you get out this way."

It was an honest offer, I could tell. This was a man who had kindness bred into his bones.

"Thank you for your hospitality," I said. "And for letting me be part of the sweat."

"It's good to sweat together," he smiled.

"Donnie is a talented man," I continued. I wanted to underscore my respect and admiration for what he had done with his family.

"He's on the red road," Orv answered. "He'll do okay."

"Well, we'd better get on the white man's road," Grover said. "It's already hotter than hell."

Donnie and Angie had come out and were standing with their baby by the front steps of their trailer. The child was still crying and squalling.

"Let me see that baby," Dan said.

He walked over and touched the infant on its chest and arms. "What's this baby's name?" he said.

"Shantell," Angie answered shyly.

"You should give her an Indian name," Dan said. He put his

hands gently on either side of the child's head. Almost immediately, the infant stopped crying. Dan made several cooing sounds, and the baby broke into a tiny, toothless smile.

"This is a good baby," he grinned.

Angie looked away and blushed.

"I'm going to say a little prayer for it now."

He touched his lips with his fingers and began speaking slowly and softly in Lakota. Shantell watched him intently, as if she knew what the old man was saying. The rest of us stood quietly while Dan spoke. When he had finished, Grover and Orv responded with a quiet "*hau, hau.*"

Donnie was standing nearby, keeping his eyes on the ground. Dan put his hand on the young man's wrist. "You raise that little girl to be strong," he said. "You stay with the mother. A child needs its father."

"I will, *Tunkashila,*" Donnie answered softly.

Slowly Dan turned back toward Angie. He reached up and touched her cheek with his worn chestnut fingers. "You be a good mother. Stay away from the bottle and raise your child in the old ways. Make sure she learns the language. And get her an Indian name."

"I will, *Tunkashila,*" Angie said quietly.

"Well, let's get going now," Dan said. "We've got a long way to go."

Another round of handshakes and laughter, and we got in the car and started our way down the rutted path. As I stopped to open the first of the cattle gates, I could hear a distant, rhythmic metallic "clink" coming from the direction of Orv's *tiospaye.* At first I could not identify it. Then I realized — it was the sound of a hammer on steel. Donnie was in his workroom carving on his sculpture.

DAN WAS SILENT AND DISTANT as we bounced down the path toward the highway.

"That baby was sick," he said.

"You think?" I said.

"I can tell. There's something wrong with her little spirit."

"Shouldn't they take her to a doctor?"

"She doesn't need a doctor. That baby's remembering something, and she's trying to get to it."

His words sent a vague shudder through me. That was the same thing Angie's grandmother had said.

"What do you think it is?" I asked.

"I don't know. They need to go to the medicine man. He can find out."

He turned away. I could see that he was thinking.

"Sometimes it's hard to tell if the sickness is in the body or the spirit," he said. "That's why they should go to the medicine man. White man's medicine is okay for sickness in the body. But it can't do anything about a sick spirit. It's good for curing, but it isn't any good for healing."

He looked out at a red-tailed hawk circling in the sky. "I think they should give her an Indian name, see if that helps."

Prairie Secrets

CHAPTER TEN

◇◈◇◈◇◈◇◈◇◈◇◈◇◈◇◈◇◈◇◈◇◈◇◈◇◈◇◈◇◈◇◈◇

CHARLES BRONSON

So, where're we going?" I asked. Now that we were back on the road, it was time to get some answers.

Dan turned toward the window, letting me know by his posture that he didn't want to be part of this conversation.

"Just keep driving," Grover said.

I was about ready to slam on the brakes and put the two men out on the highway when Grover tapped me on the shoulder and pointed to a small dot in the distance.

"Turn in there," he said.

"What is it?" I asked.

"You'll see."

As we got closer I could see that the dot was actually a small oasis of human habitation. There was a battered house trailer sitting about a hundred yards off the highway up a small dirt path. An abandoned school bus with a tattered black and white prisoner of war flag fluttering above it on a makeshift flagpole stood in the tall grass behind it.

"Good place to stock up," Grover said.

I didn't like the sound of *stock up*. It spoke of a longer journey than I had in mind. And I couldn't imagine what kind of "stock" we could get at someone's house trailer.

I assumed this was the residence of one of their friends, until I saw the small hand-painted sign in the window: Lila's Place.

Dan stepped out first. The heat was overwhelming.

"Christ, it's toasty," he said.

A scroungy little dog wormed its way out from under the stoop and wiggled its way toward us through the heat and dust. Dan made a few *tsuk* sounds, and the little dog ran over to him, wagging its scrawny tail vigorously. Unlike most rez dogs, it seemed trusting of people and hungry for affection.

"This is a good dog," he said.

In the field near the school bus I could see six children's school desks set in formation in the weeds. Old teddy bears were seated in three of them.

"School's in session," Grover said.

"Or a teddy bears' picnic," I offered.

We walked together through the dusty scattering of overturned tricycles and old tires and climbed the single wooden step into the trailer. Dan actually took the lead, though Grover and I stayed close behind him. There was no doubt that the sweat and the time in the open air had improved his mobility.

Lila's Place was nothing more than a few racks set up in the living room of the trailer. A few cans of Spam and SpaghettiOs sat on the otherwise empty shelves. Several bags of potato chips and other junk food lay on a card table, along with a selection of cheap candy. A few locally made God's eyes hung on the wall with hand-lettered price tags reading $4.50.

An old refrigerator was whirring and wheezing in the corner. A sheet of paper with "bottles of water. 50 cents" written on it was pasted on its door.

Dan tapped me on the shoulder. "Amana," he said, pointing.

"Don't look inside," I said.

A woman, who I assumed was Lila, was sitting behind a makeshift counter playing solitaire with a worn deck of cards. The little dog had followed us in and made its way behind the counter.

"Shoo," the woman said. The dog flattened its ears and ran out the door.

I looked around for something that would serve as lunch. The cans of Spam and SpaghettiOs didn't appeal to me, but I didn't see a lot of other options.

"Got any baloney?" Grover said.

"Just the Spam," the woman answered. She was focused on her solitaire game.

"Get it, Nerburn," Grover said to me.

"No," I said. "I'm not buying Spam." I knew the purchase was going to land on me.

He gave me one of his mock punches in the shoulder. "What? You a vegetarian now?"

Dan was nosing around, peering at the various shelves and looking at a painted turtle shell hanging on the wall. He shuffled over to the door and stared out at the little dog sitting on the front stoop.

"What you want for that dog?" he said.

The woman looked up slowly. "Well, I don't know."

She shouted into the back room, "Carlene, want to sell that little dog?"

Another woman's face emerged from a room in the back of the trailer. "Oh, I don't know. How much you give me?"

"I'll give you twelve dollars," Dan said.

"That's good."

"Nerburn, give her twelve bucks," he said.

I was dumbstruck. I didn't want to say "yes," but I couldn't say "no." Not only was Dan spending my money, he was spending it on a dog that appeared to have a dangerously contagious case of mange.

Grover stepped out from behind the shelves. "We don't need the dog, Dan," he said. "They've got Spam."

Dan shot him a withering glance.

"I got a pack of wieners in back," the woman said, "if you don't want Spam."

"We'll take the wieners and the dog and a loaf of bread," Dan said. "You want anything, Nerburn?"

"What else could a guy want?" I said.

Dan cackled. Then he turned toward the door and made a few *tsuk* sounds. The little dog nosed open the screen door and squirmed its way in. It wormed over to him, squinting as if it hadn't opened its eyes in days.

The little fellow was a mess. He looked like a chemo patient, with tufts of hair alternating with bald spots. His eyes were rheumy, and what hair he had was dirty and matted. His provenance was dubious, if not utterly impossible to trace. There was some kind of terrier involved, but beyond that it was anyone's guess. His ears stuck almost straight out like airplane wings, and he had sad and soulful little eyes and a droopy Yosemite Sam mustache. His spindly little tail wagged his entire rear end as he dragged himself on his belly across the floor toward the old man.

"Looks like a rat," Grover said.

"Just a mixed-blood," Dan said, slowly lowering himself toward the floor with the aid of the counter edge. I ran over to offer him assistance, but he brushed me aside. His attention was on the dog, and the dog's attention was on him. He was speaking to it in Lakota, and the dog was wagging its tail like it had just met the best friend it had ever had.

"You pay for the stuff, Nerburn. We're going out to the car." He scooped up the little pup and cradled him in the crook of his arm. He ignored me as I helped him to his feet, then shuffled off toward the car, making little cooing sounds to the dog that sounded for all the world like the gurgling of a pigeon. Grover followed close behind.

"I don't suppose you have any, like, mange medicine?" I asked the woman.

She looked at me uncomprehendingly, so I just paid the bill, then picked up the wieners and white bread and hurried out the door.

Dan and Grover had already situated themselves in the car. Once again, Dan was in the front seat. I had hoped the little dog would be sequestered in the back area of the station wagon, but he was curled up on Dan's lap, breathing contentedly.

I wanted to feel sorry for the little fellow, but my time on reservations had inured me to tragic dogs. Almost every convenience store had at least one arthritic, pus-eyed old hound scavenging around the parking area, and spinal, heavy-dugged mothers with no pups, loping along the ditches on the sides of highways, were an all too common sight. I remembered the first time I had driven to Red Lake in the winter and seen the frozen carcasses of dead dogs propped up against trees as some kind of winter sport. At a certain point the heart just hardens.

"Dan, that dog's got mange," I said.

"You're not looking so good yourself," Grover said from the back.

"I know. But mange is catching. For humans, too."

"Then we'll just wash him in kerosene," Dan said.

"You can't wash that little dog in kerosene," I said. "It'll kill him."

Dan snorted contemptuously. "It was good enough for us kids in boarding school. So now it's not good enough for some little dog?"

I gave up the fight. I'd find some way to clean up the little dog, and it wouldn't be with kerosene. But it wasn't worth an argument.

"So, you going to give him a name?" I said, trying to be conciliatory.

"Already have," Dan answered. "Charles Bronson."

"Charles Bronson," I said. "Of course. What else could you name a little dog?"

Dan saw no humor in my comment. "Could have named him something else. But I didn't. I named him Charles Bronson."

"Maybe the Great Spirit told him that," Grover said. In the rearview mirror I could see him grinning broadly.

There was nothing else I could say. I put the car in gear and headed off into the afternoon sun. Dan sat in stubborn silence. Grover blew smoke rings across the seat.

"I know something about dogs, Nerburn," Dan said testily. "You just drive."

"Hope you know how to give them baths," I groused.

Grover blew another smoke ring. I stared grimly at the straight-line highway extending into the distance. Charles Bronson was nestled in Dan's lap and sleeping happily. This was his lucky day. It was rapidly becoming obvious that it was not going to be mine.

◇◆◇◆◇◆◇◆◇◆◇◆◇◆◇◆◇◆◇◆◇◆◇◆◇◆◇◆◇◆◇◆◇

PRAYER FOR A HOT DOG

The day had reached its hottest point. A breathless haze had dropped over the hills.

"Probably should eat those wieners before they get too gamey," Grover said.

I had been entertaining the same thought; even with the air conditioning on full, the sun through the windows was brutal.

"Are we planning on eating them raw?" I asked. It was only half a joke.

"What, you think I'm some kind of savage?" Grover shot back. "Find some place with some shade, and we'll roast 'em up."

I surveyed the scorching panorama of dips and swales stretching toward the horizon in all directions. There was no reasonable place to stop, no place that offered any shade, and no likely place to safely build a fire in the tinder-dry landscape.

"We probably should have gotten the Spam," I said.

"That's what I told you," Grover said. "White man's pemmican. Stays good for years."

Dan was scratching the scabrous head of Charles Bronson and making the *tsuk*, *tsuk* sounds. The little dog was rolling in the old man's lap like a kitten.

"Bronson's getting hungry, too, Nerburn," Dan said. "Hurry up and find a place to stop."

I kept scanning the horizon for any natural barrier that would offer us some protection. But the hills were as bald as Mongolian steppes. Finally, we saw a narrow row of trees stretching like a snake along a gully far in the distance.

"Go down there and pull in," Dan said. "Should be a creek in there."

We turned off the highway and bounced down a rutted path toward the trees. Dan was right — in the middle of the thin oasis of birch and cottonwood was a small trickle of water moving through an almost dry creek bed. It wasn't much, but together the trees and the creek offered a moment of blessed shade and coolness against the relentless sun.

"Maybe I can spruce up Bronson here, too," I offered.

"You got kerosene?" Dan said.

"No, but I've got shampoo."

"White man's shampoo can't make a dent in a rez dog," Grover said. "Use rez shampoo, and maybe you've got a chance."

"Rez shampoo?"

"Bar of Lava," he said, rubbing his hand across his ash gray crew cut.

"I generally don't carry Lava with me," I said, recalling the gray pumice-laden soap that my father had used to get grease off his hands after working on the car or the lawn mower.

"The nuns used to make us eat Lava soap if we didn't know our lessons," Dan said.

"At least they didn't make you drink kerosene," I offered.

"Couldn't afford to. Had to keep it for our hair."

We parked the car near the line of trees and walked to the edge of the creek. The thin trickle of brackish water wound its way through a dry bed of rocks. Here and there it puddled into small, shallow basins.

I grabbed my shampoo, picked up Bronson, and carried him to one of the puddles. He yelped and squirmed and scratched mightily in an attempt to get back to Dan.

"Bronson's not very cooperative," I shouted. "Can one of you help me out?"

"Nope," said Dan.

"I got to dress out the meat," Grover said.

Bronson was shredding my arm with his claws. He was as strong and fierce as a baby bull.

"Damn it, Bronson," I shouted. "Take it easy." But he squirmed and wriggled with an even greater intensity.

I managed to get the shampoo open and rubbed all over him. It mixed with the blood from my scratches and filled the pool with a pink bubbly foam.

For ten minutes I alternated dipping Bronson in the puddle and relathering and rubbing him down. When I could no longer put up with his scratching, I gave him one final rinse and dropped him on the bank. He shook himself violently, then ran over to Dan.

"Good job, Bronson," Dan said. "You really held your own."

"Rez dogs are tough," Grover added.

Dan was toweling off Bronson with his shirttail. "This little guy fought as good as I did when them boarding school matrons tried to cut off my hair. They had to call the priest. I jumped on his back and bit him in the ear. You should have tried that, Bronson."

"He put up a hell of a fight," Grover said.

"Why do you think I named him Charles Bronson?" Dan said.

Bronson was looking back at me with an expression of confused betrayal.

Grover had managed to get a small fire going with some twigs and deadfall. "You're going to need some red meat after that scuffle." He sliced open the pack of hot dogs with the point of his knife. "Pink meat, anyway."

He quickly whittled points on the ends of three long sticks, shoved hot dogs on them, and propped them up over the fire. I was doing my best to wash the shampoo out of the cuts on my arm to stop the burning.

"You can use my knife if you want, Nerburn," Grover said. "Just tie off, take a shot of whiskey, and get rid of that arm. Just like the old days."

"Well, I don't have any whiskey," I said. "And this is one of my two favorite arms. I think I'm going to try to save it."

"Suit yourself."

Bronson was still staring up at me, unsure whether to hate me for his rough treatment or love me for the fact that I'd been willing to pick him up and hold him.

"I'm sorry, Bronson," I said. "But someday you'll thank me for it."

The little dog wagged his tail. I *tsukked* several times, and he moved tentatively toward me. I picked him up gently and held him. He nuzzled against me and licked the scratches on my arms. All was forgiven.

We sat in the shade of the huge cottonwood trees listening to the wind move through the leaves and branches.

"When them hot dogs gonna be ready?" Dan asked.

Grover pulled one of the limp wieners from the fire and held it toward Dan. "Just the way you like them. Medium rare."

Dan took some convenience store packs of ketchup from his pocket and slathered them on a piece of the white bread, then used it to pull the hot dog off the stick. He touched his thumb to the forefinger of his right hand and held them to his mouth for a second while he closed his eyes and mumbled a few words. Then he broke off a piece of hot dog and threw it into the fire.

"Here, Nerburn," Grover said, handing me a wiener that had been set too close to the flames and was burnt to a crisp. "This one's medium well."

I looked at the charred object, shrugged, and wrapped it in a piece of the bread. I didn't even bother with the packs of mustard and ketchup; the hot dog was too far gone to be salvaged by any condiments.

I bit into it hungrily. The center was still cold, and the meat was spoiled. There was no telling how long it had been in Lila's refrigerator.

I spit it onto the ground. "Should have gotten the Spam," I said.

"Told you," Grover said.

Dan was glaring at me.

I threw the rotten hot dog toward Bronson, who wolfed it down as if he hadn't eaten in weeks.

Dan's expression didn't change. It occurred to me that maybe he was upset with the harsh way I had restrained Bronson while I washed him.

"Bronson looks pretty good now," I said. "It was worth the scratches." I pointed to my arm.

Still he said nothing.

I was tired from the drive and from the struggle with Charles Bronson, and not at all satiated by my tepid, spoiled hot dog. I didn't know what had set Dan off, but I was in no frame of mind to deal with one of his dark moods. So I just got up, went back to the car for a piece of Wenonah's fry bread, then walked over to a small patch of grass by the trickle of stream to lie down for a rest. The quiet afternoon stillness soon had me drifting into a dreamlike haze.

I lay there listening to the soft rustle of the cottonwood leaves and the faint murmur of the brook when I felt a presence beside me.

At first I thought it was nothing and let myself drift deeper into my reverie. But the palpable sense of another presence wouldn't leave me.

Slowly, I opened my eyes. Dan was standing over me holding the remnants of his hot dog.

"You should have given thanks," he said.

"What?"

"You should have given thanks. I've been watching you. You never give thanks."

I pushed myself up on my elbows. "You mean for the hot dog?" I recalled his gesture of what looked like quiet prayer before he had torn the first chunk from his ketchup-soaked bread.

"For everything."

"Dan, that hot dog was spoiled."

"It was a gift from the Creator."

"I'm sorry. I'm hot, it's dusty, that hot dog was rotten, and the Creator wasn't on my mind."

"Should have been."

I tried to keep my exasperation in check.

"Dan," I said, "you're making more of this than it deserves."

He tossed a chunk of his hot dog and bread toward Charles Bronson.

"No, I'm not," he snapped. "You should always give thanks. White people don't give thanks enough. Too busy or something."

Charles Bronson was tearing into Dan's bread chunk and wagging his tail feverishly.

Dan's tone and presumption were not sitting well with me. I was tired, sweaty, wet, and scratched up. All I'd had to eat all day was Kool-Aid, a couple of cookies, and a bite of spoiled meat, and I hadn't had any coffee worthy of the name. I was not in the mood for one of his lectures, especially when it began with a broad-brushing of all white people.

"Dan. You don't know what thanks I give or when I give it. I don't know what other white people do, and I don't know when they do it. Some of them probably scrape their knees along the ground in prayer all day long, for all I know. Others put a nickel in the collection plate on Sunday and call it a day. Now, will you just let me take a little nap?"

"Bronson was too tough for you?" he said.

"Maybe. Bronson and the driving and the heat kind of took the stuffing out of me."

He looked down on me with disdain. "Ninety years of living have taken more stuffing out of me than you ever had to begin with. That doesn't stop me from giving thanks. Now get up and offer some tobacco."

He whacked me hard on the shoulder with his walking stick and threw a small buckskin pouch onto my chest.

I was completely taken aback. He had never done anything like this before. Had he been a younger man or someone for whom I had less respect, I probably would have confronted him.

"What's this about?" I said.

"Go down there," he said, gesturing toward the creek with his walking stick. "Down where you washed Bronson."

I stretched a bit and tried to shake the weariness out of me. I was in no mood for some kind of spiritual charade, but I wanted to bring this confrontation to an end. I picked the pouch off my chest and walked the dozen or so yards down to the creek.

I felt angry and self-conscious, like a little kid who'd been caught stealing candy and was now being sent back to the store to apologize. I was certain Dan was watching, but I didn't want to turn around to find out.

I stood there on the edge of the creek with the pouch in my hand, trying to decide what to do. If there was a proper ritual, I didn't know it. I knew only that one should always offer gifts to the four directions, then down to Mother Earth and up to Father Sky. A retroactive ritual thanks for a rancid hot dog seemed too forced and bizarre, so I took a pinch of tobacco and offered a simple prayer of thanks for the coolness and the water and the beauty of the day.

Slowly, I turned in each direction and offered thanks for something of beauty that I found in the moment — the buzz of the insects, the wind whispering in the trees, the murmuring of the creek, the little animal I heard rustling in the grasses. By the time I had made a full circle I had searched my heart and senses for everything of goodness and beauty around me.

I looked over to see if Dan was watching. He had turned his back and was waiting for me to finish my prayer.

I walked back up to him and stood by his side.

"Did you do it?" he asked.

"Yes," I said. "I didn't know the right way, but I did it as best I could."

"There isn't any right way," he said. "Not for you. For me, yes. But you don't speak Lakota. You don't have the tradition. You've just got to do something to acknowledge the Creator. What matters is that your heart is good."

He walked over to an old fallen cottonwood trunk and sat against it. His manner toward me had softened.

"You don't need to make a big deal of it. Just do something to turn your heart toward the Creator. Maybe leave a little bit of food on the plate, like your favorite part. Throw a bite of your food on the earth if you're outside. Maybe say a little prayer before you do something. Just make a little ritual."

"But aren't rituals part of the tradition?"

"Nah, those are ceremonies. A ritual's just something you do over and over. It's just a way to focus your mind. Now, a ceremony is something you have to do right. It's a way to call to the Creator to pay attention to what you're doing.

"We Indian people, we've got a lot of ceremonies. Things given to us by the Creator to get in touch. But there's a lot of rituals we do just to keep our minds on the Creator's gifts. You know, the prayers we say after a hunt, before a hunt . . ."

"Or before eating a rotten hot dog."

Dan flashed me a wry grin. "Or before eating a rotten hot dog. It's a way to turn your mind to the Creator and to make sure you're dedicating everything to him. Get up in the morning, give thanks to the Creator. Have a chance to do some good, give thanks to the Creator. Whatever you do, make a little gesture to remind yourself that you are doing it in the presence of the Creator."

He reached down and hoisted Bronson onto his lap. The little dog lunged toward the last piece of hot dog that Dan was holding.

"Does that make sense?" he asked.

"Yeah, I guess," I said. "It just sounds like prayer to me."

He gave me a playful poke with the end of the stick. "It is. Just a different word. You got to be praying all the time, or else you're just thinking about yourself."

He opened his palm so Bronson could grab the final piece of hot dog. The little dog wagged his tail wildly and tore into the chunk of rubbery meat.

"Charles Bronson here, he knows that. He's always giving thanks. See, he hasn't had nothing in his life, so he's always giving thanks for everything. You don't see him making a face about this hot dog. For him it's the greatest gift in the world. Sometimes you've got to learn from the things around you. Keep an eye on Bronson, and maybe you'll get just a little bit smarter."

Bronson had finished the piece of meat and was occupied with licking the last remnants from Dan's hand. Dan gently lifted him down and placed him on the ground. "Of course, sometimes it's easier to give thanks if you use a little ketchup."

CHAPTER TWELVE

◇◇◇◇◇◇◇◇◇◇◇◇◇◇◇◇◇◇◇◇◇◇◇◇◇◇◇◇◇◇◇

INDIANS AND CAVEMEN

By the time we got back on the road, heat mirages were rising in shimmers from the highway.

"Damn, it's getting hot," Dan said. "Doesn't the air conditioning in this car work?"

"It is working," I said.

"Well, it's not doing a very good job."

"It's a little car with a little engine. It's probably a hundred degrees outside."

I tried adjusting the knobs to increase the cooling, but the Toyota was doing the best it could. The sun beat in through the windows as if it was coming through a magnifying glass.

"Just open the windows," Grover said. "Use Indian air conditioning. Besides, it'll get rid of some of the smell of that shampoo on little Dog Soup up there. You really wash your hair with that stuff, Nerburn?"

I didn't bother to answer. My exhaustion was wearing on me,

and their glib refusal to give any shape to the trip was getting under my skin.

"Just give me my hat," Dan groused.

Grover reached into Dan's suitcase and pulled out what looked like an old khaki fisherman's cap. Dan pulled it down over his head and tilted it toward the window so it would block the direct rays.

"Pretty sporty," I said.

"We should have taken Grover's car," he grumbled.

"Or maybe Shitty's truck," I said. "That had a lot of Indian air conditioning."

Grover sat back and folded his hands behind his head.

"I've been thinking about getting myself a hat," he mused. "Maybe one of those Cleveland Indians baseball caps."

"Like Delvin had," I said. Delvin was the husband or boyfriend of one of Dan's granddaughters we had met last time out. He had been proudly sporting a Cleveland Indians baseball cap with its caricatured logo of a leering Indian.

"Yeah. But I'd change the logo from an Indian with a big nose and buckteeth and a feather to a black guy with big lips and white teeth and an afro pick."

"You'd probably make it about five blocks in any city in America before someone killed you," I said.

"I don't go to cities."

"It's probably just as well."

He picked away at his fingernails with his buck knife. It was clear he was mulling something over.

"Nerburn, I want to ask you something," he said.

"Ask away."

"How is it that you guys get all worked up about stuff that insults black folks but don't give a damn about all that Washington Redskins crap and the other stuff that insults us?"

"I don't know, Grover," I said. "Maybe because there are so few Indians and so many blacks?"

"Nah, you won't mess with Chinese either, or Arabs, or anyone else. One bucktooth Chinaman with slanty eyes, and there'd be lawyers lined up around the block. But put a bucktooth Indian with a big nose on a baseball cap, nobody says a thing."

"Maybe it's because you guys are mostly off the radar, living out here in flyover country. There's not enough of you in the big cities to bang the tin cups on the bars."

"There's plenty of Indians in cities."

"I'll tell you what it is," Dan said, piping up from under his fisherman's cap. "It's because when white people think of Indians they think of guys wearing feathers and war paint and riding around on horseback. They can't connect guys like us with guys like that."

He hoisted himself upright in the seat, suddenly interested in the conversation. "When I was a little kid," he said, "we used to play cowboys and Indians. I always wanted to be a cowboy because the cowboys were the good guys. I didn't think of myself as one of those Indians with hatchets and headdresses and all those war whoops.

"Hell, we didn't even think those were the same people as us. So, if we didn't make the connection, why should we expect you white guys to make the connection, especially when you don't even see hardly any of us anymore? To most white folks, Indians are just a bunch of welfare cheats and drunks getting rich off casinos."

"I wish to hell I was getting rich off some casino," Grover said. "I can't even make the nickel slots pay out."

Dan continued undeterred. "We don't look like we used to. We don't dress like we used to. We don't talk like we used to. So white folks don't see any connection. With black people, you see the connection every time you look at their faces."

"Interesting theory," I said. "But that doesn't explain the big blind spot. It would seem obvious that we shouldn't have teams

named the Washington Redskins and do stupid things like that tomahawk chop."

Grover held his hand up and rubbed his thumb and forefinger
together in the universal gesture for money.

"It's deeper than that," Dan said.

"Hey, old man, this is America. You never have to look any
deeper than money."

"Maybe so, but I'm going deeper anyway. Here's what I think it
is. America feels guilty about slavery. But they never had to give
anything back to black people that was hard for them to give. What
they'd stolen from the black people was their freedom, so they just
said, 'We'll give it back to you.' That was easy. Let them go to the
front of the line now and then, let them do everything white people
can do, and America could stop feeling guilty.

"But it wasn't that easy with us Indians. Look what you stole
from us. You took our land, our houses, everywhere we lived. The
only way you can make it right is to give the land back to us, and
you can't do that, because all of America's our land.

"If you wanted to give us back what you stole from us, you'd
have to give us all of America. Here, here's New York. Here's San
Francisco. Here's all of South Dakota."

"Here's Nerburn's house," Grover said.

"Hell, here's everywhere," Dan said. "But you can't face that.
So you have to say, 'Those were different people, that was a different
time.' Instead you tell us, 'You can have some chunks of land we don't
want, and here's some casinos so you can make some money to shut
you up.' Then you just go on your merry way doing what you want."

"That's a little simplistic," I said. "We did a lot more to black
people than just take their freedom. Besides, I still don't see what
that has to do with bucktoothed Indians and tomahawk chops."

"Look," Dan said. "If you see a black person and someone tells
you all the slaves were black people, you see the shadow of slavery

every time you see a black face. But we Indians, we mix up pretty well. There's been lots of intermarriage, there were lots of rapes in the old days.

"You see an Indian who looks almost white and is driving a pickup truck and shopping at Wal-Mart, you don't make the connection to someone who looked like Sitting Bull or Chief Joseph. So the Washington Redskins and that bucktoothed son of a bitch Cleveland Indian don't connect in your minds with us today. Those are old Indians, and we're supposed to be new Indians. We're supposed to not care. What you don't see is that those old Indians were our grandmothers and grandfathers."

He shifted in his seat. "It's just like the cavemen," he said.

"The cavemen?" I said. "What do cavemen have to do with it?"

"Just wait," Dan said. "I'm getting to it. You got to be patient. Now, let me explain it to you this way. If you see a picture of a caveman all hairy and hunched over carrying a club, do you say, 'Hey, that bothers me. Those are my ancestors'? Of course not, because you don't feel any connection to that.

"That's how most white people think we should think of all those images of Indians with headdresses and tomahawks. They don't have any connection to Indians today, so we shouldn't be bothered by them.

"Well, you know why they don't have any connection to today? Because the white man stole our children, cut their hair, made them learn English, wear white man clothes, and worship the white man's god. They did everything they could to break that connection. They wanted to make it so we didn't see any more connection between us and those old Indians than you do between yourself and a caveman. But we do. Those are our ancestors, our great-great-grandparents. Those are our heroes in our history."

It was a classically odd Dan argument — at once absurd and

insightful. My amusement must have shown, because Dan shifted upright in his seat and poked me several times in the bicep.

"Now, I've got some more stuff to say, too," he continued. "There's no way you can feel it's okay to bring folks over from another country in chains. That's wrong, and you know it. But with Indians, you can say, 'We beat you in a fair fight. Get over it,' or you can say, 'You signed those treaties. You made the deal.'

"What you don't say is that there was never any fair fight because you were beating us with smallpox and other diseases, and we made those deals with cannons pointed at us, or with some interpreter lying to us, or with you calling some guy a chief who wasn't a chief and bribing him to sign a treaty by promising him money and a big house."

He rolled down his window and expelled a large wad of spit. It flew back and attached itself to Grover's window in a long string.

"Jesus, old man," Grover said.

Dan shook his hand to shut him up.

"But none of that really matters. What matters is that you've got a way to lie to yourselves about what you did to us, while you don't have a way to lie to yourselves about what you did to black people. Do you follow me?"

"I do, Dan," I said. "But there's not a whole lot I can do about it. I'm not giving my house back to the Ojibwe any more than you're giving your country back to the Cheyenne or the Crow or whoever lived on that land before you moved onto it. What good is feeling guilty going to do?"

Dan slammed his hat against the dashboard. Bronson scuttled off his lap and crouched on the floor.

"Let's get something straight, Nerburn. We didn't take over anyone's land because we wanted it. We were pushed onto it by all the damn boat people from Europe filling up the east and pushing us west. We didn't try to take other people's land. Stealing other people's land is a white man's invention.

"Besides, I'm not telling you to feel guilty about it. I'm saying to take responsibility for it. Guilt's just an inside-out way of feeling good about yourself by saying how bad you feel, and I don't have any time for it. Taking responsibility is something different. It's saying that some of the good you got is because of some of the bad that you did and that you're going to do something to make up for the bad that was done."

His self-righteousness was starting to irritate me. "Okay, that's fine," I said. "But what am I supposed to do? Sit and listen to you beat up me and every other white person for things that General Custer did a hundred and fifty years ago?"

"Well, you could start by telling the truth about what Custer did. You could start by stopping people from naming towns things like Chivington when all that son of a bitch did was shoot down little girls and women and come riding into town with their private parts stretched over the pommel on his saddle. It's like naming a town Hitler."

I didn't know where Chivington was, or even if there was such a town.

"I didn't name any town Chivington, Dan, just like you didn't scalp any settlers."

He seemed to sense that he was pushing his argument too far. He took a deep breath and stared out the window. From his place under the dashboard Bronson thumped his tail as if to ask if the coast was clear.

"Okay, let me try to lay this out straight for you," Dan said. "I'm not saying any of this is your fault or even that your grandparents did any of it. I'm saying it happened, and it happened on your people's watch. You're the one who benefited from it. It doesn't matter that you're way downstream from the actual events. You're still drinking the water.

"I don't care if you feel guilty. I just care that you take some responsibility. Responsibility's about what you do now, not about feeling bad about what happened in the past. You can't erase the footprints that have already been made. What you've got to do is take a close look at those footprints and make sure you're more careful where you walk in the future."

"And how am I supposed to do that?"

"You could start by speaking up a little. No one listens to us anymore when we complain. They just call us whining Indians or some kind of radicals. Think about what Grover said. What if you had a baseball cap with a bucktoothed Chinaman or a black guy with big lips and white teeth chomping on a chunk of watermelon? You've got to start making people see us as human beings, not cartoons. It's seeing real Indians, not wise men or bucktooth savages on baseball caps."

"I do my best, Dan," I said. "I really do."

My conciliatory tone had begun to soften him. I thought for a moment he was actually going to put his hand on my shoulder, but he drew back.

"I know that. And I don't mean to be pointing my finger at you. But something's wrong when white people twist themselves into knots to keep from making black folks mad but keep calling sports teams the Washington Redskins and putting big-nosed Indians on baseball caps. It's telling us we don't matter, or that we don't exist, and it makes me damn angry."

Grover pulled himself up in the backseat and leaned in between us. He had obviously been enjoying the discussion he had started.

"You got it wrong, old man," he said. "They're honoring us with all that stuff. 'Warriors,' 'braves,' tomahawk chop. Those are signs of respect. They're keeping our memory alive."

Dan snorted in derision. He had no time for irony.

"It hurts the little kids," he said. "It tells them they don't matter and that they don't have any say, just like it's always been. Then we wonder why they kill themselves."

"Well, you know what the white people always told us," Grover said. "We're supposed to become like them. So maybe we could get one of those rich tribes out east to buy a baseball team and name it the New York Jewboys. Put a logo on their hats with a grinning Jew with a big hook nose, just like that Cleveland Indian. You could have the Jewboys against the Redskins. It would show that we're learning the American way."

Grover had moved into territory that made me extremely uncomfortable. I wanted out of this conversation, and he knew it.

He leaned closer until his head was only a few inches from my ear. "What do you think about that, Nerburn?" he said.

"I'm not touching this, Grover," I said.

"Too hot for you, huh?"

"Frankly, yes."

"Six million Jews got killed, and you give them a country. Twenty million 'Skins get slaughtered, and you put big-nosed Indians on baseball caps. You think that's fair?"

I didn't want to question his numbers, and I didn't even want to get near the issue of how many of those deaths had been the unintended result of diseases to which the Native people had no immunity. I just wanted to put an end to the conversation. Grover had made his point, and so had Dan. I think Dan realized this, too.

"I don't think Grover's saying that you should start putting cartoons of black guys or Jews on baseball caps," Dan said. "That would be as bad as what they're doing to us. Those folks have had plenty of suffering. We understand that. Hell, we understand suffering better than anybody. Indian people aren't about dragging other people down.

"But here's what you've got to understand. When you look at black people, you see ghosts of all the slavery and the rapes and the hangings and the chains. When you look at Jews, you see ghosts of all those bodies piled up in the death camps. And those ghosts keep you trying to do the right thing.

"But when you look at us you don't see the ghosts of the little babies with their heads smashed in by rifle butts at the Big Hole, or the old folks dying by the side of the trail on the way to Oklahoma while their families cried and tried to make them comfortable, or the dead mothers at Wounded Knee or the little kids at Sand Creek who were shot for target practice. You don't see any ghosts at all.

"Instead you see casinos and drunks and junk cars and shacks.

"Well, we see those ghosts. And they make our hearts sad and they hurt our little children. And when we try to say something, you tell us, 'Get over it. This is America. Look at the American dream.' But as long as you're calling us Redskins and doing tomahawk chops, we can't look at the American dream, because those things remind us that we're not real human beings to you. And when people aren't humans, you can turn them into slaves or kill six million of them or shoot them down with Hotchkiss guns and throw them into mass graves at Wounded Knee.

"No, we're not looking at the American dream, Nerburn. And why should we? We still haven't woken up from the American nightmare."

◇◇◇◇◇◇◇◇◇◇◇◇◇◇◇◇◇◇◇◇◇◇◇◇◇◇◇◇

CHAPTER THIRTEEN

SNAKES AND BEARS

We continued down the road in silence. The mood in the car had gotten even more somber after that burst of conversation. I couldn't know what Dan and Grover were feeling, but I was bothered by the fact that my own discomfort had increased dramatically when they had started talking about "Jewboys" and images of black folks with big lips and watermelons.

Why, I wondered, did those images make me more uncomfortable than the image of the bucktoothed Indian of the Cleveland baseball team? Had I, who cared more about Indian issues than almost any white man I knew, become so hardened to racist imagery of Indians that it no longer affected me? And if that was the case, what was it like for most of the American public who, as Dan had so rightly pointed out, neither knew nor cared anything about Indians or their lives or their history?

I knew that Dan spoke the truth about them seeing ghosts. I had seen it in Native people's eyes many times over the years when they talked to me. How many times had I wanted to scream out, "I'm not the oppressor. I didn't do any of those things." But the look was still there, because the ghosts were still there.

At the same time I was bothered by the way Dan had broad-brushed all white people with his indictments. I was no more responsible for what had happened to his ancestors than he was for what had happened to mine. Still, there was truth in what he said. I was downstream from the events that had shaped us both, and I was the beneficiary of the many cruel and unjustifiable actions that had been visited on his people by mine. Like he said, my house was on land where his people had once lived.

I wanted to change the mood, but I wasn't sure how.

"Dan, I'm sorry," I said. "I know that all this is hard for you."

He answered without looking at me. "You don't know how hard."

He chewed on his mouth a bit like a man adjusting false teeth. He, too, was feeling conciliatory.

"I don't mean to blame you for stuff that's not your fault," he said. "But you've got to understand. It's not like it's just big-nosed Indians on baseball caps. It's everywhere.

"Like last week. Wenonah's grandkids went on a field trip to a museum that was supposed to teach them about their culture. There was a case with some little bowls full of corn and other stuff. The person running the tour was a white lady. She really cared about Indians. She took the kids up to the case and said that the Plains Indians ate a diet of corn and berries and buffalo meat that was high in protein.

"Nerburn, my grandma was one of the best cooks on the reservation. She had a recipe for *wasna* that she wouldn't share with anybody. It had all kinds of special berries and fruits in it. Folks would come over to try to get it, and she would just laugh and say she wasn't giving it away.

"It was like that everywhere. The grandmas had special recipes.

Some of them could whip up a meal out of nothing that would make your head spin. So what sort of thing is it to say that we ate a diet of corn and berries and buffalo meat that was high in protein? That's anthropologist talk. It makes us seem like we're something in a museum. Why can't they say we had really good stews and soups and wild berry pies?"

"I don't know, Dan," I said.

He shook his finger in the air like a schoolteacher calling me to attention. "Let me ask you. What did your grandma make for dinners?"

"Well, she liked to make mashed potatoes and gravy. And fried chicken. And I think she made spaghetti and meatballs. I don't remember exactly. And bread. She liked to bake bread."

"Okay," Dan said. "How would you like it if someone told a kid that your family lived on grain and poultry and beef that was high in protein? Doesn't that seem kind of wrong? Doesn't that make you feel like they don't even look at your life as real?"

"Yeah, I guess it does."

"See, the kids at that museum didn't even know what was going on. It was only because Wenonah was along that I even learned about this.

"And there was a case with a little bow and arrow and a grass ball in it. I know what that was for. It was for a game we played when I was a kid — 'the grass ball game,' we called it. You'd wind grass around some bark and make a mark on it, then throw it in the air and shoot at it. The one who came closest to hitting the mark got to throw it the next time. We'd play that until it got so dark out we couldn't see. It was one of our favorite things.

"But you know what the card next to the case said? Let me see if I can remember it now. Wenonah told me. It said, 'These were objects used in a young boys' game that helped them develop eye-hand coordination.' Eye-hand coordination!"

He tapped me on the knee. "Did you ever go out to develop eye-hand coordination when you were a kid?"

"Wasn't high on my list," I said.

"Maybe you just didn't know it. Maybe somebody should have written a card about it. Put it next to a baseball bat and glove in a museum and have it say, 'These were objects used in a young boys' game that helped them develop eye-hand coordination.' Or we could put a bicycle in it and say, 'This was an object used to develop balance and decision-making skills.'

"This kind of stuff gets me worked up even more than that Indian on the baseball cap. We can tell the kids about how that hat shows prejudice. But how do we protect them from stuff that turns their history into some old dusty museum junk and a bunch of anthropologist gobbledygook?"

"I don't know what to say, Dan," I said.

"That's the problem. There's nothing you can say, and not a lot you can do besides what you're already doing. It's everywhere, and people don't even see it.

"My grandpa used to say that we had to be more afraid of the snake than the bear, because you can see the bear coming. Well, the stuff like the big-nosed Indian on the baseball cap is like the bear. You either kill it or get out of its way. But this other stuff, it's like the snake. It can poison you before you even know it's there."

I could sense that he was trying to bridge the gulf that had developed between us. I wanted to bridge it, too. After all, I was trying to be his ally, not his adversary. I wanted to reach out and let him know that I was on his side.

"I hope I don't do those kinds of things," I said.

"Well, you do," he said. "But it's not your fault. It's how you were raised."

My cheeks burned at the rebuke.

"What do you mean?"

He waved his hand in a gesture of dismissal. "Ah, maybe later," he said.

"No. Please. I want to know."

He spoke back across the seat to Grover. "You saw the handshake, right?"

"Sure, I saw it," Grover said.

"What handshake?" I asked.

"We got time," Dan said. "I'll tell you about it later." He straightened his fishing cap and stared straight ahead. "I'm done talking. I need something to eat. That hot dog didn't quite do the job."

"Yeah, I could use some grains and protein myself," Grover said. "Try to find a McDonald's."

UNFORTUNATELY, OR FORTUNATELY, there were no McDonald's to be found. We were in the middle of a long, empty stretch of open road that cut through an ocean of thirsty rolling grasslands. Aside from an occasional pathway off into the hills, there had been no sign of human habitation for miles. Small clusters of cattle gathered under shriveled trees or wandered through dusty dry washes. A few birds floated high in the empty blue sky. Now and then there would be a faded sign hanging on a piece of barbed-wire fence, or a black and white roadside highway sign that said, "Why Die? Drive Safely." Beyond that, there was only the high heat of the Dakota plains and the thin ribbon of roadway stretching toward the horizon.

We contented ourselves by eating the remnants of Wenonah's fry bread and sharing slugs from Orv's jug of warm Kool-Aid. Bronson joined in quite willingly, and Dan soon had him standing on his hind legs in an effort to procure pieces of fry bread to satiate what appeared to be an almost limitless hunger.

"That's a real rez dog," Grover said. "He appreciates fine dining."

"Going to have a rez belly if you keep feeding him that way," I observed.

"I've been meaning to ask you about that," Grover said. "Are you part Indian? Like your middle part?"

Dan laughed heartily at Grover's joke. "You should take a lesson from the ant, Nerburn," he said. "Works its ass off, stays thin around the middle."

The tone in the car had lightened sufficiently that I decided to pursue the handshake comment that Dan had made so offhandedly a few minutes before.

"What did you mean about the handshake?" I asked. "About how it showed I'm prejudiced?"

"I didn't say it showed you were prejudiced. I just said it showed that you miss some things."

"Like what?"

He gave Bronson a final piece of fry bread and wiped the grease on his pants leg.

"Let's go back down the trail a bit," he said. "You remember when we left Orv?"

"I remember there was a lot of joking and he gave us this fine vintage Kool-Aid."

"You remember that you shook his hand?"

"Right. Like I always do."

"Do you remember anything about it?"

"Nothing in particular. It was kind of soft, I guess."

"Here," he said, reaching his hand across to me. "Shake my hand."

I took his hand in my own. His grip was soft and loose.

"What can you tell me about my handshake?"

"It's soft, like Orv's."

"What you white guys call a 'dead fish,' right?"

"You said it. I didn't."

"Well, yours is hard. It's like a vise. What we call 'the white man power grip.'"

I looked at him quizzically.

"That's right," Dan said. "I was watching you with Orv. You gave him the white man power grip."

"It was just a normal handshake — the way my daddy taught me: 'Look them in the eye, shake their hand firmly to let them know you're there.'"

"That's my point. It's the way your daddy taught you. But it's not the way my daddy taught me. When I shake your hand, I hold it real loose. I keep my touch soft, just so we can touch each other. I don't want to grab you hard. That would be like trying to own you, to control you. I don't need to lock you down to let you know I'm there. That's the way my daddy taught me. It's the way Orv's daddy taught him, too.

"See, this is just one of those things," Dan continued. "Since your culture won, you guys make the rules. Because your guys' handshakes came from some armor knights gripping each other's arms hard so you couldn't reach for your swords, we're supposed to do the same thing. But that's not our way.

"You feel my handshake, and you think it's weak. But it's not weak. It makes you think we're soft, like some hard handshake makes you a man. But a hard handshake doesn't make you a man. All a hard handshake does is keep someone from pulling free.

"I don't want to keep someone from pulling free. That's not showing respect, it's showing power. Real strength is letting a person keep their freedom."

"That's quite a hefty bunch of conclusions to draw from a handshake," I said.

"No, it's not. A handshake is the first meeting between people. It's like the doorstep to your heart. How you do it means a lot.

"Now, let's go back to that thing about prejudice. I meet white folks, and they say, 'I'm not prejudiced. I treat everyone the same, regardless of their race.' But what they don't see is that they're still judging everyone by their own rules.

"Like the handshake. They think it's supposed to be done their way. If an Indian guy comes up and looks them in the eye and gives them the white man power grip, they say, 'Now, there's a real man.' If he comes up and takes their hand real soft in the Indian way, they think he's weak. They say he's got a dead fish handshake.

"See, that's where the thing about the snakes and the bears comes in. These are good people. They aren't like those people who don't like you because of the color of your skin or your religion or something. They just see you through their own eyes and judge you in their own ways. They don't even know they're doing it. It's just the way they were raised. You understand?"

"Yeah, I do."

"Good," he said, and reached his old, trembling hand across for me to shake. I touched it lightly, then grabbed it in a tight, hard grip. He looked surprised, then broke into a wide smile.

"You're a real bastard, Nerburn," he said.

"I know," I said, "and I'm in good company."

◇◈◇◈◇◈◇◈◇◈◇◈◇◈◇◈◇◈◇◈◇◈◇◈◇◈◇

CHAPTER FOURTEEN

MESSAGE FROM A DOG

I was enjoying the conversation. This was the Dan I remembered. But the waning afternoon light had turned my mind to thoughts of home. The mood was convivial enough that I thought it might be time to probe for some answers.

"Dan," I said. "I want to be serious for a moment. It's good to see you. In fact, it's more than that. It's a gift to be able to spend some more time with you. I'd always felt bad about not keeping in touch after our last visit."

Dan shook his head violently as if to say, "I don't want to hear this."

I took a breath and tried again.

"I really need to know where we're going. I told my wife I'd be home..."

I felt a sharp kick in the back of my seat. Grover was glaring at me in the rearview mirror. I ignored his look.

"I want to help you find out about your little sister, Dan. I really do. I've been thinking about it, and I really think you've given me a

rare opportunity. This is my chance to give something back to you
for all you've done for me. But I don't see how this trip is going to
help. I need names. Dates. Anything you can tell me. It doesn't do
any good to be driving around out here in the sun."

Dan stared straight ahead as if he hadn't heard me. He had
placed his fisherman's hat back on his head and pulled it down low
over his eyes and ears.

Grover leaned forward and said something in Lakota. Dan nodded slightly, then Grover moved up close and spoke quietly in my ear.

"You just need to drive. About another hour," he said. "Then
we're going to have a talk."

"I don't need to wait another hour to have a talk," I said.

"Yes, you do. Maybe sometimes you should just listen instead
of trying to know everything all at once."

THE HOUR PASSED SLOWLY. I had no idea why Grover had insisted
on the delay.

Dan sat motionless under his pulled-down cap, rubbing Bronson's head and belly and staring into the brutal afternoon sun.
Grover paged through a road atlas I had stuffed into the pocket
behind the driver's seat.

The heat was getting lethal. The sun had baked all moisture
from the earth, and everything from the grass to the trees had fallen
into a lifeless wilt. The pavement shimmered, and telephone poles
marched in lonely cadence toward the horizon. Here and there a
flock of small birds would rise up from the side of the road and peel
off into the colorless sky. Other than that, there was no movement
anywhere — no cars, no people, no life. Just an endless succession
of brown, rolling hills receding into a breathless, shapeless haze.

"The next town — it's about ten miles up on the left," Grover
said. "I want you to pull in there."

He said a few words to Dan in Lakota, and the old man pulled himself upright and became very alert.

The two of them engaged in a long, animated conversation while I scanned the horizon for any signs of civilization. The land was empty, hot, and barren.

Soon a few scattered homesteads began showing up on the side of the road. Then, as we crested a hill, a small town emerged in the bottom of a distant valley. It wasn't more than a few streets wide.

"This is it," Grover said. "Go down there and find a place to stop." Dan sat upright and craned his neck, as vigilant as a terrier. Even Charles Bronson sensed the change in attitude. He stood up on Dan's lap with his paws on the dashboard and stared out at the road.

I dropped into the great empty bowl of land and turned onto the town's single main street. A dozen or so abandoned buildings stood lifeless on either side of the street. The year 1889 was carved on the door lintel of a low brick building that might once have been a bank, and a faded sign reading "Laundromat" hung over a corner storefront with soaped-up windows and a "For Sale" sign in the door. A few of the buildings had old crumpled fliers tucked under the door handles. Trash blown in by the relentless winds had collected in doorways and against weathered fences. I fully expected to see a tumbleweed come rolling down the center of the street.

At the far end of town, an old gas station and feed store gave the only hint of human habitation.

"Stop there, Nerburn," Grover said.

I was happy to comply. I was concerned about the Toyota, and I wanted to check under the hood. Besides, I wanted to grab something to eat, and I needed to gas up. It was dozens of miles between towns, and my gas gauge showed we had less than a quarter of a tank.

Grover went inside while I washed the grit from the windows

and pumped the gas. I could see him talking to an old man in bib overalls who was sitting in a chair just inside the door.

As he walked back past me I reached out to stop him.

"Are we going to talk now?" I asked.

He ignored my question and pointed to a place on the windshield. "You missed a spot," he said, and got back in the car.

The comment pushed me over the edge. I threw down the squeegee and walked around to his door. "You said we'd talk in an hour, and it's been an hour. You owe me some explanations."

He looked up slowly, like a powerful animal that had just been disturbed.

"Nobody owes you anything," he said. "Just pay for the gas and get in the car."

There was something chilling in his tone. I did as he said.

"Now go down to the corner and take a left," he said. Dan was sitting motionless in the passenger's seat.

I put the car in gear and drove to the corner.

"Left, now. Go two blocks, and then pull over."

I followed his instructions and crunched onto the gravel shoulder. We were on a lonely stretch of road on the outskirts of town. An abandoned rural railroad station stood on one side of the street, and a tired, unkempt park stood on the other.

"Get out," Grover said.

Dan remained motionless in the seat beside me.

"Get out," he said again. His tone was flat and without emotion.

For the first time a wisp of fear rose up in me.

I stepped out into the blazing heat.

Grover stepped out behind me. Dan stayed in the car. "Go over there," Grover said.

He gestured to the park with its few wilting trees and brown, lifeless grass. There was nothing in it but a bent jungle gym, a gray weathered teeter-totter, and a swing set with a red rubber swing hanging by a single chain from the crossbar. On its far side a wooden shelter with a single picnic table created the only shade anywhere.

"Go to that shelter. You want to talk? We're going to talk."

For the first time in all the hours I had spent with the two men, I felt alien and threatened. Dan's silence had an uncomfortable edge, and Grover's manner bordered on violence.

We crossed the scorching street and headed toward the shelter. The air smelled of creosote from a pile of baking railroad ties lying haphazardly by the abandoned station building.

Grover took a seat at the picnic table and took out his hunting knife. With its point he gestured to the seat beside him.

"Now, what exactly is it you want to know?"

I was nervous, but I knew I had to speak my mind. "I want to know where we're going, what we're doing. Dan said he wanted me to help him find out about his little sister. Now, all of a sudden, we're off on some trip, and you guys seem to be making a game out of it."

Grover gathered himself and looked across at me. When he spoke, he was very deliberate and direct.

"This is no game. No game. Now, I want you to listen to me, and I want you to listen to me good. The old man calls you. He gives you the privilege of burying his old dog. He gives you the honor of helping him find out about his lost sister, and all you can think about is your damn car and getting home. You can't even do him the honor of showing that you care."

"I do care," I said. "And I want to help him. But driving around isn't getting us anywhere."

"Maybe not. But it's what he wants to do."

"That's fine. But how does it help us find out anything about his sister?"

"That's not your business."

"Yes, it is — if he wants me to help."

He jabbed his knife hard into the table.

"Look. The old man's not stupid. He knows what he's doing. It doesn't matter if you do. All that matters is that an elder has asked for your help. Your job is to shut up and give it."

"But none of this makes any sense. Yellow Bird's been gone seventy-five or eighty years, and all of a sudden he decides to look for her? Why didn't he look for her before? And why is he asking me? You could have helped him. Wenonah could have helped him. Lots of people could have helped him."

Grover flicked a piece of the picnic table out with the blade of his knife.

"He asked you because you're the only white man he trusts. You've been to college. You know the white man ways and can talk the white man talk."

He paused for a second before continuing. "And he said that Fatback told him he could trust you."

"A dog?"

"That's right. A dog."

He stood up and walked out of the shelter into the baking heat. His eyes moved slowly along the edge of the horizon. "You think the world is only about the things you can see."

I got up and followed him.

"But why now?"

"He got a message that he's dying. He wants to set things right."

"What kind of a message?"

Grover shook his head in disgust.

"Just do what he says. Like I do. You ask too many questions, and they're all the wrong ones."

He pointed across the street to the car where Dan was sitting, staring straight ahead like a statue.

"Now, I'm going to go get the old man, and the three of us are going for a walk. And you're just going to keep your mouth shut and listen."

The sweat was pouring off me, and the air was so hot that it burned my lungs.

"You're going to make him walk in this heat?"

"He's Lakota. Just keep your mouth shut."

He walked back to the car to talk to Dan. The old man turned toward him and began conversing. I could see that the discussion was animated and serious. Finally, Grover opened the car door and helped Dan out of the seat. Charles Bronson jumped onto the ground behind them.

"Get over here, Nerburn," Grover shouted. "We're going up to that station."

I tried to jog to catch up to them. I didn't want Dan to be out in this heat any longer than necessary.

Before I'd made it ten steps my hair was dripping with sweat and the back of my shirt was soaked. Dan and Grover were already a hundred feet up the tracks.

The rail yard was as abandoned and desolate as the park. It felt like no one had been there for years. Some huge metal storage tanks with peeling paint and rusting seams stood next to piles of rusting steel rails and empty black buckets of dried creosote. Canvas bags full of railroad spikes and hold-down plates had rotted open, spilling their contents onto the ground. Beyond them the tracks stretched off in both directions toward the distant hills.

The station where Dan and Grover were heading was about a quarter mile from where we had parked. It might at one time have been almost cute — white with a broad overhanging roof and rough-cut ornate finials. But now the whitewash had flaked and faded, and the two windows on the side had been boarded up with weathered plywood, giving it the appearance of a building that had gone blind.

I hurried after the two men as best I could. My clothes were sticking to me, and the acrid smell of creosote burned my nostrils and stung my eyes. Grasshoppers jumped on my legs and fluttered up onto my shoulders and into my face.

"Where are we going?" I wheezed as I caught up to them.

Grover glared at me — a reminder that I was supposed to keep my mouth shut.

Dan was walking carefully, using his willow walking stick. Every once in a while he would stop and look around like an animal that had just stepped from a dark room into the light. He seemed confused, concerned, unable to comprehend. I felt sorry for him and wondered why Grover was putting him through this ordeal.

We made it up to the abandoned station and took refuge under the overhang. Dan was squinting and staring every which way. I had never seen him look so lost and confused.

I started to speak, but Grover locked his eyes on me and stared me into silence.

Dan continued looking around. He poked his walking stick at the two massive wooden beams that served as steps up to the locked and boarded-up freight doors of the station.

"Yeah," he said slowly. "Yeah. I remember them steps. That's where we sat and waited for the train."

He hobbled across the rotting platform and pointed up the tracks. "There," he said. "That's the way." I followed his hand with my eyes. The two rails wavered in the heat before disappearing into the empty hills and the afternoon haze.

I looked at Grover, hoping for an explanation. But none was forthcoming.

Dan tapped the edge of the tracks with his stick. They made a hollow clang in the still afternoon air. "Yeah, here's where it came from," he said. "That way."

"You sure?" Grover said.

"Hell, yes. I'd never forget this place."

Grover grabbed me by the arm and pulled me aside.

"Okay, Nerburn," he said. "Go back up to that gas station and fetch us some water. The old man and I are going to take a rest and wait for you. When you get back you're going to get what you want."

I nodded like a child being sent on an errand by his mother and turned toward the car. Dan and Grover sat down on the steps and leaned back into the shade of the overhang.

"Get a move on it," Grover said. "It's hotter than hell."

"Bring some water for Bronson, too," Dan shouted.

The temperature must have been 110 degrees.

THE OLD MAN IN THE BIB OVERALLS and the feed cap didn't have any bottles of water to sell, but he let me fill the Kool-Aid jug with water from the tap. It was a cloudy, brown liquid, but he assured me it was safe to drink. "Been drinking it for seventy years," he said. "Ain't killed me yet."

I wetted down a towel I'd grabbed from my bag and put it around my neck and hurried back to the station. I wanted to know what was going on, but more than that I was worried for Dan. Lakota or not, this was killing heat for someone his age. I didn't share Grover's casual approach to the situation.

Dan and Grover were sitting quietly in the shade of the overhang. Dan took the jug and drank hungrily from it, then slapped some water on his forehead before pouring a little into his hand and offering it to Bronson. The little dog lapped at it ferociously. Grover sat on the far edge of the steps drinking nothing.

"Okay, tell him, Dan," Grover said. "It's time he understood."

The water seemed to bring Dan back into focus. He leaned back against the peeling paint on the boarded-up door of the station and pulled a half-smoked cigarette out of his shirt pocket.

He lifted his hand over his shoulder. "Give me a light, Grover."

Grover pulled a Zippo from his pocket and placed it in the old man's hand. Dan lit his cigarette unsteadily. It was the first time I'd seen him smoke since I'd come to the reservation.

He took a long, thoughtful inhale, then went quiet. He sat motionless for so long that I thought maybe he'd fallen asleep. Finally he took another draw on the cigarette and crushed the ash between his thumb and middle finger.

"When I got to that boarding school, I was really scared." It was as if he was picking up a conversation that we had stopped only minutes ago. Grover looked hard at me to make sure I didn't interrupt.

"I had this eagle feather. An old man from our village had given it to me so I'd remain strong. He'd earned it when he was young. He said he'd been saving it his whole life to give to someone, and that I was the person the Creator had wanted him to give it to.

"When I got to that school, the first thing the priests did was take that eagle feather and break it up. They just tore it up right in front of me. They broke it up and threw it on the ground."

Dan's hands were shaking. He could hardly get the cigarette up to his mouth.

"From that moment I hated that school. I knew it was bad for my spirit. But I was there for Yellow Bird.

"I fought everything they did. But they knew how to control you. For a long time, they punished me when I did something wrong. When I wet my bed they made me carry my mattress around the schoolyard on my back. When I ran away, they tied a log to my legs with a chain and made me march around a field. But when none of that stopped me, they started punishing Yellow Bird. One time I ran away for a few days to try to get my spirit right, and when they caught me they shaved Yellow Bird's head.

"I hardly ever got to see her. They kept the boys and girls separate. Sometimes I'd see her outside on the playground, and she'd try to run to me. She'd be crying, and they'd grab her and hit her."

He stood up abruptly and walked toward the tracks. The air was motionless. "This is where we came to get her," he said without turning back toward us. He gestured down the tracks with the walking stick.

"I came home that summer, but she got sent out to work for some white family. We got told she'd come home at the end of the summer. We came up here to get her. Me, my mother, my father. We borrowed an old wagon. We got up here and waited for her to get off the train. We had a new little doll one of the grandmas had made for her, all beautiful with a little buckskin dress and beads on the moccasins, and my momma had made her a new dress with special beads that had been given to her by the grandma. She had worked on it almost all winter.

"When the train got here, Yellow Bird didn't get off. I was the only one who spoke any English. I asked the train men if there was a little girl on there and they said there wasn't. No little girl had been on the train at all.

"My mother started to wail and pull on her hair. My father shouted at the men but they couldn't understand what he was saying. They just got back on the train and went away."

Dan uttered something in Lakota and limped slowly up the tracks. Bronson scuttled behind him. I turned toward Grover and put my hands out like a man asking for more explanation. He shook his head and put his finger to his lips.

Dan was staring up the tracks into the afternoon haze. "My mom sent letters. I wrote down everything she said and mailed them. We talked to the government people. We did everything. No one knew anything. The only thing we ever found out was in a letter from the school that she had gotten sick and hadn't been able to come home. When I went back the next year I asked everyone. The school people said she was staying with the family who had taken her for the summer. That's all they'd tell me."

"Didn't you ask the name of the family?"

"They wouldn't tell us. They said it wasn't allowed."

"So you don't know what happened to her?" I asked.

"Indian kids disappeared all the time. Got killed. Kidnapped. Just ran away, maybe lived with another tribe."

He dug the end of his walking stick into the dust and started back toward the car.

"I think about her every day, Nerburn," he said. "I think about my little sister every day."

CHAPTER FIFTEEN

YELLOW BIRD'S GHOST

I t's hard to explain the feelings that were swirling inside me as we got back in the car. There were so many unanswered questions, so many things that made no sense. I looked over at Dan's old, lined face as he sat in the seat next to me. There was a weariness about him, a kind of resigned resolution. It was as if he had dropped the keen vigilance that always characterized his expression, and in the process had lost the twinkle that had always made him seem youthful and mirthful and full of life. He seemed emotionally, physically, and spiritually spent.

We drove into the waning afternoon without speaking. The sun had lost its brutal edge, and the light on the hills was beginning to soften. Grover smoked silently in the backseat, while Dan idly scratched Bronson's head. Even the little dog seemed to know that something had changed. He lay flat on Dan's lap with his ears out and his head on his paws. He stared up at me with questioning eyes.

"Do you want to stop somewhere, Dan?" I asked. "Get something to drink?"

The old man waved me off.

"Just keep driving," Grover said.

I was deeply bothered and upset. The cat-and-mouse game had worn heavily on me, and Grover's dark edge had made me nervous and ready to go home. But the image of the old man standing on that lonely railroad siding, staring up the abandoned tracks in that ragged fisherman's cap, his white ponytail hanging down his back and his spindly, bowed legs supported by the long willow walking stick, had pulled me back. He had looked so small and forlorn, so lonely and without hope.

I thought of my own sisters, and how it would have been for me if they had disappeared without a trace when they were young, and the shadow it would have cast over my life. I could not escape the echoing resonance of Dan's words: "I think about her every day, Nerburn. I think about her every day."

Gradually, the sky darkened and the night winds began to rise. Dan slipped sideways in his seat and began snoring softly.

Grover looked closely at him, then leaned forward close to me.

"Did that answer your question?" he said. The edge seemed to be gone from his voice.

"It helped me understand, but it doesn't get me any closer to finding out what happened to Yellow Bird."

"Maybe it wasn't for you," he said. "Maybe it was for him. Like I said, the old man knows what he's doing. He's just old, he's not dumb. He wouldn't have done this for nothing."

Dan rustled in his seat. Charles Bronson was squirming and wiggling and trying to get comfortable.

"But why'd he wait all these years to do this? How could he live with it?"

"There's still a whole lot you don't understand about Indian people. Sometimes things just hurt too much to talk about."

"But eighty years?"

As we were talking, Dan began making a strange gurgling sound.

I looked at Grover with alarm. "Is he okay?"

Grover raised his hand to silence me. "Shut up." He put his head close to the old man's. Dan was mumbling and whispering in Lakota.

"What's he saying?" I asked.

Grover gestured me to keep quiet.

Suddenly, the mumbling turned into some kind of chant.

"Is he having a dream?"

"Yeah, but not your kind of dream."

Bronson was upright and alert, his ears pulled back. Dan's singing was eerie and sepulchral.

Grover had his ear almost at the old man's lips. I could not understand the words, but they sounded like "sayyay sni yo, sayyay sni yo."

"*Wakuleyo*," Dan said. "*Wakuleyo, wakuleyo*."

"He's talking to someone," Grover whispered.

Dan kept up his strange utterings. Occasionally he would switch to English for a few words, then switch back. I caught something about "little boy" and "sister" but nothing else.

He kept this up for about three minutes, fading out, then jerking bolt upright, then fading out again. I couldn't tell if it was a dream or a trance. Grover had become vigilant in a way I had never seen before, and Bronson had become strangely quiet and attentive.

Finally, Dan settled back and slouched against the door. His breathing became regular, and the snoring started up again. Bronson closed his eyes and relaxed into the old man's lap.

"Well, there's your answer," Grover said.

"What?"

"He was talking to Yellow Bird. Telling her he was sorry, that he should have come looking for her."

He lit a cigarette and sat back in his seat.

"He kept saying that he was afraid, that he'd always been afraid."

"That doesn't make sense," I said. "Dan doesn't seem like a frightened kind of person. What was he afraid of?"

Grover sucked hard on his cigarette as if he was thinking.

"You don't know?"

"No, I don't."

He looked over at the old man. Dan was sleeping quietly; his breathing was as soft and gentle as a baby's.

"Well, you would if you were an Indian."

"But I'm not."

He took one final drag and threw the cigarette out the window.

"He was afraid of what every Indian who lost someone in the boarding schools is afraid of."

"And what's that?"

He cleared his throat and spit into the dark.

"He was afraid of what he was going to find."

THE NIGHT WAS MOVING IN AROUND US. Clouds obscured the moonlight. Now and then the sky would break, and a pale illumination would fill the sky, revealing a world of blacks and grays like the negative of an old photograph or a half-remembered memory.

I peered at Grover in the rearview mirror. His face was shrouded in shadow. I wanted nothing more than to be free of this situation and headed back to my home and family. But Dan's burden was slowly becoming my burden, and there was no escaping the haunting presence of Yellow Bird's ghost.

"How much further do we have to go?" I asked.

Grover lit his lighter and opened the atlas.

"I can turn on a light," I said.

"Zippo's fine," he said. "The old man needs to sleep."

He checked the page in the wavering flame of the lighter, then closed the atlas.

"Road marker 63," he said. "About thirty miles."

"What's up there?" I asked.

"The boarding school."

The information sent a shiver through me. Up until now the journey had been an abstraction — a shapeless journey into dark and haunted memories. Now suddenly it was becoming very real. We were going to the place where it had all happened — where Dan had lost his little sister, where he had been made to kneel on broomsticks and had his hair cut off and kerosene poured on his head.

I looked over at him. His long ponytail hung loosely over his shoulder. It was like a flag of defiance, a silent claim on what the boarding school had tried to beat out of him.

"It's not still in operation, is it?" I asked, hoping that perhaps I could find some clues that could help Dan in his search.

"Nah. It's been shut down since the fifties."

"Then what does he want to find?"

"I don't know. I didn't ask. He just said he wanted to go there, and I said I'd get him there. You should do the same."

Outside, the sky was a great purple shroud pierced by specks of light. The Milky Way moved down its center like a river of diamonds. The eyes of small animals appeared on the side of the road, then disappeared. Once something large jumped across the roadway. "Pronghorn," Grover said. But it had moved too fast for me to recognize.

The mileage markers on the road moved by in rhythmic cadence. They rose up in my headlights, revealed their number, then disappeared into darkness. Grover kept flicking on his Zippo to check the atlas. In the momentary bursts of light his face would be illuminated with a wan, unearthly glow.

"Coming up," he said.

The mileage marker 63 appeared out of the darkness.

"Should we wake him up?" I said.

"Not yet," Grover said, glancing at the old man. "Let him sleep. We'll take a look and see what's up there."

I turned on to a scabrous, buckled asphalt road that led off to the right. It looked like it had once been an entrance drive to somewhere, but now it was littered with old mattresses and a couple of fifty-five-gallon drums and white plastic garbage bags with soiled baby diapers spilling out of them. Weeds grew knee-high through the cracks in the asphalt. It appeared that no one but vandals and trash dumpers had been here in years.

I proceeded cautiously. Broken beer and whiskey bottles lay shattered on the roadway.

"This is it," Grover said. "Yeah, this is it."

I kept squinting into the darkness, hoping to see some sign of habitation. But nothing revealed itself. Several times I had to stop to remove pieces of twisted copper pipe from the roadway. I was tempted to tell Grover we should turn around.

Then, as we rounded a curve, there it stood: a brooding, dark monolith outlined against the moving nighttime sky.

Grover leaned forward and stared through the windshield. I could feel his breath on the back of my head.

"Jesus," I said. "This is it?"

"This is it."

I drove slowly through the trash and broken glass toward the entrance.

The building was two stories tall with two wings on either side of a main entrance. All the windows had been broken out, and detritus littered the ground. A few gang symbols had been spray painted on the walls, along with various obscenities and illegible scrawls. It looked like a ghost ship looming on the top of the hill.

As we got closer we could see that the front door was gone and a two-by-four had been nailed across the opening.

"Let me out," Grover said.

"You're not thinking of going in there?" I asked.

"Just let me out."

"You don't even have a flashlight."

"I've got a Zippo."

I stopped the car, and he walked out through the boards and old water heaters and pieces of piping that lay scattered along the crumbling sidewalk. He poked his head in the dark opening of the doorway, then ducked under the two-by-four and disappeared. I could see the tiny flame of his lighter pass from window to window as he moved down the hallway. Soon he reemerged and made his way back to the car.

"Too dark," he said. "Holes in the floor. Junk everywhere. We can't let the old man in there. Find us a place to stay for the night."

I turned the car around and headed back to the highway. My relief was palpable. There was something ominous and foreboding about the place. I wanted nothing to do with it in the dark.

Dan continued to snore gently in the seat beside me. Bronson had awakened and was standing on Dan's lap, staring out at the shadowy structure.

"Map shows a town a few miles up," Grover said. "Get us a place to stay. In the morning we'll bring the old man up here. It'll be safer in the daylight."

We approached the town under the pale glow of moonlight. Like the town with the railroad station, it appeared to be almost abandoned. The few buildings on the main street were dark, with the exception of a grim bar with a small oval neon beer sign in the window.

I knew that small towns like this often had a last, lonely mom-and-pop motel on their outskirts. They were usually worn down and gritty, surviving on road construction crews and the occasional traveler who had wandered too far from the interstate.

A mile past the bar I saw what I had been looking for: a small roadside sign that read "Ko-Z-Rest. Singles $23."

"That'll do," Grover said.

I pulled in under the harsh sodium light that illuminated the gravel parking area in front of the office. The rooms themselves were set farther back from the road in a long, low-slung building with a narrow overhang like a cowboy bunkhouse.

I made a deal with the bleary-eyed proprietor, and we unloaded our few belongings into two rooms at the far end of the building. Blessedly, the man at the desk had claimed to have only one room with two beds and one with a single, though there were no other cars anywhere in the lot. Since Grover wanted to stay with Dan, this left me alone for the first time since we'd started the journey.

I was just about to crawl into bed and get a long-overdue full night of sleep when Grover appeared at my door. "Come on, Nerburn," he said. "Let's go down to that bar and get some food. That hot dog's already moved on through."

"What about Dan?" I asked.

"He's okay here," Grover said. "There's a cop show on TV. He likes those. We'll bring something back to him."

We got in the car and crunched our way across the parking area. Through the open door to Dan's unit I could see him sitting on the edge of the bed about two feet from the television screen, pushing buttons on the remote with one hand and scratching the top of Bronson's head with the other.

With the old man situated for the night, Grover seemed to relax. He leaned back in the car seat and put his hands behind his head, like a man in a lounge chair.

"So, how you doing, Nerburn?" he asked.

"Not very well," I said. "In all honesty I just want to go home."

"So do I. This isn't any fun for me either."

"So, why are we doing it?"

"The old man asked. That's enough for me. Remember, I'm old military: 'Need to know.'"

"Well, I'm not. And I've got a family."

"He had a family once, too. He had a little sister named Yellow Bird."

The comment put me in my place. "Sorry," I said. "I just have a hard time understanding how you can lose your sister and not look for her for your whole life, then suddenly want to find out about her."

"I told you. He was afraid."

"But what exactly was he afraid of? The worst he could find out is that she was dead, and he's probably been assuming that anyway."

"You don't know much about the boarding schools, do you?"

"I know they were bad. 'Kill the Indian, save the man.' I know there's been lots of talk recently about sexual abuse."

"Tip of the iceberg. Murders. Mass graves. It's just starting to come out. We've known about it for years. But no one believed us."

"Murders and mass graves?"

"Oh, yeah. Kids were beat to death, pushed into scalding baths, left outside in the winter as punishment until they froze to death. They've found corpses of babies buried in walls."

"Corpses of babies?"

"Sure. Some of those little Indian girls can be really pretty."

Grover's revelations were mind-numbing. And his offhanded way of mentioning them was even more chilling.

"Did stuff like that happen when Dan was at that place?"

"I don't know. I suppose it did. But he doesn't talk about it. He'll joke about some things, tell a few stories. But the hard stuff? No. That talk back at Orv's was the most I'd ever heard him say. Most Indians, they just push it away. They say there was some good and some bad, and that it helped them learn English, and stuff like that. That's mostly how he is.

"Think about it. If you were a little boy and some old priest comes up and makes you take down your pants and starts messing with you, you think you'd want to talk about it? Hell no, you'd be too ashamed.

"What if you were a little girl, and you had a baby, and that baby came from a priest? What are you going to do? Say that your baby's father was a priest? No. You're going to kill yourself or you're going to shut up."

He looked over at me for my reaction. "You think I'm making this stuff up?"

"No, Grover. I just don't know what to say."

"There's nothing you can say. You're not going to find this stuff in books. You've just got to believe us."

"I do. It's just hard to imagine."

"Well, you better imagine it," he said. "We all do. Every night."

He exhaled slowly into the darkness. "Yeah, the stories I could tell you."

"Like what?"

He thought for a minute, then shook his head. "Nah," he said. "It ain't worth it."

"Please. It helps me understand."

He remained silent for a few seconds more, then sucked a breath in through his teeth. "Okay. Just one. But this is all I'm going to say.

"There was this little kid. I'm not going to say who or where. He was just a little guy, maybe eight or nine. He was pretty quiet because he couldn't learn English.

"On Fridays in this school they used to get a change of clothes. They'd have to take off all their old clothes and put them in a pile on the floor, then they'd get clean clothes. They'd have to do this in front of the sisters — take off everything and stand there naked until they got the clean clothes. Those sisters would look and make sure they put all their dirty clothes in the pile.

"One of the things you got with your clean clothes was a clean

handkerchief. Well, this little guy, he couldn't find his old handkerchief. One of the bigger boys probably stole it. So the sisters asked
him where his handkerchief was.

"'I don't know,' the kid said.

"'You used it to wipe yourself,' that sister told him.

"'No,' the kid told her. 'I didn't do that.' Like I said, he couldn't
speak very much English.

"She didn't believe him. She went and got the priest and told
him that the kid had used his handkerchief to wipe his butt.

"They made him get dressed, then they took him out to the outhouse. It was really long, maybe thirty feet. All the kids used it.

"'We know you used that to wipe your butt,' he said, 'And now
you're going to find it.'

"'They had an Indian guy who worked there pry some boards
from the outhouse. 'Now get down in there and find it,' they said.

"The little boy kept saying, 'No, no,' but they didn't care. They
dropped him down in there, right into the shit. 'Now you're going
to find it,' they said. They made him crawl in all that shit from one
end to the other, reaching around trying to find that handkerchief.

"'Did you find it?' they asked.

"'No,' he said. He was all covered with shit.

"'Then you got to do it again.'

"They made that little boy keep crawling back and forth on his
hands and knees, down there in that outhouse, looking for that handkerchief. They just watched him and laughed."

He flicked his cigarette out the window. "Is that enough story for
you?"

"Did you know that kid?" I asked.

He turned his face toward the window and looked out into the night.

"Don't matter," he said. "It was just another Indian kid."

❖❖❖❖

WE GOT TO THE BAR JUST BEFORE CLOSING TIME. We ordered a couple of hamburgers and an order of fries. The place was empty, and the stools were up on the counter.

Normally I would have started up a conversation with the bartender just to pass the time, but Grover's revelations had moved me inside myself. Suddenly I was seeing Dan through different eyes — no longer as the sharp-eyed, humorous observer of life's foibles but as a wounded old man, trying in his last years to put some shape to a life he had not chosen and had barely survived. I still could not imagine how his family had let his sister go missing for all those years.

Grover seemed to read my mind.

"Listen," he said. "I don't know if your grandparents came on boats or if they were a bunch of farmers. But you've got to understand something about the old man. His folks weren't more than a few years from Wounded Knee. The government still shot people. It stole the kids, performed experiments on them, sterilized the little girls. If you made too much noise you just disappeared. That's just the way it was. You didn't make trouble."

"Sounds like the Nazis," I said.

Grover just shrugged. "I'm just trying to make you understand. This is a big thing he's doing. I'm telling you again, he's counting on you because you're the only white man he trusts."

The bartender came out through the swinging doors and placed a grease-stained brown bag on the counter in front of us. "I gave you extra fries because we're closing up," he said.

"Thanks," Grover said. "The old man really likes fries."

I paid him and left a few dollars on the counter for a tip. On the shelf behind the bar in front of all the liquor bottles was a sign that read "When I Left Nam, We Were Winning."

"No we weren't," Grover said when he saw me looking at the sign. "That's the problem with America. Always have to think

you're winning. We Indians know better. Sometimes you lose. Sometimes the best you can do is try to survive."

BY THE TIME WE GOT BACK TO THE MOTEL it must have been close
to two. The door to Dan's unit was closed, but the lights were still
on. I could see the pale flicker of the TV screen shifting the light
inside the room.

"Keep it quiet," Grover said. "It looks like he fell asleep again.
No need to wake him up if we don't have to."

We opened the door slowly. Dan was curled up on the bed with
his clothes on. For the first time I noticed that his shoes had no laces
and he wasn't wearing any socks. He reminded me of my father in
his last days — so sallow and sunken that he almost seemed a corpse.

A late-night talk show was blaring from the television. Bronson
was curled up in the old man's arms. When he heard us enter, he
stuck his head out from under Dan's elbow and wagged his tail.

Grover walked over softly, turned off the TV, then reached in
the bag and gave me a hamburger. "You can take it back to your
room and eat it there."

"You going to wake Dan up to eat?" I asked.

Grover shook his head. "Nah, he'll get by." He looked down at
the little dog, who was sniffing expectantly at the newfound odors in
the room.

"I'll give Dan's burger to Bronson," he said. "He deserves it."

He flashed me a last wicked grin.

"Besides, he always gives thanks."

◇◇◇◇◇◇◇◇◇◇◇◇◇◇◇◇◇◇◇◇◇◇◇◇◇◇◇◇◇◇◇

CHAPTER SIXTEEN

TALKING STONES

I sat in my hotel room, staring at the flickering screen on my television and nibbling at my burger. But despite almost an entire day without food, I had no appetite. The weight of the day still burdened me. Grover's comments about mass graves and little children being dropped into outhouses upset me more than I had realized. And the idea that Dan had felt compelled to keep this secret about his sister for all these years saddened me beyond measure.

I kept seeing an image of little Yellow Bird standing mute and accusing on the front steps of a boarding school in a taffeta First Communion dress. It was not even a real image; I had no idea if she had even made a First Communion.

But the image wouldn't leave me. It rose out of the thousand expressionless faces I had seen in old sepia-tone boarding school photos like the fragment of the photo Dan had given me — little children dressed in European clothing staring blankly at the camera as the priests and nuns stood behind them, controlling everything about them except the fierce emptiness of their gazes.

Did those priests and nuns really do those terrible things that

Grover had claimed? Had they happened to Dan? Had they happened to little Yellow Bird?

I covered my head with my pillow and tried to occupy my mind with thoughts of home. Eventually, after an hour of tossing and shifting, I fell into an uneasy sleep. The last images I remembered were the face of little Yellow Bird, mute and accusing, staring at me as if I were an enemy, and a small boy standing by an empty railroad track, looking off into the hills.

I was awakened by a sliver of light coming in around the edge of the blinds. I sat bolt upright, uncertain where I was. I lifted the corner of the blinds and peered out through the open window onto a panorama of rolling hills backlit by a pale lavender illumination. The air was already picking up heat, and birds were chirping and trilling in the morning grasses.

I'd had a good night of sleep. The phantoms of the previous evening had dissipated, and I was filled with new resolve. I reached over to grab my shaving kit from the bedside table. A strange scratching noise was coming from outside the unit.

I opened the door a crack, and Charles Bronson came bounding in.

"Hey, Bronson," I said. "Enjoy your burger?" The little dog wagged his tail and jumped up on my bed. He stood on his hind legs and tried to lick my face.

"Not so fast," I said. "We barely know each other."

He wiggled and bounced like some kind of cartoon animal, with all four legs leaving the ground at the same time.

"You know, you're not so bad," I said, scruffing the patchy fur on the top of his head. "I can't say much for your gene pool, but you're okay."

The attention sent him into an ecstasy of wagging. I had the distinct feeling that he must have had a human family at some time. His hunger for affection was too earnest and unprotected.

"You just wait here," I said. "I've got a little cleanup to do. Let me take a quick shower, and then I'll take you for a walk." But he was already nose-first into my trash basket, snuffling in the greasy piece of butcher paper containing the remnants of my hamburger. His tail was wagging like a metronome.

When I came out of the bathroom he was sitting with an old brown cotton glove in his mouth. The burger bag and wrappers were scattered all over the room. His Yosemite Sam mustache was covered with ketchup. He wagged his tail and held the glove up like a prize.

"Where'd you get that, Bronson?" I said. It was an old work glove I had once used for changing the oil filter in the car. I hadn't seen it for years. It must have been stuffed in one of the side pockets of the aviator bag.

He wagged his tail and held it aloft.

"You can do better than that," I said, and reached for one of the ragged motel washcloths.

He shook his head back and forth, almost as if telling me, "No, this is what I want."

I was slowly getting fond of the little guy. What he lacked in physical appeal he made up for with his openness and enthusiasm. Most rez dogs were either so wary that you couldn't get near them or so tragic that you could only pity them. But Dan's attentions and ministrations had already brought out something playful and mirthful in Bronson.

More than that, he had a strangely human manner about him. He always seemed to be abnormally present to the emotional reality of a situation, and sometimes — like now — he almost seemed to be engaging you in conversation. It was unnerving. You felt as if you were not only being observed, you were being understood. It was a far cry from Fatback, who had just slobbered love and hopefulness over every event of the day.

I bent over and reached for the glove. Bronson shook his head and backed away as if he intended to keep it.

"Come on, Bronson," I said. "Give it up. It's filthy." He growled playfully and looked me in the eye.

"Give me that glove," I said. I grabbed for it, and he ran into a corner.

Before long I was chasing him across the bed and around the room. He was wagging and growling and waving the glove in the air.

Finally I trapped him under a table. He dropped the glove and smiled at me.

I got down on my knees and reached for the glove. He was sitting right behind it, panting and grinning.

"I'm taking that," I said. He barked in response, as if he had understood.

"I'm serious. It's filthy. I'll get you something else."

I reached across cautiously and put my hand on the glove. Without warning, Bronson leapt up and licked me on the face. Then he grabbed the glove and ran off into the far corner of the room, yipping and barking. He almost sounded as if he was laughing.

I COULD HEAR THE TELEVISION through the wall from Dan and Grover's unit, but there was no sign of movement.

"Come on, Bronson," I said, "Let's check out the day."

The hills surrounding the motel were radiant in the pink morning light. I sat on the stoop and breathed in the fresh high-plains air. Bronson sat next to me, alert and smiling. The glove was gripped tightly in his teeth.

"You know, you're not so bad, Bronson," I said. "You're kind of a crafty guy. But you've got bad taste in gloves."

I picked up a stray piece of wood and threw it to see if he would turn his attention to the stick. He ran off into the weeds and reappeared carrying a stone.

"A stone, now," I said. He wagged and looked at it proudly. "At least it's not the glove."

Just then, Grover opened the door and stepped out. He lit up a cigarette and exhaled into the sky.

He looked over at Bronson and me. "Christ, Nerburn, you got ketchup all over your face." He glanced at Bronson's ketchup-stained whiskers. "I thought you had a wife back home."

I wiped the remnants of Bronson's wet dog-kiss off my lips and nodded a sheepish smile of thanks.

"You ready for this?" he said.

"I guess so. But I can't imagine there's anything up at that place."

"That's for the old man to decide."

He reached in his pocket and pulled out a half-crushed cigarette pack. "I'm out of smokes," he said. "Should have got some last night. Let's take a run down to that bar."

"Grover, it's 7:30 in the morning. No bar is going to be open."

He considered it for a moment. "Got to have some smokes," he said. "Maybe the grocery store. Otherwise, we can go to the next town."

"I've been in a car long enough," I said. "If you want to go look for some, go ahead. I'll stay here with Bronson."

"Puppy whipped, eh?"

Bronson wagged his tail and stared up at me. His ears stuck out like airplane wings. "Yeah, I guess so. You go ahead."

Dan emerged from the darkness of the motel room wearing a clean shirt with a string tie.

"Come on, old man," Grover said. "Let's go get some smokes."

"Nah, I'm staying here," he said. "It's too damn early to be driving around chasing cigarettes."

"Suit yourself," Grover answered.

I threw the keys across the hood of the car. "Bring me some coffee."

Grover climbed in the Toyota and headed off toward town. Dan and I sat watching the light fill in behind the hills.

"Sleep okay?" I asked.

He touched his hands to his lips and raised them to the sky in a gesture of thanks.

He looked down at Bronson and said something in Lakota. The little dog dropped the stone at his feet.

"That's a good dog," he said.

"He seems to have sticks confused with stones," I said.

"Nah, he knows it's a stone. He's just helping it out."

Even for Dan this was an odd comment.

"How's he helping it out?"

"That stone probably wanted a little excitement. He'd probably been sitting there for years. Wanted to take a little trip."

"A trip."

"Sure. Stones get bored, too."

He took the stone from Bronson and flipped it a few feet into the grass. Bronson surged after it.

"You ever been walking along a beach and reached down and picked up a stone?"

"Sure, who hasn't?"

"Why do you think you picked up that particular one?"

"I don't know. It was pretty, or it had an interesting shape, probably."

He shook his head. "No. That stone called to you. It wanted to move. What if you had to sit somewhere for a million years?"

I chuckled softly.

Dan yanked on my sleeve. "You think I'm kidding. I'm not. Stones can talk. You've just got to know how to listen. That's the trouble with you white folks. You only know how to listen with your ears. There's lots of things talking out there. Sometimes even too many. Sometimes you can't even get them to shut up. Bronson just heard that stone and brought him over to you. He's a rez dog. He knows how to listen."

Bronson wagged and held the stone in his mouth. Dan took it from him and put it in his pocket. "Let's go around back, find a better place to sit. It's better than going back in that motel room. A guy should always try to have sky over his head. Besides, it increases my odds."

The reference eluded me. "For what?" I asked.

He jabbed me in the ribs with his elbow. "That I won't die looking up at a lightbulb."

THE MOTEL BACKED UP AGAINST A SHARPLY RISING HILL. Behind the building, next to the dumpsters, someone had placed an old spool table and a couple of chairs. A seat from a van rested next to them, surrounded by a jumble of beer cans and cigarette butts. It must have been the place where the housekeepers came to smoke during their breaks.

Dan ignored the mess, sat down on the van seat, and pointed up at a bird gliding on the wind. Bronson disappeared, snuffling, into the brush.

"This is going to be a good day," Dan said. "Look at the bird, how he's gliding. Wind from the east. It brings understanding."

He glanced at me for a response. I could think of nothing appropriate to say, so I just remained silent. He whacked me playfully on the shin with his walking stick.

"East. Dawn. When you're in the dark the light comes up, get it? That's the direction of understanding. Didn't they teach you anything in those white schools of yours?" He shook his head in mock frustration.

"Didn't teach me that."

"They should have. Different directions, different kind of knowledge. East brings understanding. That's the way the elders taught," he said. "They taught us the old knowledge. They taught us how to understand the original teachings, the ones from the Creator."

He leaned back on his elbows and let the morning sun warm his face. "Yeah, that was good education. Not that stuff we got in the boarding school."

He turned his head toward me. "You want to hear how the elders taught us?" he asked.

"Sure," I said. It was a good way to pass the time until Grover got back.

"Well, I'm going to tell you, then," he said. "Let's start with that bird up there. What do you see?"

"Looks like a hawk. Some kind of predator."

"Good," Dan said. "Now, what's it doing?"

The hawk, or whatever it was, was riding on the wind currents, rising and falling and never moving its wings.

"I don't know. Hunting? What do birds do, anyway?"

"They do a lot, if you pay attention. There!" he said. "Look."

The bird had ceased its gliding and was hanging motionless, as if suspended in the sky.

"Watch now."

Suddenly the bird dropped down as if the sky had fallen out beneath it.

"Saw something," Dan said as it disappeared behind a ridge. Soon it rose up again. We could barely see some small object in its talons.

"Okay, what does that tell you?" Dan asked.

"I have no idea," I said.

"It tells you that if you want to hunt small things, you've got to remain absolutely still. It says you're better off watching from a distance if you want to catch something than following up close."

He tapped me again with the edge of his walking stick. "You're a pretty bad student, Nerburn. My grandpa wouldn't have been very impressed."

"I'm not surprised."

"Now, when my grandpa used to send me out in the morning, that's the kind of thing I would have to look for. 'I want you to watch everything, and then when you get home, I'm going to ask you about what you saw,' he'd say. If I came home and said I saw a bird in the sky, he'd ask me everything. 'What color was it? How high did it fly? Did it move its wings? How did it ride the wind?'

"He'd ask me a hundred questions. He wouldn't let me get away with answers like yours. Then he'd tell me a story about that bird and what it meant to the people. He'd tell me what to watch for the next time I saw it, and what I could learn from it.

"By the time I went to bed I'd be worn out. But I'd know something. It was that way every day. There wasn't anything we did that wasn't learning."

I sat back in my chair and closed my eyes. "Smart grandpa," I said.

"You bet. And it wasn't just seeing," Dan said. "It was hearing, smelling. Everything. I remember we used to walk by the edge of a little creek. He'd make me cover my eyes then ask me how deep the creek was.

"I'd have to sit and listen. If the creek giggled, it was shallow because it meant there were rocks close to the surface. If it whispered, it was deeper, but not so deep you couldn't walk across it. If it was silent, you had to be careful. That's how you knew where to cross in the darkness — by listening to how the creek talked."

"Sounds like a good way to learn," I said. The fresh morning air, with its whisper of wind and chatter of birdsong, had lulled me into an easy peace.

"Damn right. And everybody learned that way. You watched the birds, you watched the trees, you watched the animals. You watched everything and you listened to everything, and then you had to answer about everything. It was damn tough.

"But if the grandmas or grandpas saw that you had a special talent — maybe you listened closely and hardly ever spoke, or maybe you talked a lot to the animals in a private language — they might send you to one of the elders or medicine people who would teach you more secret things, things that carried big responsibilities, like how to interpret signs or cure illnesses. Then you'd really learn about that hawk, because they'd teach you the secret knowledge of that hawk."

"Did you get to learn any of the secret knowledge?" I asked, more to keep him talking than to learn anything in particular.

Dan sucked on his teeth for a minute, then breathed out heavily.

"No. I can read signs pretty good. But that's all. I was sent off to the white man's school. They thought my white eye gave me a different power. They wanted me to learn the white man's ways. That was supposed to be my gift to the people."

I could sense a faint air of melancholy coming across him as he spoke of the "white man's school" and what he had missed, so I remained quiet to see where he wanted to take the conversation. Even so, this was the most relaxed and happy I'd seen him since I had arrived on the reservation.

"See, that's the other thing," he said. "For Indian people, everything is a message. Like the wind from the east. That's a message."

He pointed to his milky eye.

"Or my eye. For you, a kid gets hit in the eye by an arrow and it's a tragedy. You say he's handicapped. But for us, it's a message. That arrow was a gift. Like I told you, it took me a long time to understand it as a gift. I still sometimes wonder about it. But the elders understood the way it was a gift because it offered a message.

So they kept reminding me. 'You got one white eye,' they'd say. 'That means you've been given the power to understand the white man's ways. That's the Creator's gift to you. You've got to use it for your people.'

"And that's another thing."

His thoughts were tumbling out now, like kittens from a bag.

"We weren't supposed to do learning for ourselves, we were supposed to do it for our people. When I got to that damn boarding school they put us in rows, made us all learn the same things. They said that you could only learn when you were sitting down, that it was all in books and that we were all supposed to learn the same thing. They'd give us a test and say, 'You're smarter, you're dumber.'

"That's one of the reasons those schools were so hard for us. You told us we all had to learn the same thing and we had to learn it in the same way. What if a kid has some special skill or talent? What if he seems to have a special connection to the hawk or the trees or the waters? Why shouldn't he learn about them and then bring that knowledge to his people? Everyone doesn't have to know the same thing. You know what I mean?"

"Yeah, I do, Dan," I said.

This was the first time since I'd arrived that he had let his mind wander freely. I was happy Grover had left us alone. This was the old man I remembered, floating on his thoughts like that hawk in the sky, rising and falling, then swooping down when he saw an idea and bringing it back to share with me.

"Do you know what Wapashaw said?" he asked.

"Wapashaw?"

"You called him Wabasha. He was a chief over your way."

I knew something of Wapashaw, or "Wabasha," as we had known him, from my school days. He had been one the chiefs of the Dakota people who had lived in southern Minnesota and had been

part of the tragic battle with the U.S. government in 1862 when their
people had been denied food and payment for their land. The struggle, called the "Dakota Uprising" or the "Dakota Conflict," had
resulted in the hanging of thirty-eight Dakota men — the greatest
governmentally sanctioned mass execution in U.S. history.

"Wapashaw said that if you keep your mouth shut and watch the
world around you, maybe in your life you will have one idea that
will be of service to your people. Think of that! One idea! Not a
thousand ideas. Not one idea a day. One idea in a whole life!"

"Reminds me of Leonardo da Vinci," I said offhandedly.

Dan screwed up his face. "Who?"

"Italian painter, inventor. One of the greatest minds who ever
lived."

"So what does he have to do with what I'm saying?" I could see
he was a little upset at my injection of some European into the conversation.

"One day a man came to watch him work on a painting he was
doing of Jesus and his disciples. The man sat there all day, and
Leonardo only made one stroke the whole time. 'You stood there all
day and only made one stroke,' the man said. Leonardo just looked
at him. 'Yeah, but it was the right stroke,' he said."

Dan sat quietly for a second. I was not sure if he was angry or
if he didn't see the relevance of the analogy. Then, all of a sudden,
he burst out laughing.

"That's pretty good, Nerburn," he said. He reached over and
pushed me playfully. "What was that guy's name?"

"Leonardo da Vinci."

"I've got to remember that. Leonardo Duvishhi. You sure he
wasn't an Indian?"

"Might have been Wapashaw's long-lost uncle," I said.

Dan laughed heartily. "This is a good day, Nerburn. I'm glad
you came to visit me."

The hawk cut great arcs against the towering sky. The eastern horizon was filling with pinks and lavenders.

"So am I, Dan," I said. "It's been too long."

THE MORNING UNFOLDED IN A CALM, relaxed rhythm. Dan continued to talk about the old ways of teaching — how sitting and watching and learning from nature were the keys to a child's education; how the elders, not some hired teachers, were the ones who taught the children. He talked about the things his grandfathers used to do; about birds in the sky and animals on the ground; about the classification of living things into creatures that crawl, creatures that fly, creatures that walk on two legs, and creatures that walk on four.

I was happy to see him so relaxed, and I was eager to hear his thoughts. But despite my pleasure at Dan's company, Grover's absence was beginning to weigh on my mind. He was a good driver and the roads were easy, but he'd been gone long enough to find a pack of cigarettes. My concerns were beginning to rise.

Dan seemed completely at ease with the situation. He just kept rolling along in his thoughts, like a dog snuffling through tall grass.

"Yeah, birds," he said. "You really have to pay attention to birds. They're two-leggeds, like us. But they can fly up to the heavens, so they're messengers, too. Go back and forth between the Creator and the people. Like that hawk up there. He's one of the special messengers. Almost as strong as *wanbli* — who you call the eagle. *Wanbli* always brings understanding."

He sat back and turned his face to the growing morning sun. The hawk kept up its motionless vigil high above the eastern horizon.

"Now, my grandma," he said, "she really could talk to birds."

He put his fingers to his lips as an indication that I should stay silent. The fields around us were a symphony of chirps and rustles and small ground sounds.

"You hear that?"

"What?"

"That song. Listen."

A small bird whistle rose and fell.

"That," he said. "That's *tasiyagnunpa*, the meadowlark. Likes to sing a lot. My grandma could understand them. Sometimes I'd be outside playing while she was hanging clothes on the line, and I'd hear her talking to them, using their language."

"She actually whistled? Sounded like a bird?"

"Kind of. Not exactly. It's hard to explain. One time I remember she was talking to the meadowlarks and she got real angry. She started shouting at them and picked up some rocks and threw them at them. She died that summer. I think that meadowlark was telling her something she didn't want to hear.

"This was the way it was all the time. Everything talked to us. Everything was giving us a message. The stones, the trees, the birds, the grass. That's why we were trained to keep our mouths shut and our ears and eyes open. I never thought anything of it. It was just the way it was supposed to be."

"The Creator's teachings," I said.

"That's right. And we were good learners. We could have taught your people, too. But they never listened. Thought we didn't know anything. They just looked in their Black Book. They said it had everything they needed to learn the Creator's lessons." He shook his head like a teacher frustrated by a dullard schoolboy.

"Why would the Creator put everything in a book and only give it to one people? That doesn't make any sense. If people didn't have that Black Book, they wouldn't know about the Creator. People have been around for thousands of years. Did they all have to wait until your people showed up with their Black Book to learn about the Creator? That's stupid. And what about the people who lived before that Black Book was discovered?

"The way we see it, the Creator put his lessons everywhere. Built them right into the earth before he even put people here. Our job is to learn those lessons in the place we were given, and the way to learn those lessons is to sit still and listen."

He reached in his pocket and pulled out the stone Bronson had given him.

"Look at this." He kept it cradled delicately in his hand like an egg. "Some of the wise ones, they could actually hear this stone talk. It would help them find out where an illness was in someone's body, or they could walk along with it and it would pull their hands toward a medicine plant. You can't even imagine something like that, I bet."

"Not very easily."

"Well, I'm not surprised. It's not in that Black Book. But I remember back in boarding school those priests told that story about the guy who went up on the mountain and got those tablets."

"Moses. The Ten Commandments."

"Yeah. That's right. So what were those tablets made of?"

"Stone."

"What did they have on them?"

"God's words."

He poked me again. "See. Even you people have God talking through stones. But the way you figure, he's got to write on them. We just listen."

He gave me a great, wide grin.

"Not bad, Dan," I said. "Not bad."

He flipped the stone out into the grass again. "Enjoy your trip," he said as it rolled off into the weeds.

"I think your people used to be this way," he continued, "but you forgot. I used to listen real close when they talked about religion in that boarding school. You had those tablets. You had that guy who got talked to by that burning bush."

"That was Moses, too."

"There were lots of things in nature giving you messages. Trees, oceans. How about that snake with that apple? But somehow you got lost and forgot all about those things.

"The Creator stopped being a teacher who filled the world with lessons. Instead you turned him into some kind of judge or police- man who's sitting way up in heaven keeping track of everything. When you die, if he thinks you've been good he sends you to a good place. If he thinks you've been bad he sends you to a bad place. I don't like that. I like our way, where the Creator was a teacher who gave us the earth to discover. I'd rather think of the Creator as a teacher than a policeman."

He looked over at me with a sly grin. "What do you think of that, Nerburn?" It was obvious he was pleased with himself and his little homily.

"I like it, Dan. It's good."

I thought perhaps he was done. I sat back and stared up into the blue morning sky. But then he spoke again.

"See, here's another thing. For us, the Creator's always here. He's always sending us something. Not for a test, but to see if we're paying attention. Like little Bronson. Know why I took him?"

"No, not really," I said. "It came as kind of a surprise to me."

"Came as a surprise to me, too," Dan answered. "But I was pay- ing attention. Remember when we buried Fatback? How I made you go away and leave me alone?"

"I do."

"I knew that was a time I needed to do some close listening, because when we buried Fatback we let her spirit loose. I knew she was still nearby and that she'd have something to say to me. So I stayed there and listened. Pretty soon I heard her talk. It wasn't like words, but it was like an understanding.

"She said, 'There's going to be another little friend coming to you soon. That friend will find you. You won't have to do anything. That friend will find you.'

"Now, when we stopped at that store, who did Bronson come to? You like dogs just fine. Why didn't he come to you?"

He answered his question before I had time to respond.

"Because he was looking for me."

Bronson came trotting out of the weeds and sat down in front of us. He had retrieved the glove and had it clamped tightly in his mouth.

"God, Bronson," I said. "Leave that thing alone. It's probably full of diseases."

"See, that's the difference. You see this little dog, and all you think of is diseases. You probably figure the old man's feeling bad about Fatback and just wants another dog. That's how white people think. All kinds of psychiatrist stuff. You don't pay attention to the spiritual. Don't hear the messages from the other places.

"But I'd done my listening, just like the elders taught me. That Fatback had strong power. I knew something was coming to me."

He pushed himself upward and flexed his shoulders and arms like he was trying to loosen up some muscles.

"Yep, knew something was coming. Turned out to be Bronson."

He reached down and rubbed the little dog's head. Bronson glanced at me sideways. He was still clutching the glove in his mouth.

"You better let him keep it," Dan said. "Everything has a reason."

"There's no good reason for carrying an oily glove," I said.

Dan sucked on his teeth and stared up into the sky. "Maybe he's going to bring it to Shitty." Bronson wagged his tail and pushed the glove forward. "Of course, he might just be trying to trade it for a hamburger."

CHAPTER SEVENTEEN

◇◈◇◈◇◈◇◈◇◈◇◈◇◈◇◈◇◈◇◈◇◈◇◈◇◈◇◈◇

A CLOCK IN THE HEAD

The sun was moving toward midday. As much as I was enjoying Dan's verbal meanderings, Grover's absence was really beginning to concern me.

"I'm a little worried about Grover," I said.

Dan was shuffling back toward the motel room. He flapped his hand dismissively. "You worry too much," he said. It was a familiar refrain whenever I expressed concern about something to do with time or schedules. "Just enjoy the day. If you gave more thanks instead of always thinking about time, your life would be a lot easier."

"But he's taking a long time just to get a pack of cigarettes."

Dan stopped his shuffling and wagged a finger in my face. "You know what your problem is? You got a clock in your head. 'It's twelve o'clock — time to eat.' 'Ten o'clock — time to go to bed.' 'It takes twenty minutes to go to the store. Grover's been gone twenty-five. Time to get worried.'

"That's one of the things I used to like about you. You didn't wear a watch. But I was just being tricked. You got a clock in your head."

I just shrugged. There was nothing I could say.

"You know," he went on, "that's one of the reasons we could always get away from your soldiers. We knew you always ate by the clock. Our people, we ate when we were hungry or when there was food. Your folks, it was always the same — morning, noon, and night. You're in a damn war, and you still lived by a clock. All we'd have to do is keep running for a whole day and we'd get away from you, because we knew you had to stop three times to eat.

"That clock stuff even got us in trouble in boarding school. They'd tell us to hurry up and come down for breakfast. Then there'd be lunch, then supper. Didn't matter if we were hungry or not. If it was time to eat, we had to eat.

"And in class, everything was about that clock. After all that time with my grandpa, being sent out in the morning and having to come back at dark, now I was sitting in rows having to look at a clock.

"Spelling? Do it for an hour. Arithmetic? Do it for an hour. Everything had to fit inside an hour. When I went out to follow that bird for my grandfather, did it do all its teaching in an hour? Did the creek stop teaching me after an hour? Or the buffalo, or the snake?"

"Probably not," I said.

"I remember in that boarding school when they made us stand up and say that pledge to the flag. There was an eagle on the top of the pole. They said that was the symbol of America. But I just looked right past that eagle. I knew what the real symbol was. It was that damn clock hanging behind it on the wall."

I could see that he was taking great delight in his rambling discourse, and I was taking great pleasure at seeing him so full of enthusiasm and energy. But I was still concerned about Grover.

"See, it's all part of a bigger thing," Dan went on, "something I could never really understand. It's how you try to put everything in boxes. I thought about this when I was a little kid sitting in my desk looking at that clock, about how you put all your learning in boxes. Spelling? That's one box. Reading? That's another box. Geography? Another box. I couldn't make any sense out of it.

"Think about it, Nerburn. My grandpa taught me to look at everything. Then all of a sudden, there I am in that damn boarding school where they broke everything down into boxes. 'Put away your spelling book and take out your counting board.' 'Put away your counting board and take out your geography book.' It's like everything was in its own separate world.

"When my grandpa sent me out to look at the birds he didn't tell me to look at their geography or their arithmetic. That wouldn't have made any sense, just like it didn't make any sense to only have me learn about them for an hour. Did that bird have arithmetic? Did it have geography?'"

He punched at the ground with his walking stick.

"Do you see, Nerburn? In the old ways we learned everything at once, then had to take it apart to understand it. When I went to white school, I had to learn everything in little parts, then try to put it together again. I thought that was backwards. I still do."

I nodded my approval, but Dan wasn't done.

"Do you think little kids want to sit in seats all day? Do you think they want to be in rows and have all their learning in boxes? Kids need to run and play. They need to watch everything around them and ask questions. They need to watch the grown-ups and see what they do and try to do it. Learning's about watching and think-ing and asking and practicing and doing it again and again and again. Everything is here to teach us. Let the little kids learn the world whole, then take it apart and put it into boxes. Don't make them learn the boxes first, then try to put it all together."

He turned toward me for a response. Basically, I agreed with him, but I decided to push him a bit.

"But what about things like world history?" I asked. "What about literature? Those are individual subjects. You need books for those. You can't just learn them wandering around out in the forest or up on some hill."

"Aha!" he said, as if I had walked into a trap. "I'm glad you said that, because it gets me to something important. You're right, those things need books. But that's white man's learning. It's about collecting everything and analyzing everything and putting it in order and saving it. Just like the way you live your lives. But that's not what Indian people are about. We're here to look for the Creator's purpose and to honor what's placed before us."

We reached the overhang in front of the motel. Dan eased himself into a chair sitting next to a coffee can full of cigarette butts. He shook a crooked finger at me.

"Now I'm going to tell you something," he said. "Something Indian people know and your people never seem to figure out. What do you call the Creator?"

It seemed like an impossible logical leap.

"God, I guess."

"What does God mean?"

"I don't know. Just God. The one who's above everything. 'I Am Who Am,' I guess. At least in Hebrew."

"Now, what do we call the Creator?"

"*Wakan Tanka*, I think."

"Right. Now, what does *Wakan Tanka* mean?"

"The Great Mystery."

"Right," he said. "So, there you are."

This seemed to constitute some kind of finality for Dan, but it brought me no closer to any kind of understanding.

"Okay," I said. "So?"

"Just let that thought take a little rest so you can take a look at it."

He sat back and folded his arms. I remained quiet and acted like I was thinking.

"Did you figure it out?" he said.

I shrugged my shoulders noncommittally.

"I thought so," he said, as if talking to the class dunce. "If the Creator is the Great Mystery, that means you can't understand him, right?"

"If it's a him," I said.

He slapped at the air as if shooing away a fly. "That's a white-people problem. Stop trying to put logs in my path."

"Okay."

"So, saying that the Creator gave you a Black Book doesn't mean that you understand everything, does it?"

He answered his question before I could respond.

"No. Because if you understood everything, the Creator wouldn't be a mystery. We're not talking about a little mystery, here. We're talking about the Great Mystery —*Wakan Tanka* — the mystery that's behind everything, before the beginning of life and after the end of death. The mystery that's behind the sky, the birds, the stars, everything. *The Great Mystery. The Great Mystery.*" He said it twice as if by repeating it he was going to drill it into my thick skull.

"I understand," I said.

"Good. I figured you would. Now, remember when I said that it wasn't fair for the Creator to put all his teachings in a book, because then no one could have those teachings until they got that book? It's the same for the Buffalo Calf Woman or Jesus or anything else. That would mean that the people who don't have that teaching wouldn't have connection with the Creator. But everyone has connection with the Creator because everyone is part of creation, see?"

"I do." I had no idea what this had to do with learning literature or world history, but Dan was in good spirits, and it seemed best just to let him talk.

"Now, sometimes the Creator might send something special to help a people learn or to give them some special knowledge. He might give one people the skill to keep track of things in books. He might give another the skill to listen to nature. Our people's history is in our stories. Your people collect history from everywhere and put it in books. Those are different skills, just like there are different ways of understanding the Creator.

"You need to think about this. What if the Creator gave every people something special, something that other people don't have? What if he put his teachings in different hearts in different ways, like he put different teachings in the rocks than in the animals?

"What if your Black Book way had one part of the truth and our *Inipi* way had a part of the truth and other people had a different part of the truth? How would you look at the world, then? Would you try to kill the ways of other people? I don't think so, because you'd be killing a part of the Creator's truth.

"It's the same with learning. Maybe we aren't the collecting people; maybe we are the listening people. Maybe we can't take everything apart as well as you can, but maybe we can help you remember how it went together. We are all fingers on the hands of the Creator. We must learn to work together to make this a better world. We must learn to work together to be the Creator's hands here on earth."

"That's beautiful, Dan," I said.

"Everything that's true is beautiful," he said, "because everything that's true is from the Creator."

I LEANED BACK AND STARED INTO THE BLUE vault of the midday sky. Great, billowing clouds were moving like dreams above the rolling landscape, casting shadows that raced like phantoms across the hills. It was a beautiful day, and I wanted to appreciate it. But I had become so fixated on Grover's absence that I was not giving as much heart to Dan's musings as they deserved. I was worried about Grover, and I was worried about my car. The day was turning toward afternoon, and I was concerned that we wouldn't have enough time to get up to the school and do whatever it was that Dan felt compelled to do.

But none of this seemed to be on Dan's mind. It was as if he lived in a constantly moving present that was alive with the ghosts of the past and the generations of the future but had no connection to the obligations and responsibilities of the moment. As Wenonah had once said to me years ago, "When you're here, you're here. When you're not, you're not."

For Dan, I was here, Charles Bronson was here. Grover would be here when he got here; until then, he was completely absent from Dan's consciousness.

I was about to say something about Grover when I heard the telltale whine of the little four-cylinder Toyota engine in the distance.

"I told you," Dan said, as the sound of the approaching car grew louder.

"Say," he added. "Do you think maybe your worrying made him come back faster?"

"No doubt in my mind," I said.

He let out a little chortle. "You're a good boy, Nerburn. A little slow sometimes, but a good boy."

"Not much boy left in me."

"Oh, yeah, the boy is in all of us. That's why we got to be good to the children. The boy always lives inside the man."

In a moment the familiar form of the gray Toyota wagon emerged from between the hills and crunched into the gravel parking area.

Bronson, too, had heard the sound and was sitting upright in anticipation. He had already learned the distinctive sound of the Toyota's motor.

"Bronson's got a good ear," I said.

"I told you — he's a rez dog," Dan answered. "He knows how to listen."

Grover wheeled across the parking lot and came to a stop right below where Dan and I were sitting. He stepped out carrying two white Styrofoam cups of coffee. It took every bit of willpower I had not to ask him about the reason for his long absence. But I didn't want to sound like I had a clock in my head.

He handed me one of the cups. I took a quick sip. The coffee was so hot it burned my tongue.

"Where'd you get this?" I asked.

"Got it with the cigarettes, right down the road at the grocery."

"You must have had to wait a long time until they opened," I ventured, hoping to get some information indirectly.

"Nah, they were open as soon as I got there."

Clock or no clock, the temptation was too great.

"So what took you so long?" I asked.

He pointed up at the sky. The hawk had been joined by several others. They were floating and rising and cutting circles on the breeze.

"Wind from the east. Brings understanding. Figured you guys needed a little time alone."

CHAPTER EIGHTEEN

◇◈◇◈◇◈◇◈◇◈◇◈◇◈◇◈◇◈◇◈◇◈◇◈◇◈◇◈◇◈◇

TWENTY-EIGHT FRENCH FRIES

A s Dan packed his belongings in the car, I pulled Grover aside. "Did you tell him what's up there?" I asked.

"He'll find out."

"Grover, that place is a ghost ship. He's not going to discover anything about something that happened seventy or eighty years ago."

"Maybe he doesn't expect to."

"Well, then, why are we doing it?"

"Because he wants to."

I walked away in disgust. Grover's evasions only increased my frustration about the shapeless nature of this trip.

Dan had positioned himself in the front seat and was trying to buckle his seat belt.

"Come on," he shouted. "Sun's past noon."

I slid into my seat and prepared to make the futile drive up to the vandalized boarding school. I wanted to tell Dan what we had seen last night to prepare him for the disappointment, but since Grover had chosen not to say anything, I decided to do the same. It was, I assumed, like the stop at the railway siding — more about Dan's desire to revisit his past than an actual visit in search of clues about his sister. Still, it was one more journey into abandonments and disappointments, and my heart went out to the old man as he sat there in his rumpled fishing cap fiddling with his seat belt and staring at the surrounding hills.

As we approached the town, Dan tapped me on the leg.

"Sun's past noon. I told you that before."

"I know. That's why I'm hurrying."

"No. Sun's past noon. Time for lunch."

"I thought you guys didn't have to eat three meals a day."

"Boarding school influence. They didn't put a clock in my head, but they sure as hell put one in my stomach. Damn Bronson snuck up on my burger last night. A guy needs his nourishment."

I shook my head in amazement. We had driven for a day and a half and were within a few miles of a place that had haunted his dreams for almost eighty years, and now we had to stop for lunch.

"Find a place with French fries," he said. "I like French fries. You can count them."

"Well, I guess that's important."

"It is. I like to eat twenty-eight."

"Go back to that bar," Grover said. "Those fries were pretty good."

"Bronson thought so," Dan said. "I didn't get a damn one."

I drove down the highway to the bar. The heat of the day was building, and the wind was blowing hot across the hills. The only other vehicle in the lot was an old pickup with its tailgate plastered with bumper stickers for bars and rodeos.

The place smelled of stale alcohol and cigarettes. Except for a sharp shaft of light coming in through a single window next to one of the booths, it was as dark and depressing as it had been the night before.

"Back again?" the proprietor said as Grover walked in. He was a heavyset white man who looked like a retired farmer.

"Can't stay away," Grover said.

"Can I bring my dog in?" Dan asked. Bronson was nosing around cautiously like an animal that had learned not to cross thresholds unless invited.

"As long as he pays cash," the proprietor laughed. He was a good-natured man who seemed happy to have the company.

We slid into the single booth that looked out the window. A few tumbleweeds bounced their way across the gravel lot, and a single wilted tree stood baking in the sun.

"Where's the lunchtime rush?" I asked as the proprietor came over with his order pad.

"You're it. Things don't pick up until dinner."

I was left to contemplate what "picking up" meant. The place had been almost empty the night before, and I had not seen more than five moving vehicles anywhere in the town.

"You got French fries?" Dan asked.

"Yes, sir," the man answered.

"I'd like twenty-eight," Dan said.

"Twenty-eight it is," the man said, as if it were an everyday request.

I looked up at the menu scratched on the chalkboard. My choices appeared to be a burger or chili, and I didn't want any more burgers.

"I'll have the chili," I said.

"All out. I'm waiting on a delivery."

"Then I'll have a burger."

"Grill's not ready. I can throw a burrito in the tub with the French fries."

The thought of a deep-fried burrito cooked in the grease with French fries didn't do much for me, but it was better than nothing. "Some coffee, too," I added.

"Nothing for me," Grover said. "I live on cigarettes."

The proprietor disappeared through two swinging doors into the back room. I could hear the hiss of frozen French fries hitting a vat of boiling grease.

"Hope I get twenty-eight," Dan said. "That's how many I like."

Grover pushed himself out from the booth. "I'm going outside. Let me know when you're done."

He disappeared through the door, leaving me alone with Dan.

"What's with the twenty-eight fries?" I said.

"It's a good number," he said. "Not too many, not too few."

"Like Goldilocks's porridge."

He shook his head like a man trying to get something irritating out of his hair.

"An old story," I said.

He ignored me and began talking to Charles Bronson in Lakota.

With Grover gone and the twenty-eight French fries still in the fryer, it seemed like a good time to broach the subject of what Dan expected to find up at the old boarding school.

"So, what do you want to do up at the school?" I asked.

"I want to look around."

"For what?"

"Oh, I don't know. There'll be something."

I decided to tell him the truth.

"Dan, we stopped up there while you were asleep last night. It's abandoned. All boarded up."

He ruffled Bronson's neck. "Oh, there'll be something," he said. There was something odd in his manner; something distant and distracted.

I was about to ask more when the proprietor backed through the swinging doors from the kitchen carrying Dan's French fries and my naked burrito.

Dan looked closely at his fries. "This is good," he said.

"If you need more, I'll make them," the proprietor answered.

"Nope. I just want twenty-eight."

"That's what you got. Twenty-eight exactly."

I looked at the burrito sitting on the white plate in front of me. It looked like a fried gopher. "One of these is fine for me," I said.

The proprietor brought me a white mug of coffee and went back to wiping down the bar. "You just holler if there's anything you need."

"Decent fellow," I said.

"Yep," Dan answered. He was already engaged in separating his French fries into piles.

Bronson stood up on his hind legs and placed his front paws on the edge of the table. He was examining the fries with undisguised interest.

I watched in amazement as Dan meticulously separated his French fries into four piles of seven. His hands were so stiff he could barely move them. I could hear him counting under his breath.

"What are you doing?" I asked. "Do you always put them in piles of seven?"

"No. Sometimes I put them into piles of four."

There was no rhyme or reason to what he was doing, so I just picked at my burrito until he had finished his culinary housekeeping.

Finally, with his food in the proper order, he picked up one of the French fries, broke it in half, and rubbed the two pieces together.

"Giving thanks?" I said.

He looked at me like I was the dumbest person in the world.

"No. Getting the salt off. Doctor said it ain't good for me."

"You could have just asked the guy to hold the salt."

He had stuffed the first one in his mouth and was gumming it around. "Who ever heard of French fries without salt?"

I tried to steer the conversation back to the subject of the school and his little sister. "So, that's the school Yellow Bird went to, too?" I asked.

He took a fry from the second pile, snapped it in half, and rubbed the pieces together until he had most of the salt off them. Then he mumbled something and put one piece in his mouth and gummed it around for what seemed like a minute before swallowing it.

"These are good French fries," he said.

I tried again. "I don't know what I'd do if one of my sisters disappeared."

He held the other half over Bronson's head. The little dog did its circus dance on the seat to reach up and grab it.

"This Bronson likes fries," Dan said.

Through the window I could see Grover standing in the mottled shade under the lone tree at the far end of the parking area.

We sat in silence while Dan moved around his plate, eating a fry from one pile, then moving to the next. It was obvious that he wasn't ready to talk about his sister, so I decided not to push it, even if we sat there without speaking for the rest of the afternoon. I stared out into the sun and watched Grover smoke his cigarette.

"So, you want to know something about the boarding schools?" he said suddenly.

"Absolutely." I brightened. Perhaps this was his way of moving around to the subject of Yellow Bird.

"I'll tell you, then," he said, snapping a fry in half and performing his desalinization ritual. "It all started with the boats."

"The boats? What boats?"

"The ones you people came on."

"What? Like Columbus and the *Mayflower*?"

"All of them."

"That seems like a long way back to get to the boarding schools."

His eyes narrowed. He pointed at me with a French fry. "Are you telling this story, or am I?"

"You are."

"Then I'm telling it my way. And I say it all starts with the boats."

"Okay," I said. "Back to the boats."

He moved to another pile and stuffed another fry in his mouth. "Here we were, sitting around in our houses when we looked out into the ocean and saw these big boats way out at the horizon. Pretty soon a couple of little boats come rowing in with men on them who looked like dogs — all hairy and dirty."

"Like a prewash Bronson," I offered.

"Worse. We could smell them from the shore. But we figured they were hungry, so we brought them in and gave them something to eat."

Dan had told me this story before, and I knew from experience that once he slipped into one of the well-worn grooves of his memory he was going to proceed along it for as long as he liked. So I just settled back, sipped at my coffee, and stared at the shadows moving across the hillsides. The sun had passed its zenith and was turning toward the western horizon.

"It was that Columbus guy. They were all sick, teeth falling out. We did what we could to help them out.

"Well, pretty soon other folks came. All sorts of them. Puritans. Spaniards. Frenchmen. All coming on boats.

"Now, you've got to remember — we were lots of different peoples, too, speaking lots of different languages, maybe not getting along so well in everything. But we all lived here on the land, mostly trying to leave each other alone. We'd fight with each other, sure, and for a lot of reasons.

"But these boat people, they were really different. They wore hard shoes. Had different clothes, different food, different weapons. They kept putting flags up everywhere and talking about some God who lived in a desert and died on a cross. We didn't even know what a desert was, and we sure as hell didn't think much of a God who died on a cross."

"Are you sure this is going to get us to the boarding schools?" I asked.

He waved another French fry at me. "You got somewhere to go?" He pointed to my head. "Tick tock, tick tock."

"Okay. I'll shut up."

"Good. Now let me get moving. I've picked up the scent."

I sat back and dug at the edge of my burrito with my fork.

"So along come all these guys on boats, carrying flags, shooting guns, waving Bibles, wanting things. We fed them, taught them how to live, showed them what was good to eat. We wanted to get along with them. In fact, we felt kind of sorry for them. I mean, we figured if they'd come on boats they must have been a long way from home.

"So we said, 'Okay, you can stay here with us. There's lots of room.' We figured you were a strange tribe who got lost out on the ocean and needed a place to rest up. You seemed friendly enough, and you had guns and flints for starting fires and lots of things we had never seen before.

"So we let you stay around. We even tried to learn your ways, just like some of you tried to learn ours. It was working out. We figured you'd move on when you wanted to.

"But pretty soon we got this strange feeling that you weren't moving on. You were staying. You were moving in all around us, chopping down trees, building hard houses. And you were bringing your friends."

"Hard houses?"

"Yeah. Houses that couldn't move, that you couldn't take down.

Made out of logs so big it took ten men to move them. And you made fences — started dividing the land into 'mine' and 'yours.'

"Well, that didn't go over so well, because we didn't believe the land was ours or yours or anyone else's. It belonged to the Creator and had been a gift for us to use. We were trying to share that gift with you, and now you were trying to say it was yours."

I was staring out the window trying to stay interested. Dan, as always, had a way of putting things that made him engaging, but I could see no end to this harangue. Outside, I could see Grover leaning against the tree, blowing smoke rings. He noticed me watching and gave me a tiny salute on the edge of his cowboy hat.

"You listening?" Dan said.

"I'm right here."

"Yeah, well, I feel you drifting away. I can tell when a guy's floating off."

I straightened myself in my seat like a schoolboy and turned my attention back to him. "Sorry. I'm back."

"Okay," he continued. "Now stay here." He stared at me pointedly to let me know he was watching.

"Pretty soon there were more and more of you coming. Boats coming in. People coming in. And everyone doing the same thing — building hard houses and fences. You started cutting our paths into streets. You wanted special buildings where people could sell and buy things. You wanted a special tall building to worship the Creator with a point on it as high as the trees.

"We could see what was going on. It was pretty simple — if you were making buildings so heavy that you couldn't move them, it meant you weren't going anywhere.

"We tried to talk to you and explain that we were happy to have you visit. We were even okay to have you as neighbors — that the Creator must have brought you here for a reason — but if you wanted to build hard houses and wide roads you should go back to your own land. The Creator must have put you somewhere, so maybe that was where you belonged.

"But here.'s where we got a surprise. You didn't believe the Creator had *put* you somewhere. You believed the Creator had *sent* you somewhere. And the somewhere you believed he had sent you was right where we lived.

"When we tried to tell you that this wasn't right, you'd point to your Black Book and say that everything was right in there.

"We had a lot of talks about what to do. Some of us wanted to kill you. Some of us wanted to move away from you. Some of us even wanted to try living like you, because we thought maybe you had some powers that we should learn. All we knew for sure was that we had to do something, because you were filling up the forests and killing all the animals, and our people were dying from all the sicknesses you brought."

I shifted in my seat and stared out the window in desperation. Dan had barely gotten Europeans to the East Coast, and we still had at least two centuries to go before we got to the boarding schools. My only hope was that Grover might come in to hurry us along or that Bronson might start acting up. But Bronson was seated comfortably next to Dan waiting patiently for French fries, and Grover was resting under the tree, smoking a cigarette and carving contentedly on a stick of wood.

"Well, we tried some fighting, but that didn't work. We tried joining up with some of the other boat people, but that didn't work either. So we figured we'd try to come to understandings with you, like we did between ourselves. Whenever we had problems with other people, we just met together, talked until we reached an understanding, then sealed the understanding by smoking together in the presence of the Creator. We figured we could do the same with you folks.

"But that wasn't the way you did things. For you, everything had to be written down, just like those rocks had to have writing on them before you'd believe what they said. So you would come with pieces of paper all full of scratches and read us what you said was written on them. Then you'd ask us to touch the end of the writing stick while you made another scratch to show our agreement. That was the way you wanted things done.

"We were never sure of what those pieces of paper said unless one of your people could speak our language or one of our people could speak yours. But we figured they were pretty much what you told us, so we'd touch the end of the writing stick, and that would be that. We figured it wasn't that big a deal, because mostly we figured what we were agreeing to was letting you stay in your hard houses in exchange for some of the guns and blankets and other good things you had. It seemed fair enough. The way we looked at it, the land still belonged to the Creator. We were just making agreements about how we would share it.

"But you weren't thinking this way. You believed that when we touched the end of the writing stick we were letting you make all the rules on that land. And not just for a while, but forever. You could say who could go there and who couldn't go there, who could hunt and fish there. You even said it gave you the right to say who owned the animals and the water on that land.

"This made us angry. We figured the Creator didn't give anyone the right to own the animals or the water or anything else on the land. Now suddenly you're drawing lines and making rules and saying that this is what the Creator wanted because it was in your Black Book about the guy in the desert who got nailed up on a tree."

He smashed a French fry hard into his plate. "You got a house, Nerburn?"

"What do you mean? Of course I have a house."

"Well, think about it. Someone comes into your house for a visit, you feed them and treat them right, and pretty soon they say they're staying and that they're going to make all the rules. They eat all your food and break up all your furniture and tell you which rooms you can go in and which rooms you can't. They say it's all written down in a book they've got and that you've got nothing to say about it. That's how it was, and we didn't much like it."

"I probably wouldn't like it, either," I said, secretly trying to count the French fries remaining on his plate.

"You're damn right you wouldn't! You'd probably try to chase them out. And, if they wouldn't go, and they started having all their friends move in, you'd probably figure things were going to get a little hot."

It seemed that the conversation had wandered so off course that Dan had forgotten what he had even intended to talk about.

"Come on, Dan, let's finish up," I said. "We can continue this in the car."

He pointed at his plate. "Do you want to hear about the boarding schools or not? We've still got a lot of French fries to go."

Outside I could see Grover asleep under the tree. His legs were stretched out and his cowboy hat was pulled down over his eyes. He did not look like a man who was preparing to move anytime soon.

"Well, pretty soon the house that the Creator had given us was so damn full of you boat people that something had to be done. We weren't much for getting together in big groups of all the tribes, but some of us thought it was probably time. You've heard of Tecumseh?"

"Yes."

"That's what he thought. We should have listened to him. We were still strong enough. We could have driven you all back to your boats. But while we were trying to figure it out, all you boat people got together to figure out what you should do with us. And you'd come up with a pretty simple plan: all the Indian people had to go.

You didn't care where we went. All you cared was that we got the hell out of all the places you wanted to live. And if we didn't go, you were going to move us.

"So, that's what you did. First you tried to buy our lands. But when that didn't work fast enough, you started coming with guns and rounding us up and sending us off to places where you didn't want to live."

"You mean Jackson's policy of removal?" I said, trying to keep him on track.

"Policy of removal?" Dan said. "Policy of removal? Is that what you call it when you kill thousands of men, women, and children by breaking into their houses and chasing them out at gunpoint and marching them off to some place hundreds of miles away where they can die of starvation and disease? You call that a 'policy of removal'? I call it a death march."

"Are you talking about the Trail of Tears?"

"That was just one. One that you let into your history books. You did it to the Creeks, too. Lots of others. You did it any time you wanted our land. You didn't care that we lived there. You didn't care that we had sick people and old people who could barely walk. You didn't care that we had gardens planted and that this was the place where our parents had taught us how to fish and hunt and that this was the land where our grandparents were buried."

He jabbed at me with a French fry. "Have you heard of the Doctrine of Discovery?" He pronounced it "doctryne" as if the word was as foreign to him as the concept it expressed.

"No," I said.

"Well, most people haven't. I sure hadn't. And the rest of our people hadn't either. Some pope from way back where you boat people came from waved some stick around and said that since we weren't Christians we didn't have the right to our land. If you found it, you could take it. That's like me coming over a hill and seeing your house and saying, 'Hey, I discovered Nerburn's house. Now it's mine.'"

Bronson had been jostled by Dan's shouting and gesticulating. He put his forepaws on the edge of the table. "Have a couple, Bronson," I said, pointing to the French fries. "Help him out."

Dan glared at me. "This isn't a joke, Nerburn."

"I didn't say that it was. I just think we ought to get going."

"We'll get going when I'm damn good and ready to get going," he said. "Now, shut up and listen."

"So, anyway, Jackson and his bastard friends tried to get rid of us by sending us off. Apparently we weren't dying fast enough on our own. He wanted to send us to the other side of the Mississippi, where none of you boat people lived. He thought it was a desert. He didn't care if we could live there or not. For him, dead was as good as alive. You'd probably have finished us off if you hadn't gotten into that war."

"Which war?"

"The one with yourselves."

"You mean the Civil War?"

"Yeah, that one. It pretty much took your attention away from us. You tried to make us choose sides, but mostly we didn't. We wanted to help the white people who were our friends, but mostly we just wanted to protect our own people. We figured it wasn't our fight and that it couldn't be anything but good for us, because it kept your mind off destroying us and taking our land.

"But, boy, were we wrong. All that war did was help you sharpen your killing skills. Once that war was over, you had all these soldiers with nothing to do and you'd gotten a taste of how to take care of problems. So you sent your armies out to the West. You decided to take care of the Indians once and for all.

"This time there wasn't any sending us somewhere. It was just flat-out killing. If we wouldn't sign pieces of paper giving up everything we owned and go live on little pieces of land, you'd just kill us. You figured it would be easy. We had our women and elders and little children, so we couldn't move very fast, and we didn't have as many weapons as you did. So you figured you'd just roll us up or kill us all.

"But you figured wrong. You guys with your three meals a day and soft beds didn't know what to do out here where there wasn't any water and you could see an army coming for a hundred miles. It wasn't like fighting in the forest and stealing out of farmers' gardens and catching a few fish and animals to keep going. Out here it was all big space and Indians on horseback and herds of buffalo. And even when you came across folks who had settled down, like the Pueblo people, the land was so big and full of places to hide that you didn't know what to do.

"Well, that's when the second real bastard showed up — that General Sherman. He picked right up where Andrew Jackson left off. But he'd been in that Civil War and he was smart about killing. He knew you couldn't chase everybody down. The way he'd whipped the other boat people in the South was to destroy everything they needed to live — their houses, their food, everything. It worked. You take away people's food, and pretty soon they lose their will to fight.

"So he gets out here, looks around, gets an idea. He sees that *tatanka* is the only real food we have."

"The buffalo."

"Right. He doesn't care about *tatanka* being a sacred animal, and he doesn't even know that we use the fur for clothes and the bones for needles and the horns for drinking and the brain for tanning leather. All he knows is that *tatanka* is what we eat, and he figures if he kills what we eat, then we're all either going to starve or do what he says. So he decides to kill all the buffalo. All of them."

He reached across and grabbed my arm. "Do you know how many there were?"

"Dan," I said, "we really ought to get going." He disregarded me as if I hadn't said a word.

"There were millions of them. The herds were so big that it would take days for them to pass. There were so many of them that the earth shook like thunder when they went by. Who'd have ever thought that you could kill them all? But he figured killing them was easier than killing Indians. He just had to have patience, and he just had to have a plan.

"That plan was simple. He'd hire people to kill buffalo and pay them for the tongues. There were all these trappers that didn't have anything to do anymore now that the people in Europe were wearing silk hats instead of beaver hats, and these men knew where the buffalo herds were. The railroads helped, too. *Tatanka* didn't like to cross over metal rails, so the more railroads that were built out here, the more *tatanka* got trapped and cut off from escape."

"Dan," I said, "if we're going to get up to that school and look around, we should really get going."

He slammed his fist on the table.

"I've waited almost eighty years to do this. You think a few more minutes are going to bother me? Just get that clock out of your head and wait until I'm done."

He split another desalted French fry and shared it with Bronson.

"Anyway, it became a big sport to kill buffalo. White men from the East would come out on their trains, then get in wagons and be carried to camps where there were scouts with guns and tents who would take them out to shoot *tatanka*. It was like they were going on vacations. They even came from Europe.

"Some of them never even got off the trains. They just waited until the buffalo got close enough, then they'd shoot into a herd. But mostly they had to go out to where the herds were. Lots of times, they'd just go camp by the watering holes. *Tatanka* would come with their little babies and see the hunters, then run away. But after a while they'd get so crazed from thirst they'd have to come back, then the vacation people would kill them.

"They'd take a tongue or some body part for a trophy. Other than that, they'd just leave them lie. Sometimes they'd take the skins, but mostly they just got back on the train and left.

"One bunch of white men came up with an idea to shoot *tatanka*, then they'd cut around the neck and around the legs and down the belly, so the skin was cut like a jacket ready to open. Then they'd pound a metal stake through *tatanka*'s skull into the ground, really deep, so the body was anchored really strong to the ground.

"When they had it really firm to the ground, they'd tie a rope around the skin at the top of *tatanka*'s neck and attach it to a yoke between some horses or the back of a wagon. They'd whip the horses and the horses would get frightened and start running and yank the skin right off. They pulled off all sorts of flesh, too. Then they'd just leave the rest of the body lying out there to rot.

"It made our people sick. *Tatanka* was our sacred animal. We would say prayers before taking its life. Now these white people were ripping its skin off and leaving its body everywhere. The prairie looked like it was covered with boulders. It stunk so bad you had to cover your nose. Flies were everywhere so thick you could hardly walk.

"Our people would go out into the fields and cry. One man said, 'What do you expect from people who have a God that they nailed to a tree?'

"But even if it broke our hearts, we never believed you'd be able to kill them all. But you just kept killing. I've seen pictures where there were *tatanka* skulls piled as high as a house."

"I've seen them, too," I said.

"Well, then you know. That Sherman said he was going to wipe us out, and he damn near succeeded. He shot our men, he shot our women, he shot our children, and he shot our food. He told his commanders to have his soldiers kill us any way and any place they could. So that's what they did."

Dan put his hands on the table and exhaled deeply. I could see that he was shaking, though I couldn't tell whether it was from exhaustion or anger. I was hoping he would stop, as much for his own sake as for mine. But he took a deep breath and continued.

"Well, you happy?"

"What do you mean?"

"You wanted the boarding schools?" he said. "Well, now you got the boarding schools."

I was confused. "How is this about the boarding schools?"

He cracked another French fry in half, desalted it, and split it with Bronson. He had systematically been moving around his plate, taking a fry from each pile. There were about twelve left.

"They were just the next idea. The next way to get rid of Indians. If you can't kill all the Indians, you just kill the Indian inside all of them."

"'Kill the Indian to save the man.'"

"Exactly."

"So, now I'm going to tell that to you. Sherman was doing a pretty good job of getting rid of us. We were dying like flies. But some white people had a new idea — church kind of people. They didn't think we were animals; they just thought we were like little children. They thought we needed to be taught the right way to live, and that once we heard about it, we'd change to be just like them.

"They convinced your President Grant that there had been too much killing. He was pretty worn out with the killing himself, because he'd done so much of it during your Civil War. And he was a church guy, too. So he went along with them when they convinced him to give the Indians over to the churches. He dealt us out like a bunch of playing cards. 'These Indians go to this church, those Indians go to that church.' My people got dealt to the Catholics.

"By now most of us who hadn't been killed had been hustled onto reservations. There weren't that many of us left, only a couple hundred thousand. There'd been millions of us when you'd first come on your boats. Millions. So, for the government, this was really a mop-up action. But the churches took it real seriously.

"They came out in their wagons with all their Bibles and their do-gooder ideas. We were supposed to put on their clothes, eat their food, farm like they farmed, speak their language, and worship their God. They thought they were saving our souls.

"But let me tell you something. They were just being used. The government didn't care about our souls, it cared about our land.

"So while the do-gooders were all concerned about making us pray to that god nailed up on that tree, the government was only concerned about making us into farmers. Hunters need a lot of territory. Farmers only need a little land inside of fences. Make Indians into farmers, they figured, and they won't need so much land. You can sell the rest of it to the white folks.

"Well, the church people bought into this. They believed their god wanted everyone to be farmers. I don't know where they got that idea. All the people in their Black Book were wandering around out in that desert. They sure weren't farmers. But somewhere along the way the church people had got the idea that hunting and picking food off the land was savage, while growing things inside fences was civilized and Christian.

"The truth was, we'd been farming for years. But we did it our own way where we all worked together. What the government really wanted was to break us apart, make us work by ourselves. One of the do-gooders named Dawes was some kind of senator, and he got a law passed that broke up the reservations into little pieces. They were going to give a piece to each family, start us thinking all about 'mine' and 'yours' like the white folks. Forget about listening to our leaders, forget about working together and sharing everything.

"Once they got that law passed, they were almost there. We

Indians were mostly killed; those of us who were left were stuck on little pieces of land way off where white men didn't want to live. We'd been given little squares of property and told we had to build fences and become farmers. The government had churches and government agents looking over us to make sure we didn't try to live the old way. All that was left was to beat the memory of those old ways out of us.

"That's where the boarding schools came in. You can't make the elders learn new ways. They aren't going to speak a different language. They aren't going to change the way they do things. So you just take away the children, beat them if they talk their own language, cut off their hair, take away the clothes their mothers and grandmas made for them, make them pray to the white man's god, and pretty soon you'll turn them into white men.

"The boys will forget how to hunt. The girls will forget how to tan hides and make food from the plants and the berries. They won't know the sacred stories, they won't know the ways of the elders. Instead, they'll learn to laugh at the old ways and call their elders 'savages.' They'll think they're better than their parents, smarter than their elders.

"And if the parents try to hide their kids so they won't get taken away and have their spirits poisoned at one of these schools, the police put the parents in jail. All the while the church people keep thinking they're doing it to save the poor Indians' souls.

"It was a hell of a system, I tell you, Nerburn," he said. "The government could call it whatever it wanted — boarding school, education, civilizing the Indian, whatever. But it was really just the last big Indian killing. It was the killing of the Indian heart. They killed it by trying to turn it white."

He picked one of the few fries left on his plate, split it in half, and desalinated it, then closed his eyes and lowered his head like a man saying a silent prayer. When he spoke again, his voice was distant.

"They took us kids hostage, Nerburn," he said. "That's all it was. They took us kids and held us hostage and tried to brainwash us, and our parents didn't dare do anything."

He raised his head and looked vacantly out onto the empty, burning landscape. "If someone has your kids, you'll do whatever they say."

"Is that why your parents never tried to find out about Yellow Bird?" I asked softly. "Because they were scared?"

He kept staring out the window. His eyes had that faraway, misty look that I had seen every time he spoke about his sister.

"Oh, they tried. But they had to be careful. It had only been a few years since Wounded Knee — soldiers mowing down women and children with Gatling guns and rifles. People remembered that. They remembered their parents and grandparents being killed. They remembered the stories of that Chivington son of a bitch at Sand Creek making a little girl run across a field and chasing her on his horse and shooting her dead. The white man cruelty wasn't just stories to them. It was real, and they weren't sure it was over."

He chewed on the piece of French fry and fed the other half to Bronson. "My parents weren't stupid," he said. "They knew what would happen if they started nosing around. You don't want to get branded a troublemaker, not if you want to eat or you want to work or you want your other kids to be treated okay."

He looked across at me with his lined, tired face.

"I was that other kid, Nerburn."

He put his head in his hands and looked down at the table. "Leave me alone for a minute," he said.

I slid out of my seat and walked quietly toward the door. He was absently stroking Bronson's scruffy head and speaking softly to him in Lakota.

Bronson looked over and gave me that knowing, too-long stare. He nuzzled up to Dan and burrowed deep into the old man's lap. He seemed to understand what was going on far better than I.

CHAPTER NINETEEN

◈◇◈◇◈◇◈◇◈◇◈◇◈◇◈◇◈◇◈◇◈◇◈◇◈◇◈◇◈◇◈◇◈

RATBERRY SANDWICHES

I walked out the door and stood under the overhang. Grover saw me and ambled over.

"How's he doing in there?" he asked.

"His mood's gotten real dark," I said. "One minute he's talking about wanting to get up to the boarding school, the next minute he's organizing his French fries into little piles and rambling on about the whole history of the United States. I don't know what's going on."

Grover pulled out a cigarette and lit it with his Zippo. He reached over to me with the pack and pushed a cigarette out with his thumb. "You sure you don't want one?"

"No. You know I don't smoke."

"You should give it a try. Might calm you down."

"I don't need to be calmed down. I'm just trying to help him out, and suddenly he's talking about General Sherman and buffalo skulls and the Indian policy of Andrew Jackson. He's doing everything except going up to the boarding school he claimed he wanted to visit."

Grover spit expertly between his teeth. "You know, Nerburn," he said, "you're like those treaty negotiators we used to have to deal with. Always in a hurry. Sometimes there are preliminaries."

"There are preliminaries and there are evasions," I said. "Look out there." I swept my hand across the blazing, parched horizon. "We've got to get moving if we want to get up there before it's a hundred and ten degrees."

"Just relax. He's just doing it the Lakota way, by laying out the history. That's how we remember our history, by telling our story."

"But does the story have to start with Columbus?"

"Everything starts with Columbus. At least everything to do with white people."

"But what's with the French fries?"

"He likes to get rid of the salt."

"No, the piles. First he insists on getting exactly twenty-eight, then he divides them into piles. It doesn't make any sense."

A small smile crept across Grover's face. "How many piles?" he asked.

"Four."

He spit one more time onto the ground. It made a small puff of explosion in the dust. "Mmm. Twenty-eight French fries. Four piles of seven."

He made a great charade of counting on his fingers. "Let's see. Four seasons. Four directions. Four stages of life.

"Seven council fires. Seven sacred rituals. The moon lives for twenty-eight days. Yeah, I guess it doesn't make any sense."

"That's crazy," I said. "What is it? Some kind of Lakota French fry rosary?"

Grover glared me into silence. When he spoke again, his words were clipped and precise. "It's what he wants to do. And it's how he wants to do it. Can't you ever just be patient and show some respect?"

I started to speak, but he stared me down. His eyes had lost their mirthful edge. I realized I had pushed too far.

"Sorry," I said.

He flicked his cigarette ash into the dust and crushed it with the toe of his boot. "Being sorry's for people who don't think. If you think before you talk, you don't have to be sorry. Now, I didn't ask you *what* he's doing, I asked you *how* he's doing."

I gathered my thoughts and tried to give an objective answer. "Like I said, he's all over the place. One minute he's angry, the next he's joking. It's like these great waves of emotion wash across him and take him over. By the end he was getting pretty dark. I was starting to get worried."

Grover nodded like a doctor who had just had his diagnosis confirmed.

"Come on," he said. "Let's try to pick him up."

We walked back into the cool air-conditioned darkness of the bar. Dan was still sitting in the booth looking out the window into the afternoon sun. He was down to four fries fanning out in the four directions. Bronson was splayed out on the seat next to him, chewing on several half-masticated pieces of French fry. Grover nudged Bronson over and slid into the booth next to Dan.

"Damn, you're getting old," he said. "You used to be able to down twenty-eight fries in twenty-eight seconds. Now you can't even eat twenty-eight without help. I knew there was a reason you picked up that rez dog."

"Twenty-eight's twenty-eight," Dan said. "It doesn't matter how big they are. Besides, Charles Bronson's hungry. I'm just building up his strength."

"Maybe we should have gotten him two burgers last night," I said. It was clear that Grover was trying to lighten the mood, and I figured I'd try to help.

Grover grabbed one of the remaining fries on the plate and held it up to the light. "That's naked," he said. He grabbed the shaker and doused the entire plate with a shower of salt.

He popped the fry in his mouth and licked his fingers. "Healthy living will kill you. Now, Nerburn said you were wandering in the woods."

Dan looked at the fries and snorted. "I wasn't wandering. He just doesn't know how to follow a trail."

"Well, it must have been a hell of a long trail. I was getting pretty toasty out there while you were cutting through that prairie grass up in your brain."

Dan picked up one of the last remaining fries and split it in two.

"You're getting to be just like Nerburn. Tick tock, tick tock. I was coming." He rubbed the two pieces together and took a bite.

He spit the fry onto the floor. "Christ, you ruined it." Bronson lunged down and snapped it up.

Grover winked at me. He had Dan engaged again.

"So, what was this trail you were cutting?"

Dan gulped some water in an attempt to wash the salt out of his mouth.

"I was trying to explain about the boarding schools and how the damn government used them to try to wipe us out."

"They were just trying to make us into good Americans," Grover said. He nudged me with his elbow to let me know I should play along.

Dan's eyes flashed. "Don't make jokes about this," he said.

"Who's joking?" Grover continued. "I got good memories of those ratberry sandwiches."

Dan snorted in disgust.

"What are ratberry sandwiches?" I asked.

Grover grabbed another fry and shook about a teaspoon of salt on it. Then he split it in two and gave half to Bronson. Bronson took one bite and backed away.

"Ratberry sandwiches were what we got when the government inspectors weren't around. See, there wasn't any refrigeration, so food was just kept in the cellar under the stairs. Bugs, worms, all sorts of stuff got into everything. Rats got into the flour. When we got our bread we'd have to look for the little black dots. 'Ratberries,' we called them. You remember those, don't you, old man?"

Dan scowled a bit, but he couldn't resist being drawn into the conversation. "Yeah, I remember them," he said. "We called them 'rez raisins.' I remember one kid even found a whole rat tail in his bread."

"Protein, Nerburn," Grover said. "That's Indian protein. That's why we liked it when the government folks visited. Damn, we got good food then. I'd stick stuff in my pocket, save it for later. No ratberries during government visits. No Indian protein."

"I didn't even know what half the stuff was that we had," Dan continued. "One time they gave me a banana, and I bit into it without peeling the skin. The matron whacked me on the head. She thought I was trying to be funny. I'd never seen a banana before."

"A least it was better than what the folks back home got," Grover said. "That's one of the reasons they'd let the kids go to boarding school. They knew at least we wouldn't starve."

He grabbed the last French fry and stuffed it in his pocket.

"Old habit," he grinned.

He stood up to leave.

"You should get that dog some water, old man," he said. "The little guy seems kind of thirsty."

BY THE TIME WE WERE BACK IN THE CAR, Dan's mood was almost jovial. Grover's teasing and joshing had brought him out of himself. I had to marvel at how Grover had just the right touch with the old man. He knew when to prod him, when to joke with him, when to support him, and when to be silent. He truly was Dan's protector, and the way he performed his role was something to behold. I thought of what I'd once been told were the four prime Lakota virtues: bravery, generosity, respect, and wisdom. In relation to Dan, Grover had them all.

"Tell Nerburn that story about the priest and the bells," he said.

Dan shook his head. "Nah, it's not much of a story."

"Sure, it is. It's a good one."

"Yeah, come on, Dan," I said. "I like stories about priests. I did my time in the church."

"I'll give Bronson the French fry," Grover said.

Dan shifted in his seat. Bronson looked up at him.

"Okay. I'll tell it. But you knock the salt off before you give it to him. It's not good for him.

"There was this one old priest. A real gruff guy. I was scared to death of them priests anyway, wearing those black dresses and strings of beads with crosses on them. But this guy was the worst. He had this long white beard, and his teeth were all yellow. He was always growling, sounded like a bear.

"Well, we used to have to go to church every morning. I never paid much attention. I just followed everyone else, standing up and sitting down and kneeling. When they'd say prayers I'd just put my head down and mumble.

"One day one of the kids was sick, so that priest grabbed me by the collar and threw me up toward the door. 'You got to serve Mass,' he said, all grufflike.

"'Father, I don't know Mass,' I told him.

"He just growled some more and made me put on a white dress and gave me some bells and shoved me up there. God, I was scared. So I just kneeled up there and every time that old priest looks over at me I ring those bells like there's no tomorrow, and I say, real loud, 'mea culpa.' I'd heard them saying that a lot in the Mass, and it was the only thing I could remember.

"The old priest looks at me again, real mean, so I ring the bell again and say 'mea culpa' again, this time a lot louder. He kept looking and I kept ringing and shouting. I must have rung those bells five hundred times during that Mass. Oh, did he beat the hell out of me."

Grover burst out laughing. In spite of myself, I found myself laughing, too.

"See, I told you it was good, Nerburn," Grover said. Even Dan was chuckling at the memory.

"Did stuff like that happen to you in boarding school, Grover?" I asked.

He ran his hand over his crew cut and scratched the back of his head.

"Oh yeah, we all had stuff happen to us. But things had changed pretty much by the time I got there. It was still rough, and some of those old priests still had some funny ideas. But there were some good priests, too, and I could always outrun the bad ones. I was pretty quick on my feet.

"Besides, I already knew English a little. That made a big difference. The ones who didn't know English, they had it rough. Me, I had a head start. I just had to learn how to work the system. Like I joined the track team so I wouldn't have to wear those heavy white man's pants. And I went into the band. If you were in the band, they wanted you to march. So you got outside. The first day they gave me some kind of horn, told me to blow in it. I didn't know what they were talking about, so I spit in it. They beat the hell out of me that day."

"So you got beat, too?"

"Everyone got beat in those days," Grover said. "White kids, too, in their schools. The guys in the navy told me. That's just the way they did things back then."

"Yeah, it was better when we got outside," Dan mused. He was watching the brown hills pass as we headed out of town. "Outside we could talk Indian if there was nobody around. We had this drill yard, like in a prison. They'd take us out there and make us march in formation, do all sorts of stuff. We had these little wool uniforms made out of old soldiers' clothes. It got hotter than hell in them.

"But even when we were marching I liked being outside better than being in the classroom. In the classroom we had to sit in desks in rows and do everything by the bells. For a long time I thought the only way white people knew when to do anything was when a bell went off."

"Sometimes I think that's the way they still are," Grover said.

Dan was staring idly out into the bleak sweltering terrain.

"It must have been hard for you after the way your grandpa had taught you," I said.

"Yeah," he answered.

"Yeah, it was hard. All of it was hard. But it's like Grover said, the English was the hardest. You could drop the ratberries on the floor and hide the bugs under your plate. But you couldn't hide from the English they made you talk.

"From the first day they were shouting at you in English. You didn't know anything. If you said anything in Indian they'd hit you. Our parents never hit us, now here's some white person whacking us every time we turned around."

"Did it scare you?"

"Hell, yes, it scared me. When you're just a little guy, getting hit all the time for things you don't understand — of course it scared me. But you know what really scared me? It was that damn globe. We had this big globe in the room, and the teacher said that was what the world was like. I'd never thought about the world being round.

"How'd they know that? Where did they stand to get a look at the world that let them know it was round? For us, there were the four directions. If the world was a ball, what happened to the directions? And they said the world was spinning. I was scared we'd fall off when we got to the bottom."

Grover laughed and stretched out in the seat. He was enjoying the memories.

"Weren't there any nice teachers?" I asked.

Dan thought about it for a minute. "Yeah, there were a couple. There was one priest who let us talk Indian when he was around. He even tried to learn some of our words. He was okay. But most of them, they'd whack you for looking cross-eyed. Hell, they'd whack you until you went cross-eyed.

"They used to lock us in a closet if we didn't know something. Little place. All dark. No light. There were always kids crying in the closet. But if you cried too much, they'd yank you out of there and beat you with a belt. You learned pretty quick to keep your mouth shut. Better to be scared in the dark than bent over a table and beat with a belt."

"Did you get put in that closet much?"

"No, I just kept my head down all the time. I let them think I was dumb. Mostly I ended up on the stool."

"The stool?"

"They had this stool in the corner. It was for kids who didn't know something. They made you face the wall and put a big paper hat like a cone on your head. It made you ashamed, but it was better than being beat or left all day in a dark closet. I spent a lot of time on that stool."

He steepled his hands in front of his face and closed his eyes, as if retreating into his memories.

"There was this picture of George Washington that hung right over my head. I'd sit there on that stool and look at that picture and think, 'I wonder if that's Jesus?' They always told us George

Washington was the Great Father and that Jesus was the Great Father, so I wondered if they were the same.

"But then there was a picture of Jesus on the other wall and he had brown hair and a beard, and the picture of George Washington had white hair and no beard. I thought that maybe George Washington was Jesus when he got old. These are the kinds of things I thought about when I sat on that stool."

Grover laughed and slapped his knee. "See, Nerburn, that's what it was like being an Indian kid in those days. It wasn't like those white-people books you read as a kid showing a bunch of little bucks running around wearing deerskin suits and shooting bows and arrows."

"It doesn't sound very nice," I said.

"It wasn't very nice," he said. "But those weren't very nice people. In fact, it was pretty damn bad."

"You know what I hated the most?" Dan said. His tone was suddenly quieter and less jocular. "Bedtime. I hated it worse than the meals. I hated it worse than the beatings. There were all of us in that room in those metal beds. They'd put out the lights, and everything would be lonely and dark."

He exhaled slowly. "Just lonely and dark."

His voice had gotten so low you could hardly hear him.

"At home, every night my mother would tuck us in. She'd come in and tuck my blankets around me and hug me and sing a little song to me, real soft. I used to wait for bedtime because it was so soft and warm when she'd come into the room and tuck me in.

"In that place, there was nobody to tuck us in. I'd just lay there thinking about how hard it was for me. Then I'd think about little Yellow Bird over there on the other side of the building in the girl's rooms, and how she couldn't talk English and couldn't hear anything.

"More than anything, I wanted to go over there and tuck her in. But I couldn't. All I could do was lie there. Lie there and listen to the floors creak and the wind blow outside.

"It was so dark, so goddamn lonely and dark."

THE MENTION OF YELLOW BIRD was like a change in the atmosphere. I glanced at Grover in the rearview mirror. He held his hand up to indicate that I should let things be.

We drove in silence through the hills toward the boarding school. The silence only grew as we turned onto the buckling asphalt drive that wound up to the abandoned building.

Now, in the daylight, I could see the full measure of the decay. The pavement was laced with fissures and potholes. Weeds grew from cracks in the roadway. Trash was everywhere. Books and papers were scattered on the ground, all decayed into mush. It was as if the whole place had been abandoned, then vandalized, then simply left to rot. Graffiti was everywhere — gang signs, odd symbols, hearts with names in them — all spray painted in crude, quick strokes. It was obvious that this was still a place where young people came to drink or party or just hang out. It was amazing to me that it had lain this way for years, never cleaned up, never salvaged, never repaired or removed.

As we turned the last corner, the abandoned building loomed before us, hollow as a skull. Broken chairs and desks lay on the ground beneath smashed-out windows.

Dan said nothing; I couldn't imagine what he was thinking.

I harbored no illusions that we would find anything in an abandoned building that would help Dan find out about his sister, and I doubted that he did either. But Grover was right: this wasn't about Yellow Bird, it was about Dan. This was a journey into the wreckage of his past.

"So, what do you want to do?" I asked as we approached the crumbling walkway that led up to the boarded-over front door.

"I'm going in," he said.

"You sure you want to, old man?" Grover asked. "I checked it out while you were asleep last night. There's nothing here."

"I've waited eighty years for this," Dan answered. "I'm going in."

Grover snuffed out his cigarette. "Let's do it, then," he said.

Dan had the car door open even before I had come to a complete stop. He swung his feet out on the ground and pushed himself upright.

"Give me my walking stick," he said. "Just one of them. And there's a bag in the back. Buckskin. Give it to me."

Grover grabbed the bag and handed it to Dan, then passed the walking stick across the seat to me. I tried to help Dan get his balance, but he just slapped my hand away.

Bronson was already snuffling around in the grass and the trash.

"Grover, this is nuts," I whispered. "He could get hurt."

"Or maybe healed," Grover said. "We've just got to do what he says."

The pavement was blistering. Flashes of light glinted off shards of broken glass lying everywhere in the dirt and the grass. The afternoon had taken on a breathless torpor, and shadows cut in on angles from the corners of the building.

Grover helped Dan duck under the two-by-four that had been nailed across the empty doorframe. Dan paused a second to let his eyes adjust, then started down the hallway, sweeping his walking stick before him like a blind man swinging his cane. Grover stayed in front of him, keeping a close eye on the floor, pushing junk out of the way with his feet and testing the boards to see that they were solid. I followed behind, keeping as close as possible so I could catch Dan if he slipped or fell backward.

Dan seemed oblivious to our presence. He kept turning his head, looking at walls and doors and ceilings. He paid no attention to where he was walking or to Grover's efforts to remove trash from his path.

Occasionally he would utter a low "hnn," as if in acknowledgment of some discovery or some particularly poignant memory.

Grover kept the pace slow. The afternoon light shafted in through the broken windows, creating pools of illumination in the dark interior.

At one point, about fifty feet into the darkness, Dan stopped and gestured with his walking stick.

"That's where the old priest was," he said, pointing to a doorless room with sickly green walls and junk strewn across the floor. "That's where they'd send you if you were bad."

He shuffled over to the doorway and peered in, as if even after all these years he was still afraid to enter. "The first time they sent me here — God, I was scared. That old priest was standing there beating his hand with a ruler. He looked about ten feet tall, with that long white beard. He looked like all those pictures of God they had on the wall.

"I'd never seen a man wearing a dress before. He didn't say anything. Just whacked me hard on the side of the head and made me sit in the corner. I sat there all day while he read books at his desk. I didn't dare talk, didn't dare ask to go to the bathroom. Finally I couldn't hold it, so I wet my pants. He didn't say anything. Then when it was starting to get dark he opened the door and sent me out. I had to wear those piss pants until Saturday washing. He never said anything about it."

I could sense Dan moving deeper and deeper into his memories. I had no idea where this journey was going to take him or how it was going to heal the wound in his heart. But I followed Grover's instructions and said nothing — just kept close to offer assistance if he needed it.

He moved further down the hall to a classroom. Remnants of a blackboard still hung on the wall.

"That was the room for the little kids," he said. "I remember one time walking by this room and seeing a little girl standing up next to the desk with one of them chalk erasers stuck in her mouth. She was crying really hard. The teacher was just sitting there, like she didn't even know the little girl was there. That little girl was about five."

I pulled a piece of faded paper out from beneath a pile of boards on the floor. It was a grade sheet of the sort that teachers used back in the thirties, with categories like "deportment" and "posture." Most of it was rubbed away or faded by age. My guess was that vandals had found some old cabinets and scattered the contents over the floor before making off with the cabinet itself or mindlessly smashing it into splinters or using it to start a bonfire out on the grounds for some late-night drinking party.

I showed the sheet to Dan. "Did you get papers like this?"

"What is it?" he asked.

"It looks like a grade report."

"Read it to me."

I read the few words that were still legible.

"Yeah, I remember that kind of stuff," he said. "We had grades for everything. How to sit, how to stand, if we ate right, if we talked right. That's how the white man did things. They divided up every-thing, then they gave you a grade. I couldn't understand it. Every-thing was divided. The day was divided. The food we grew was divided. Everything was weighed and measured and counted. I think that's why they made us learn arithmetic — so we could measure and count everything."

He stared up at the blackboard. "We couldn't understand any-thing."

He wandered further into the darkness. Far ahead of us at the end of the hall we could see the bright light of an open doorway to the outside.

"You know, they even had the school day divided into two parts. In the morning we did all the book stuff, like arithmetic and geography. In the afternoon we went out and worked in the shops. In some ways, that was better. I didn't care about learning how to cut fence posts or fix wagons, but at least we weren't sitting in desks.

"Pretty soon we realized that the afternoon really wasn't about learning, even if they said it was. They just needed us for work. They'd have the girls standing at ironing boards all day, or they'd have us digging holes for fence posts. You tell me what sort of learning that is."

"I had a navy buddy who went to school out near Montana," Grover said. "He said their school made them dig coal. They had to dig a hole in the ground taller than a man just to get down to it, then they had to chop that coal out and bring it up and carry it back to the school building. The white man in charge said they dug up a hundred tons. Training to be coal miners, I guess."

"We didn't have coal, but we had to haul ice," Dan said. "Forty below zero in the middle of winter, and they'd make us go out to the river and chop ice and bring it back. We didn't have gloves that were any good, and our feet would get wet. Lots of guys lost fingers and toes."

He stopped before a stairwell that led to the second floor. "I want to go up there," he said.

I looked at Grover. "Let me check it out," he said, and loped up the stairs.

In a few minutes he came back down. "Can't make it," he said. "There's holes in the floor and wire and junk everywhere. You can't even walk."

"Did you see any beds?" Dan said.

"Nope. Just wires and junk."

"That's where the boys slept. It was just one big room, all full of beds. There was all kinds of coughing and crying. We knew if one kid started coughing, pretty soon every kid would be coughing. There'd be kids spitting up blood all over the place.

"They'd give us medicine in a spoon. White man's medicine. It tasted so bad we'd try to spit it out, but they'd just hold us down and force it down our throats. We wanted to go back home to get our grandma's medicine, or maybe have our parents take us to the medicine man. But they wouldn't let us."

He walked toward the shaft of light streaming in through the rear doorway.

"One time Yellow Bird was sick. I saw her outside." He pointed to a field to the right of the building. "That's where she was standing. She was just crying and coughing. I ran over to her, and they caught me and hit me. That night I jumped out a window and ran away. I was going to go home and get some medicine. I didn't even know where home was. But I was going to help my little sister.

"Some white man saw me running along the road and caught me. When they brought me back they made me carry that damn log for a whole day. They told me they were going to make me carry it as far as I had run, and if I ran away again they were going to do it again with a bigger log. That's when they shaved little Yellow Bird's head. Here she was, sick and coughing up blood, and they cut off her hair because her brother had run away."

We had reached the end of the hall. I looked at Grover for a signal about what we should do next. He pursed his lips and shook his head. Dan continued toward the bright afternoon light that was streaming in through the doorless rear entry.

He began a low chant. He closed his eyes and started weaving back and forth. I started toward him to steady him. Grover held me back.

Dan reached in the buckskin bag he had slung over his shoulder, pulled out a small pouch, and lifted it to his lips. He started pulling at his chest like he was removing something and throwing it away. We stood behind him, watching him in silhouette against the bright illumination of the doorway.

I turned again to Grover, mystified and concerned. It was as if the Dan who had been talking to us about the harsh ways of his school days had suddenly disappeared. Grover was silent and motionless.

Dan's singing got louder still. It was like he was crying out to someone, sending his song high onto the hillsides in an effort to be heard.

Grover was still as stone. His full attention was focused on Dan. The rooms around us echoed with the old man's song. It was not the voice of a ninety-year-old man; it was young, strong, almost as if it was coming from someone else. It rose and fell like the undulation of the hills, swooped and climbed like a bird in flight.

My concern and curiosity had disappeared. In their place was something that bordered on fear.

Suddenly Dan stopped. The silence of the abandoned building rushed in around us. He put the pouch back in the buckskin bag.

"There," he said.

We stepped through the doorway into the light.

At the top of the hill in front of us stood a cemetery. A metal archway marked its entrance, and in the distance, backlit by the sun, stood a huge, white crucifix.

CHAPTER TWENTY

◇◇◇◇◇◇◇◇◇◇◇◇◇◇◇◇◇◇◇◇◇◇◇◇◇◇◇◇◇◇

A GIRL NAMED SARAH

We stood on the crumbling concrete steps of the gutted school building and stared up at the distant graveyard.

The sun glinted behind the crucifix, reducing it to a silhouette against the afternoon sun. It was like a mirror image of Dan silhouetted in the doorway, and I wondered if maybe his chanting had been directed to the large stone figure on the cross on the hill above us.

A narrow, dusty pathway led from the school toward the top of the hill. It was almost completely covered over with weeds and prairie grass — less a trail than the ghost of a trail. It reminded me of some of those old pioneer wagon trails out west — so overgrown as to be unnoticeable up close, but worn so deep that you can see their ghostly presence from a distance.

I didn't know if this was the cemetery for the school or just a lonely graveyard that happened to be nearby. The path unnerved me. I had visions of small schoolchildren carrying the caskets of their schoolmates up that path in the remorseless afternoon sun.

I was about to ask Grover if there were children buried in the graveyard when Dan said, "Let's go. Someone help me."

I looked at the narrow, rutted trail. "It's a long way up there, Dan," I said.

"I made it up the hill to bury Fatback," he said. "I can damn well make it up this hill, too."

Grover took Dan's arm. Dan did not resist.

The wind had picked up. It was dry and desiccated, like an old man's breath. The prairie grass cut at our ankles. Grasshoppers jumped and scattered as we passed.

I could not believe the two men could keep up such a pace. I was panting and sweating. The hot wind leached the moisture from my skin as soon as it formed.

The sun burned down on us and shone directly into our faces. Grover pulled a pair of sunglasses out of his pocket; I just squinted and covered my eyes. Dan pulled his fisherman's cap tighter on his head and continued upward as if he didn't even notice the heat.

When we reached the top of the hill the sun was shooting shafts of light from the western horizon. As far as the eye could see there was no movement, only the shifting shadows on the distant hillsides beneath the incessant hissing of the wind.

A few rounded tombstones poked their way above the whispering grasses; old handmade wooden crosses stood canted in the blistering wind. There was an air of abandonment about everything, as if the place was seldom visited and had started to fade back into the earth. Had it not been for the bent chain-link fence with its wrought-iron arch and the looming crucifix, anyone passing on the road below would not have known that the graveyard even existed.

The cemetery was small — maybe fifty feet by fifty feet. The fence was meant to mark it off from the rest of the vast, rolling landscape. But all it did was make it seem isolated and lonely. The few stones and wooden crosses were all leaning in the same direction, blown into strange and lonely formation by the relentless prairie winds.

Small dolls and plastic flowers lay faded on the graves. A few humpbacked white stones sat canted in the earth. Several others had fallen over and lay on their backs. On the far side of the graveyard a gathering of small homemade wooden crosses stuck out of the ground like flowers. They had once been painted white, but the winds and the dust and the blowing winter snows had reduced them to an ashen, bone gray. Above it all, and strangely out of place, stood the white marble crucifix, with its ghostly Christ figure looking sky-ward in frozen agony.

I had never had such a feeling in a place before. The small plastic flowers and children's toys seemed like cries of love and grief. The looming crucifix looked as alien as something from outer space.

I stared out over the landscape. There was nothing in any direction except rolling hills and the abandoned shell of the school far below us. A single road snaked from one horizon to the other. Somewhere in the distance, a dog barked.

Dan peered through the rounded metal arch. "Let's go," he said.

Grover moved closer. "I told you he was up to something," he whispered.

We walked slowly into the fenced area, with Dan taking the lead and Grover and me following behind. The crucified figure of Christ loomed directly in front of us at the far end of the graves, staring up into the blue, lifeless sky.

From the middle of the graveyard it was possible to see for miles in any direction. The great winds blew hot and dusty across our faces. Birds of prey floated lazily above the distant hills.

Dan stepped unsteadily along the small pathway that led to the crucifix.

"Start looking," he said.

Charles Bronson stood at the arch, refusing to enter.

"Come on," I whispered. He wagged his tail and yipped but would not cross the boundary.

"You look along the edge of the fence, Nerburn," Dan said. "Grover and I will work back from here."

"What am I looking for, Dan?" I asked.

"Anything that says Yellow Bird or Sarah. If she died in the school, they'd probably have used her school name."

The sound of the name *Sarah* shocked me. It seemed so biblical, so European, so wrong.

"They gave us all Christian names," Dan said. "That's how I ended up being Dan."

Grover was already walking among the grasses looking at stones. "They're pretty worn," he said.

"Just look," Dan said.

I went to the perimeter of the fence as Dan had instructed and began pulling back grasses and weeds that had grown over some of the graves. Bronson ran around the outside of the fence next to me, yipping and mewling.

"Come on in, Bronson," I said. But he refused to cross the boundary, even where there were holes in the fence that he could easily have crawled through. It was as if some presence was keeping him at bay.

The graves were not in any orderly arrangement. It was less a cemetery than a burial ground, despite the effort to contain it within the boundaries of the fence.

In some places there were little flat gravestones completely hidden by the overgrowth of grasses. Some graves were only marked by piles of rocks with no identifying headstone or marker of any sort.

Where there were markers, the names were mostly in English. Some sounded Lakota, like Horn Cloud and Looks Back. Others were anglicized — Jackson, Taylor, Smith.

It was obviously not just a graveyard for the school, though far too many of the dead were children. There was a tragic note to them — "infant daughter, dearly loved"; three children, ages two, four, and six, whose graves were marked by three vertical wooden stakes with a single crossbar forming a weathered cross with three legs; two children of different ages who both died on the same day.

The whole place had the feel of a poor person's cemetery where makeshift graves had been shaped and tended by loving hands. On one you'd find a framed and faded picture of a man in a military uniform; on another there'd be a torn rag doll or stuffed teddy bear sitting on a rough mound of dirt and wiregrass. On one grave someone had built a small village of plastic Indian figures arranged around a plastic teepee. One headstone was nothing more than a poured puddle of concrete into which someone had scratched "my loving dad" while it was still wet.

I moved from grave to grave, examining each to see if anything indicated that it had belonged to Yellow Bird. I was uneasy walking among these unknown dead; it seemed wrong to be looking so clinically at these private statements of love and grief. I tried to bow my head and say a small prayer of forgiveness at each to honor the love and sadness that it contained.

Many of the graves could not be identified. Some were but slight depressions in the earth where the ground had settled, with no headstones to mark them. Others had broken stick crucifixes from which the painted names had worn off or were marked by pieces of paper with long-faded messages written in pen or pencil.

An air of impermanence hung over everything. The few marble stones seemed like futile attempts to defy the pull of the earth to reclaim these people for its own.

I worked my way around the perimeter. Dan and Grover were fanning out from the central path that led from the metal arch to the crucifix.

"You see any Sarahs?" Dan asked.

"No," I said.

"Keep looking."

His throat was tight. His voice was tinged with desperation.

In the distance the unseen dog kept up his incessant barking.

Out of the corner of my eye I could see Dan lowering himself onto his knees. I thought perhaps he was collapsing in the heat. But he began crawling slowly through the wiry grass.

I glanced at Grover, who was staying close by his side. He looked back at me with a flat, indecipherable expression.

Dan was speaking strangely, in almost a singsong fashion. I could not make out his words through the keening of the wind.

I turned to move toward them. Grover gestured me back.

Dan moved from grave to grave, brushing back the grasses covering the names, then running his fingers over the carved letters. His songs were getting more urgent. I strained to make out what he was saying.

Suddenly, I had a feeling that something was wrong. I started toward Dan. Grover gestured me back more violently.

The old man kept crawling from grave to grave, making a strange wailing sound, like an infant or an animal.

Then I realized. This was not a song or a prayer.

The old man was crying.

CHAPTER TWENTY-ONE

◈◇◈◇◈◇◈◇◈◇◈◇◈◇◈◇◈◇◈◇◈◇◈◇◈◇◈◇◈◇◈

"GO HOME TO YOUR FAMILY"

At the sound of Dan's crying I backed out of the cemetery and made my way down the hill. It seemed wrong to be standing on land hallowed by Lakota deaths. This was their place; this was their grief. The spirits that spoke here spoke their language. I was an interloper, an unwilling witness. I did not belong here.

Charles Bronson rushed up to me the second I stepped out of the graveyard. He leaped at my pants leg and yipped until I picked him up. All the way down the hill he nuzzled into my chest and made small gurgling sounds.

"It's okay, Bronson," I told him. "Dan will be along in a bit."

He wagged his tail and nuzzled ever closer.

I walked around the outside of the school and sat down against the side of the Toyota. High above, the birds of prey carved distant circles in the empty sky.

Bronson kept looking at me with soulful, knowing eyes. I scruffed him under his neck and held him like a baby. In the far distance the dog continued to bark. The hills rolled like waves toward the burning western horizon.

Finally, Dan and Grover emerged, walking slowly around the side of the building. They were silent and uncommunicative.

"Did you find her?" I asked.

"She wasn't there," Grover said curtly.

We all got in the car, and I drove down the cracked asphalt drive toward the main highway.

"Just take us home," Grover said.

Dan sat motionless in the passenger's seat holding the buckskin bag in his lap.

I turned to the south and headed back toward their reservation. Even without stopping it was going to take us seven or eight hours to get back.

I tried several times to make casual conversation just to relieve the heaviness. But neither of them responded to my comments, so I ceased talking and drove in silence into the fading afternoon haze.

By twilight no one had said a word. Dan was within inches of me, but the wall around him was as insurmountable as if it had been made of stone. He kept looking at the bag and speaking silently under his breath. Bronson licked his hand, as if to remind him that there were still those who cared about him. But Dan did nothing in response. Grover sat silently in the backseat, neither speaking nor moving.

Night crept in with the waning of the light. The hills loomed heavy on either side of us. The moon cast a ghostly glow on the passing landscape, making everything seem like an old tintype or silver print.

I wanted to reach out to Dan, but I didn't know how. I felt that I had failed him. He had seemed so buoyant and full of good humor as we drove up to the school. It was obvious now that he had

assumed that Yellow Bird would be in that cemetery. That's why he
hadn't been concerned about giving me information. He simply had
wanted me to bear witness to this final act of closure in his almost
century of life.

I felt honored that he had wanted me to share this with him. But
now that the search had been a failure, his words spoken by the fire
— "I lost little Yellow Bird. Now I want you to help me find her
again" — weighed even more heavily on my heart.

Bronson lay quietly in Dan's lap, curled up in the old man's
gnarled, arthritic hands. Whenever I looked over at him, he turned
his face toward me and stared with his brown, knowing eyes. He
seemed completely aware of what was going on. He reminded me of
one of those dogs who sits patiently by its master's grave, knowing
that the person will never return but feeling that it is his duty to
remain there in eternal vigil.

I reached over and petted his head; he licked my hand in
response, then burrowed deeper into Dan's lap. Dan never moved.
He just clutched the bag and sat as motionless as a statue.

We drove this way all through the night. When I stopped for
gas, Dan stayed in the car. Grover stood outside and smoked, his
orange cigarette ash glowing in the darkness.

We reached the edge of the reservation just as the first light of
morning was creasing the hillsides. No word had yet been spoken.

As we turned onto the old familiar highways, Dan broke the
silence. "I know she was there," he said. "I know she was there."

Grover puffed on his cigarette and said nothing.

"I'm going to keep looking, Dan," I said. "I'm going to get you
an answer."

He turned to me with eyes that seemed to contain the weariness
of five hundred years of betrayals and broken promises.

"You just go home to your family," he said.

"No, I mean it. I'm going to find out what happened to her."

He smiled weakly and stared out the window. Bronson looked up at him and licked the back of his hand.

"I just wanted to find her," he said. "I just wanted to find her so I could honor her. I just wanted to turn my sadness into peace."

We passed the rutted clay trail that led to Orv's *tiospaye*. It seemed like a roadway to nowhere. Everything was empty and forlorn.

WENONAH WAS WAITING AT THE DOORSTEP as we churned up the path to Dan's house. Her look of expectation changed to sadness when she saw Dan slumped in the front seat.

I could see her bite her bottom lip to hold back her tears. Then she ran down the steps to meet him at the car door.

The two of them spoke for a few minutes in Lakota. I stepped out and stood mutely on my side of the car.

She walked over to me as Dan wandered off toward the house.

"I'm sorry," I said.

"It's not your fault."

"Yes, it is," I said. "I said I'd help him find her."

"Sometimes things just don't work out."

Her fatalism and acceptance almost broke my heart. "He was so full of hope," she said. "I had never seen him so full of hope."

I could see the old man climbing slowly up the steps using his willow walking sticks. Bronson was right behind him. Dan opened the screen door, and the two of them disappeared into the darkness.

Grover had been shadowing Dan to make sure he made it into the house safely. Once the old man was inside he walked over to us and propped himself against the fender of the car. He pulled a pack of Lucky Strikes out of his top pocket, lit one, and drew deeply.

"I thought we had it," he said.

Wenonah twisted the dishrag she was holding in her hand.

The fluorescent light came on inside the house. Through the

doorway we could see Dan padding back and forth in the kitchen. He had put down his walking sticks and was pushing his hospital chair in front of him. Charles Bronson was right behind him, following his every step.

"I'm going to find her," I said.

Wenonah smiled softly, like a mother listening to a child who promises to one day buy her a big house.

"Just go home to your family," she said.

She reached into her dress pocket and pulled out the photo of Yellow Bird. "He said to give you this." She placed it in my hand and closed my fingers around it.

I looked at the little face staring up at me. "As God is my witness I'm going to find out what happened to this little girl," I said.

"Well, that's between you and your God. I hope you're right."

Grover walked over and extended his hand. I took it and held it softly. "Nice handshake," he grinned. Then he whispered, "Keep at it. Something will happen."

Through the doorway we could see Dan standing under the flickering light, his hand above Charles Bronson. The little dog was jumping on his hind legs, turning in little circles, with the glove held tightly in his mouth. In the wan light of the early dawn, it reminded me of nothing so much as the stories of the ghost dance, where the Lakota spun in frenzied circles in the hopes that their dancing would bring the dead back to life.

Grover gave me one final cuff on the shoulder. He reached in his pocket and pulled out the French fry from the restaurant.

"I better go give this to Bronson," he said. "A person should always keep his promises."

Forest Silence

◇◈◇◈◇◈◇◈◇◈◇◈◇◈◇◈◇◈◇◈◇◈◇◈◇◈◇◈◇

CHAPTER TWENTY-TWO

A HAUNTED HEART

For the next few months I lived with a haunted heart.

The photo of Yellow Bird was like a weight on my spirit. I carried it with me constantly, as if by looking at her closely and frequently enough I would gain some kind of insight that would lead me closer to her. But all I ever saw were those sad eyes and that hard, defiant expression. She became like my own child — a child I could not reach but whose unreachable loneliness brought me to the edge of tears every time I looked at her.

I could not get over the fact that Dan had wanted me to have the picture. It was more than a gift; it was a passage. Photos are precious to Indians, especially to the old ones who believe that photographs capture the soul of a person. By putting that photo in my hands, Dan had also placed Yellow Bird's spirit in my hands. It was up to me to keep that spirit strong and to bring it back to life.

I couldn't shake the memory of Dan lying curled up on that motel bed under the harsh glow of the overhead light. I kept seeing those white, sockless ankles and those untied shoes. He had looked like a corpse or an abandoned child. Some nights I would wake up filled with that image and not know if it had been a dream or some kind of a vision destined to haunt me the rest of my life.

As winter descended, my darkness deepened. Each little girl in the supermarket, each mention of the name *Sarah* brought a rush of images of little Yellow Bird. I could not pass cemeteries. I could not read obituaries in the newspaper. One time, as Christmas approached, I saw a pile of old dolls in a bin in a local thrift store. One of them was a homemade rag doll of a little Indian girl. I almost started crying and had to leave the store.

I did what I could to continue the search. I contacted the national archives in Kansas City, looked into databases, and spoke with officials from churches, tribal centers, and state historical societies. But try as I might, I could not find information that shed any light on the fate of the little girl staring out at me from that photograph.

The task began to seem hopeless. No one wanted to be my ally. The Indian archivists distrusted me, thinking I was one more anthropological researcher digging into the private lives of Indian people; the churches, dealing with lawsuits born of the long-hidden actions of their priests, said their records were sealed or nonexistent; historical societies, unsure of what was considered sacred and what was considered public record, shunted me off to committees. When I was actually able to sit down with documents, the print was faded and the script often illegible. Many records had simply been destroyed.

If that wasn't enough, the records themselves were confused and inaccurate. Indian names had been recorded in dozens of ways. Yellow Bird's Lakota name could have been miswritten or mistranslated. The arbitrary name *Sarah* could have been changed when she left the school and possibly changed a final time by a family if they had taken her in and adopted her.

If she had subsequently married a white man and had wanted to hide her Indian roots, she might have changed her name again, as well

as taking the family name of her husband. It was a track that was difficult to follow under the best of circumstances. Under these conditions, trying to find a little girl who had disappeared from a boarding
school almost eighty years ago was proving to be almost impossible.

I lived in constant fear that every ring of the phone was a call
from the reservation, and that an Indian voice on the other end
would say, in a flat, unemotional tone, "Dan's walked on," making
my failure irrevocable and absolute. Grover's final comment — "A
person should always keep his promises" — echoed like an indictment at the center of my being.

More than once I almost got in my car and drove out to the reservation. But the journey made no sense. What was I after? Reassur-
ance? Absolution? I had no news to give, and there was nothing
more to be gained by revisiting the site of the old boarding school.

As January deepened, the pall over me became even darker. I took
to driving through the snows to nearby reservations, partly just to be
with people who might sympathize with my dilemma, and partly in
the faint hope that someone I met could tell me something that would
lead me even one small step farther down the path to an answer.

In convenience stores, at gas stations, in bingo halls, in tribal
offices I brought out the photo, told my story, and asked if anyone
could offer me assistance or guidance. Often my inquiries were met
with silent, empty stares. Other times I was met with sympathetic
nods and stories of their own family histories — stories that were
every bit as tragic and inconclusive as Dan's.

It gradually became obvious that almost every family carried a
wound from the boarding school days. Children having their mouths
washed out with lye; little boys strapped to tables and beaten with
belts or locked for days in rat-infested root cellars for speaking their
own language; girls being raped by staff and having their infants
buried in unmarked graves in hidden corners of the school grounds
— stories like these were commonplace, and they only furthered my

realization that little Yellow Bird's disappearance was neither unique
nor unusual. She was just one more anonymous casualty in the government's war against a people and a way of life.

Saddest of all to me was the fact that many of the Indians themselves seemed to accept this. "What can you do?" one man told me.
"I can't unlearn what I was taught. They ripped the Indian out of me
and filled me up with a white man."

The strangest responses came from the clergy and the churches.
So many of the ministers and priests and nuns I spoke to had devoted
their lives to working with the Indian people, and they had loved
them and lived among them as family. Some even spoke the Native
· languages better than the people themselves. But when the subject of
the past wrongs in the boarding schools came up, a quiet passivity
came over them. It belonged to a different, darker era to which they
were heir but for which they would take no responsibility. It was
as if they were living in the presence of an echo, but refused to
acknowledge the sound from which that echo had come.

I brooded on this strange, dark stain on the heart of our national
experience. It was as if no one could face it directly, and no one
wanted to. The Native people found it too painful; the churches
found it too volatile. It was rapidly becoming apparent that there
was no easy route to an answer, if, indeed, there was any answer at
all. I very well might have given up if it were not for Grover's words:
"Stay with it. Something will happen."

Finally, and quite unexpectedly, that something did happen. It
came in the form of an encounter in a small convenience store on an
isolated reservation highway in the deep pine forests of nothern Minnesota up near the Canadian border. As I was standing at the check-
out counter, I got talking to a woman about the boarding schools in
the Canadian reserves, where the treatment of children had been, if
possible, even worse than it had been in the boarding schools on the
American side of the line.

I showed her Yellow Bird's photograph and mentioned the boarding school she and Dan had attended. The woman brightened. "Oh, I've heard of that school," she said. "I think my great-grandma went there."

The answer stunned me.

"She did?" I said. "Did she ever talk about it?"

"You could go ask her. She just lives up the road a few miles."

My heart started racing. This was the first hopeful news I had received in months.

"She's still alive?"

"Oh, yeah."

"How old is she?"

"Oh, I'd guess about ninety. She still lives alone up there. We keep trying to get her to move in with us, but she says she likes it out by the lake."

"I'd really like to talk to her," I said, trying to contain my excitement. "If you think she wouldn't mind."

"Oh, no. She likes company. She'll probably talk your ear off. You could go up there right now."

Winter had reached its deepest point. Already, at 4:00 p.m., the day was fading toward twilight. By 5:00 it would be completely dark, and the sky was heavy and foreboding. But the chance to talk to an old woman who knew that boarding school and was about Dan's age was too exciting to resist.

"How do I get there?" I asked.

"It's kind of hard to explain. Here's what you should do. Head up this road out here. Don't take any turns. After about twelve miles you'll see a little house trailer on the right. There'll be Christmas lights on it. That's Lori's store. Go in and ask there. Tell her I sent you. My name's Donna. She'll help you out."

The weather was worsening as I headed north into the twilight. The wind blew skeins of snow across the highway, and passing gusts lifted clouds of snowy mist that enveloped the car and blinded my view. Here and there, when the wind died down, I could catch a glimpse of a great snow-covered lake through the breaks in the heavy banks of pine trees.

The heater blew a thin and fragile warmth. Ravens as big as small dogs picked at frozen, half-buried animal carcasses on the side of the road. Here and there, flat expanses of frozen swamp and bracken opened into broad distances that revealed a lonely horizon of waning afternoon light.

Off to the right, toward the great lake, one lone ancient pine, its top snapped off in a long-forgotten storm, towered high above a line of barren trees. At its zenith, an eagle's nest as big as a child's mattress sat triumphant and isolated. I could see the great birds circling in the swirling mist far out over the frozen lake.

I had almost decided that the drive was too dangerous when a strange, muted glow of reds and blues and greens appeared ahead on the right. As I drew nearer, I could see a small hand-painted sign on the side of the road that said "Lori's Store." Far back in the trees, almost at the edge of the lake, an old, square aqua-colored house trailer stood on cinder blocks. It was trimmed with strings of Christmas lights. Old tricycles and tires lay half buried in the snow on either side of the door.

I crunched into the parking area, pulled my collar up, and stepped out of the car. The wind felt like shards of glass against my flesh as I hurried to the door and pushed my way in. A woman in her early twenties was seated behind a counter watching a small television set. On the floor next to her sat a young girl of about seven. She was wearing dirty pink moon boots and a torn pink parka. She was playing with a blond Barbie doll that was missing one leg.

"Getting stormy," the woman said. She seemed unsurprised to see me.

"More than I'd like," I said.

I wiped the condensation from my glasses and shook the snow from my collar. The child was staring at me with undisguised interest. The presence of a strange white man was clearly an event in her life.

"Hi," I said. "What's your name?"

"Amber," she answered. She had a big gap in her smile where one of her baby teeth had just come out, and thick, black hair, shiny as a raven's wing, that fell almost to her waist. She thrust her doll out in front of her.

"This is Sabrina," she said.

"She's very beautiful," I answered.

"Are you going to buy something?" she asked.

I was anxious to get going, but the little girl was taking such pleasure at my attention that I couldn't be dismissive of her.

"Of course," I said. "This is a store, isn't it?"

"It's my mom's store. I help her." She beamed up at the woman behind the counter.

"Well, I'll bet you're a good help. Maybe you can help me."

I was about to ask how to get to Mary's when the little girl ran over and took a position next to the cash register. It was obvious that she wanted to be a salesperson like her mom. Not wanting to disappoint her, I turned my attention to a metal candy rack that held a few chocolate bars and assorted boxed candies.

"Well," I said, "I've got a problem. I'd really like a candy bar, but I don't know what I want. Is there one that you'd recommend? A favorite of yours?"

The little girl whispered intensely to her doll, then marched the one-legged Barbie across the counter and brought it to rest on a Hershey bar.

"Is that the one Sabrina recommends?" I asked.

The little girl nodded and bounced her doll up and down.

"Sabrina's got a good idea," I said. "I think maybe I'll get one."

I made a great charade of pondering the issue. "But now I have another problem."

The little girl nodded seriously, as if preparing to offer me counsel.

"I can only eat half a candy bar before I get full, and it's too cold to take it with me in the car. Can you think of anyone here who might be able to help me by eating the other half?"

Amber looked up at her mother. Her mother nodded slightly. "Sabrina and I can," she said.

"You can? Do you think it's okay with your mom?"

Amber nodded vigorously.

"Well, then, we should do it," I said. "Why don't you have Sabrina pick out the best one, and we'll divide it up."

Amber pointed Sabrina's nose at the first Hershey on the rack. "This one," she said.

"Well, that one it is," I said. "Now, I've got one last question. Could you maybe help me figure out where Mary Johnson lives?"

"I know where she lives," Amber said, jumping up and down. "I know where she lives."

Her mother quieted her with a glance. One does not give out information thoughtlessly to a strange white man seeking personal information on the reservation.

"It's okay," I said. "I talked to Donna down at the trading post. She said I should ask you for directions."

"You talked to Donna?" the woman said.

"Yeah. I'm trying to help an old man who went to the same boarding school as her great-grandma. Donna said she'd probably be happy to talk."

The woman softened. "Oh, yes. Mary likes company. She lives down by the lake. Her house is kind of hard to find. What you do is go down the road a couple of miles. Look for the tree with the eagle's nest. It's easy to see."

"I know. I passed it on the way in."

"Turn into the road just past that. It's just a path. Do you have a truck?"

"No," I said, "only a station wagon."

"Well, it's probably okay. There hasn't been much snow lately." She looked out the window at the swirling mist. "Just lots of wind."

Amber was looking up at me in wide-eyed anticipation. I unwrapped the candy bar, broke it in two, and handed her the bigger half, along with a dollar.

"I hope you and Sabrina enjoy the candy bar," I said.

Amber bounced Sabrina up and down on the counter as if to say, "We will."

"It's not often I get waited on by two such beautiful women," I said. Amber looked away shyly. She thrust Sabrina toward me while keeping her eyes averted. "She's the prettiest," she said.

"Oh, I don't think so," I answered. "I think you are."

Amber giggled and ran behind her mother. She reached Sabrina out where I could see her.

"Yes, she's very pretty, too," I said. "But not as pretty as you."

"No," Amber answered, peering out from behind her mother with wide, dark eyes. "She's prettiest. She's got really pretty hair."

◇◈◇◈◇◈◇◈◇◈◇◈◇◈◇◈◇◈◇◈◇◈◇◈◇◈◇◈◇◈◇

CHAPTER TWENTY-THREE

FADING TRACKS

A s if on cue, the snow started up again as I walked back to my car. At first it was just a small dusting, and then it turned to big heavy flakes. My every instinct dictated that I should hold off on the visit. But, for the first time since I had left Dan last summer, I felt I might be moving closer to little Yellow Bird. The prospect of a lead that I could actually follow made me willing to take the risk.

I watched closely for the eagle's nest. Though I had seen it on the way in, I hadn't paid any real attention to its specific location. With the wind picking up and the sky swirling with snow, I was afraid I would miss it on the way back. Finally, after about five miles, I caught a glimpse of the lone pine with its huge nest standing ghostly in the fading winter light.

About a half mile past the broken pine, a small path with two single tire tracks cut off on a diagonal from the roadway into the snowy forest. It was like a tunnel into the trees, sparsely traveled, and otherwise unmarked.

I turned into the path, felt the crisp crunch of snow under the tires, and began my careful journey toward what I hoped would be Mary Johnson's house. The branches from the low-lying scrub and bushes scraped along the side of the car. Globs of snow, dislodged by my passing, fell from the branches of the surrounding trees and hit the hood and windshield in heavy clumps.

I was filled with trepidation. I had driven such roads before, but never in winter. I knew that they could stop abruptly or simply fade out into nothing. If I had chosen wrong, or if I were to meet another vehicle, there was no way to turn around, and I would be forced to back out — something I didn't think I could accomplish in the growing dark. Worse yet, if these tracks had been made by a four-wheel-drive vehicle, and I got caught in a hollow or slid off the path, I could be facing a night alone in a frozen car in a northern winter — the kind of experience I read about each year in the local newspapers. Very often they turned out badly.

After about a half mile of bumping and slipping down the path I was consumed with panic. I couldn't stop, I couldn't turn around. There was no way I could ever back up. The tracks behind me were filling in with snow as I passed.

Night was descending faster than I had anticipated. In the darkening forest the light had almost ceased to exist. My headlights only accentuated my isolation. They shone like flashlights on the trunks of the surrounding trees, revealing in frightening close-up how dense the woods really were.

Once I thought I saw a hint of movement off to my right. A deer, perhaps. Or something else. I remembered the Ojibwe stories of the "little people" who lived in the forests and seldom let themselves be seen. But I couldn't let my imagination overtake me. I needed to concentrate on the two narrow, fading tracks.

After what seemed an eternity, I saw a faint glow in the distance. It grew brighter as I approached, until I could see that it was a single yard light hanging from a utility pole high above a double-wide trailer. Tracers of snow were cutting through the ghostly cone of illumination it cast on the house below.

An old van sat half buried at the edge of the parking area. Snow had drifted around it up to its door handles.

I parked in a small turnaround area, making sure to get myself aimed outward before shutting off the engine. A single path, poorly shoveled and barely wide enough for one person, led from the parking area up to the door. The snow was piled fully three feet high on either side of it.

The curtains were drawn. Through them I could see flickering images from a television set.

I tucked a pouch of Prince Albert into my pocket and stepped tentatively from the car. The wind was strong and gusting, making me reach reflexively for the collar of my jacket.

Mary must have seen the lights of my car coming down the path. She was peering through the small window in the middle of the door as I reached the top of the steps.

I heard the door unlatch, and then it opened a crack.

"Yes?"

"Are you Mary?" I said.

The wind from the lake almost ripped the flimsy metal storm door out of my hand.

"Donna gave me your name back at the Trading Post," I said. "She told me you might be able to give me some help regarding a little girl who went to the same boarding school you did." I was trying desperately to establish my bona fides. All I wanted was for her to let me in from the wind and cold. But she was being cautious. She lived far off the road, and an unfamiliar man at her door, especially a white man, was cause for wariness.

"How'd you find me?"

"Lori gave me directions to your house."

"Lori did?"

"Yeah. Amber's mother. At the store."

"What do you want to know?" she said.

I pulled my jacket tighter against my neck. "I'm trying to help a friend of mine. A Lakota man whose little sister went to boarding school about the same time you did. Donna thought you might know her. I have a picture."

The answer was sufficient.

"Come on in," she said. "It's getting pretty cold out there."

She pulled the door open, and I hurried inside. My fingers were numb, and the tips of my ears were burning.

She closed the door behind me and beckoned me toward a chair. She was a tiny, birdlike woman, standing no more than five-feet-one or -two and weighing barely a hundred pounds. She had a severe widow's hump and was wearing a thin, shapeless housedress and a black button-up sweater. Her hair was completely white and tied loosely with a ribbon. It hung to the middle of her back.

I brushed the snow off my shoulders. "Thank you," I said. "I know this is an intrusion."

"No, no. That's fine," she said.

I was about to hand her the Prince Albert when she turned and headed toward a back room. "I'll make some tea. Does your car have four-wheel drive?"

"No."

"Well, we need to keep an eye to the weather, then," she said. "That path covers over pretty easily, especially in the wind."

I slipped the pack of Prince Albert back into my pocket. The trailer was filled with cheap dime-store bric-a-brac, and a crucifix hung on the wall. I didn't want to embarrass either of us by involving us in an inappropriate or uncomfortable ritual.

"Do you like sassafras tea?" she called from the kitchen. "My mother used to make it when I was little."

"That sounds great," I said. The wind was screaming outside the windows.

She continued her activities in the kitchen. "We used to drink a lot of tea when I was a little girl. My grandma would go out in the woods and pick different leaves when we were sick. I used to go with her. I don't think the kids today know about these things."

"No," I said. "These are different times."

"I liked the old ways better," she said.

I wanted to move the conversation toward the subject of Yellow Bird.

"So, you went to the boarding schools?" I said.

"Oh, yeah," she answered. "I went to a couple of them. They were pretty good. We had good meals. I liked the nuns. They taught us how to sew on machines."

She emerged from the kitchen carrying a plate of sugar cookies. "The tea will be done pretty soon. You eat some of these."

I took one and smiled my approval.

She sat down across from me and put her hands in her lap. She was old in a way that I had only seen a few times in my life — not elderly, but ancient. Her face was completely covered with wrinkles running in all directions. There were no smile lines, no furrows of anger. She was like a piece of dried clay that had baked too long in the sun.

Her comment about the "old ways" emboldened me. I pulled the tobacco from my pocket and handed it to her.

"I don't want to seem inappropriate," I said. "But I brought you this."

She took the pouch of Prince Albert in her bony hands and smiled up at me.

"Thank you," she said. "This is very kind of you. How can I help you?"

I breathed a quiet sigh of relief. She had taken the tobacco as it had been intended: as a gift and a request to ask a question. Her response indicated that the gift had been accepted.

"I'm trying to find out some information about a little girl. She went to boarding school about the same time you did. I think it might be one you went to. Her brother's pretty sick. He's trying to find out what happened to her."

"How old is he?" she asked.

"Eighty-nine. Ninety."

"Then he doesn't have much time."

The teapot started whistling on the stove. Mary got up and walked slowly toward the kitchen.

I waited impatiently for her return. The wind was howling on the lake and rattling the siding on the trailer.

"Do you think the path out will be okay?" I asked.

"Just a minute," she said from the kitchen. "I can't hear you."

Soon she returned carrying a tray with two small teacups and an ornate red and blue china teapot. "My friend brought these back from Korea. She said it was very nice there."

"They're very interesting," I said, trying to feign interest in the china.

"Do you like honey?" she asked.

"Yes, please. That would be fine." I was willing to agree to anything to get the conversation moving.

I pulled out the faded photo as she ladled honey into my cup of tea.

"This is the little girl," I said, pushing the photo across the tea tray. "Her name was Yellow Bird. Or Sarah."

Mary picked up the faded photo and stared at it for what seemed like five minutes.

"It's not a very good photo," I apologized.

She said nothing but just squinted silently at the small fragment of photograph.

Then, very deliberately, she handed it back to me.

"Yes, I remember that girl," she said. "Yes, I remember her. She was different. She couldn't talk very well. She played with dolls all the time."

"That's the one," I said. My heart was beating with excitement.

"She didn't play very much with anyone," Mary said. "Just with her dolls. She sewed dolls a lot. The nuns let her do it because she couldn't talk. She made really beautiful dolls. I thought she was really sad."

She took the picture again and held it close to her face. I realized that, like many old Indians, she didn't wear glasses.

"Yes, that's her," she said. "I'm sure of it."

"Were you friends with her?"

"No, I don't think she had any friends. She was Lakota or Nakota. Most of us were Ojibwe. We couldn't understand each other. I didn't speak very good English, and that little girl, she hardly spoke at all, so I never talked with her."

She kept staring at the photo as if it was going to reveal a secret.

"I do remember a story about her, though."

I pulled myself closer.

"One day we were out on the road. Just walking. There was a farm down there. There was this farmer, a white man. We got milk and things from him, so we went there sometimes. I think they wanted us to see how a white man's farm worked.

"Well, on the way, there was this big field. Wide — almost like a swamp — maybe a mile across. That day there were four of us — two other girls and the sad little girl and me. And one of the matrons, a really mean one. We were just walking."

I sipped my tea and kept my attention on her. This was the kind of information I had dreamed of finding.

"Well, anyway, when we got by that field, that little girl, she started crying. She fell down and put her hands over her ears. She was just crying. The matron got really mad at her and tried to pull her up. The little girl said something in Indian, so the matron hit her.

"'Talk English,'" she said. "'Or I got to hit you.'

"But the little girl couldn't talk English. We all knew that. She couldn't learn things. The matron kept hitting her. 'Talk English,' she said.

"Well, that little girl, she kept crying and holding her hands over her ears. She kept shouting, '*Shunka*'-something. It was Indian for *horse* in her language. Some of the other kids told me that.

"The matron, she got really mad. She thought the little girl was crying because she wanted to ride on horses. She kept hitting her with a strap, but that girl wouldn't stop crying. She just kept saying that *shunka* word.

"Later we found out that some white man had brought horses there once and had tied them up and then didn't come back for them and they all froze to death in the winter. That place was called 'dead horse field.' We didn't know that. That's why I remember that little girl. I remember her from that field."

"You mean the little girl didn't know that, either?"

"No. None of us knew that."

The story, with its vague echoes of the supernatural, was unsettling, especially with the swirling winds and the darkness and looming presence of the great frozen lake.

"That's a sad story," I said.

"She was a sad girl," Mary answered.

"Do you remember what happened to her? Where she went? What her name was?"

"No. Like I said, I never talked to her. The next year I went to a different school."

She reached for the teapot. "Do you want some more tea?"

"No, thank you. I'd better get going."

I ate another cookie to show my appreciation for her hospitality. She kept staring at the photograph, as if it might open some doors in her memory.

"I didn't help you much," she said apologetically.

"No, you gave me another piece of the puzzle."

"I do remember that she was sick a lot," she offered, trying to give me some last piece of information. "You know, there were lots of diseases there. They'd make us all take baths in the same water, so if someone was sick it got in the water and we all got sick. We all had to use the same towels, too."

"What kind of sickness did she have?" I asked.

"I don't know. Maybe that one in the lungs. Tuberculosis. Lots of kids got tuberculosis. They'd send them off to the tuberculosis place. Sometimes we'd never see them again."

"A tuberculosis place?"

"Yeah. It was somewhere up near Canada. Near Turtle Mountain, I think."

"Do you think she might have been sent there?" I asked.

"I don't know," she said. "It could have been anything. You know, in summer they'd send us off to live with white families. They'd make us be their maids and do all their work so we would learn how to be like white people. Sometimes girls ran away. They'd get homesick and didn't like having to do all the work for these people, so they'd run away. Maybe that's what happened to her. I don't know."

The wind was picking up outside, and it was clear that Mary was now just casting about in search of information that might be helpful.

I reached out my hand to shake her birdlike fingers.

"Thank you very much," I said, taking her hand softly in mine.

"You're welcome," she answered. "I hope you find something about that little girl for your friend."

"I do, too."

She removed her hand from my grasp.

"You know, it's sad to lose a sister or brother," she said.

"I can't even imagine."

She smiled warmly and nodded. "Yes, it's very hard." Her smile never wavered, but her look was distant and her voice seemed far away.

MUCH TO MY RELIEF, the path out was no worse than when I had come in. The trees had blocked the snowing and drifting, and, at least for the moment, the storm had lessened and the clouds had cleared. The sky had turned an inky purple and was alive with an unearthly glow. Through the openings in the branches overhead I could see the faint hint of the aurora borealis moving sinuously above the horizon.

I was excited by what Mary had told me. It gave me hope that I could follow the trail a little further. But her stories about Yellow Bird filled me with a deep sadness. It was the first glimpse I'd had into the little girl's life other than the few snippets Dan had shared with me.

I took out the picture of Yellow Bird and stared at it in the dim illumination of the dome light. There were those lips clenched tight in fierce defiance, that ragged little pageboy haircut, and those wounded eyes with their untouchable melancholy. What had her life been like in that boarding school, hundreds of miles from her home, friendless, isolated, unable to speak, with only a few dolls for playmates?

I thought of little Amber with her bright eyes and her gap-toothed smile, holding up her one-legged Barbie. She was about the same age as Yellow Bird had been in the photo.

I turned onto the main road and made my way south through the pillow drifts and snow-silenced forests.

"I'm going to find you, little Yellow Bird," I said out loud. "I promise."

In the darkness of the advancing northern night, with my imagination moving like the aurora borealis, it was almost as if she was out there, listening and waiting.

CHAPTER TWENTY-FOUR

◇◇◇◇◇◇◇◇◇◇◇◇◇◇◇◇◇◇◇◇◇◇◇◇◇◇◇◇◇◇◇

A GLOW IN THE DISTANCE

W here are you?" Louise said. There was something close to panic in her voice. I put my mouth closer to the receiver to drown out the sound of the wind.

"I'm outside a little reservation store up by the border," I said. "I'm sorry I couldn't call. There's no cell service here."

"Have you been listening to the radio? There's a huge storm blowing in from Canada. They've shut down everything west of Winnipeg."

I didn't need a radio to tell me something big was coming. The calm on the way out from Mary's house had been ominous, the glow too bright and unnatural. It was as if the sky had been gathering a quiet power in preparation for something dark and threatening. In the twenty miles between Mary's and the trading post, the wind had picked up again. Small, hard flakes of snow were blowing almost on a horizontal, and the air was strangely unsettled.

"Look," I said. "I'm okay. I think I'm going to push a little farther to the west. I met an old woman who knew Yellow Bird and

went to the same boarding school. She mentioned a sanitarium out
by Turtle Mountain."

"Turtle Mountain? That's in the middle of North Dakota.
You're not going to try to make it out there?"

"What am I supposed to do? I can't make it home. There's no
town anywhere around here. Turtle Mountain's about the same distance as heading back. I might as well give it a try."

"But at least heading this direction you've got the trees. You
drive west, you're going into the prairies."

I knew she was right. Half an inch of snow with a strong wind
on the prairies can be more dangerous than a foot of snow in the
forests. At least trees serve as markers. You find yourself driving
through a tunnel of white. On the prairies the road simply disap-
pears and leaves you staring at a shapeless landscape of undifferen-
tiated whiteness. A false turn or a slip, and you can find yourself
stuck in a ditch with no traction, no phone service, and no way to get
out. You can't walk for help, and you can't stay in your car. More
experienced travelers than I had lost their lives in such circumstances.

"Look. I'll make it to the nearest town, find a place for the night,
and stay put until the plows get out in the morning. It's the best I
can do."

"Sometimes I wish you'd never gotten involved in this," she
said.

"So do I," I said, as the snow swirled around me. "But it's a little late for that now."

"Just call when you find a place to stay. I'll keep the phone by the
bed."

I hung up and walked back to the car. The windshield and hood
were already covered with snow. The road beyond the parking lot
was almost invisible in the growing storm.

I pulled a map from the glove box and plotted the distance to
the next town. It was about forty miles directly west.

I turned onto the roadway and headed into the storm. The thick pine forest offered protection from the wind, but before long the road had drifted over, and I was cutting tracks through fresh snow. The trees loomed ghostly on either side of me.

Several times I thought of turning around, but when I checked the rearview mirror, I saw that my tracks had filled in behind me. Even if I made it back to the trading post, there would be no place to stay. I would end up trying to sleep in my car, and I had only my jacket to keep me warm in temperatures that were rapidly dropping below zero.

With no better options, I continued on the road toward the little North Dakota town.

Gradually, the forests thinned, then gave way completely to shapeless, treeless prairies. It was as I had feared — the relentless winds were blowing the snow on a horizontal, sending skeins across the roadway and obscuring the pavement with finger drifts. Patches of asphalt were still visible, so I could navigate my way from dark spot to dark spot. But I knew I didn't have much time before the road completely disappeared.

More than once I thought of stopping at a farmhouse to ask for a place to stay. But the few scattered farmsteads were set far back from the road, and their long driveways were already hidden beneath a featureless blanket of snow. With the windchill dropping and the snow increasing, parking the car and attempting to walk to one of them could produce disastrous results. There was nothing to do but continue westward until I could find safe harbor in the small town I had seen on the map.

I inched my way forward, decreasing my speed as conditions deteriorated. Soon I was going no more than ten miles an hour. I kept on this way for about an hour until a faint glow appeared on the horizon. I wanted to speed up, but I knew that without proper winter survival clothing — an oversight I was regretting more and

more by the minute — skidding off the road a mile from the town
could have the same result as skidding off the road on the uninhab-
ited prairie. I had to remain patient.

By the time I reached the outskirts everything was buried in
snow. The town was only one street long, and it appeared to be completely shut down. There were a few lonely tire tracks cutting through
the fresh layer of white. But other than that, there was only the
ghostly haloed glow of the few streetlights casting their weak illumination on the empty main street.

There were no hotels or motels other than one darkened roadside inn on the edge of the highway leading out of town. I pushed the
nose of the Toyota through the fresh snow and banged on the door
until a disheveled old man who smelled of alcohol opened it a crack
and peered out at me.

"Everything's taken," he said. "Construction crew." He nodded
toward the parking lot. There were about ten pickup trucks sitting in
front of the units, all half buried in snow.

"I'll sleep on a couch. Anything," I said.

"Sorry. There's just no room. There's a place about twelve
miles up. You should be able to make it. But you'd better get going.
This feels like a big one."

He shut the door and turned off the porch light.

I was close to panic. Once again, I thought of pulling onto a side
street and sleeping in the car. But the wind was so raw and the air so
cold that I doubted I could survive. I considered going to the police
station to see if I could sleep in the jail, but then I realized that this
tiny prairie outpost had no police station or any other public services,
for that matter.

Finally, against my better judgment, I decided to make a run for
it. I tried to tell myself that it was only twelve miles, but in the back
of my mind were the stories of the old North Dakota farmers who
strung lines between their houses and their barns so they could make

it between the two during snowstorms without getting lost. Twelve miles was a lot farther than the distance from a barn to a house.

Within minutes of leaving the town I regretted my decision. But I dared not try to turn around on the snow-covered, featureless highway. If I slid off the shoulder, I would be trapped in the ditch until morning.

Visibility was approaching zero. My headlights did little more than illuminate the raging snowstorm a few feet in front of me. More than once I had to step out into the ripping wind to brush snow off the road to find the yellow line.

It took me almost three hours to make the twelve miles. I don't think I would have made it had a semi not come roaring by, kicking up a cyclone of snow and disappearing quickly into the night. How he was navigating I don't know, but I didn't care. I followed the red glow of his taillights until they disappeared into the mist, then set myself in his tracks and limped my way forward.

By the time I reached the town it was well past midnight. I was so weak with panic that I could barely hold the steering wheel.

The town was little bigger than the last one — a single main street with a few side streets. It could not have had a population of more than several hundred.

The silence of the great storm had overtaken everything. The roofs of the buildings were buried in huge drifts. The main street was dark except for a few streetlights casting feeble circles of light through the swirling snows. The only sound was the howling of the wind.

I drove through the town, searching desperately for any sign of life.

I did not see a motel anywhere. Finally, on the outskirts where the highway resumed, I caught sight of a small glow behind a darkened service station and café. A few semis had pulled over there and sat rumbling in the darkness with their trailer lights on. Across the

lot was a small cement building with a red and white painted sign
that read "Motel and Laundromat." The lights were off, but I could
see several cars in front of the units.

Almost giddy with relief, I pulled in, tightened my jacket around
my neck, and ran to the door.

A light came on inside, then a man with a long gray ponytail
peeked out from behind a curtain. I mouthed, "I need a room."
Slowly, he opened the door against the pummeling wind. "Thirty
bucks. No credit cards," he said.

I gratefully traded three tens for a key and fought my way
through the snow to my unit. I could barely stand up against the
gale. After I had made several futile attempts to fit the key into
the frozen lock, the door creaked open. I stepped inside, turned on
the space heater, and collapsed on the bed. My hands were so numb
I could barely pick up the phone. No sound came from the receiver.
The storm must have blown down the phone lines. I tried my cell
phone, but there was no service. I knew that Louise would be frantic, but there was nothing I could do.

I pulled off my shoes, crawled under the covers, and fell into a
deep sleep, wondering how the Native people had ever managed to
survive on a land like this.

I AWOKE TO A SEA OF WHITE OUTSIDE MY WINDOW. I could see the
occasional faint flashing light of a snowplow as it moved along the
highway. Other than that, everything was a whirling maelstrom of
wind and flakes.

I pulled on my boots and gloves and stepped out of the motel
unit. My car looked like a snow-covered boulder. Across the lot the
muted lights of the adjacent trucker café glowed in the morning
darkness. Apparently someone had managed to make it in to work
the morning shift.

The wind was cruel and steady, punctuated by vicious gusts that cut and burned the flesh. I had to lean into it to keep from being blown backward. I thought of Dan's grandmother huddling in the gully at Wounded Knee creek with winds like these screaming across the landscape. It was impossible to imagine the terror and suffering she must have experienced as she hid from the soldiers and the raking fire of their Hotchkiss guns.

Whoever had made it in to the café had gotten a pot of coffee going. Five or six truckers were hunched over on stools, trading stories and waiting for the storm to subside. Their rigs idled outside, rumbling like huge animals.

Someone's walkie-talkie was scratching in from Brandon, Manitoba. It issued forth unintelligible squawks that the truckers seemed to ignore.

"Anyone know how long this is going to last?" I asked. I assumed they had radios and weather bands that gave them decent information.

"Snow should be done by noon," one of the truckers said. "But there's ice under everything west. Where you trying to go?"

"I'm trying to get to the sanitarium up by Dunseith," I said.

The waitress looked at me strangely. "There's nothing up there," she said. "It's been closed for years."

"I'll go anyway," I said.

"Not today, you won't," the trucker said. "Not unless you want to slide off the road and freeze to death."

"That wasn't plan A," I said.

"Well, for today it's plan A, B, and C."

He turned away from me and resumed drinking his coffee. He had no further interest in a foolhardy traveler who thought he was bigger than the weather.

I sat glumly on my stool. The wind outside was blowing the snow in sheets.

"Well, I guess plan D is to sit and wait," I said.

"Better than the others," the trucker said distractedly.

I paid for my cup of coffee and walked over to the ancient pay-phone that hung on the wall by the restrooms. At least I could call home and set Louise's mind at ease. I picked up the receiver. The line was dead.

"Everything's down," the waitress said. "Probably ice on the lines."

I took my coffee and hurried back across the lot to my motel room.

I tried the TV, but it offered nothing but static. The only book in the place was the Gideon Bible. I sat morosely on the stiff-backed chair, drinking my weak truck stop coffee, listening to weather and farm reports on the bedside radio, and wondering what I had done and what I should do next.

THE TRUCKER WAS RIGHT. By noon the snow had stopped and the wind had abated. The storm had passed, leaving a glistening blue sky arching over a sea of white flatness that stretched as far as the eye could see. Plows were going by on the highway kicking rooster tails of snow twenty feet into the air. A few pickup trucks with four-wheel drive had ventured out and were cutting tracks through the fresh snow. Slowly, life was returning to normal.

I wanted to try to make it to the sanitarium. Perhaps there was nothing there, but I wanted to see it. And I might be able to find some archives in the local library or some old photos at the newspaper office. But I had to trust the truckers, who said that the roadbed was covered with ice. I had driven enough on such roads to know that ice could be more treacherous than snow. It could be almost invisible — "black ice," as it was called — and could spin your car off the road without warning. Those guys were the pros. If they said not to drive it, I wasn't going to drive it. The best counsel was to wait things out. The radio would alert me when the roads were passable.

I tried the phone in the room one more time. I was desperate to get to Louise to let her know I was all right, but there was no way I could contact her until service was restored. The line offered a few clicks and nothing else. I put the receiver back on the hook and went out to clear the snow off the car.

A few blocks of Main Street had been plowed. With the sky clear I could get a better feel for the town. It didn't offer much in the way of entertainment. There was a café, a grocery store, a few second-hand shops, and a bar. The roads heading out of town were still snowed under, so there was no way I could drive out to look at the surrounding landscape, even if I wanted to risk the ice. I was stuck either in my motel room, in a bar or restaurant, or in second-hand stores looking at ceramic ducks and old magazines. None of the options seemed very appealing.

A few shopkeepers were out with snowblowers, and several pickups were parked on diagonals in front of the stores. Other than that, nothing moved.

At the corner of one of the cross streets there was a small sign that said "County museum. Two blocks." Lacking anything better to do, I decided to see if it was open. I turned onto the side street and fishtailed my way through the snow in the direction the sign had pointed.

The museum, too, was completely snowed in. It was housed in an old two-story school building constructed of yellow brick — a remnant of better days when the small towns hadn't lost all their young people and children still grew up to take over the family farms. Now, like so many others in the Dakotas, it had been con-verted to a secondary use — in this case, a repository for the vari-ous artifacts of farm life that had been donated and bequeathed by locals over the years. A cardboard sign taped to the window read "Closed until Spring. For Winter entrance inquire next door."

An old 1880s farmhouse in a state of substantial disrepair sat on the lot next to the school. It probably had once been the principal's home but now it appeared to be the residence of someone who was either too old or too poor to put any effort into upkeep. The roof of the porch sagged, and the white siding was peeled and flaking.

I waded through the snow and knocked on the door. A woman with white hair pushed back a lace curtain and stared out at me. I pointed toward the school and mouthed the word *museum*. She smiled and unlocked the door.

"Sorry to bother you," I said. "But I'm stranded here for the day. I'd love to get a look at your museum."

"Oh, I'm sorry," she said. "I should have shoveled. Just a minute. I'll get the key." She hurried back into the house and returned wearing heavy boots and a green army parka. "You caught me by surprise," she said. "We don't get many visitors this time of year."

We trudged through the snow toward the old school building. The woman kept up a running commentary on how the town used to be such a thriving place and how the residents had gotten together and purchased the building when the county was going to tear it down. She was obviously proud of the museum and pleased to show it to a visitor.

"It'll be kind of cold until the heat gets going," she said. "It's the original furnace."

"I'll be fine," I said. "It's actually rather pleasant now that the wind has died down."

Instinctively, we both looked up at the cobalt blue sky. There was a sparkle to everything, and the air held an invigorating freshness.

"Yes, it's a good place to live," she said. "It's just too bad all the young people are moving away."

CHAPTER TWENTY-FIVE

◇◇◇◇◇◇◇◇◇◇◇◇◇◇◇◇◇◇◇◇◇◇◇◇◇◇◇◇◇◇

ONE WHITE EYE

The schoolhouse door creaked as she pushed it open. She was right; the place was cold — cold and musty. If they heated it at all in the winter, it was only minimally. You could see your breath in the dark, frigid air.

The woman pressed an old round-buttoned light switch, and a few overhead bulbs flickered on, illuminating a long hallway lined with oak display cases.

She pushed another button, and somewhere far below me an old gravity furnace boomed once and kicked into life.

"We don't generally open in the winter unless someone asks," she said. "It costs too much to heat."

Chuffs of warmth began to come up through black metal floor grates. They blew balls of dust before them.

"Is there anything in particular you'd like to see?" she asked.

"Not really. Unless you have something about the sanitarium up by Dunseith."

"We might have a few newspaper articles. Everything else would probably be up at St. John."

"That's fine," I said. "Maybe we can look at them before I leave. I'll just wander around, if it's all right with you. It looks like an amazing little museum."

The woman beamed. "Take your time," she said. "I've got nothing I have to do."

I wandered from room to room. The woman stayed close behind me, making frequent apologies and offers of assistance and explanation.

The schoolrooms had been divided into smaller cubicles, and each one was filled with display cases and wall shelves stacked high with a confusing welter of historical artifacts that ranged from old frontier rifles to spinning bobbins. Rough efforts had been made to establish some sense of order to the collection, but the sheer profusion of objects had defied any attempts at meaningful categorization.

One room was filled with old army uniforms and bayonets and a few Nazi helmets and insignia that some local soldier had brought back from World War II. In another there were shelves of kitchen utensils and old mannequins wearing faded lace dresses. What might have once been the gym contained several model T's, some old tractors, and an ancient threshing machine.

"That was Mr. Tanglen's," the woman said proudly. "He got a patent on it. One of the first anywhere for a threshing machine."

I continued through the building, marveling at the spears from Borneo, the tea sets from England, and the boxes of bones that were allegedly pieces of a dinosaur skeleton that had been unearthed during a sewer excavation. The woman stayed close to me, turning the lights on whenever I entered a room, and turning them off as I left.

I entered one small room and found myself face-to-face with a giant grizzly bear in a glass case. It was rising up on its hind legs and must have been nine feet tall. "Mr. Thorvaldsen was a big game hunter. We have a leopard in the back room. We don't have it on display right now because it's coming apart."

There were collections of dental tools, framed newspaper clippings about a grain elevator fire and a visit from Alf Landon, and a clumsy re-creation of an old post office, complete with a stiff, life-size dummy wearing a postal uniform and sticking a letter into a postal box.

"This is quite a place," I said.

The woman beamed even more broadly. I was spending far more time and showing far more interest than she had expected. "Oh, yes, we've had a lot of interesting people in this town. You know how farmers love to collect things."

She turned on the light in a room full of stuffed birds and Indian artifacts. There were several heavily beaded buckskin dresses hanging on the wall and two old ornately carved pipes lying on their sides in a glass case.

"You shouldn't have the stems attached to the bowls," I said. "They're supposed to be kept separate except when they're being smoked."

"Are you Native American?" she asked.

"Hardly," I laughed. "It's just something I picked up along the way."

I walked to the far corner, where a small glass cube sat on a display stand. It contained a little doll positioned on a piece of red velvet. The typed display card said "Sioux doll, 1890–1930." It was sewn from a rough burlaplike cloth and dressed in a worn buckskin shirt and pants with fringes and delicately applied beadwork. It was flopped forward like a marionette whose strings had been cut.

A wave of wistfulness came over me; this was very likely the exact kind of doll that little Yellow Bird had played with during her days at the boarding school.

The woman was watching me from the doorway. "They were very talented people, weren't they," she said.

"Yes," I said. "Very talented."

I bent down to examine the doll more closely. Even in the shadows the precision of the workmanship was evident. The buckskin shirt had a perfectly sewn line of white beads down its center, and the cuffs of the shirt and pants were decorated with a delicate border of alternating sky blue and deep ebony beadwork.

I felt close to tears. I could imagine the "grandmas," as Dan called them, sitting in the room with Dan's little sister, using dolls like this to carry on a conversation with the little girl who could barely hear and had lost the courage to speak.

"I can turn on the light in the case if you like," the woman said.

"Please."

She plugged in an extension cord in the far corner of the room, and a small light in the top of the display cube flickered on. With the cube illuminated I could see the little doll more clearly. It was little more than a cloth gingerbread man sewn from two pieces of rough fabric and stuffed with cotton or mattress ticking, but each stitch had been sewn with accuracy and love. On its feet were two little moccasins, each delicately beaded. Fringes of leather, perfectly cut and perfectly spaced, hung down from the shirt cuffs to approximate fingers.

I tried to look at the face, but it was hidden in shadow. I could see a thin line of black beads forming a simple half-smile, and two large almond-shaped eyes made from tightly spaced, pearlescent white beads. Even in the half-light I could feel its simplicity and sadness.

"Would you like me to bring it out?" the woman asked.

"I'd like that very much," I said.

She walked over and carefully removed the doll from the back of the case. She cradled it gently in her hands and held it toward me.

"Doesn't it have a lot of feeling?" she said.

"Yes, it's amazing."

She shifted it in the light so I could see its face better. As she turned it, I felt a shock of recognition. One eye had a single black bead in its center, and the other was completely white.

"Have you ever noticed that this doll has one white eye?" I asked.

"Yes," she answered. "I've wondered about that. I just figured maybe the person who made it ran out of black beads."

"I suppose that's possible. What do you know about its history?"

"Not very much. It was donated by a woman who used to live around here. Would you like me to pull out the accession materials?"

"Please."

She placed the doll on the counter and went into another room. With the woman gone I was able to examine the doll more closely. It lay on its back staring up at me. The edges of its eyes were turned slightly downward, giving its expression an air of ineffable melancholy.

"Yellow Bird," I said quietly. The little doll stared back at me in mute loneliness. I was tempted to pick it up but chose not to. There was something inviolable about its sadness.

I could hear the woman shuffling some papers and closing some file drawers. Soon she returned with a small note card.

"This is all we have. It doesn't say much," she said, squinting at the small card covered with typing. "Just that this was a children's doll and that the woman who donated it had wanted the museum to have it. She worked out at the sanitarium you mentioned. The one near Dunseith. She was very interested in Indian affairs."

"Does it say anything else about her? About the doll?"

The woman examined the card closely. "No," she said. "The doll was the only thing she gave to the museum. It doesn't say if she died or went back to the old country. Maybe she was German. Germans weren't too popular around here after the wars."

"Thank you," I said. "You were very kind to show this to me."

"You're very welcome."

She cocked her head and stared closely at me. "You're sure you're not Native American?"

"No, not even a bit. I'm just a traveler. And a father."

She nodded kindly, as if she understood. "Yes, it is very beautiful. Someone was a very lucky child."

"Yes. Very lucky." Far below us the furnace huffed and boomed. The woman put the doll back in the case and turned off the light in the room.

I took the hint and headed for the door.

"Could I make a donation?" I said.

Her face brightened. "That would be wonderful. It costs a lot to heat this old building."

"And a good building it is," I said.

I pulled out my checkbook and began to write.

"Just out of curiosity, do you know where the woman lived? The one who donated the doll?"

CHAPTER TWENTY-SIX

◇◈◇◈◇◈◇◈◇◈◇◈◇◈◇◈◇◈◇◈◇◈◇◈◇◈◇◈◇◈◇◈◇

SECRET IN THE SNOWS

I made my way out of town toward the west. The plows had made a first pass through the snows, and the road was marginally drivable.

The woman had been mystified by my interest. "There's nothing out there," she said. "No one has lived there for years."

Nonetheless, she had given me very specific and accurate directions. "It's about six miles out," she said. "It will be pretty well hidden by the brush and trees. Watch for a big oak with a broken branch. The house is back in about a quarter of a mile."

I was alive with anticipation and excitement; I was convinced that the doll in the museum had been made by little Yellow Bird. Part of my certainty had to do with the white eye, but part of it had to do with the ineffable sadness of its expression.

In the months since I first visited Dan, Yellow Bird had become as alive to me as my own children. I had revisited the stories Dan had told about her, stared at the faded photo, and even encountered her in my dreams.

I often felt I could feel her presence. The loneliness of her deafness, the sadness of her separation from her family, rose up from behind the fierce defiance of the face in the photo and gave me no rest. The father in me kept seeing past that hard gaze to the little child, so alone, so frightened, so bereft of human connection. When I had looked at that little doll, in some way that I couldn't explain, I had felt I was staring into the face of little Yellow Bird herself.

The day had turned bright and beautiful. The landscape was a sea of glistening white. About every half mile a windbreak of trees led up to a dense copse of cottonwoods and oak that sheltered an old farmhouse. Some had smoke coming from the chimneys. Others were cold and abandoned. A few had drives that were already plowed out, allowing the residents to make their way carefully into town.

I kept track of the distances on my odometer until I caught sight of an old oak sticking its spiny fingers into the sky. A single branch hung down from one of its limbs, as if the limb had been hit by lightning and had split almost in two. An abandoned farmstead stood about a quarter mile from the road, set off from the surrounding fields by a perimeter of perfectly spaced trees that had been planted generations ago to serve as a shelter break against the relentless prairie winds. Through the trees and brush I could see a gray weathered two-story farmhouse set back in the shadows. A few small outbuildings were hidden farther back in the brush. Snow had blown up to their sides, half covering them in frozen waves of white. The windows on the house were gone, and the front door stood partially open. It was obvious that the place was empty and unvisited; aside from a few animal tracks, the snow was undisturbed.

I stopped my car on the side of the road and made my way toward the house. The snow was almost knee-deep. It crunched as I broke through its crust and burned my ankles as it soaked through the cuffs of my pants and made its way down into my boots.

More than once I had to stop to catch my breath from the effort of breaking tracks through the heavy drifts. But I had to get to this house. I sensed that somehow it would lead me to some answers about Yellow Bird.

I made it up to the front porch and stood bent over with my hands on my knees, breathing hard. The wind in the trees made a hollow, rushing sound.

I pushed at the front door. It creaked on its hinges and gave way slowly into a gutted, trash-strewn living room.

The windows all were broken out. Shards of glass stuck up from their frames like jagged teeth. Drifts of snow had piled up in corners. All the furniture was gone except for a few broken wooden chairs. Tongues of wallpaper hung ragged from the walls.

An old wood cookstove had been dragged from the kitchen and tipped over in the middle of the room. The floor was covered with books and papers and pieces of clothing that had been scattered by vandals who had ransacked the house. Animal scat was everywhere.

I wandered among the detritus, trying to find something that would give the place an identity or a life. But the rooms were decayed beyond recognition.

In the kitchen the cabinets had been torn from the walls and the drawers pulled out and scattered on the floor. The window was broken, and a ragged piece of lace curtain flapped in the wind.

I knew it was dangerous, but I felt compelled to climb to the second floor. If this had been Yellow Bird's house, her bedroom would have been up there.

I walked carefully up the broken stairs. In some places the risers were cracked and broken. In others, you could see all the way through to the basement stairway below.

All the doors on the second floor had been torn from their hinges. The wind blew in through the empty windows, skiffing snow across the bedroom floors.

In one room a rotting mattress had been pulled into a corner by some long-departed squatter or vagrant. Weathered magazines and a melted candle lay next to it on the floor. In another, the sloped ceiling had been pulled open, revealing the boards and framing. There was nothing anywhere to give the place a character and an identity except for the intricate flower pattern on the faded wallpaper. The years and the vagrants and the rot had erased all remnants of its personality.

I stepped carefully down the stairs and out the door. I was filled with an overwhelming sense of loss. It was just one more abandonment, one more place of memories and ghosts. For the first time I was truly beginning to understand why Dan had not pursued the whereabouts of his little sister. His lament by the fire — "too many deaths, Nerburn. There's too many deaths" — echoed with every footstep.

I moved carefully among the rotted boards on the porch and stepped into the yard. The brush and trees surrounding the property had kept the snow to a minimum. I crunched around the side of the house and into the back area. It was large and open — the kind of yard that once had been alive with family gatherings — and was surrounded on all sides by the protective perimeter of ash and elm.

Beyond the shelter break the endless fields stretched toward the horizon. Snow devils swirled and danced across them, lifting squalls of blowing snow above the featureless landscape. The wind moaned as it moved through the frozen fields.

On one tree a child's wooden swing hung by a single rope from a branch. It twisted and turned slowly in the wind. In one of the collapsing sheds a rusted cultivator lay half buried in snowdrifts on the frozen floor.

I tried to imagine life here — a child in the swing, someone digging in the garden, the summer afternoons spent staring into the distant flatness of the fields that stretched to the horizon in all directions.

It was equal parts loneliness and peace, and I was overwhelmed by an almost unbearable melancholy.

I pushed my way into a small pathway that cut through the bushes and brambles at the rear of the property. Perhaps, I thought, this led to a secret child's area where Yellow Bird had played.

The underbrush was thick and tangled. I had to hold my hands in front of my face to keep from being scratched by branches as I walked. Off to my left an old tin washtub lay filled with ice and frozen leaves. A rusted hand plow with its forked handles and curved blade lay buried in the snow to my right.

I was nearly to the edge of the property when a small fence sticking up from the snow caught my attention. Its pickets were weathered to the same gray as the frozen trees and were almost completely hidden in the underbrush and branches. Had it not been for their formal geometry I never would have noticed them.

I pushed my way through the snow until I reached the fence. It seemed a strange place for a garden, but I could not imagine what else would have prompted someone to frame off this little square in the middle of a thicket.

The garden was overgrown with brambles. I stepped over the low boundary into the center. The area was small — no more than fifteen feet on a side. The brambles were hard and sharp and formed an almost impassable tangle.

I put on my gloves and began pushing my way through them, when my boot hit something hard and I fell forward into the snow. I felt around with my hand and felt another hard shape. I brushed away the snow and saw a round hump of white stone.

I cleared more snow away. It was a gravestone. I kept brushing. Soon three more humped stones revealed themselves. They were small, only a foot or so tall, and no more than an inch or two thick. They were made from marble and were so weathered that the writing on them was almost unreadable.

I wiped the snow away from one that seemed the least weathered; it had a crude carving on the top of two hands clasping each other. The writing was in an archaic script and had been worn almost beyond recognition. I recognized the word *mother* and a name that looked like Thorvilson or Thorwaldson.

I cleared the snow away from the others. They, too, were weathered almost beyond recognition. I got down on my knees and began pushing snow away from the whole grave area. On the ground I could feel several stones lying flat. I uncovered them as best I could, trying to read the names and the dates.

Out beyond the trees the afternoon light was fading, and the wind was gaining strength.

I dug into the snow more forcefully. I felt desperate — almost dirty — as if I was in violation of something sacred.

Ingvar. Nikolai. 1897. 1913.

The snow soaked through the knees of my pants, got beneath the cuffs of my gloves, and cut into my wrists.

Mother. Wilhelmina. Two crudely carved figures facing outward. *Infant. Brother.*

One by one, the stones revealed themselves. The growing wind blew the snow back across them almost as quickly as I could brush them free. It was almost as if nature herself wanted this place to remain undiscovered. But I couldn't stop. If Yellow Bird was buried here, I had to know.

Through the spidery branches I could see the daylight fading. The sky had turned a brittle, lifeless copper, and the graveyard was sinking into shadow.

I crawled to the edge of the fence; only the perimeter remained to be checked. I moved along it in the growing darkness. But there were no more stones. All the graves were in the center.

Without warning, the loneliness and the cold overcame me, and I began shivering uncontrollably. I suddenly had a vision of myself on my hands and knees in the snow, several hundred miles from my home, crawling through some family's forgotten graveyard in an abandoned homestead on the North Dakota prairie, trying to find the remnant of some little girl who had disappeared from everywhere except an old man's heart. It was a ghostly echo of Dan's fruitless search on that lonely hilltop cemetery months before.

Without meaning to, I started to cry. I took the glove from one hand to wipe the tears before they began to freeze. The sky in the distance was losing its light.

"I'm sorry, Dan," I said out loud. "I tried. I did the best I could."

The wind keened and whistled and rattled through the branches. I brushed the snow from my knees and stepped toward the fence. I was filled with an overwhelming sense of violation and shame.

Then I saw it — a small, handmade wooden cross sticking out of the snow in the far corner of the graveyard. It had weathered to the color of old bone and was almost invisible among the drifts. It was not attached to a grave but was merely propped up against the fence, as if it had fallen over and someone had not wanted to throw it away.

I knelt down in front of it. Though the night was turning dark and the whole graveyard was in shadow, it was possible to see the words written crudely on the cross member in fading black paint: *Sarah, Indian Girl.*

On the vertical stick was the date, 1927.

❖◇❖◇❖◇❖◇❖◇❖◇❖◇❖◇❖◇❖◇❖◇❖◇❖◇❖◇

CHAPTER TWENTY-SEVEN

A HARD WINTER

I stood in the wind outside the bar digging through my billfold for the small slip of paper that Orv had given me the previous summer. I could barely contain my excitement to get in touch with Dan and let him know what I had found.

Phone service had been partially restored at the motel, and I was able to get a quick call through to Louise before the conversation was drowned out in a welter of static and crackling and the line went dead.

The motel manager had suggested the payphone outside the bar. "They get good service there," he said. "The owner's brother works for the phone company."

I stood in the frigid night air trying to read the numbers on the piece of paper. It had worn through along the crease where it had been folded, and the digits were almost illegible. A few flakes of snow drifted slowly down through the arcing glow of the streetlight. The night sky had burst forth into a wonderland of stars.

Eventually I was able to decipher the number and place the call using an ancient phone card that had been tucked in a corner of my billfold. I was nervous and excited. This was the phone call I had dreamed of making.

The phone on the other end rang and rang. I expected an answering machine to pick up, but the ringing just continued. I started to feel sheepish for letting it go on so long.

I was about to hang up when I heard a click on the other end of the line.

"This is Orv."

It was the same soft tone that I remembered from our time at the sweat. His gentle manner seemed a million miles from the star-drenched darkness of the North Dakota night.

"Hi, Orv, this is Kent Nerburn. I was out there with Dan and Grover and Jumbo last summer. We did a sweat together."

"Yeah, I remember. The guy who likes trees."

"Yeah, that's me. Listen, I'm way up by the Canadian border at an outside pay phone. It's colder than hell, and I need to get a message to Dan."

I could hear labored breathing on the other end of the line. The pause went on longer than I liked.

"Dan's okay, isn't he?" I asked.

The phone line remained silent.

"Orv?"

"Yeah?"

"He's okay, right?"

"He's had a hard winter," he said. His voice was slow and deliberate.

"But he's . . . I mean, he's making it?"

"He's doing better."

A thousand thoughts ran through my mind. Perhaps Dan had fallen ill. Perhaps he'd slipped into senility. Maybe my failure to contact him had sent him into a decline.

"I think I've found something about his little sister," I said, hoping to justify my being out of touch for so long a time. "I met a woman who remembered her from boarding school."

I started to explain about the doll and the museum and the graveyard by the house, but Orv interrupted me.

"You probably should talk to Wenonah," he said.

"Sure. I'm sorry. You're right." I was fumbling for words. "Do you have her number?"

"Her phone's been cut off. Call back tomorrow morning. I'll see what I can do." Then the phone went silent.

I placed the receiver back on the hook. The abruptness of the conversation had come as a shock. I had hoped for something more — some excitement, some warmth. But all I'd felt was distance.

I walked back to my car under the canopy of stars. I knew that Dan was not central to Orv's life, but still, this was not what I had expected.

A few flakes floated down through the pale glow of the streetlight. A solitary pickup churned its way down the snowy main street and disappeared into the night. The snow on the sides of the sidewalk was piled as high as my waist.

I drove back slowly in the direction of the motel. Maybe Orv was just not at ease with the telephone, I told myself. Or maybe I had interrupted him in the middle of something important. But I couldn't shake the sense that his curt manner spoke of something deeper.

I let myself into the motel room and lay down on the hard bed. Television service had not been restored, and I had nothing to read. I turned on the bedside radio and listened to some distant evangelist go on about salvation, then turned it off and stared up at the ceiling.

The wall heater coughed out a dusty warmth. I tried the phone again, but it was all clicks and crackles. I was left alone with my thoughts about Orv and the tiny farmstead graveyard and the little cloth doll slumped over in a dark display case in the corner of a cold, unvisited museum.

THE NIGHT PASSED SLOWLY. I thrashed and tossed, unable to sleep. Orv's manner had sapped me of all confidence. Was that really Yellow Bird's doll? Was that really Yellow Bird's grave?

More than once I almost got up and drove out to the farmstead to reassure myself. But it made no sense. There was nothing I could find, and the night was too dark, the roads too uncertain.

By morning I hadn't slept more than half an hour. I wanted to call Orv as soon as the light came up. But I knew I had to wait. His house was many miles from Wenonah's. And winter there could be as brutal as it was here. If he had to talk to her in person, there was no reason to think that he would get to her before late morning.

I sat in the half light of my dingy room drinking weak motel coffee and listening to farm reports on the radio.

I kept trying the phone, hoping for a dial tone. By eleven I could wait no longer. I tried one last time before going back to the phone outside the bar. There were a few clicks, then a long dull buzz. It was hollow and scratchy, but it was a connection.

I dialed the number and waited. I could feel my pulse racing.

Again, the phone rang interminably before someone picked it up. Finally, a voice came on the other end of the line.

"This is Orv."

"Hi, Orv. It's Nerburn again. I hope I didn't wake you up."

"Nah, I get up with the roosters. If I had a rooster."

I breathed a sigh of relief. This was the human touch I had wanted.

"Did you get a chance to talk to Wenonah?"

There was some muffled conversation on the other end of the line.

"Here," he said. There was more muffled conversation, then

clunking and banging as the phone was passed from one hand to another.

"Nerburn?"

It was Wenonah's voice. She sounded distant and accusatory.

"You should have called. He's been waiting."

"I know. I'm sorry. But I didn't want to get his hopes up."

"You didn't need to get his hopes up. You just needed to let him know that you hadn't abandoned him. He's had bad luck with white people in his life."

"I know. And I didn't want to be one of those white people."

"You would have been if he had died. Now tell me what's going on. Orv said something about a doll and a grave."

I told her about the museum and the doll and the old grave marker.

"Tell me more about the doll," she said. Her manner remained cold and distant.

I described the fringed hands and the face and the delicately beaded moccasins. "And it's got one white eye, just like Dan."

"Maybe she ran out of beads."

It was the same thing the museum caretaker had said. But Wenonah's tone was derisive, almost abusive.

"Come on, Wenonah," I said. "A cross with the name *Sarah*? A little doll with one white eye? A woman who worked at the sanitarium and took in Indian kids? What more do you need?"

Her voice remained flat and unemotional. "I need to be sure," she said. "This will be grandpa's last journey. It had better be a good one."

"It will," I said. "I promise."

There was a long pause on the other end of the line, as if she was considering what to say next.

"Well, he can't come now. He got pneumonia over the winter. He's pretty weak."

"But he's going to be okay, isn't he?"

"Nice of you to ask."

"I'm sorry. I just want him to see this."

"So do I. But he has to be able to get there."

"When do you think that will be?"

"I don't know. Whenever he gets well. He's waited this long. If it happens, it happens. If he dies, well, then that's what happens."

Her tone and manner angered me. They seemed filled with blame directed at me. It was not my fault that Dan had waited eighty years to look for his sister. It was not my fault that the path had gotten cold or that the old man had fallen sick. If anything, I deserved some thanks for staying with the search and some praise for what I had discovered. I was tempted to tell her so, but I resisted. It was more important that we work together to get Dan healthy and up to the gravesite.

Besides, she was his granddaughter. She wanted him to have peace and resolution as much as I did. If she thought he couldn't travel, she was probably right. But I wished I could talk to Dan to see how much risk he wanted to take. I was sure he would have wanted to come, no matter how infirm he was.

I hung up the phone and stared out the window.

The storm had passed. The roads were clear. There was nothing to do but return to my home and wait.

The Gathering Dawn

◇◇◇◇◇◇◇◇◇◇◇◇◇◇◇◇◇◇◇◇◇◇◇◇◇◇◇◇

CHAPTER TWENTY-EIGHT

VIGIL

February came, then March. At first I met each day with anticipation. I was certain that, despite her brusque manner, Wenonah wanted Dan to see the gravesite as much as I did. She knew how much it meant to him; she had been the most upset about the failure of our journey to the boarding school and the cemetery.

But slowly, as the days turned to weeks, I realized that this was going to be neither a short nor an easy vigil. As I sat in my home, day after day, occupying myself with other projects and waiting for the phone call, I saw far too clearly how much burden my silence must have been on the old man. Every ring of the phone had me rushing to the receiver; every call that was not about Dan filled me with disappointment.

Several times I almost called Wenonah simply to apologize for my insensitivity, but I knew it would involve contacting Orv or Jumbo and waiting for a return call, and when the call came there would really be nothing I could say. Wenonah would listen, give some terse answer, and hang up, convinced that my real purpose had been to pressure her to force Dan to take the journey. And, in some sense, she would have been right.

So I went about my life, allowing my anticipation to settle into a dull yearning and wondering if there was more I could have done — more I should have done — to have learned about little Yellow Bird's fate more quickly.

Once I did call Orv to ask about Dan's health, and I even put in a call to Jumbo. But neither of them had anything more to offer than, "He's doing okay." In each case I hung up feeling sheepish and intrusive.

Eventually, I decided that I had no choice but to accept Wenonah's fatalistic position that "if it happens, it happens. If he dies, well, then that's what happens." Still, it was not easy for me. To occupy my mind, I set about researching everything from Lakota dolls to childhood tuberculosis to the background of the woman who had donated the doll.

I learned more about the strange sanitarium on the hill in the middle of North Dakota and about the outing program where young Indian children were sent to live in white homes instead of being allowed to return to their families. Everything I discovered made my heart ache even more for the sad fate of little Yellow Bird, but nothing shed more light on her life. She truly had disappeared into the shadows of history.

By late April I had almost decided to go back to the farmstead and take some photos to bring to Dan just to give him some feeling for his sister's fate, when I received a phone call early on a Sunday morning.

"It's an Indian. A woman," Louise mouthed as she handed me the phone. "I think it's Wenonah."

I was torn between anticipation and dread. This was either the phone call I longed for or the phone call I feared. I grabbed the receiver and tried to answer as normally as I could.

"Hello."

"Nerburn?"

"Wenonah?"

"We can come now." There was no explanation or elaboration or casual conversation.

"So, your grandpa's feeling better?"

"He's good. Where is this place?"

"It's in North Dakota, up by the Canadian border."

I told her the name of the town and started to give her directions.

"We'll be there Tuesday," she said.

"This Tuesday?"

"We'll leave tomorrow."

"You want a phone number? Some way to get me?"

"Grover knows your car. And he knows the kind of place you stay."

I started to say something, but the line went dead. I stood there staring at the receiver as if it were some kind of alien animal.

Louise had been watching from the doorway. "Was it about Dan?" she asked. "Is he okay?"

I put the phone down and looked out the window. Our yard was just beginning to green up after shedding its blanket of winter snow.

"I guess so. Wenonah says he's ready to travel. They want to meet me up in North Dakota on Tuesday."

"At least he's alive."

"You could hardly tell from Wenonah. God, she's harsh."

"She's probably just being protective. Besides, it's not about her. It's about Dan."

"They're like fingers on a glove. You can't separate them."

"Maybe that's the way they have to be to survive."

She picked up her trowel and the flat of perennials she was preparing to plant. I looked longingly out at the garden and the trickling waters and the softly budding aspen.

"You'd better go pack," she said.

TUESDAY MORNING ARRIVED LIKE SOFT MUSIC. The sky was a gentle pastel blue, and the wind, for the first time since autumn, was warmer than the air. Sunlight flashed off the remaining snow patches like reflections off diamonds, and the puddles of water rippled and lapped in the breeze.

I was almost giddy as I packed the car. I had been so worried that Dan would not make it through the winter. But he had survived, and now his lifelong nightmare was about to come, if not to an end, at least to a resolution.

I knew it would be a bittersweet moment, but none of us had expected a joyous conclusion. I think we had all known that we would not find Yellow Bird alive. But what we had hoped and prayed for — some definitive knowledge and the blessed finality of closure — was finally upon us.

I was mildly apprehensive about showing Dan the doll in the museum and the cross in the graveyard. I hoped they would heal old wounds, not open new ones. But those were things I could not control. He had lived far longer than I and had played out these moments in the privacy of his imagination many times. How he responded was between him and his heart. I was merely the courier, and I had done the best I could.

I was most concerned about how he would respond to the little cross. I wished it had been something more — there was something pitiful and almost discarded about a makeshift wooden cross among the solidity of the weathered stones. But perhaps that was the way it was meant to be — a harsh reminder of how the Native people were slowly fading back into the earth while the Europeans were claiming it with the permanence of stone.

All I knew for certain was that I had found Yellow Bird and had gotten the information to Dan before he died, and that within a day he was going to be standing closer to his little sister than he had in the last eighty years.

I grabbed a few small gifts for Dan and whoever else came along with him, and set out on the day-long journey across the prairies to the lonely farm country on the border between North Dakota and Manitoba.

The change in season had wrought a magical transformation on the land. When I had last made this journey, I had been in danger for my life. Now the rich moistness of the air and the blue clarity of the sky lent a joyful brilliance to the day. The ditches on the sides of the lonely country roads danced with shimmering water. Songbirds rose in clumps from the fields and fluttered off toward the newly budding trees. Winter loneliness had turned to springtime hope. The entire landscape was alive with possibility and promise.

I wanted to arrive by early afternoon and get situated in the motel. Wenonah and Grover and Dan all knew the Toyota, and there was only one motel in town. I had no doubt they'd be able to find me.

My biggest concern was that they'd be met with the kind of steely indifference that often greeted groups of Indians driving across the country. Questions would be answered tersely, if they were answered at all, and every tone and gesture would be directed toward sending the single, unambiguous message, "Keep going. You're not welcome here."

I needed to forestall this, at least at the museum. Most of the old farmers preferred their Indians as artifacts and historical displays, not as real people with real interests and real needs. I had no idea how the woman at the museum, or whoever was now in charge, would respond to their presence.

I arrived in the town shortly after three and went directly to the old school building. The woman next door was raking last autumn's dead grass from her lawn. She was wearing a housedress and old black buckle overshoes. She recognized me immediately.

"Come back for another visit?" she asked.

"I couldn't stay away. One day wasn't enough to see all the sights."

She laughed cheerfully and leaned on her rake. "Now you're seeing our town at its best," she said. She held her hand out toward the horizon. "The peace of God's land." Songbirds hopped around in the tree branches above her head.

"An undiscovered treasure," I said.

"I think so. So did my husband. I wish we could convince some of the young people to stay, though."

"If you did, then you wouldn't have the school building for a museum," I said.

She stared off through the trees at the cloudless blue sky.

"Yes, I guess you're right. But still, it was so nice to hear the laughter of young children." She smiled at some private memory, then turned her attention back to me. "So, what can I do for you? Have you come to see the museum again?"

I told her about Dan and how I believed that little doll had belonged to his sister.

"He's about ninety now," I said. "This will be very special to him."

"I'll get the heat on," she said. "Those old buildings stay cold long into the summer."

I looked at the old swing set rusting in the yard behind the building and went off to get myself a room for the night.

◇◇◇◇◇◇◇◇◇◇◇◇◇◇◇◇◇◇◇◇◇◇◇◇◇◇◇◇◇◇◇

CHAPTER TWENTY-NINE

COLLECTING RENT
ON THE HOMELAND

The motel was as uninviting as I remembered it. But even it seemed less spartan in the gentle warmth of a springtime day.

A stale blast of must and mildew greeted me as I entered my unit. I opened the window to let in some fresh air, then took off my boots and lay down for a short nap. It was unlikely that Dan and Grover would arrive before early evening, and I was tired from the drive.

But I couldn't sleep. The hours alone in the car had given me time to think, and the approaching meeting had given life to my lingering doubts. How did I know for certain that it was Yellow Bird's grave that I had found? What if the doll was completely different from the kind Yellow Bird had played with, or if the one white eye was simply part of some stylistic tradition that was completely unrelated to Dan's affliction?

Wenonah's terse comment, "This will be his last trip," echoed in my mind. It was supposed to be a journey to peace and resolution, not one more journey of disappointment. I kept seeing Dan crawling around in that graveyard on his hands and knees, whimpering and crying like a lost child. I had to fight back the thought that I might be summoning him for one final betrayal.

I lay there watching the clock tick off the minutes. I had not anticipated this wave of self-doubt, and I berated myself for not having dug more deeply into the history of the woman and the sanitarium and the farm. But all that was past now. I had to trust that my initial instincts had been correct.

I fell into an uneasy sleep.

When I awoke the room was dark. The clock said 10:15.

I assumed Dan and the others had arrived while I had been sleeping and had booked themselves into another unit.

I looked out the window. The sky was dark, and there were no other vehicles in the lot.

I cursed myself for not having insisted that Wenonah give me some contact number. They could be lost, or the car could have broken down, or worse.

I tried to comfort myself with the thought that this was often the way it was with Indians. They might promise to be somewhere at a certain time, then just not show up. When pressed for an explanation, they'd say, "My cousin came over," or "I didn't have enough money for gas." Or they'd show up the next day, or two days later, and offer no explanation at all. I'd seen it a hundred times. This could easily be such a circumstance.

But in my heart I knew better. This trip had been so crucial to Dan; the sense of his time being short had been so much on everyone's mind. To blow it off as one more example of people operating on "Indian time" seemed like a forced explanation. Something had to be wrong.

I was about to contact the police when I heard the heavy rumble of a car outside the unit. I ran to the window and peered through the space between the curtains. It was Grover's old pea-green Buick,

followed closely by the big white four-door pickup I had seen parked
by Orv's on the night of the sweat.

I was about to open the door to greet them. But something
stopped me. I didn't want to appear as if I'd been waiting, and I felt
I should watch Dan for a moment to get a feel for how fragile he
really was.

I watched from behind the curtains as Grover parked next to my
wagon, got out, and went around to his trunk. In the flickering glow
of the dome light I could see Dan hunched in the passenger seat with
a blanket over his shoulders. He had lost a great deal of ground physically and was barely able to open the heavy car door and slide his
feet out onto the ground.

The sight took me aback. I had known he was sick, but this was
a far greater deterioration than I had expected. He looked old and
frail and helpless. I could understand why Wenonah had been so
insistent that he build up his strength before attempting the journey.

I hurried back and sat on the bed. Dan was a proud man, and I
didn't want him to know that I had seen him struggling to get out of
the car. I would let him gather himself and present himself in the
way he felt best, and I would show him the honor and respect that he
deserved.

In a few seconds I heard a thud on the door as if someone was
kicking it with his heel.

"You in there, Nerburn?" It was Grover's voice.

"It's open," I shouted. "Just give it a push."

The door opened a crack amid scraping and cursing. I could
hear Grover grunting as he maneuvered Dan's four-wheeled hospital wheelchair across the threshold. "Christ, old man. You get better treatment than the tribal chairman."

"I cause less trouble than the tribal chairman."

"Yeah, but I can't vote you out."

"Can't vote them out either."

The scraping and cursing continued.

I jumped up and hurried over to offer my assistance.

"Can I give you a hand?"

"No, just get the mutt out of the way," Grover shouted. "If the old man wasn't so slow I could run him over."

Bronson was running back and forth in front of Dan's chair. He had my old glove in his mouth. It had been chewed almost beyond recognition.

"Hey, Charles Bronson," I said. "Good to see you." I reached my hand toward him. "You bring me a present?"

"You better not try to take that from him," Dan said. "Or you'll remember why I named him Charles Bronson."

"It's a good thing he didn't grab an old pair of your underwear," Grover said. "That thing's bad enough."

Bronson sidewindered over to me, wagging his tail fiercely and holding the glove high in the air. Dan had tied a piece of buckskin festooned with ribbons around his neck.

"What's this all about?" I asked.

Grover grunted Dan across the threshold.

"The grandkids," Dan said. "They like to dress him up."

"I thought maybe he was in training to be a Fancy Dancer."

"He should be in training to be soup," Grover said.

Bronson sat up on his haunches like a prairie dog.

"Kids taught him that, too," Dan said. "He's a smart little bugger."

In the light of the motel room I could see Dan more clearly. His cheeks were sunken and his skin was sallow, and his hands were mottled and bruised. His fingers looked like chicken bones, and his knuckles were the size of walnuts. He had a star quilt draped over his shoulders and was slumped forward as if the weight of his own body was almost more than he could bear.

"How you doing, Dan?" I said.

He looked up at me and grinned. His eyes were red and watery.

"I'm doing okay, Nerburn," he said. "There's more behind me than there is in front of me, but I'm doing okay. Just an old leaf getting ready to fall off the tree."

He reached out to give me a handshake. His hands were too arthritic to open fully, so I just took his fingertips softly in mine.

"It's good to see you again, Dan," I said.

"It's good to see you, too, Nerburn," he said.

I gave Grover a nod to acknowledge his presence. He nodded back, then stepped into the shadows by the door.

Bronson had jumped back on Dan's lap and was staring up at me.

"I think he remembers me," I said.

"He remembers your damn glove," Grover said from the corner.

Dan looked over at Grover with disgust. "Nah, he's a smart little dog. He knows lots of stuff. That old Fatback knew what she was doing when she sent him to me. He's a real comfort in my old age." At the surge in attention, Bronson thumped his tail and pushed the glove against Dan's chest.

Grover took a few steps toward the door. "I'm going to take off. The old man said he wants to talk to you alone. Which unit are we in?"

I looked at him quizzically.

He stood there picking at his teeth with a toothpick. "Well, where are we supposed to sleep? We can't all sleep in here."

"You're serious, aren't you?" I said.

"I'm always serious."

"You're always serious with my money."

"Just collecting some back rent on our homeland."

Dan shook his head as if to say, "Get this over with."

"Just tell the guy at the desk to put it on my card," I said, making no attempt to hide my disgust.

Grover stepped over and gave me a mock punch on my shoulder. "That's the spirit," he said. "Respecting the elders."

He put his hand on the door handle and started across the threshold.

"You could order a couple of pizzas, too. That would be a real sign of respect."

He gave me a little salute and walked out into the night.

CHAPTER THIRTY

◇◆◇◆◇◆◇◆◇◆◇◆◇◆◇◆◇◆◇◆◇◆◇◆◇◆◇◆◇◆◇

THE LONGEST NIGHT

With Grover gone, Dan's whole manner changed. He exhaled heavily and looked up at me with tired, smiling eyes.

"It's been a hard winter, Nerburn," he said. "Really hard. I think I might have crossed over a couple of times."

Though said without malice, his comment cut deep.

"I'm sorry I didn't call, Dan," I said. "I should have been more considerate. I just didn't have anything. I didn't want to get your hopes up."

He waved his hand several times as if to silence me. "That's okay. I knew you'd call when the time was right. It probably kept me alive. I just wasn't sure whether you or the Great Spirit would get to me first. I was afraid maybe you were working on Indian time."

He broke into a phlegmy cackle that rattled far down in his lungs.

"Damn," he said. "Can't seem to kick this thing. Get me a cup of water."

I hurried to the sink, unwrapped a motel drinking glass, and filled it with water. He took a couple of sips, cleared his throat again, and spit a wad of speckled green phlegm into the glass before handing it back to me.

"Is there anything else I can get for you?" I said.

"Nah. Water's good. I'm just glad I made it here."

"So am I."

I wanted to be respectful, but I was anxious to tell him what I'd discovered about his sister. "You want to know what I found out about Yellow Bird?" I said.

He flapped his hand again and spit into the cup. "Nah, not tonight. I've waited eighty years. I can wait a few more hours. I just want to sit and talk a bit."

His lack of urgency took me aback. I had thought that he'd want to hear about his little sister right away.

He pointed to the back of his left hand. An old dirty bandage of the kind they put on you when you have an IV in a hospital was stretched across a purple bruise, and he still had a plastic hospital bracelet around his wrist.

"I spent a couple of weeks in one of those white-man hospitals," he said. "You get a lot of time to think when you're in there. They won't let you do nothing or go anywhere, and they got tubes in you and wires on you and they're staring in every hole you got. I went down a lot of old trails in my mind while I was there. Met up with a few things that I want to get off my mind."

He dug his heels into the worn motel carpet and pulled himself across to a little table at the edge of the room.

"Come over here," he said, pointing to the chair on the other side of the table. "Sit down there."

I pulled the chair out and sat down in it. "Nah, not there. Right across from me. I don't like it when people listen to me sideways."

He broke into another paroxysm of coughing.

"Let me get you some more water," I said.

"Just give me that one," he said, pointing to the cup full of phlegm. "It's the same stuff coming up as it was going down. Just a little thicker."

I ignored his comment and placed a fresh glass of water in front of him. He took a sip from it, then spat again into the glass.

"A high-class motel would have a coffee can for this stuff," he said.

He rolled himself closer to the table. "You got them white man's ears with you?"

I reached in my shirt pocket and pulled out my old cassette recorder. Its battered plastic case was now held together with duct tape.

"Starting to look like an Indian machine," he said.

"Going Native," I answered.

He chortled a few times and hacked up some more phlegm.

"Christ," he said, "it's rattly in there. I better get going. Get those ears working."

I pressed the "Record" button, and the wheels of the old tape recorder squeaked into life.

Bronson heard the squeaking and lifted his head. He put his front paws on the edge of the table and looked curiously at the recorder. "He keeps track of things," Dan said. Bronson looked up at Dan, then back at the machine, then back at the old man. Dan nodded, and the little dog relaxed and took his place back in Dan's lap.

Dan exhaled deeply and lapsed into a long silence. He mouthed some words in Lakota, then touched his thumb and finger to his lips and began to speak in English.

"I'm going to speak now," he said. "These are things I want you to hear."

He had assumed the formal manner of speech that he used when talking about something important.

"I have been alive a long time. Almost a hundred years. I have seen many things. I have seen the old people pass and the old ways pass. I have seen our connections to the old knowledge become like threads ready to break.

"But a river does not run backward. That is one of the Creator's laws. We must accept what has happened and pay attention to what is going to happen downstream. We must pay attention to what is going to happen to the children."

He peered over at the tape recorder.

"You sure those ears are working?"

I pointed to the wheels whirring behind the small plastic window.

"Good," he said. "Because I want you to get all of this.

"See, Nerburn, it's the children who are most important. People get old and die, but the children keep coming. They keep coming with their little faces and their smiles. They come with pure spirits and open hearts. Then something happens. Their eyes change. Their mouths get hard. They move way back inside and don't let anyone in. They lose the way of the heart."

He took another sip of water.

"We cannot let this happen. They have just come from the Creator. They remember things they do not even understand. We must protect that. We must keep their little hearts from getting hard."

He looked down at the table, as if he was examining his thoughts to make sure he was speaking truly.

"I know that we Indian people are not the only ones who love the children, Nerburn. All people love their children. But we know our love in a special way, because we are now so few.

"We were once a large nation of many peoples. We stretched from one ocean to the other. But now we are only a small handful, struggling to hold on. Each child is a gift, each death is a loss. We cannot afford to lose our children. We cannot afford to lose them to death or to drugs or to a sadness that kills their spirit. We cannot afford to see them disappear into the brown bottle, because they come back with violence in their hearts.

"But what I say is true for all the children — the children of your people and my people and all the people in the world. We need to help them set their feet on the path of kindness so they do not raise their hands in violence against each other."

He looked me directly in the eye — something he did not often do. "Do you understand what I am saying?"

I nodded quietly.

"Good, because this is an important trail I am trying to walk.

"You see," he continued, "the Creator has given me a gift. It was not an easy gift. But the Creator's gifts are not always easy. Sometimes they are hard. But we must accept them and use them to help the people.

"The gift the Creator gave me was to have an open heart for the children. He gave it to me when he took Yellow Bird from me. From that moment, I could not think of anything except her. Whenever I saw children playing, I thought of Yellow Bird. Whenever I heard a child cry, I thought of Yellow Bird. Now, for all my years, every time I see a little child I think of Yellow Bird."

"It must have been hard," I said.

"Yes," he answered. "It's been hard. Life is hard. But life is good, too. Because of little Yellow Bird my heart has always been open to the children. When I have wanted to lie down I thought of the children and kept walking. When I have wanted to take the bad road I thought of the children and stayed on the good road. I knew that I must live for little Yellow Bird, and that little Yellow Bird was present in every child I saw.

"Perhaps that is why I did not look so hard for her. If I found her, I might have taken an easy rest. I might have closed my heart to the other children. But because of her, my heart remained open to them all."

He reached across and grabbed my sleeve again. He was touching me more than he ever had in his life.

"Are you sure you're understanding me?"

"Yes, Dan," I said. "It's a privilege for me to hear these things."

"It is not a privilege," he said. "It is a responsibility. You are the one I have chosen to help me speak. You are the one who must help me pass these things along.

"Now I will continue."

He steepled his gnarled fingers in front of his face.

"Now the trail begins to get difficult. It gets difficult because there are things that are difficult for me to say and things that will be difficult for you to hear."

He touched his fingers to his lips, as if seeking to consecrate his words.

"When your people first came here, we reached out our hands to each other. We showed you our ways, and you showed us yours. We taught you about the animals and the plants and the medicines. We showed you how to live on this land — how to make clothing and grow crops and build houses for the weather. You thanked us and showed us all the amazing things that you had created, like guns for hunting and glasses that could make far things look close, and special medicines that could cure sicknesses our medicines could not.

"Those were good times. They were not always easy times, but our hands were extended to each other in the hope of friendship. We were living together inside the Creator's promise.

"But then something changed. Your hunger for our land became greater than your hunger for our friendship. What had been a sharing became a struggle for a way of life.

"We did not want such a struggle. We have always believed that the Creator's knowledge is too great to fit inside one people. We believe he gave different knowledge to different people, just like he gave different knowledge to different plants and different animals. We believe it is our task is to be open to the Creator's knowledge and to honor it wherever it is found.

"From the first, we saw that your people had a special kind of knowledge. It was knowledge that was difficult for us to understand, but we had to respect it, because it was your gift from the Creator. It was the knowledge of the restless spirit.

"You were always seeking. You did not want to stay still — in your lives or in your minds. You were always trying to change things, to make them better, to make them different. It was like the world that the Creator had made was not good enough for you. You wanted to know what was inside of stones and what was beyond the stars. You took everything apart then tried to put it back together. You never rested.

"This seemed to us like an unhappy way to live. We believed that what the Creator had given us was enough and that the place he had put us was where we belonged. We wanted to learn the Creator's original teachings in the land that he had given us. We were an honoring people, a guardian people, not an exploring and discovering people. For us the world was a mystery to be honored, not a puzzle to be solved.

"But we saw that you had accomplished great things in your way, and we respected that. We thought that we could share our knowledge with you, and that you would listen to us and learn from us, like we were learning from you. But that was not your way. You believed that the Creator had put all his knowledge in a Black Book and it was your task to bring that Black Book to other people and make everyone live in the way that you lived.

"As you became more and more powerful, you tried to force this way of life on our people. You tried to destroy our languages. You took our children. You would not let us practice our beliefs or live in the way we had been taught by our ancestors. You tried to silence the voices of those who had lived here long before you and replace them with the sound of your language and your own way of life.

"This was a mistake. Our Indian people have been here for ten thousand seasons. We have a deep knowledge. We have been born on this land; our bodies have returned to this land. We have an understanding that comes only from deep listening and long patience. You needed to hear what we had to say, but your ears were closed and your hearts were hard.

"Now the earth is passing through a difficult season. A strong wind is shaking all the trees. Everyone is wondering what will happen. But our people are not worried. The tree of our life is strong; the roots of our knowledge go far into this earth.

"Your people's roots do not run so deep. You grew fast and tall on this land, faster and taller than we had thought possible. But your roots have just started to become one with this soil. These winds could harm you. They could damage your little children. That is why I am talking to you. Perhaps now you will listen to us. Perhaps now you will open your hearts to what we have to share."

His hands were shaking. I had never seen him so desperate to communicate.

He took another sip of water. "I need you to understand these things, Nerburn," he said again. "I need you to pass them on."

"I'll try, Dan," I said.

He slammed the glass back on the table.

"No," he said. "No. You will not try. You will do it. You will do it for me, and you will do it for Yellow Bird. I am telling you this. You think I let you close to my life so you could choose what you want?"

"I'm sorry, Dan. I didn't mean it in that way."

"I don't care how you meant it. I only care that you do what you are called on to do. It is like I said — not all gifts are easy gifts. This gift I give you is not an easy gift. People will challenge you. White people will say that you lie. Indian people will say that you try to steal our words and put them in your own mouth.

"Grover says I should not have talked to you. He says you're weak. He says you fear anger. He thinks I chose poorly.

"I don't believe that. I think you are strong. I think you have the strength of a camp chief, not the strength of a war chief. You are not a leader, but you make sure that no one is left behind. We Indian people are the ones who have been left behind. That is why I talk to you. Because you will not let the little children be left behind."

I was taken aback by his vehemence. But I was honored by his willingness to stand by me.

"I won't let you down, Dan," I said. "I won't let Yellow Bird down. I won't let any of you down."

He poked my arm with his crooked finger. "You just worry about the children downstream," he said.

He pointed at the tape recorder. "Now, check those white man's ears. Make sure they're still awake."

I held up the recorder so he could hear the whirring of the wheels. "They're still awake," I said.

"Good. Now let us go a little farther on this trail.

"The greatest weakness of your people is that you do not know how to listen. You have closed your ears to other voices. Not just the voices of other people, but the voices of all creation. This is wrong. The Creator has placed knowledge in all things. Just because we humans have been given the gift of being able to stand outside ourselves does not mean that our knowledge is superior. We are not at the center of creation, we are just a part of creation.

"We Indians understand this. We know that the Creator placed special knowledge in everything. *Tatanka* has a special knowledge. *Wanbli* has a special knowledge. The plants, they each have special knowledge. Even little *shunka* here, he has special knowledge."

He rubbed Charles Bronson under the neck. The little dog shifted in Dan's lap and stared up at Dan with something close to love.

"It's not knowledge they can express, because they can't stand outside themselves and think about themselves like we can. Their knowledge is pure. It's inside them. They can't express it, but they live it. It's our task as humans to watch them and listen to them and learn their knowledge, just as we must listen to the winds and the rivers and the trees and the stones."

He hoisted himself upright in his seat and again looked directly in my face. His milky right eye was gleaming.

"We must stop looking at life as if we humans are at the top of everything. There's spirit in everything, not just in people. If the Creator made it, there is spirit in it. And if it has spirit in it, it has a part to play in creation.

"Here is where your people have lost the path. You have spent too much time thinking that we humans are at the top of everything. You have spent too much time trying to learn about things and not enough time trying to learn from them. You have thought too much and honored too little."

He paused and took several deep breaths, as if gathering his strength.

"Do you remember what we said in the sweat after we prayed?"

"Yes. *Mitakuye oyas'in.*"

"And what does that mean?"

"'All my relations.'"

"That's right. All my relations. Not 'all the things I can use to make my life better.' All my relations. That means everything in the world — the plants, the animals, the sky, the trees, the rocks — everything. When you feel that everything is your relation, you feel that everything is connected.

"That is the secret to living a life of the spirit. If you see that everything has spirit and that everything is connected, you honor everything because you know that it has a part to play in creation.

"Now, this is where the trail leads back to the children. The way we are living today is not good for them. It takes the light out of their eyes, because it does not teach them to see the spirit in all of life. It takes away their connection to everything else. It does not allow them to see the part they play in creation.

"Instead, they think of themselves as part of a straight line that runs from birth to death, and their task is to wait their turn until they reach the place in the line where they are strong and powerful. They are not taught that they have an important role to play just where they are, and that it is they alone who can fill that role.

"Remember when I said that the children have pure hearts because they are closest to the Great Mystery? This is their gift, and that is their part — to remember the goodness of the Great Mystery and to reveal it to us. The rest of us get hard with life; the children remain soft with hope.

"Your way harms the children because it confuses being useful with being important. The little children are not useful because their hands are not yet strong and their minds have not yet been filled with knowledge of how the world works. But they are important. They are important because of where they stand in the circle of life. Like the elders, they are weak. But like the elders, they are closest to the Great Mystery. They allow us to see the morning of creation.

"This is something we have tried to share with your people. We have tried to remind you that life is not a straight line from birth to death, but a circle where the young and old hold hands at the door of the Great Mystery.

"If you see life as a straight line, where the young and old are weak and those in the middle are strong, and if you think that to be important you must be useful, you do not see value in the young and the old. You see them as burdens, not as gifts, because they cannot lift their hands to be of use to the community.

"But the young and old both have other gifts. The young have enthusiasm and hope. They give us dreams when we get weary, and they fill the future with promise. The old have the wisdom of experience. They have traveled far on the journey of life and give us knowledge about our own road ahead.

"In our Indian way, we honor these gifts, just like we honor the gifts of all creation. We do not call our old ones 'senior citizens' and put them in buildings away from the rest. For us, they are elders. They have lived what we are still waiting to learn. We go to them; we listen to them. 'What do you know?' we ask. 'What has life taught you?' They are the keepers of the memories. Their hands have touched the hands of our grandfathers and grandmothers. Their stories are alive with the heartbeat of the past.

"And we do not look at our children as full-growns waiting to be. We see them as special beings who bring us the freshness of wonder. They keep our hearts soft and our hands gentle. They keep us from thinking only about ourselves.

"And they give the elders a reason to live, because we entrust the elders with the shaping of their hearts and with setting their feet straight upon the path of life.

"This is an important task, and one that the elders hold close to their hearts. They understand that once you have wandered far from the good path, it is hard to find it again. But they know that the children have not had time to wander far, so they share the wisdom of their life with them. And the children listen and know that what the elders say is true, because in their little hearts they know the elders are the closest to them in the circle of life, not the farthest from them on the road from birth to death.

"Do you understand this?" he said. "How the children are a gift to the elders and how the elders are a gift to the children? How they complete the circle of life like morning and evening complete the circle of the day?"

"Yes, Dan, I think I do. I think I really do."

He reached his shaking hand toward the glass of water on the table. He seemed emotionally spent.

"Good. Now, just a little more now, and I will be done. Here is why it is important that I say these things. The lives of my people and your people once ran like separate waters. But now they have come together. I am not saying that this is good or bad. Only the Creator knows such things. I only know that the stream of our children's lives has merged with yours and that all of us must now travel together on the journey of life.

"What we must do now is learn from each other — the way it was when your people first came here. We must reach our hands out to each other again. My people must keep our hearts open to what is good about your ways, and you must open your hearts again to what is good about ours. It is time for our Indian voices — the voices that have been silenced — to be heard again."

He reached across the table with both hands and grabbed me by the wrists.

"This is why I come to you. Your people do not hear us because they do not see us. They see drunks. They see shacks. They see casinos and wise men and people with their hands out. They see everything they want to see, but they don't see us. And if they don't see us, they don't hear us. And if they don't hear us, they can't learn from us."

He let go of my wrists and pounded the table. The tape recorder fell over and the water glass jumped. Little Bronson scuttled off his lap and ran to a corner.

Dan coughed several times and took a deep breath.

"I am sorry I get angry. But your people need to hear us. We Indian people know many things. We know how to wrap our arms around a larger family. We know how to be poor without thinking that we should be rich. We value our elders because we know they are the keepers of the memories, and we value our children because we know that they carry the hope for the future. We know how to

honor the mysteries of life without always thinking that we're supposed to solve them. And we know how to keep the sacred on our
lips, because we know that what is on the lips eventually makes its
way to the heart.

"These are good things. They are good things for everyone.
They are the gifts the Creator gave us, and we want to share them.
But your people need to listen. They need to learn how to listen."

I carefully set the cassette recorder back in front of him. "I
believe you're right, Dan."

"I know I'm right. But it does no good to be right when your
voice never reaches another person's ears."

"I'll try to change that, Dan," I said. "I promise."

"Don't make promises to me," he said. "Make them to the
Creator."

"All right, I make the promise to the Creator."

"Then here is only one more thing that I have to say. I have left
it for last, because it makes me say hard words about your people,
and I do not like to say hard words about another people. But where
your way has been wrong and has washed over our way, I owe it to
the children to speak the hard words.

"From the very first our people are taught to share. When one
person has something, we all have something. When times are difficult we divide what little we have and share it with others. This is
our teaching; this is our way. It fills our heart with the idea that the
people come first.

"From the beginning, you tried to take this away from us. You
taught that we should forget about the people and think first about
ourselves. It was why you put us in boarding schools and tried to
kill our language and our old ways — you did not like that we put
the people first and tried to live for the people before ourselves.

"We did not understand this. Your Jesus taught people to share.
He gave away everything he had to feed the hungry. He didn't think

about 'mine' and 'yours.' But when we lived this way, you said it was wrong. You said we had to learn to take care of ourselves and not rely on each other. You called it 'self-reliance' and told us that this was why your people were so strong and why you had accomplished so much.

"You brought soldiers and ministers to make us live this way. You took the land the Creator had given us and divided it into little squares and gave it back to us with our names on it. You told us we should sell things instead of giving them away. We did not like this then, and we do not like it now, because it harms the heart and fills it with fear."

"Fear?" I said.

"Yes. If you are living only for yourself, and you know that everyone else is living only for themselves, you know that there is no help for you if you fall. All people must fall at some time, just as there will always come rain and bad weather. You learn that you must protect what is yours, or you may lose everything.

"You put locks on your doors, locks on your hearts. You live in fear that you may lose what you have, so you spend your life getting more and more and trying to build walls around what you have. You learn to protect rather than to give.

"In the old way there were no locks on our doors. We had no fences to make lines between 'mine' and 'yours.' To be great among our people was not to gather the most for ourselves, it was to be the biggest giver and sharer and to protect the weak. We honored those who could help the most, not those who could have the most.

"Once a person starts to live in your way, everything changes, because everything has to be protected. You start making rules about what people can't do, not what people should do. Look at those Ten Commandments you tried to teach us in boarding school: 'Thou shalt not, thou shalt not.'

"I'd rather have rules that say, 'You should, you should.' It

teaches us who we should be, not who we should not be. All your
way does is tell someone how not to be bad. It doesn't tell them how
to be good.

"When we teach the children this fear way, we set their feet on
a bad path. We teach them to grow up thinking about themselves.
Sharing is just a small stick they hold out to other people, not the
strongest branch on the tree of their lives. They learn to protect, not
to give, and it builds a wall around their hearts.

"We need to change this. We need to teach them a helping way,
to give them a vision of what is right, not only of what is wrong. We
need to teach them that the way to be strong is to help the weak; the
way to have wealth is to give things away; the way to lead is to serve.
We need to let them know that they are an important part of the circle of life, and if they do not play their part, no one else can.

"If we teach them these things they will have hope in their
hearts. If we don't, their hearts will become hard. They will gather
things to them and watch life from a cold distance. They will see the
world as something to use, not something to honor. Their ears will
stay closed to voices of creation, and the words of the sacred will die
on their lips."

He closed his eyes and grabbed my arm tightly, as if by holding
it he would keep me from losing the understanding of what he had
said. We sat this way for several seconds. Then, slowly, he loosened
his grip and sat back in his chair.

"That is enough for now," he said.

The little tape deck whirred on the table. Bronson moved cautiously back from the corner and jumped into Dan's lap. Dan rubbed
the little dog's head and closed his eyes.

I didn't know if he was finished, or if he was merely resting. His
words had exhausted me, but they had touched me; I had seldom
heard him speak so purely from the heart. I wanted him to know that
I understood, that I honored what he said, and that I would carry

his message forward to the best of my ability. But his eyes remained closed, and I didn't want to disturb him.

I went to the sink, washed out the cup, and placed a glass of clear water before him.

He opened his eyes slightly and drank deeply from it.

"*Pilamaya*," he said. I did not know whether he had forgotten who I was or if he just chose to speak in Lakota. Then he closed his eyes again and let his head drop to his chest.

I touched him softly on the arm. "Would you like to get some sleep?" I asked.

He waved me off without opening his eyes.

I sat quietly for a few minutes to see if he would wake, but his breathing was steady and his hands had relaxed at his sides. I gave Bronson's glove a tug and tousled him on the head, then crawled into the bed on the far side of the room. The light through the curtains spoke of the coming of another day.

CHAPTER THIRTY-ONE

REACHING ACROSS

I awoke from a dream about wandering through weeds and briars, only to find Bronson curled up against my chest. His bristly fur was pressed against my skin, and he was breathing tiny blasts of carbolic dog breath directly in my face. The glove was lying between his front paws. At the first sign of movement he jumped up and licked my cheek.

I rubbed my eyes and looked around the room. The light was still on, but Dan had gotten out of his wheelchair and was asleep on the other bed. He was fully dressed and had not even crawled under the covers. The star quilt partially covered his midsection, but his bony ankles and worn leather shoes lay exposed in the harsh motel light.

I tried to move silently toward the door to switch off the light.

"It's okay, Nerburn," he said without opening his eyes. "I'm not sleeping. Just thinking."

"You sure you don't want to get under the covers and rest for a while?"

"Nah. This is the day I've been waiting for. I'll be taking the big rest before long."

He pushed himself upright and reached for the wheelchair next to his bed.

I could see he was having trouble getting up.

"Here, let me help you," I said.

I got behind him and put my arms under his and lifted him to standing. He didn't protest or resist.

"Getting old's rough," he said. "It's like you shut down every night and you've got to start over every morning."

He pointed across to the tape recorder. "Did you get everything?"

"Every word." I gestured toward the glass with its mixture of water and phlegm. "And a few other sounds, too."

"Good," he said. "Now I'm ready to hear what you found out."

It was as if the talk of last night had completed something for him, and he was now prepared to move forward.

I told him the story of the old woman by the lake and the doll in the museum, and the abandoned house with the overgrown grave-yard. I did not tell him about the broken wooden cross with the name *Sarah* on it, because I did not want to upset him. Instead I told him only that her grave was there and that he would soon be able to touch the earth where his sister lay sleeping.

He listened intently without interrupting.

"Let's go see that doll," he said.

GROVER WAS STANDING OUTSIDE the unit next door puffing on a cigarette.

"He fell asleep," I said.

Grover nodded and blew a stream of smoke into the air. He put his hand to his forehead and shaded his eyes like a cavalry scout scanning the horizon. "Still don't see that pizza man," he said.

"Could be any minute," I said.

The white pickup I had seen at Orv's was parked on the far side of Grover's Buick.

"Is Orv here?" I asked.

"Orv. The rest of them, too."

"All waiting for pizza, right?"

"All waiting for pizza."

Despite the levity, I felt a tightness in my stomach. Whoever was in the next room had come along to be part of this moment. Wenonah had said it: this would be the old man's last journey. If I was wrong it would be one of the biggest failures of my life.

Dan pushed past me into Grover's unit, using his wheelchair for support. "I'm going to wash up," he said.

Bronson pattered after him holding the glove. Grover gave the little dog a shove in the rump with his foot.

I moved closer to Grover.

"I'm worried about Dan," I said. "He seems so fragile and weak."

"He is," Grover said.

"He kept talking about the children and crossing to the other side. He seemed almost desperate."

"He is."

"Is he that sick?"

"He knows his day. The old ones are like that. They can reach across."

Grover took a last drag on his cigarette and flipped it between the cars. "Yep. He's just an old wolf wandering in the twilight getting ready to lie down."

He spit a long stream of tobacco-laden saliva onto the gravel. "I hope you're right about this doll thing and that graveyard."

Through the doorway I could hear the clanking of Dan's metal walker and smell the wafting sweetness of cheap cologne.

"I'm ready, Nerburn," Dan said from inside the entry. "I'm taking my metal legs. Let's go."

He emerged from the darkness of the unit wearing his fisherman's cap and a black nylon baseball jacket with "Warriors" written on the back. It was patched in several places with silver duct tape. A beaded doeskin bag was slung over the front of his walker.

As he stepped into the daylight we were hit by the full force of his cologne. "Jesus, that's as bad as Nerburn's dog shampoo," Grover said.

"You could use a little of it yourself," Dan said.

He clacked past us toward the car, using his walker for support. "I guess you should bring the chair, too, Nerburn," he said. "Just in case."

Bronson scuttled across the threshold behind him. As he passed, Grover reached down and swooped him into his arms.

"If the pizza guy doesn't come, I'm thinking about making sacred puppy soup," he said.

Bronson squirmed and struggled to get loose. Grover ripped the glove from the little dog's mouth and shoved it in his back pocket. "Time for you to make it on your own," he said. Then he flipped Bronson harshly onto the ground and shooed him off with his foot.

It was a strangely aggressive act, even for Grover. But I knew he disliked the little dog, and I had no idea what had gone on between them since I had seen them last.

Dan glared at Grover and hustled Bronson into the front seat. Bronson looked back at Grover and bared his teeth.

Grover waved the glove just out of Bronson's reach. The little dog lunged and snapped at it. "You make it on your own," Grover taunted.

Dan paid no attention to the exchange.

"Come on, Nerburn. Let's get going," Dan said. "I want to see that doll."

"You coming?" he said to Grover.

"Nah. I'll wait for the others. They need their sleep."

I scribbled a rough map to the property on the back of a gas receipt and handed it to Grover. "We'll swing back here to get you. But take this just in case we don't connect."

"We'll probably be at the café," he said. "Unless the pizza man gets here."

I ADJUSTED DAN'S JACKET AND BUCKLED HIM IN. Charles Bronson had taken his traditional spot on Dan's lap. He was nervous and unsettled without his glove.

"What was that all about between Grover and Bronson?" I asked.

"They got some stuff going on," Dan said, dismissing my comment with a wave of his hand. "How far's that museum?"

"Just a couple of blocks."

He shifted nervously in his seat.

"This is an important day for me," he said.

"I know."

"I don't want you to talk too much."

"I won't."

"Good. That will be a sign of respect."

We drove the rest of the way to the old schoolhouse without speaking.

"This is it," I said as we pulled up in front of the old brick building. The caretaker was pulling weeds in her front lawn.

Dan looked around curiously. The woman came over to greet us.

"This is the man I told you about yesterday," I said.

She reached out her hand in greeting. Dan took the end of her hand in his fingers. He did not look at her.

"Mr. Nerburn said you'd like to see the doll," she said. She had obviously gotten my name from the check I had written last time I was here.

Still, Dan said nothing.

I helped Dan from the car and positioned him in his walker. He moved up the walk without speaking. Bronson trotted along behind him.

The woman looked at me, confused. She had expected more engagement, more animation. I nodded and motioned her forward.

She led us into the building, turning on the lights as we moved through the hallway. Dan kept his head down.

"Is it warm enough for you?" she said.

"It's fine," I said. "Lots better than last winter." Dan pushed his way forward in his walker and kept his eyes on the floor.

"It's right around this corner," she said. Dan's silence was obviously making her uncomfortable.

She turned on the light in the room with the display case containing the doll. Dan shuffled in and went directly to it, as if he had known where it was all along.

The woman flicked on the light in the case. The doll was flooded in bright yellow light.

Dan bent over and put his face about an inch from the case. "I want to hold it," he said. These were the first words he'd spoken, and they were less a request than an order.

The woman looked distressed. I nodded silently to her and mouthed, "It's okay."

She looked around nervously, as if trying to find someone of higher authority to help her make the decision. "He's Lakota," I said, hoping that his cultural tie to the doll would set her mind at ease.

"I don't know," she answered.

"He'll treat it as gently as if he was holding his little sister," I said. "I promise."

Sensing that there was something more at stake than she understood, she moved to the back of the case and unlatched it. "Since you're Lakota," she said, "I suppose it would be all right."

She carefully removed the doll from the case. Dan reached his shaky hands forward and took it from her.

"Are you sure you don't want some help?" she asked nervously.

"This is good," he said.

She looked around again, almost frantic.

"Come on," I said. "He needs to be alone."

She glanced over her shoulder as I ushered her from the room. Dan was holding the doll in front of him, cradled in his trembling hands as if he was holding a baby bird.

I DON'T KNOW HOW LONG THE WOMAN and I stood outside in the dusty hallway. It was probably only minutes, but it felt like hours. She kept fidgeting and twitching, wanting to return to make sure the doll was okay. But to her credit, she resisted.

From around the corner we could hear Dan speaking softly in Lakota. It was a complicated sound, plaintive and filled with emotion. The two of us stared uncomfortably at each other. Dust motes filtered through the light as the old man's words echoed in the empty hallways.

Just when I was beginning to wonder how long this would go on, Dan appeared in the doorway. He was still holding the doll in front of him in cupped hands. He moved unsteadily over to the woman and handed her the doll. She took it from him gratefully.

"You take special care of that," he said. His voice was filled with hard authority.

He turned toward the front door.

"Get my legs, Nerburn," he said. "It's time to go."

I grabbed the walker and slipped the woman twenty dollars. She stared at me in utter confusion.

"Was it Yellow Bird's?" I asked as we got back in the car.

"Take me to that farmhouse," he said.

"Should we get Grover and Orv?"

"Just get me out there."

I drove past the motel, hoping to find Grover and Orv to let them know what was happening. But their cars were gone. I went through the café lot. But that, too, was empty.

"We should find them," I said.

"Find them later," Dan said.

He took the doeskin bag and placed it on his lap. Bronson jumped up and positioned himself next to it like its guardian or protector.

WE DROVE OUT OF TOWN ON THE GRAVEL ROAD that led the several miles to the abandoned homestead. I kept scanning the horizon for any sign of Grover's car or the big white pickup.

Dan refused to speak. I had no idea what he was thinking and was preparing to ride all the way to the farmstead without exchanging a word, when he suddenly tapped me on the knee with his finger.

"Pull over," he said.

I crunched the car to the side of the road and put it into park. Dan reached into the doeskin bag and pulled out a long buckskin roll that was tied on each end with a red ribbon. He touched it carefully and with reverence. I assumed it held his pipe, though this seemed like a strange time to stop to smoke.

Slowly, with unsteady hands, he undid the ribbon on one end. The roll was old and brittle. It looked like it hadn't been opened in a long time.

"You need some help?" I asked.

He shook his head and fumbled with the tie. Eventually he got it free and folded back one of the buckskin flaps.

Wrapped inside, like an infant in swaddling clothes, was a small burlap doll. It had the same buckskin clothing, the same sad simple smile as the doll in the museum. The fingers were made in the same manner, by cutting the fringe, and the moccasins were decorated with the same blue and yellow beads.

He turned it toward me so I could see the face more closely. The left eye had a single black bead for a pupil; the right eye was completely white.

"This is Yellow Bird's," he said. "She made it with the grandmas, when she was just little. This was how she could talk to me," he said. "Because she made the little doll into her brother."

CHAPTER THIRTY-TWO

◇◇◇◇◇◇◇◇◇◇◇◇◇◇◇◇◇◇◇◇◇◇◇◇◇◇◇◇◇◇◇◇◇◇

ZINTKALA ZI

W e drove the rest of the way in silence. On either side of us the fields lay black and fertile, waiting for the moisture to recede so the plowing and planting could begin. Patches of snow hugged the margins of the ditches. The trees in the copses and shelter breaks had begun to take on the fuzzy softness of new buds, and the first small songbirds of spring flitted from tree to fence post and pecked at seeds on the side of the road.

I wanted to say something about the beauty of the day — something to bring Dan out of himself — but I didn't wish to intrude on the privacy of his thoughts. Whatever had taken place in the museum had moved him to a deeply private place. This was his time; this was his journey.

We drove without speaking — two men, only inches from each other, separated by worlds and cultures and driven by dreams and demons the other could never fully understand.

I looked over at Dan. He was holding the little doll in cupped hands and mouthing words in its direction. Bronson lay curled in his lap, staring toward the doll with unabashed curiosity.

I was concerned about how I would get Dan back to the gravesite. I had not counted on the heavy moisture of a North Dakota spring. I knew he couldn't walk far, and I didn't think I could push his old wheelchair through the spongy earth. I had to hope there was a path along the outside of the shelter break that would allow us to drive directly into the back clearing and up to the thicket.

As I approached the farmstead I saw what I was looking for: an old trail, probably once used by farm machinery, running along the outside of the trees. It was little more than two ruts through the dirt, and it was filled with ice-covered puddles. But it looked passable.

I splashed the wagon across the icy low spots until I found a break in the trees that allowed me entry into the yard.

Dan held the little doll close to him, as if he feared that the pitching and jostling would dislodge it from his grasp. His breathing was shallow and fast.

Bronson sensed that we were coming to our destination and stood on Dan's lap with his front paws on the edge of the window.

I drove cautiously through the soft wet ground of the backyard. I wanted to get as close as possible to the tangle of bushes that surrounded the small graveyard. Bronson growled and pawed at the window.

"He knows something," Dan said.

Bronson kept up his growling and scratching.

We passed near the frayed rope swing that hung from a branch of a huge old oak in the center of the yard.

"Is that part of a swing?" Dan asked. "Yellow Bird loved to swing." He was alert in his seat now, turning his head from side to side.

"Let Bronson out," he said.

I stopped the car and opened my door a crack. Bronson bounded across me and bolted into the brush.

"Do you think he'll get lost?" I asked.

Dan stared at the rope swing.

"He won't get lost."

He carefully replaced the doll in its buckskin swaddling and returned it to the doeskin bag.

"Get me my metal legs," he said.

I went around to the back of the wagon, pulled the walker out of the cargo area, and positioned it next to the passenger door.

"Hook the bag on it," he said. "Make sure it's tight."

I hooked the doeskin bag on the front of the walker and helped Dan to his feet.

"Where's the grave?" he asked.

I pointed to the thicket. "It's hard going. Lots of brambles."

He ignored my comment and pushed the walker toward the tangle of brush and bushes. The front wheels dug into the muddy earth, almost causing him to fall. I grabbed his arm as he lurched to the left, but he brushed me aside. I had not seen him so purposeful since we had been at the graveyard on the hill behind the boarding school.

I looked out over the empty fields and the straight-line gravel road cutting off into the distance, hoping one last time for a sign of Grover and the others. But the landscape was silent except for the twittering of the songbirds and the soft breathing of the wind. I had to hope that my map was adequate and that they would find their way out here by themselves.

Bronson came running out of the thicket from the direction of the graveyard. He growled and barked and spun in circles.

"It's over there, isn't it?" Dan said, pointing toward Bronson.

"Yes," I said.

"I figured."

Bronson was wild with excitement. He looked up at me, then back at Dan, then bounded back into the bushes. We could hear him barking and yipping as he rustled around in the underbrush.

"He can't find the grave, can he?" I asked, almost embarrassed to propose something so mystical.

"He can find what he can find," Dan answered.

Dan pushed his way to the opening in the bushes that led to the burial site. The path was so overgrown that there was barely room for a child to pass through, much less an unsteady old man with a walker.

I stepped in front of him and began clearing away branches and ground cover. He ignored my efforts and pushed deeper into the path. I tried to stay in front of him, but he kept lifting his walker and moving forward, hitting my heels with its frame and knocking against me if I didn't move quickly enough.

The distance from the beginning of the path to the burial area was only about thirty feet, but the going was almost impossible. Dan was as unsteady as he was adamant, and more than once he almost fell as he pushed against me with the walker. I kept listening for a car engine in the distance, hoping for some help. But there was no sound other than the birds, Bronson's barking, and Dan's labored breathing.

I began to fear that I had given Grover the wrong directions and that he and the others were lost on some unmarked gravel road while Dan was moving closer to one of the most important encounters of his life.

The birds hopped down to lower branches to observe us. More than once they lighted on Dan's walker before lifting off and flying off into the bushes. It was unnerving how close they were willing to come to us.

Dan said something in Lakota, and they stopped their hopping.

He kept pushing forward and speaking quietly under his breath. Charles Bronson continued his snarling and growling from somewhere up ahead in the bushes.

Dan spoke again in Lakota — he was speaking only in Lakota

now — and Bronson came crashing through the brush and jumped at his pants leg. I was worried he would knock Dan over, but Dan seemed unconcerned.

Bronson locked his eyes on mine. It was the most disconcerting look I had ever received from a dog — part wildness and part wisdom — and he stared at me until it made me uncomfortable. Involuntarily, I nodded at him, as if he were a person. He barked once at me and rushed back into the thicket. The songbirds perched on branches only inches above our heads.

"Are we almost there?" Dan asked.

"Just a little farther," I said. "Right inside that fence."

Through the brambles and spreading underbrush we could see the rough perimeter of the small cemetery. The old gravestones stuck up like gray toadstools from the soggy earth.

With the snow mostly melted it was possible to see the stones clearly. There were probably twenty of them scattered almost randomly throughout the graveyard. Some stood upright; others were canted at strange angles. Still others were flat on their backs, the victims of vandals or the ravages of time. They looked even more forlorn and abandoned than they had when they were covered with snow.

I looked to the corner where the wooden cross had been propped against the fence. I didn't see it.

I looked again. Perhaps it had fallen over and was hidden by the brown grasses and melting snows. But there was no sign of it anywhere.

A shudder of dread came across me. What if someone had stolen it? Without the cross there was no way to prove to Dan that this was his little sister's gravesite.

A sick feeling rose in my stomach. Why hadn't I anticipated such a thing? I had just assumed that no one came out here. I should have realized that the vandals and vagrants who had destroyed the house could just as easily have come out here and destroyed the cemetery. What better souvenir from a night of drinking than an old wooden cross with the words *Sarah, Indian Girl* scratched on it? Right now it was probably hanging on the wall in some college dorm room in Grand Forks or lying charred in a fire pit on the outskirts of Winnipeg amid a pile of empty beer cans.

I looked frantically around the edge of the graveyard. Dan was pushing his way among the stones, oblivious to my searching.

I was close to panic. I could hear Wenonah's words, that her grandfather had not had good luck with white people in his life, and that this journey had better be worth it, because it would be his last.

The silence from the great, empty landscape echoed like a great indictment. Grover was out there somewhere, driving around, unable to find us. Wenonah was probably with him, worried sick about her grandfather and enraged at me for getting them lost. I had made Dan come four hundred miles to stand in the brush behind an abandoned farmhouse, surrounded by fields that had been plowed up by white men who had taken this land from his ancestors, on the promise that he would finally see the grave of his little sister. And now he was wandering among the tombstones of white settlers while the only white man he had ever really trusted was preparing to tell him that his sister's grave had been here last winter, that he was sure it was here somewhere, that we probably just needed to look harder, that there must be some sort of mistake. It was as if the whole event had become a cruel, mocking joke, and I had been its author.

The sun had moved directly overhead. It cut a pattern of shadows through the overhanging trees, stippling the ground with a confusing lacework of lights and darks. Dan was moving carefully among the shadows, squinting at the headstones and snow patches and trying to distinguish one from the other. He was too infirm to bend down, and the stones were far too worn for him to read them. The rattling in his chest was getting worse, and his breathing was labored.

"Show me where it is," he said. "I can't read these stones."

I was about to confess that his sister's grave had been marked only by a crude wooden cross, and that the cross appeared to be lost, when Bronson bolted from the woods and began barking and yipping at my pants leg. He yanked on my cuff as if he wanted to play.

I gave him a hard push with my foot. "Get out of here, Bronson," I said. "I'm not interested in your games." I was angry at him, at myself, at the entire world. I knew I couldn't stall much longer.

I practiced apologizing to Dan in my mind, explaining about how the marker had been here, about how I was certain this was the place. But it all rang hollow without the cross.

Dan was making his way among the stones, using his toe to push brush off the ones that had fallen over. Bronson yipped and yapped and ran back into the woods.

I hurried over to Dan to offer him support. The ground was uneven and the branches were sharp. If he fell, he could cut himself badly or injure himself on the gravestones.

In the shadow of the bushes I could see Bronson growling and digging and pulling at a pile of brush.

I guided Dan toward the corner where the cross had been propped against the fence.

"It's right around here," I said, having no further way to avoid the issue.

Bronson came bounding out of the brush again and almost knocked Dan over.

"Damn it, Bronson," I said.

Bronson yipped and pulled at my pants again.

"What's he after, Nerburn?" Dan said.

"I don't know. He wants to play fetch or something."

"Go see," Dan said.

For the first time since we'd found him I was ready to strangle the little dog. Grover's angry treatment of him no longer seemed so out of place.

"Go see what he wants," Dan said again.

I didn't feel like following a dog into the woods, but I was willing to do anything to buy time. Perhaps, with just a few more minutes, Grover and the others would arrive and we could all join forces in the search for the cross.

"Wait here," I said to Dan, and pushed my way through the tangle of branches to where Bronson was digging in a pile of twigs and sticks that were stuck in a mound of dirty gray snow. He was shaking his head and ripping at a stick that was lodged under a large stone.

"So this is what all the barking's about," I said, giving him another shove. "Get out of the way. I'll get your damn stick." I didn't want to leave Dan unattended for more than a few seconds, but I wanted to shut Bronson up. I could hear Dan clanking his walker toward me as he made his way around the gravestones in utter disregard of my instructions.

"Just stay where you are, Dan," I shouted. "I'll be right back."

Dan ignored me and pressed forward.

I brushed Bronson aside and pulled hard on the stick. It was stuck tightly under the stone and was almost impossible to dislodge. Bronson kept surging forward trying to grab it.

Finally, I was able to move the rock enough to pull the stick free. It was rotten and muddy and had a filthy piece of cloth bound to it by a tight winding of fish line. At first I thought it might be a part of Yellow Bird's cross, but a quick examination showed it to be nothing more than a broken piece of tree branch.

"So all this is about some stupid stick," I said, tossing it deep into the brush. Bronson shot after it like a dog possessed.

I didn't know what its attraction was, and I didn't care. Behind me I could hear Dan's clanking and muttering.

I was just about to go back and tell him what was really going on when I noticed that moving the stone had exposed the corner of a flat slab. It appeared to be a gravestone, but I couldn't be sure.

I pushed the snow aside and dug into the dirt. I was curious as to why a grave would be outside the burial area, if indeed it was a grave. I hadn't seen it the last time I had been here because I hadn't looked outside the perimeter of the fence. Besides, it was almost invisible beneath the brush and undergrowth. I wouldn't have seen it this time had it not been for Bronson's persistent digging and barking.

Dan had made his way through the brambles and was standing right behind me.

"I didn't see any grave," he said. "Where is it?"

"Just a minute. I'll come and help you look."

He prodded me with the tip of his walker.

"What's down there? What did Bronson find?"

"I don't know," I answered. "It looks like another gravestone."

"Well, just leave it. Come and show me Yellow Bird's grave. I don't care about these other ones."

"Just let me clear this off," I said. "Out of respect." I was still trying to buy time until Grover and Wenonah arrived.

I swept the snow and dirt off the surface of the slab until I could see some writing.

An odd apprehension came across me.

"Isn't *Zintkala* Lakota?" I said.

"What?" Dan said abruptly.

I brushed more snow away.

"*Zintkala Zi*. Isn't that Lakota?"

Dan gripped the handles of his walker with both hands. A strange sound welled up inside him. It came from deep in his chest and passed through his throat — a kind of wailing ululation that was half jubilation and half sob. It made the hair on the back of my neck stand up.

Bronson came running out of the brush with the stick in his mouth and stared up at the old man.

Dan paid no attention to either of us. His eyes were closed and his face was turned skyward. He reached into the bag on the front of his walker and lifted out the buckskin roll that held the little doll. He held it in front of him as if making an offering.

"What does *Zintkala Zi* mean?" I asked. I had a fair idea, but I wanted to hear him say it.

Dan kept his eyes closed and continued his chant.

I looked down at Bronson. He had that strange, laughing, wild-dog look in his eye. He grinned at me and held the stick aloft like a prize. His paws and whiskers were covered in mud.

I was not sure what to do. Dan's chant — if indeed it was a chant — sent chills through me. It was like a ritualized shaping of the wail you hear from family members at the closing of a coffin — a wounded cry of finality and loss, too big to be absorbed, too deep to be voiced.

"Leave me alone, Nerburn," Dan said. His voice was shaking. "Go on. Let me be."

I didn't want to leave him. He was too frail and unsteady. But I remembered his anger when I had resisted leaving him on the hill when we had buried Fatback.

He flapped his hand at me. "Just go. Just go," he said.

Bronson moved over closer to his leg, as if to tell me he would take over as the old man's protector.

Hesitantly, I moved across the graveyard. The wail had begun again. I was confused and distressed.

I made my way through the tangle of brush, trying to keep my eyes on Dan. Through the branches I could see him standing above the grave with the little doll extended in front of him in offering or supplication.

I stopped as soon as I made it into the yard. I wanted to give him his privacy, but I needed to stay close enough to help him if he wavered or began to fall.

I looked up and down the road in the faint hope that I might see Grover's car or the pickup in the distance. But the road was empty, and the fields were silent and still.

A glint of sunlight flashed off something silver on the far side of the house. At first I thought it was a piece of glass. But when I looked more closely I saw that it was the front bumper of a car.

I glanced quickly back at Dan to see that he was all right, then hurried toward the front yard. Perhaps the others had arrived while I had been digging out the gravestone.

I rounded the corner to find the white pickup parked on the far side of the house. The glint of silver had come from the front bumper of Grover's old green Buick that was nosed slightly into the back-yard. Grover was sitting on the steps of the porch smoking a cigarette and playing mumblety-peg. Orv and Wenonah were sitting behind him on a pile of boxes. Shitty and Donnie were standing by the pickup drinking cans of Mountain Dew. Inside the pickup cab I could see Angie feeding her baby. They all seemed perfectly relaxed and nonchalant.

"God, I'm glad to see you all," I said. "I thought you'd gotten lost."

"Indians don't get lost," Grover said. His flipped his knife off his thumb into a circle he had scribed on the porch.

"The map was okay? I was afraid it made no sense."

"Indians don't need maps."

"Listen, the old man's out in back. He's standing . . ."

Wenonah jumped up. "He's out there alone? You left him alone?"

She pushed past Grover and hurried down the steps. "You should never leave him alone. I thought you had him in the car."

"He wanted to be by himself," I said. "I think we found Yellow Bird's gravestone."

She shoved me out of the way and disappeared around the corner. "You should never have left him alone," she shouted.

I tried to explain that he had sent me away, but she was out of earshot.

I turned to Grover, hoping for some sign of support. "He told me to leave him," I said.

Grover flipped his knife blade off his thumb and watched it spin once, then land, point first, in the porch boards.

"Two points," he said.

He gestured to the step next to him. "Sit down, Nerburn. Take a load off."

"I think I should go help Wenonah," I said.

He pulled the knife out of the boards and scribed a tally mark next to the circle. "Wenonah can take care of the old man. Sit down."

I looked at Orv for guidance. He smiled and gave me a thumbs-up. Donnie and Shitty lifted their cans of Mountain Dew as if in greeting.

I was convinced that they misunderstood the gravity of the situation.

"Listen," I said. "I think I found Yellow Bird's actual grave-stone. It was under some bushes. *Zintkala Zi* — that's Yellow Bird, right? It's got Dan really upset. He started wailing as soon as he saw it. "

Grover sliced a sliver of wood from the edge of the step and stuck it between his teeth. "You're like an old woman," he said. "Worrying all the time. Just sit down."

Orv smiled kindly at me. Donnie nudged a rock with the toe of his tennis shoe. Shitty swilled his Mountain Dew and looked toward Orv with a toothless, cat-whisker grin.

I couldn't comprehend their indifference to the situation. They had just come four hundred miles to help Dan bear witness at his little sister's grave, and now they seemed more interested in mumblety-peg and Mountain Dew than in what was going on with their ninety-year-old friend.

I took a step toward the path around the house. "I'm going back out there," I said.

Grover pointed his knife blade toward me. "Sit down," he said. There was no humor in his voice. "We'll know when it's okay to go. Now take a seat."

I looked helplessly toward Orv. He smiled and nodded toward the place next to Grover.

Reluctantly, I moved over and sat down on the step.

We sat quietly listening to the wind rustle in the grasses and the trees.

"You play mumblety-peg?" Grover asked.

"No," I said.

He stuck his knife in the porch next to me.

"No cards, no mumblety-peg. You're not a lot of fun."

"I didn't come here for fun," I said. "I came here to help Dan." I looked at the others. "It seems like maybe I'm the only one."

Orv leaned forward from his seat on the boxes. "It's okay, Nerburn," he said. "Grover's right. Wenonah can take care of things."

Orv's measured tones calmed me a bit. I knew he didn't take pleasure in toying with me like Grover did. If he thought it was all right, it was probably all right, even though none of it made any sense.

"Okay," I said. "I'm trusting you guys."

"When have I ever steered you wrong?" Grover grinned.

Glumly, I accepted the situation. I leaned back and rested my elbows on the step behind me. No one was saying anything.

After about five minutes I couldn't stand it any longer.

"I'm sorry," I said. "I'm going back out there. I want to see if the old man's okay."

Grover shook his knife at me. It was done in jest, but his meaning was clear. "Just take it easy," he said.

"Geez, Nerburn," Shitty said. "You're in a pretty big hurry for a guy who took so long to get here."

"What do you mean?"

He looked from Grover to Orv to see whether he should say more.

"We were here when you got here," he said proudly.

"You guys have been here the whole time?" I said.

"Buick's faster than a Ti-yota," Grover said.

"Then why didn't you come out in back? Didn't you see me drive up?"

Grover flipped his knife off his thumb and watched it stick in the porch boards. "Hadn't finished my game."

Orv was obviously feeling sorry for me. "It was better this way," he said. "When we saw you drive in the back way we decided to stay put. We thought Dan could use some time alone."

"Well, it's clear Wenonah didn't think so."

"Wenonah worries too much," Grover said. "The old man's a pretty tough character."

As we were speaking, Charles Bronson came bounding around the corner with the stick in his mouth.

"Hey, Dog Soup," Grover said. "Come on over here." He *tsukked* several times, and Bronson ran up the steps and jumped into his lap. Grover chucked him under the chin and tousled the top of his head.

I was mystified. I had never seen the two of them relate to each other in any positive way.

"I thought you hated him," I said.

"Nah, I don't hate him. At least not all of him. He's a mixed blood. Got some coyote in him, I think. That part I like." He yanked on the stick. Bronson yanked back. "Besides, we've got an understanding."

Bronson put his front paws on Grover's chest and thrust the filthy stick toward his face. It was a mess of mud and cloth and string and saliva.

Grover laughed and lifted him down onto the ground. Bronson ran over to the pickup and peed on the back tire.

"He never pees on your truck, Shitty," Grover said. "He must not like Chevvies."

Shitty adjusted his glasses and snorted several times through the rotten stumps of his few remaining teeth.

Orv was still staring at me and smiling. "You should feel pretty good, Nerburn," he said. "You've done a good job."

"The old man's out in back sobbing and wailing, and his grand-daughter's ready to kill me? That doesn't feel much like a good job."

"Nah, the old man is happy. It's good when you make an elder happy."

"He didn't seem happy when I left him."

"Oh, there's 'fun' happy and there's 'peace' happy. We watched him on the drive up. You've done good."

I strained my ears to hear if any sounds were coming from behind the house.

"You're sure we shouldn't be out there?"

Grover flipped his knife into the circle and scratched a mark on the step near his feet. "You're still thinking like a white man," he said.

"Well, that shouldn't come as a surprise."

"It doesn't. But I want you to give it a rest." Lacking any other option, I slumped down and put my chin in my hands. They were going to do this their way, and all I could do was follow.

A ribbon of yellow butterflies crossed in front of the porch. A few songbirds chirped back and forth to each other in the bushes. Bronson lay in the shade under the truck chewing at his filthy stick. Everyone seemed completely at ease except me.

After a few minutes a meadowlark hopped on a fencepost in the side yard and gave its distinctive trill.

"Okay, that's it," Grover said, getting to his feet.

The meadowlark trilled again.

"Yep. *Tasiyagnunpa*," he said. "Time to go. Come on."

"Because a meadowlark sang?" I said.

"Sure? Why not?" he grinned.

Orv shook his head. "You're a good sport, Nerburn."

Everyone sprang into action. Shitty threw his empty Mountain Dew can into the pickup bed. Orv grunted his way off the box and stepped stiffly down from the porch. Donnie ran to the front of the pickup and helped Angie and the baby onto the ground.

With Grover in the lead, we moved quickly around the side of the house. I hurried up to Orv, who was hobbling along about twenty feet behind Grover. "What's going on?" I asked.

"Time to see the old man," he said.

"Because of a meadowlark?"

"Grover's just playing with you."

"Then how'd he know?"

"He just decided."

"Is there going to be some sort of ceremony?"

"It's up to Dan. Whatever he wants."

We made our way through the moist grass of the backyard to the opening into the thicket. Through the thicket we could see Dan and Wenonah standing together near the gravestone. Dan had his hands extended with his palms facing upward. Wenonah was supporting him with her arms around his waist.

"Keep it quiet," Grover said.

We pushed through the brush, walking single file, until we reached the little graveyard.

Orv turned to Donnie. "The baby should stay out," he said.

Donnie nodded and stayed back with Angie and the baby.

The rest of us walked around the perimeter of the graveyard, keeping our distance from the gravestones, until we reached Dan and Wenonah. Dan had his eyes closed and was speaking as if he didn't know we were there.

Grover gestured us to stand still. We remained motionless until Dan stopped speaking.

Then Orv nodded to Shitty, who stepped forward and got down on his hands and knees. His manner was respectful, almost formal, as if the act he was about to perform held great significance. He carefully brushed away the rest of the dirt and snow that had covered the gravestone, making sure to get it clean all the way to the edges.

With the dirt removed we could read the stone more clearly.

Above the name *Zintkala Zi* was a relief carving of a little girl. It was done in a simple, stylized manner, reminiscent of Allan Houser's work.

I looked at Donnie, who looked away. Angie leaned against his shoulder.

Shitty was staring up at Orv with a proud, expectant look on his face. For the first time I noticed that his pant cuffs and shirtsleeves were caked with mud. Orv smiled back at him with a warm, fatherly smile.

Orv stepped forward and took a small abalone shell from his pocket. He placed it on the gravestone and filled it with some leaves from a tobacco pouch.

Grover stepped up and lit the leaves with his Zippo. The rich smell of sweet grass rose up in a thin ribbon of smoke.

Dan opened his eyes and looked around. He nodded to us all, then began to chant softly while we all stood behind him with our hands folded and our eyes down.

A young rabbit came out from the bushes and hopped across the grave area. Dan pointed to it and said something, as if its presence was expected. The rabbit turned its head toward him for a moment, then ran off into the brush. Charles Bronson, who had taken a position at Dan's side, didn't move a muscle.

Dan said something to Wenonah in Lakota, and she turned to me. "Do you have the picture of Yellow Bird?" she asked.

I pulled it from my pocket.

She took it from me and smiled — the first kind gesture she had offered since we had arrived — and handed it to Dan. He looked at it for what must have been a minute, then touched it to his lips and handed it back to Wenonah. She bent down and placed it on the smoldering sweet grass. The edges flared and curled until the image darkened and disappeared.

Dan began a long, prayerful song. It sounded different than the one I had heard before — mournful and melodic and very inward feeling, rather than a wail into the sky.

Wenonah reached into the bag and took out the little doll. Dan took it from her and lifted it in front of him.

He turned in the four directions, chanting at each turn, then lifted the doll first toward the sky, then toward the earth, as if presenting it to some unseen forces. When he finished, he handed the doll back to Wenonah and moved unsteadily back toward the graveyard. Grover stepped up and took him by the arm. He shuffled past the gravestones until he was directly in front of Donnie and Angie and the baby, who were standing outside the fence. Little Shantell was fidgeting and cooing in her star quilt.

Dan moved up close to them and placed his hand on the baby's head. He began speaking quietly in Lakota. He spoke at length, as if offering a benediction.

Occasionally Orv or Wenonah would utter a low *hau* in response to something he said. Shantell stared up at him with wide, round eyes. She seemed transfixed by the old man's soft, melodic tones.

Dan held his left hand out to the side without taking his eyes off the infant. Wenonah placed the little doll gently in his palm. He brought it in front of him with ritual care, held it to the sky, then carefully positioned it on baby Shantell's chest.

Shantell waved her tiny hands at the presence of this new object. Very slowly, Dan took her arms and one by one placed them around the doll. Shantell lay there, unmoving. She opened and closed her fingers but did not take her arms off the doll or her eyes off the old man. There seemed to be a real connection between the two of them.

Dan's hands were unsteady, but his gestures were precise. Again, he reached his hand toward Wenonah and waited. Wenonah handed him a smaller buckskin roll from the bag. He unwrapped it carefully. In its center was a small eagle feather.

He took the feather and placed it in Shantell's shock of jet-black hair. Wenonah assisted him in tying the feather to the child's hair with a strip of rawhide.

He touched the child's forehead once more, letting his hand linger there for a moment. Donnie's and Angie's eyes were cast down.

Orv moved over close to me. "You should go back to the car now," he whispered.

I BACKED DOWN THE PATH INTO THE CLEARING, then walked to the edge of the shelter break and stared out over the empty fields. The dark earth gave off a pungent musk. A few wisps of clouds floated like smoke trails across the sky. The trees above my head swayed slowly in the wind.

Looking back through the thicket I could see that the group had formed into a circle. Dan was at its center, talking and gesturing. Occasionally I would hear a *hau, hau* or catch a low murmur of some kind of response.

I was almost hypnotized by the moment when I felt a slight movement against my leg. Startled, I looked down and saw Charles Bronson staring up at me. He wagged his tail and pawed at my cuff. The stick was still clamped tightly in his mouth. It had been gnawed raw, and the string and rag were dripping with mud.

"Hey, Bronson," I said, bending down and grabbing him under the belly. "How're you doing?"

I lifted him into my arms and rubbed some of the dirt off his whiskers. "You deserve something better than that stick," I said.

I reached in my pocket and pulled out an old bandana I used for cleaning my glasses. "I'll make you a trade. My clean bandana for your slobbered-up stick."

Bronson cocked his head and looked curiously at the bandana. I held it close to his nose so he could pick up its scent. He sniffed it several times, then, with a whippet-fast lunge, snapped it out of my hands and jumped to the ground. He kept the dirty stick clamped tightly in his teeth.

"Hey," I said, "that was supposed to be a trade."

He dragged his plunder into the bushes and crouched in the dirt, wagging his tail and staring back at me with wide, gleeful eyes.

"Okay," I said. "You can keep it. It's the least I can do after Grover stole your glove." He yipped once and jumped toward me, as if daring me to chase him.

Over by the burial area I could hear rustling and movement. There was some low laughter, and one by one people emerged from the path. Orv and Grover were chuckling and talking together, and Donnie and Angie and Shitty were huddled closely around Shantell.

Only Dan and Wenonah remained behind. I could hear Dan chanting by the gravesite and smell the faint odor of tobacco mixed with sage.

Orv walked over to me and said, almost apologetically, "There was a lot of private stuff. It just seemed better that way."

"No explanation necessary," I said. "I feel privileged just to be here."

He touched me on the shoulder in a wordless gesture of thanks and hobbled off around the front of the house.

The springtime sun had turned warm and gentle. The late-morning sky was a brilliant robin's egg blue. The day was alive with a deep prairie peace.

Grover walked by and gave me one of his mock punches on the shoulder.

"I told you it would work out," he said. "You just had to have patience. Things always work out if you keep your prayer in front of you."

"I didn't know you were a praying kind of guy," I said.

He winked once and lit up a cigarette. "There are a lot of things you don't know."

"Like meadowlark talk?"

"And how to play cards and mumblety-peg," he grinned.

He looked over at Bronson, who was dug in under the bush with his newfound booty. "Christ, now he's got a bandana, too."

"Yeah," I said. "I tried to trade the bandana for the stick. But he took them both. Now he won't give either of them back."

Grover blew out a thin stream of smoke. "Must have been raised by a white man."

Through the bushes we could see Dan and Wenonah standing over the grave.

"I just wish there was something more we could do," I said. "Maybe repatriate the body or something."

Grover shook his head. "No, this is the way the old man wants it. He says that this is all Indian land even if white men live on it, and he doesn't want to disturb her."

"If that's what he wants."

"That's what he wants."

Grover looked up at the band of yellow butterflies fluttering over our heads. He held up his hand, and one of them flew down and lighted on his finger.

"Special Indian power?" I said.

"Nope. Just some sugar left over from the doughnut I had for breakfast. The pizza man never came."

He flicked his finger, and the butterfly flew off into the sunshine.

"Here, I got something for you," he said.

He reached in his back pocket and pulled out the old chewed-up brown glove he had taken from Bronson at the motel.

"That's Bronson's glove," I said.

"Most of it," he answered.

"What do you mean?"

He held the glove up so I could see that a big piece had been cut out of the palm.

"What happened?"

"Cut out a chunk."

"Why?"

"Sometimes you work with what you've got."

"What do you mean?"

He reached in his shirt pocket and pulled out a length of fish line. He wrapped the glove around his finger and mimicked winding the line around it.

"I still don't get it."

"Well, then, Dog Soup is smarter than you are." He nodded toward Bronson, who was chewing aggressively on the masticated stick with its saliva-soaked piece of cloth and mud-covered string. "If you lose something important, you'll do damn near anything to get it back. Goes for dogs with pieces of glove, just like it does for old men with lost sisters."

Bronson looked up at us and wagged his tail.

"The stick? That's a piece of glove that's tied to it?"

Grover lit another cigarette. "All those knots I learned in the navy finally were good for something."

He tossed the rest of the glove in Bronson's direction. "Nice work, Dog Soup," he said. Bronson shot out and grabbed the glove, then quickly returned to his spot under the bush.

I shook my head in amazement. "You're a crafty guy, Grover," I said.

"Well, you sure as hell weren't going to find that stone without some help," he said. "White guys never go outside the lines."

Bronson had gathered the glove into a pile with the rest of his booty and was happily chewing on what remained of the stick. He looked up at us and yipped. His eyes were wide and laughing.

"Giving thanks?" I said.

"That's right," Grover answered. "Giving thanks. That's what Dog Soup does best."

CHAPTER THIRTY-THREE

◇◇◇◇◇◇◇◇◇◇◇◇◇◇◇◇◇◇◇◇◇◇◇◇◇◇◇◇◇◇◇

A BLUE DAKOTA DAY

Orv came back around the house carrying a plastic cooler that had been in the bed of the pickup. He set it down in the middle of the yard under the big oak tree.

"You want a sandwich, Nerburn?" he said.

"What you got?"

"Spam."

"White man's pemmican," Grover said.

"Stays good for years, right?" I said.

"You got it."

"Sure, Orv, why not?" I said.

"This *wasichu*'s got good taste," Orv laughed.

Grover drew deeply on his cigarette. "He's learning."

Angie was standing at Orv's side with a cellophane pack of white bread and a can of Spam. Donnie was standing behind her cradling Shantell in his arms.

"Let's get this feast going," Orv said.

Angie took a few condiments from the cooler, along with a

plastic jug of Kool-Aid and some paper cups. She opened the can of
Spam and began cutting inch-thick slices using the top of the cooler
as a table.

"Do you like ketchup?" she asked me.

"Of course he likes ketchup," Grover said. "What's a Spam
sandwich without ketchup?"

She smiled and squirted a massive blat from a squeeze bottle
onto a slice of white bread.

Donnie moved closer to me. I could tell that he wanted to talk.

"So, how's little Shantell doing?" I asked, hoping to start the
conversation. "No more ear infections?"

"You should call her Zintkala Zi," he said quietly.

I looked into the baby's placid, brown eyes.

"Sure. Zintkala Zi," I said. "Pretty name."

"It means 'Yellow Bird.' Dan gave it to her."

The baby opened her eyes wide and stared at me. I stroked her
fluffy black hair, making sure not to touch the eagle plume. She was
still clutching the doll tightly in her tiny hands.

"That's a good thing," Grover said, "that name."

We stood quietly side by side — Grover, Donnie, and I — looking out over the rich, empty fields. Orv had moved across the yard
and was standing with his arm around Shitty's shoulder. "This is a
peaceful place," I said.

Grover nodded and snuffed out his cigarette on the sole of his
shoe.

Donnie remained motionless, softly stroking little Zintkala Zi's
cheek. There was still something on his mind.

"Was it any good?" he said finally.

"What?"

"The gravestone."

"Allan Houser couldn't have done better," I said. "The face was
beautiful. And the lettering was perfect."

"I worked on it for three months, ever since winter. I had a tough time with the A's."

"Yeah, A's are hard."

He fell silent again. There was more he wanted to say.

"Marvin helped me," he said quietly, as if revealing a secret.

"Marvin? Who's Marvin?"

"My brother. That's his real name. I think we should call him that now."

I vaguely remembered that someone back at the sweat had mentioned that Shitty's real name was Marvin.

Grover broke into a guffaw. "It'll never stick, Donnie," he said. "Some things you just gotta let be."

On the far side of the clearing Orv had taken a rag out of his pocket and was wiping the dirt off Shitty's hands. It was a gentle gesture, filled with a father's love.

"He did all the polishing," Donnie said. "He did it just like you told me — with the oil and the dust. He worked on it every night. Sometimes he didn't even sleep. It wouldn't have been so good without him."

"He did it right," I said.

"He carried it out here all by himself, too. He wouldn't let anyone help. He dug it in, too. Packed down the edges, covered it up. Put the rock on top of the stick. I think Dad's really proud of him."

I looked across at the ratty man having his hands washed by his father.

"I think he is, too."

In the distance we could hear the low edge of Dan's chanting.

"You don't think Grandfather knew, do you?" Donnie said.

Grover shook his head. "Nah, he didn't know. I think his heart was just full of joy at finding her." He reached in his back pocket and pulled out the two sticks that had formed the weathered cross with the name *Sarah* on them.

"But this" — he shook the two stakes at us — "this would have bothered him. It would have bothered him all the way to his grave."

He gave Donnie a tap on the behind with the sticks. "Nice work."

Donnie smiled shyly and looked at the ground.

We could hear the distant clanking of Dan's walker. He and Wenonah were making their way down the path to the yard. Bronson shot out from under the bush and ran up to them with the old glove held proudly in his mouth. He appeared to have abandoned the stick and the bandana now that he once again had his most valued possession.

"So that's why you didn't come along to the museum?" I said.

"We wanted this to be good for the old man," Grover said. "Required a little planning."

"You did a good job."

He looked at the folks gathering in the clearing. "We all did," he said. "But don't quit your day job to become a map maker."

Orv dragged a couple of old stumps from behind one of the sheds and placed them on either side of the plastic cooler.

Shitty hurried around the house and returned with a cheap aluminum lawn chair.

Angie had finished making the Spam sandwiches and was placing them on a paper plate on top of the cooler next to the jug of Kool-Aid.

"Time for the feast," Orv said.

"Good thing Jumbo's not here," Grover grinned. "Those sandwiches would be gone in sixty seconds."

"Where is Jumbo?" I asked.

"Business engagement," Grover said. "I think he's negotiating a merger."

Dan clanked his way to the middle of the yard. Shitty ran up behind him with the lawn chair, and he and Wenonah eased the old man into it.

I walked over and sat next to him.

"Feeling okay, Dan?" I asked.

"Feeling good."

Bronson splayed himself out in the sun at the old man's feet and chewed contentedly on his glove. Orv and Shitty moved over to the oak tree and sat down together beneath it.

Angie passed around the plate of sandwiches. Donnie, cradling baby Zintkala Zi in his arms, smiled up at her.

Grover handed me a sandwich dripping with ketchup. The slab of Spam was as thick as a deck of cards. "Medium rare," he said. "With all the fixin's."

Dan took a sandwich and looked over at Donnie and the baby. His eyes were shining.

He touched his fingers to his lips and held the sandwich to the sky.

"It's a good day to live," he said. "*Mitakuye oyas'in*."

From out of the thicket a cloud of yellow butterflies rose into the sunlight.

"*Mitakuye oyas'in*," we all responded, and raised our Spam sandwiches in thanks to the blue Dakota day.

ABOUT THE AUTHOR

Kent Nerburn is widely recognized as one of the few American writers who can respectfully bridge the gap between Native and non-Native cultures. Novelist Louise Erdrich has called his work "storytelling with a greatness of heart." Nerburn is the author of twelve books on spirituality and Native themes, including *Chief Joseph and the Flight of the Nez Perce, Simple Truths, Small Graces,* and *Neither Wolf nor Dog: On Forgotten Roads with an Indian Elder.* He lives in northern Minnesota with his wife, Louise Mengelkoch; an earnest yellow Lab named Lucie; and Sid, an irascible orange cat. His website can be found at www.kentnerburn.com.

FOLLOW DAN DOWN FORGOTTEN ROADS

If you appreciated *The Wolf at Twilight*, don't miss *Neither Wolf nor Dog*, the powerful story of Kent Nerburn's first journey with Dan.

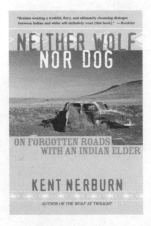

Against the unflinching backdrop of contemporary reservation life and the majestic spaces of the western Dakotas, Nerburn draws us deep into the world of the tribal elder Dan, as we journey to where the vast Dakota skies overtake us and the whisperings of the wind speak of ancestral voices. Dan speaks eloquently on the power of silence, the difference between land and property, white people's urge to claim an Indian heritage, and the selling of sacred ceremonies. An unlikely cross between Jack Kerouac and *Black Elk Speaks*, *Neither Wolf nor Dog* is full of humor, pathos, and insight. It takes us past the myths and stereotypes to the heart of the Native American experience and in doing so reveals America in a way few of us ever see.

"Realists wanting a truthful, fiery, and ultimately cleansing dialogue between Indian and white will definitely want [this book]."

— *Booklist*

"This is one of those rare works that once you've read it, you can never look at the world, or at people, the same way again. It is quiet and forceful and powerful."

— American Indian College Fund

Paperback • $15.00 • 352 pp. • ISBN: 978-1-57731-233-8